CTHULHU'S
BACK IN TOWN

KURT E. ARMBRUSTER

authorHOUSE

AuthorHouse™
1663 Liberty Drive
Bloomington, IN 47403
www.authorhouse.com
Phone: 833-262-8899

Published by AuthorHouse   02/15/2022

ISBN: 978-1-6655-5201-1 (sc)
ISBN: 978-1-6655-5200-4 (hc)
ISBN: 978-1-6655-5202-8 (e)

Library of Congress Control Number: 2022902956

Print information available on the last page.

This is a work of fiction. Characters, businesses, and locations depicted herein are either creations of the author's imagination or used in a fictitious manner, and should not be construed to represent past or present reality. This work acknowledges the continuing influence of H. P. Lovecraft as an inspiration for its creation.

This book is printed on acid-free paper.

Acknowledgements

Thank you Christopher Lott, Christopher Post, and Christina for reading and critiquing the manuscript; Don Rauf, for loyal support and encouragement; and most of all my wife Cedar, for feeding me body and spirit, and inspiring the best in me.

For Jason

The Humans are not alone upon the earth. Others have walked where we walk, and will walk when we have passed into other worlds. The forest and water are home to many whose faces we do not see. The shadow world is alive with spirits!

—S'klalth elder saying, transcribed by Dr.
Henry Smithers, Seacoma, 1856

Young men dream, and oft-times those dreams are deep, dark, and unwholesome. What spectral forms lurk in the shadows of forgotten places, eager to feed upon those dreams?

--Asanath Potter, 1872

Prelude To A Hiss

I had to be so damn curious. Me and my radar ears, always getting me into trouble. Half our world problems come aurally. I can prove it, and maybe someday I will. Just now, however, something was after me—me, a humble bass player. I reviewed my short and possibly limited musical career as I splashed down the tunnel searching desperately for an egress. All I wanted was to play music and have a little fun. But no, I was being chased by a crazy woman and a bunch of frog-men. Ahead, chinks of light. A doorway! I jerked it open, rushed up a short stairway, and burst into the alley. My boots pounded onto the old boardwalk, and with a splintering crack the rotten slats gave way and I plunged back into darkness. Great, just fucking great. I shook my head and staggered to my feet. A grunt echoed down the tube, then a hideous hissing sound. God, the stink!

1

The Hidden Ones

Her face looked carved from wood. Tall and gaunt she was, and alone. Some of the villagers shunned her and laughed at her behind her back. S'kladog saw that their laughter often seemed nervous. He wasn't nervous; he liked the woman, M'katl, perhaps because he too was tall and serious and not popular with the other young people. Nestled into the crook of the bluff, the S'klalth village had its cliques, and S'kladog and M'katl belonged to none of them. So they found each other. They both often visited the broad lagoon just outside the village, and they were there one evening when a seal broached the surface with an explosive snort. S'kladog jumped back in surprise, and M'katl laughed softly. "They come here through a passage out to the water," she said in a low, warm voice.

He did not want to stare, but S'kladog was surprised to see that up close she was not as ugly as he had thought, and maybe not as old, either. M'katl gazed into S'kladog's brown eyes. "You come here often." she said. "You gaze at the water. Like me." The softness of her voice made his spine tingle. "Are you looking for the Hidden Ones?" she asked.

He shrugged. "Just looking."

"Look and listen," she said. "Keep your eyes and ears open, and you may be surprised."

S'kladog's mother, Neot'su, frowned when he told her about his visits with M'katl. "What does that old woman want with you?"

"Nothing," S'kladog replied. "We just talk. Besides, I don't think she's that old."

Neot'su regarded him thoughtfully. "No? Well, she's an odd one. As long as I can remember, even when I was a young girl, she's lived there in that little house all alone, always keeping apart. Some people say she's a kind of witch."

S'kladog's eyes widened. "A witch, here?"

Neo'tsu chuckled. "I don't think so. I've never seen her do anything to make me believe that."

"Are people afraid of her?"

"Some are, I suppose. A woman, all by herself—people are quick to jump at shadows and blabber all kinds of rumors." In her time Neot'su had been the butt of more than one rumor, herself. "Well, anyway," she continued, "watch out for wagging tongues. If you are seen with M'katl, you will become a subject of gossip. Some will think you're strange if you hang out with her."

S'kladog said nothing. People already thought he was strange. And anyway, what was "normal"—that big dope, A'skamotl, who relished clubbing salmon violently and hung bloody skins from his house? The other young men all seemed to admire him. He did not. And if they thought he was strange for hanging out with M'katl, too bad for them.

S'kladog and M'katl continued to meet at the lagoon and pass evenings in her house, where she offered him a pipe of sage and talked about herbs and mushrooms and the time when the S'klalth village was much larger and the people kept celebration days with dancing and fancy masks. She talked, too, of Do-ki-batl—the Changer—and of the Water Beings.

"Water Beings!" S'kladog exclaimed. "Shimat'l says he saw one of them swimming in the lagoon. But he lies a lot."

"Boys love to tell stories," said M'katl. "Still, it is possible he saw one. Kekan'tu and Ts'ats'mo are well-known. She looked into the distance and her voice lowered. "I hope he did see one of them."

"Why?" asked S'kladog.

M'katl's face darkened. "Because the old ways are dying off, and I'm afraid the old beings are, too."

"Dying off? What do you mean?"

"There is a strangeness in the air these days, S'kladog. Have you felt it? No? Well, perhaps that's for the best. But look at our village: it's only a shadow of what it used to be. Families have pulled out, not so many young people are born anymore. We no longer celebrate the special days or dance the old dances."

"Why, do you think?"

"A sickness is about. I've heard that many people have died from it, far away down the coast."

"Do you think the white men bring it?"

M'katl felt a strange chill. She hoped her young friend would be spared the sickness. As for the white men—who were they but men? "I don't know. I only know that things are changing. Do-ki-batl is a great spirit. All things change."

S'kladog was uneasy hearing about the sickness, but he did not want to think about it. He wanted to ask her if she was a witch.

That evening, his mother would not be denied. "Come, son, what do you and M'katl talk about?"

"She tells me about the old days here. Do you know they used to do the mask dances?"

Neot'su smiled patiently. "I saw one as a girl." (She had told him this more than once.) "Some of the families had old masks that had been with them for a long time. Beautiful masks of whales, birds…" Her voice trailed off wistfully, making S'kladog feel strange again. "They said they left to find better fishing, but those families were always feuding, always accusing each other of stealing this and that. I think this place was just too small for both of them."

S'kladog laughed, but his mind was troubled. He wished people still did the mask dances, and wished his mother and M'katl did not sound so sad when they talked about it.

"So," Neot'su said, "what else did you find to 'discuss'?"

S'kladog heard the odd note in her voice but shrugged it off. "Do-ki-batl…Water Beings."

"Watch out for that Do-ki-batl, he'll turn you into a snake!" Her face shone in the light of the cooking fire and S'kladog felt a burst of pride that his mother should be so beautiful.

"Have you ever seen the Water Beings?" he asked.

"No," she said. "People say they've seen them, and I think sometimes I've felt them nearby"—she smiled slyly—"when I'm at the water doing our wash and no one's helping." Neot'su gazed at her blushing son and said, "S'kladog, you are wise and thoughtful, older than your years. It may be that you will see the Water Beings. You have keen eyes, maybe they see beyond what other people see. Maybe this is why M'katl has made friends with you."

That evening S'kladog went again to the lagoon. As he sat staring into the flat, dark water, M'katl came and sat beside him. She asked, "Have you seen the Hidden Ones?"

He looked into her eyes, which were a dazzling blue, and asked, "Who are the Hidden Ones?"

"Water beings…spirit beings that live all around. If you are quiet and patient, they may show themselves to you. Or, they may not. That does not mean they're not here. They are shy with humans."

S'kladog raised his eyebrows. "They watch us?"

"Always."

"Now?"

"Listen. Listen to the trees, the stones, the birds, the water. Listen and hear. They are of us, and we are of them. All are one."

S'kladog looked at M'katl and said, "I'm going in." He stripped off his clothes and slipped into the lagoon. Spreading his arms like wings, he knifed through the cold water, plunged deep into the darkness, then shot into the light, delighting in the power of his body. He caught M'katl's eye as she watched him, proud to be friends with this handsome woman standing like a cedar by the water. He went under again, and wondered if a seal might come in through the passage and swim with him. At last, S'kladog slid from the water and stood trembling. He smiled at his grave-faced friend and she returned his smile, revealing teeth white as bone. "Come to my house tonight," she murmured. Then she walked away into the trees.

That evening after supper, S'kladog excused himself.

"Are you going to her house?" his mother asked.

"Yes."

She gazed solemnly at him, then nodded and kissed his forehead. S'kladog walked through the quiet village in the misty evening air, his body tingling as he recalled M'katl's voice, so warm and full of hints of mysterious things. M'katl welcomed him smiling. Her house smelled of fresh pine boughs and herbs, tallow lamps flickered. "Would you like to eat?" she asked.

"Mom and I ate."

"Does your mother approve of your coming here?"

"Yes—more or less."

"She is a good woman, I think, to have such a son." M'katl moved toward him. "S'kladog, you are young and handsome. I am old and ugly." She came closer, dropping her head and her eyes like a young doe.

S'kladog felt his heart race. "I don't think you're ugly," he said, looking into her blue eyes. M'katl smiled and let her robe fall to the floor, revealing her naked body. S'kladog's eyes bulged, and something else too, for her body was not ugly. Anything but! M'katl took his hands in hers and placed them on her breasts, then wrapped her arms around him and planted her mouth on his. She was strong and her kisses swept through him like hot wind.

S'kladog felt a great force building within, irresistible as an ocean wave. He ripped off his clothes and wrapped himself around M'katl, kissing her deeply, desperately. "Ummm," she moaned, "my strong, sweet young man…"

Hours later, S'kladog lay in M'katl's warm fur bed, more relaxed than he had ever felt. He stared at the woman asleep beside him. Enveloped in thick gray-black hair, her face glowed like a vision of the spirit world. Those blue eyes: how had she gotten them? He felt a pang of sadness, knowing that she could probably never be a real wife to him. But how good she had made him feel!

Would he tell his mother? No, she would get angry with M'katl. Then again, maybe she knew this might happen. S'kladog was coming to realize that there was little his mother did not know. Awhile later they rose and drank tea. Then M'katl opened a large cedar box and pulled out a small bundle. "I've never shown this to anybody." She undid the bundle and handed what was inside to S'kladog. Dull gray-green and faintly greasy to the touch, it was a stone carving of a creature with wings and tentacles and a head like a starfish. On top of the head was an eye. "Shit," S'kladog said, "a monster!"

"It was my granny's," said M'katl. "She told me how, when she was a girl, canoes arrived at the village one day. Warriors—big, ugly brutes— came ashore without being invited. They had war clubs, and some walked around with their penises exposed." S'kladog laughed, but fell silent before M'katl's stern expression. "They pushed into the main house, shoving their privates into the faces of the elders and demanding something to eat. One of them shook a rattle at the elders and warned them that if they defied the warriors, he would use the rattle to summon great beings that would come down from the sky and kill the Humans. After the outsiders had eaten their fill, they clubbed six of the women and took them away as slaves. They left this figure behind as a warning."

"Whoaaa," said S'kladog, "I hope those guys never come back."

She cocked her head and gazed at him thoughtfully. "I hope so too. But there are things beyond us, things in other worlds, and who can say whether or not they may choose to pay us a visit. Anyway, It was a long time ago. I've always wanted to share this with someone—someone like you, S'kladog. Someone who sees things. You will see things I will not—a new world, I think." She stroked his hair tenderly. "Be ready, dear S'kladog. Be strong. Do you have a special song?"

S'kladog shrugged. "Just this and that."

"You must think of a song for yourself, one that will reach others. When you are alone and feel afraid—sing. You will feel stronger, and others will feel your strength."

He gazed silently at the little figure while M'katl fixed a meal of trout and mashed roots. Then they returned to bed.

After that, S'kladog visited M'katl often. He listened closely as she taught him words to keep away dark spirits, and he swam in the lagoon as she watched, tall and serene. Once in a while a seal joined him, and he delighted in darting and weaving with the creature deep in the pool and blowing lustily with it at the surface. S'kladog grew to manhood, and nestled in its hollow, the S'klalth village remained as it was for a long time.

One rainy night, S'kladog went to M'katl's and knocked on her door post. She did not answer. He peered inside—her house was empty. He slumped to his knees, numb all over. Next day he asked the neighbors, but no one knew where M'katl was, and she never appeared. It didn't make sense. In time, S'kladog felt the pain subside, and by talking with his mother and swimming hard in the lagoon his questions and his passions settled into themselves. Something had called M'katl away and that was that. The Hidden Ones? Maybe. He felt a growing certainty that he also would be called one day. Then, he would follow, and find her. But a short time later, several in the village fell ill and died—Neot'su among them. S'kladog again felt the searing agony, and wondered why the disease had spared him.

He knew he could not stay in the village, not with all he had loved gone. He gathered his few things into a bundle, took his mother's stout staff, and

7

walked out of the house, past the lagoon, and into the hills. A cold rain fell and the old inland trail was muddy, but he kept his gaze fixed on the way ahead, and as he walked, he sang—*I, S'kladog, walk here! I, S'kladog, sing here!* Now he knew, just as M'katl had said, that his song, the song she and his mother had inspired, would give him strength and perhaps invite a spirit to guide him.

Morning passed to afternoon as he slogged down the long valley. Thankfully, many feet had kept the trail passable. Were M'katl's among them? S'kladog hoped the other walkers were friendly, but he kept her words with him—*Be ready...Be strong*—and he kept a sharp eye out. He paused to eat some berries and dried salmon, and smoke some herbs, then he laid down and dozed. When he awoke, it was getting dark. He felt a black loneliness; he had never gone so far from home, and now there was no home. But his two women had taught him well, and he felt no fear, only excitement, as he realized that the way ahead was full of possibilities. S'kladog moved well away from the trail, found a hollow in a fallen tree, made a bed of his blankets, and fell fast asleep.

Sometime later he awoke to the sound of soft voices close by. *There he is,* they whispered—*he is, he is, hu-man, hu-man, huuuu-maaa...*S'kladog opened his eyes and his blood froze. Eyes, glowing yellow in the darkness, watched him. The Hidden Ones! He was sure of it. Trembling, he stood and raised his arms in greeting, and softly sang his song. Now, he sang M'katl's name with it, and a great warmth settled upon him. The whispering voices stilled and one by one the eyes winked out. S'kladog knew that they, and also M'katl and his mother, had heard and understood. He lowered his arms and closed his eyes. As stillness returned, he snuggled into his blankets and smiled and thought again of M'katl. *They are of us, and we are of them. All are one.*

2

Driving Miss Janet

When the rain settles in on old Port Landsend, it settles hard. It bombards the dilapidated United Wharf until the weight of one more drop must push the sagging structure into the bay. It scours the clay bluff at the entrance to the town, gouging out loose earth and leaving scabrous holes. It slants along Harbor Street as if to wash away a century of puny human accretions. And it pummels without mercy the luckless soul caught out walking. *You don't belong here*, the deluge hisses. *Go away.*

I stared into the white tunnel of the headlights. At 29 I didn't have much, but I did have a secondhand station wagon, a Kay bass fiddle, and a gig in Port Landsend.

"Port Landsend?" I said after Jeff's call roused me that murky February afternoon. "Really?"

"Yeah, this guy's opened a club there and he wants to try jazz. In fact, he'll be playing drums. Fifty bucks a night and rooms."

I had recently fallen in with Jeff and a gang of vintage jazz players, and I welcomed any excuse to call myself a musician and not a taxi driver. "Okay, I'm in. Beats hauling drunks on a Friday night."

"Excellent," said Jeff. "Brad's on reeds and we've got an excellent piano player from Bremerville. Is your car running okay? I'm going up early and we're all going to rendezvous at the Star Chamber, right on the main drag, watch for a yellow sign. Downbeat's nine, black slacks and white dress shirts."

Traffic was sparse on the peninsula highway that night and a cold rain fell, but as the city lights vanished behind me, I felt a rush of exhilaration. I was on the road plying my craft, and the swish of the swipes and the passing headlights conjured an old favorite, Bernard Hermann's hypnotic road music from *Psycho*, playing for Janet Leigh as she drove down Route 666 on her rainy night flight from one life to the next. She hoped. Yeah, the old hymn of hope, crooning its haunting refrain as we skim the cracks in life's highway, hoping they won't trip us onto our faces or swallow us whole. Sorry, baby, you got a bum deal.

At the turnoff for Port Landsend I swung onto a two-lane road carved through thick evergreen woods, the kind of forest primeval you can walk fifty yards into and never walk out of. After a few miles the trees gave way to a desolate scrubland. Isolated farmhouses stood forlorn in the gloom, windows yawning blackly, like silent cries for help. No other headlights kept me company down the lonely valley, and under the spell of the bleak countryside I tasted the first sour beads of apprehension. What did this hick town want with some doofy jazz band? This was the eighties, after all—people wanted disco. Or out here, country. We were going to bomb—I knew it.

From the back, old Kay whispered: *Can it, kid, this is the gig. So what if we bomb? Every real musician bombs at least once.* Bearing the scars of a thousand gigs, she was right. Hell, Benny Goodman bombed, just before he knocked the country on its ear. I banished doubt and sped onward. Scattered lights burned through the murk and the road plunged to a tideflat littered with the hulks of beached fishing boats. I passed an abandoned motel, skirted a pockmarked bluff, and eased off into what was obviously a main arterial.

Welcome to Port Landsend! Far ahead a blinking yellow light swung in the wind, the rain pelted the windshield. Who would turn out on this fuck-all night in this fuck-all town? A bright yellow sign loomed up: *Star Chamber*.

I slid into a parking slot and hefted the bass onto the sidewalk. The air reeked of salt water, and across the street a phalanx of blood-red brick Victorian buildings glowered down like Dickensian schoolmasters. I pushed into the small square room and headed toward an upright piano and a set of drums. The place was nearly empty, but candles flickered on the tables and the dark-paneled club was cozy and inviting. A knot of guys perched at the bar and one of them, a ruddy, silver-topped fellow, saw me and lurched to his feet. "You must be the bass man," he said, thrusting a beefy hand at me. "I'm Rick Weller, glad you could make it. Come on back to the office, the guys are all here. You bring some dress clothes?"

Rick led me down a narrow hallway and into the office. Jeff waved, "Hey, Erich, all right!" Cornet in hand, he made introductions then suggested numbers for the first set as we changed into stage wear. I knew them all and felt my confidence rise. Jeff and Brad noodled softly on their horns and I eased Kay from her canvas case and ran through some warm-up scales with bow and fingers. "Sounds good, Erich," said Rick, chewing on a fat cigar and rubbing his hands in anticipation.

"I hope they like us," I replied. "'Course, if they don't, I got something to hide behind."

Rick cackled gleefully then shot back, "Hell, they better like us. Star Chamber's the first new thing they've had 'round here in a coon's age."

Pianist Danny Fipps, an owlish little man of about sixty, squinted at us. "Never thought I'd see Landsend again. Used to work the Elks Club here. Funny old place, Landsend. Kind of a backwater."

Rick darkened slightly. "Well, I hope to change that."

In a shadowy corner, Brad poked at a chink in the paneling. "Wonder where this goes." Barely discernible in the dim light was the faint outline of a sealed doorway.

11

"Old stairway down to the cellar," said Rick. "Thought about openin' it up, but so far I haven't had the time. Prob'ly goes down to the old tunnel."

Jeff perked up. "Tunnel?"

"Drain pipes. S'posed to be a whole network of 'em under the town, from back in the old days."

Jeff wandered over and peered into the crack. "Sheesh" he said, grimacing, "that's quite a stench there."

I leaned in next to him and sniffed. A rank fetor wafted through the crack, making my nose wrinkle.

"Salt water," said Jeff, "or mold."

"Nah," I cracked, "it's just the kitchen."

Rick cackled again. "Shit, better not be, for what I'm payin' 'em! You fellas about ready to hit it?"

We quickly found a relaxed groove and my worries faded as the place filled up. Most of the patrons seemed to be friends of Rick's, but no matter, the barroom banter was lively and couples got up and danced. At one we signed off, and Rick and Danny headed for Rick's suburban home while Brad and Jeff and I tromped upstairs to the newly-refurbished apartment that was to serve as band room. I hung out for a while, then burrowed under my comforter and recapped the night. Good band, good groove, a fun night. But how long could it last? I was fed up with driving cab and anxious to make my living in music. Old-time jazz was not necessarily a forever thing, but it would do for now. As for spending the weekends in Port Landsend— why not? But what was that smell in the back room?

3

Tremor

In the year 1883 Mother Earth was feeling itchy. And when she got itchy, she scratched. Off the coast of Sumatra, a small cone-shaped mountain belched, then let go in a cataclysmic blast that all but sank the surrounding island of Krakatau and killed thousands. Ash circled the earth and the high stratosphere blushed eerily, and in the far Pacific long, restless swells and glowering sky spoke of other effects, effects felt by whales and vast schools of tuna, and felt too by a great silt-covered mound, whose layers of slimy sediment sloughed aside to reveal a jumble of titan blocks and a monolith of black stone. Deep within the ocean's bosom, the blocks shifted. And that which slept within the blocks stirred.

4

A Rotten Row

"**W**ant some?" Brad grinned as he gobbed peanut butter on a slice of bread.

"No thanks," I said, gagging at the smell. I filled a bowl with Raisin Bran and went to the window, slid it up, and sucked in delicious salt air. Port Landsend lay shrouded in a cold gray mist, the quicksilver sheet of the harbor stretched into infinity.

"So," Brad said, "what kind of place is Port Landsend, anyhow?"

"Old," I said. "Old and quiet."

Jeff looked up from his marine biology textbook. "One of those classic would-be metropoli of the Gilded Age, as I read it." Bursting with curiosity and puckish humor, Jeff was a second-year grad student who could put on a front of academic sobriety one second and spout Slobovian dialect the next. "Port Landsend was a busy seaport in the early days, but then it sort of gave up the ghost."

"Seems like the perfect place *for* ghosts," Brad said. "What about those tunnels, anyway?"

"Intriguing proposition," said Jeff. "Alas, so many of these old legends turn out to be just legends and nothing more."

"And that smell in the office?"

"Just old place stink," said Brad.

"More like old dead body stink," I said.

Jeff guffawed. "Jeez, you guys! It's probably mold. We're right on the water, after all. Anyway, most mysteries turn out to have mundane explanations."

"Tch, tch," chided Brad, "you're no fun at all."

"Nice to have a few mysteries left," I said. "What do they do here nowadays?"

Jeff shrugged. "Boat-building, fishing..."

"Embalming," said Brad, smacking obnoxiously.

I crunched the last of my cereal and said, "Well, it's definitely a shell-of-its-former-self kinda place. Let's go check it out."

We clumped downstairs and into the light of Saturday. Sporadic cars plashed down Harbor Street, tourists poked in and out of the shops, and kids congealed in front of Hot 'n Crusty Pizza. We ambled toward the blinking yellow light at the far end of the street, taking in the brave little businesses—antiques, natural foods, hardware, a book store with a cat snoozing in the window. Looming overhead, the wizened brick facades kept silent vigil over passing generations. Jeff pointed at the upper windows. "I wonder what's in there. Looks mostly empty."

"Bodies," Brad replied.

"Bradley, Bradley," objected Jeff, "these are sweet old buildings—the high hopes of the Gilded Age entrepreneurial elite all set for the big boom. Only it never happened. Sad. I'll bet some of those upper floors have never been occupied."

We reached the end of the block. "Whoa!" Brad gaped at a gnarled ruin looming at the water's edge. A witch-hatted cupola jabbed the sky and shards of broken glass glinted in the windows like shark's teeth. *United Wharf,* proclaimed peeling black letters on the moldering façade. A rusty chain link fence liberally decorated with No Trespassing signs barricaded the place.

"Amazing that a thing like this hasn't burned down by now," Brad said. The old pile seemed to exhale mold and something less definable.

Jeff sniffed the air. "Interesting bouquet."

"Psychic residue," I said.

"There's a residue here, all right," Brad said, "but it sure ain't psychic."

We stared silently a moment longer, then turned back down Harbor Street, admiring the faded advertisements on some of the elderly buildings: *Blue Label Shoes...Tables for Ladies...Dr. Silver's Golden Elixir*. Scattered tourists and locals meandered about, and in a dark alcove a leather-faced young man in stained overalls stared at us with dull eyes. Brad nodded at him and said, "Hey," but the man only looked away. "Friendly chap," Brad muttered. "I don't know, Jeff, this place is kind of creepy."

Jeff shrugged. "Rick seems to have a lot of faith in it."

"I hope he knows what he's doing," I said.

We walked on in silence. A vacant lot littered with trash made a poignant contrast with the pompous business blocks, and I pondered the fate of the little city with big ambitions. When did the first shadows of doubt disturb the slumber of its anxious boosters? What desperate words were spoken around dinner tables as the wind rattled the windows? Across the still water a line of cabins slouched along a sand spit, and beyond them stretched the slate-gray vastness of Pilot Sound. Just ahead, battered rowboats lay outside a hut with a crudely-lettered sign saying *boat's for Rent*.

"Hey," said Brad, "how 'bout it?"

In the hut we found a round man with a gray face and bulging eyes. "Dollar a hour," he croaked. Jeff took the oars and rowed slowly along the waterfront. The feeble sun lit Landsend's weather-beaten backside, and from the water the decrepitude of the city was all the more apparent. "Hey, check that out," Brad said, pointing at a large opening in the seawall, partially obscured by blackberry vines. Jeff nosed us toward the hole and pushed the blackberries aside with an oar, revealing an arched aperture in the crumbling stone. It was just big enough for a boat and rower.

"The tunnel!" cried Brad.

"Or a sewer," said Jeff.

"Let's go in."

I shook my head. "I don't think so."

Brad grinned. "Okay, guys, moment of truth: Do we man-up and enter the tunnel of mystery, or do we wimp out?"

"Wimp out," I said.

Jeff edged us slowly up to the hole and shook his head. "I would have to concur with Brother Erich. We don't know where this thing goes, or if it's safe."

"You guys are pussies," Brad said.

"Better a live pussy than a dead cat," I said. "Plus, there might be things in there."

"Things? Like what?"

"Ever see that movie about the giant ants in the sewers of LA. Sounds corny, only it scared the crap out of me. If you'd seen it, you wouldn't be so eager to go into that hole."

Brad shook his head in disgust. "Pussies, pussies..."

"Meow."

Jeff turned away from the opening and rowed toward the United Wharf. We drifted into the jungle of pilings underneath the wharf and entered a cool, dark realm redolent of creosote and seaweed. "Nice colony of giant acorn barnacles," Jeff said, pausing by a thickly-encrusted piling. Their tiny jaws poked from the shells, opening and closing in slow motion.

"Killer barnacles," said Brad, his taunting mood unabated. "They could leap right out and peck us to death."

"Funny, ha-ha."

Something banged overhead. A large gray sack fell into the water about twenty feet off and bobbed to the surface. Jeff rowed over and nudged it with an oar tip. "Something inside," he muttered, "feels soft."

"Came through a trapdoor," I said, peering up.

Snort! A whiskered head burst from the water and lunged at the sack. Another followed, and another, thrashing the water in furious rivalry.

"Shit!" Jeff yelled, "sea lions!" He shoved hard against the pilings and rowed us back into daylight. "Nasty buggers! Kill a man, easy."

"Look at them go for that sack," said Brad. "Must be food."

The beasts chomped at the bag and broke it open. Something flashed golden brown, and a tail and hindquarters disappeared beneath the surface. A dog. The water churned blood-red as the snapping heads devoured their meal. A sea lion gave one last grunt and the water was still. The ghost-gray hulk of the United Wharf glowered down in mute disdain.

5

Advent

Belching smoke from her gleaming black funnel, the steamer *La Paloma* made a majestic sight as she eased in to City Dock. Five days out of Santa Francesca, she was the fastest liner on the coast, and the crowd of passengers lining her decks testified to her popularity. High on the open bridge, the black-bearded captain barked orders through a megaphone. A telegraph jangled, deckhands hurled thick hawsers at outstretched arms, and the vessel was made fast.

S'kladog leaned on the pier railing and studied the ship. The looming hull of black steel plates bore a faint resemblance to his people's cedar-plank houses, but everything else about it was profoundly alien. The whites had worked many wonders, he thought, but the changes they had wrought... He thought again of old Do-ki-batl-the-Changer, and shook his head. Men horsed a gangplank up to the rail and the passengers began trooping ashore: sober-faced gentlemen in black, women shepherding squabbling children, and sports in loud suits, all peering wide-eyed and wide-awake for the main chance. Every day in this year the white man called 1888, more settlers disembarked at Port Landsend. The Board of Trade had done its work well.

S'kladog grunted. How many white people could there be in the world? All the spirit power of the Humans had been powerless against the invaders.

And yet, he knew who some continued the old ways—even going into the water and giving themselves to the Water Beings, thinking to become immortal. He had seen them do it. Some said that, in return for the sacrifice, the people living along the water had plenty of fish to eat. And some said that those who practiced the sacrifice became invisible to the whites, and immune to their diseases and their weapons. Had any whites joined in? Probably not—shit, the Water Beings would probably throw them back!

The thought made him chuckle softly as he watched the newcomers file down the gangway. He pitied them in a way, for while they possessed great powers, they did not have Tahmanous, the spirit-power that could make one strong against cold and fatigue. They did not know Do-ki-batl, who could transform a man into an eagle, a wolf, or even a slug. They did not know of the other worlds, or of the secret places ruled by black spirits: the Wind-walker, the Dweller-within, the Burrower, and others even more terrible. The Humans knew. And they also knew that even the Tahmanous did not always hold against the black spirits. S'kladog squinted narrowly across the water. What would happen, he wondered, when his people were gone and no one was left who knew the dangers of these other worlds? What would happen if the whites angered the black spirits?

Trailing the line of debarking passengers came a stern-looking man with a black beard, followed by a handsome woman with a thoughtful face. Holding her hand was a small boy who walked steadily down the plank and looked about with a bold, clear gaze. S'kladog watched the boy who, as if sensing the tall Indian's gaze, turned and looked straight into his eyes. The child's face wore a sobriety beyond his years, and even from a distance the vivid emerald of his eyes gleamed. What did such eyes see—and what new changes would they bring to the world?

6

Café Society

The Lamp Post Café was quiet and charmingly charmless. Gray was the primary decorative theme, the furnishings looked left over from the Truman administration. We slumped into a booth and gazed glumly out on the bay. "So," said Jeff, "what *was* that?"

"You know what it was," said Brad, looking pale.

"Somebody dropped a dead dog out of that building," I said. "At least, I hope it was dead."

A young woman in a black skirt and white sweater strode over. "You want coffee?" she asked in a soft but husky voice.

Three pairs of eyes gaped shamelessly. Her figure was full, her black hair long and shiny, her mouth wide. Straining against the chaste black skirt, her legs were thick and taut. She regarded us coolly through big, protuberant eyes. Far from a "classic" beauty, but far more intriguing.

"Uh—yeah," I blurted, "coffee's good, thanks." No doubt used to slack-jawed male incoherence, she nodded curtly and walked away. I tore my eyes from her with difficulty and looked back at my bandmates.

"So," Brad said, "why would somebody drop a dog into the bay?"

Jeff shrugged. "Easier than burying it."

"Maybe it's some weird cult thing where they dump dead animals in the water."

"That's crazy," I said.

"Not any crazier than a lotta shit in this world," Brad replied.

A man in a worn blue fishing hat got up and came over. He was about sixty, and purple veins showed through the thin skin of his ruddy cheeks. I remembered seeing him in the bar the previous night. "Hello, boys," he said, smiling warmly, "that was good music last night."

"Oh, hey!" Jeff yelped, "glad you liked it."

"It's sure nice to get good music in Landsend," the man went on. "I hope Rick's place can hold out. We're a pretty quiet town, as you've probably noticed. Tourists come through, but you can pretty much see what there is to see in an hour. I'm Ralph, by the way."

"Nice to meet you, Ralph," said Jeff. "So, what do folks do here?

"A little fishing, boatbuilding. Mostly elderly, anymore—retired and whatnot." The back door opened and a stout, bullet-headed man sloped in. Ralph shot him a glance. "Well, guys, gotta git. I'll be in tonight." The stout man shambled into the kitchen, the waitress followed, and Ralph followed them with his eyes, then leaned in toward us and whispered, "If I was you fellas, I wouldn't go pokin' around too much. There's some here who aren't too friendly." He gave us a nod and slipped out.

"Well," said Bradley, "I guess we've been warned."

At a nearby table, four guys chomped, chewed, grunted, and belched. Their frowzy attire led me to ruminate on the evolution of the modern American male. Festooned with advertising logos and draped in baggy shrouds, they did not present an ennobling sight. "Classy joint, huh? said Brad, peering around the little hash house. "Any guesses on how long this gig will last?"

Jeff made an enigmatic face. "Rick hasn't said anything about his plans, whether he's going to have other bands come in or what. We had a good crowd last night, but I'm not sure how long he can keep it up."

"A common problem," grinned Brad.

One of the four guys, a bulb-headed guy with thin, stringy hair, was staring at me. He nudged the man next to him and they looked at me and guffawed. I was glad I wasn't alone, but even with Jeff and Brad by my side, this looked like a bunch I did not want to tangle with. They soon got up, leaving a mass of wreckage behind them, and slouched toward the door. "Nice boots" muttered bulb-head as they shuffled out. Well, shit; not a day in Landsend and I was already a marked man.

7

Persistence Of Memory

Things stirred beneath the surface, things moved in the soil, things buried, things shunned, things forgotten. But memory is not existence, and some things persisted, forgotten but not gone. Smoothly, silently they slipped through green forests and cold waters, dreaming and whispering to one another. Far out in the vast seas swam other things, their voices pinging through the depths, calling. Answers were faint and long in coming, but come they did, bearing memories and longing for communion and procreation. The thread stretched thin, but it never broke.

The old ones who had known and respected the unseen beings had dwindled, a new breed was multiplying rapidly, a breed that raised great tall houses and sailed huge smoking boats. It was said that the new beings were limitless in number and were taking over the whole world. And that they fouled everything they touched.

Voices called through the water and the forests and the air, voices weak but persistent: *Beware the new ones. They must be watched.* And within some of the drifting, dreaming things there resided a stubborn residue of memory that carried on across the trackless reaches of strange eons. *We, too, built cities*, they remembered. *We, too, were great.*

8

Roll Them Bones

The following Saturday afternoon the sun was shedding its gossamer veil and patches of blue glimmered over the bay. We ate our assorted dog's breakfasts and Jeff suggested a walk. Brad nodded eagerly. "Sure! Maybe we'll get to see more seal-feeding."

It was unseasonably warm, and a respectable lot of tourists, including some of the last night's patrons, roamed Harbor Street. The dozing cat in the window of the Grebe Bookstore enticed us in and we were greeted by a tall woman in purple. Jeff introduced us as the Star Chamber band.

She flashed us a dazzling smile. "I'll be in, I love jazz."

"Do you have anything about Port Townsend?" I asked.

She gave me a thoughtful look. "There's nothing published. Don't know why—we certainly have a colorful history. The only information I can think of is the old newspaper, the *Lector*. Been out of business for years, but I believe the Port Diablo Library has it on microfilm." We poked through the stacks a few more minutes, purchased some trashy paperbacks, and headed back out to the beach. The sun was warm but the shore was deserted. On the far sand spit the little shanties basked in the afternoon light. Now and then, a dark figure appeared and vanished.

We ambled down a long trail heading for the beach north of town, savoring the sweet tang of the underbrush and the feeling of sand under our feet. My eyes wandered from the path and lit on a clump of driftwood partially concealed in a small, shadowy depression. I stopped, blinked, and looked again. "Uhh—guys," I said. It wasn't driftwood, it was bones: thin, gray, whiplike bones. We picked our way gingerly into the brush and stood over what looked to be a skeleton about six feet long.

Jeff ran a finger over one of the bones. "Hmmm...strange texture. Almost gelatinous"

"A seal, maybe," I said.

"Yeah," said Brad, "looks like part of a flipper."

Jeff shook his head slowly. "I don't think so." He pointed toward another object nearby: a skull. With gaping eyeholes and two short horns, it looked like a prop from an old Western—except for the two nasty-looking incisors jutting from the upper plate.

"That's no kind of seal I've ever seen," said Jeff.

"A walrus?" I said, further displaying my ignorance of the marine mammal realm.

"Maybe it's Bigfoot," Brad said, grinning stupidly. You had to love him.

Jeff knelt and touched the skull. "Something very weird about this boy." He stood and said, "I think we should take these bones to a specialist. I know just the guy, right up here at Dungeness College, in Port Diablo." Jeff gently picked up the skull and asked Brad and me to gather a few of the shorter bones.

"I can save you the trouble." A tall figure stood etched against the sky. Draped in a shabby slicker, fray-bottomed pants, and not much else, he nonetheless presented a picture of solemn dignity.

"Those bones is best let alone," he said, his voice soft but firm. "It came here to die in peace."

"You know what this was?" Jeff asked.

The man glared at us with dark, unblinking eyes. "I know and you don't. Better that way." His face was saturnine, his eyes and mouth dark slits.

Jeff's academic background asserted itself. "Look, these are bones, long-dead, lying on a public beach. We only want to find out what they are. I don't mean to disrespect traditional customs, but maybe we could learn something from them."

The tall stranger regarded us a moment. "Well, then," he said, "won't try and stop you. Only, you might save yourselves trouble by leaving them lay." He moved slowly down the path and disappeared.

Jeff laughed nervously. "Sheesh, was he for real or what?"

"All the more reason to have these things looked at," Brad said.

I wasn't so sure. "Maybe the guy's right. Maybe we should just leave them here."

"I think that would be wrong," Jeff insisted. "Native customs and traditions are fine. I respect them. But we're not them, and these bones aren't, either. I'm an empiricist. I can't leave such a mystery just lying here." He wrapped the skull and bones in his jacket and we walked back toward town. I looked back, trying to see where the dark man had gone, and hoping we hadn't made ourselves one more enemy.

9

A Man Of Business

Olin Marsh did not like the house. It was too big and too dark, and he often got lost in its far reaches, where even the heat from the great furnace, deep in the forbidden cellar, did not fully penetrate. But if he disliked the house, Olin hated the tree. Though not large, it was black and ugly, and in the gray dusk its contorted limbs looked like the tentacles of a giant sea beast he'd once seen in a book. They seemed to be reaching toward the house. Toward him.

The mansion was the talk of Port Landsend, and all the more astonishing since Olin's father had at the same time erected a large new wharf on the downtown waterfront. Two contractors pressed a hundred men on the jobs, earning Mr. Marsh high regard among both genteel and laboring populations. And yet, some found the house excessive, even an affront. "Who is this Marsh, anyway?" they muttered in purse-lipped envy. "Who are his people?" To most, however, the dwelling's expansive bulk, finished in a sober brown and maroon, proclaimed better than anything else that prosperity was finally taking root in Port Landsend.

Olin remembered little of the old life in the East, but in quiet moments he vividly recalled the voyage across the rolling ocean, the grave-faced but kindly captain, the strangers talking in the dining saloon, the figures bent in misery at the railing. And he remembered pulling into the little city that was to be his new home, and the tall, dark man on the pier who seemed to look right through him. In the carriage ride to the house, Olin told his father about the man. "Most probably an Indian," his father replied. "There are a number of them about, though I daresay not for much longer."

The word "Indian" excited Olin, but his father's grim words chilled. "Why, Father?"

"They are a doomed race, Olin." With a black-gloved hand, the man gripped the silver pommel of his walking stick. His face was hard. "Doomed to give way before the new order of things."

"That's sad."

"Nonsense. I should say it is more accurate to assert that the Indians are merely evolving. Like the rest of humanity. We, all of us, shall evolve. Are evolving, even now."

These words seemed to offer hope, and this satisfied young Olin. They arrived at the big house that was to be their new home and went inside. Olin held his mother's hand and stood in the vestibule, silently taking in the wood-paneled elegance and the ponderous staircase rising into the ceiling. "And now," said his father, "I've business to attend to."

Unit Marsh sat down at his desk and pulled a letter from the top drawer. He was a grave forty-nine, tall, erect, armored in stiff black broadcloth. His wide-set blue-gray eyes were chilly and remote, his salt-and-pepper beard enclosed thick lips and a weak chin. But no one who knew him would ever call Unit Marsh weak, and though a relative newcomer, he was a power in the Gate City. Not, however, a popular power; in the office, on the street, and at meetings of prominent businessmen, his granite aloofness seemed to convey a barely-veiled contempt for society. Invitations to join fraternal organizations and attend exclusive social occasions—summonses coveted by anyone else—went coldly unacknowledged. The man was an iceberg.

The last Board of Trade meeting had not gone well. After the recent doldrums, things were showing signs of picking up, and in 1889 hopes for a new boom were running high. So, too, were tempers. The leading businessmen rounded on their strangely obdurate associate. "See here, Marsh," said realtor Moses Ash, "when are you going to get off your high horse and run for city council? We need men of your stripe leading the charge, now more than ever."

Grocer Elijah Smithers thumped his fist on the table. "Yes, indeed. Why, your innings with the Coastal Line would put paid to these dull times."

"Quite right," exclaimed Ash, "we must pull *now* to keep going. Or perhaps you are not aware how much traffic we're losing to Seacoma."

Marsh regarded them with heavy-lidded coolness. "Gentlemen, please. I have no talent for politics, only business. You want a more outgoing man to represent you."

Matt Krupper, owner of the town's largest dry goods store and perhaps the most respected of the group, could no longer conceal his exasperation. "Hang it all, Marsh," he sputtered, "that's just it! Why say, 'represent *you*' and not '*us*'? It's as if you do not feel a part of our city. One would think you feel you have no stake here at all—that you were just passing through."

"Krupper's right," said druggist Shelburne Clough. "We can hang together or hang separately. Now that the North Pacific Railroad is talking about extending, it's imperative that we redouble our efforts at civic promotion. Marsh, are you in or not?"

Unit Marsh's placid features reddened slightly. He had little use for the social puffery and vainglorious illusions of so many of the business class, and he endured these meetings only to detect, and hopefully deflect, potential trouble. Marsh held up a hand. "Gentlemen, gentlemen. I do not believe conditions are as delicate as you make out. Nor do I believe the railroad will ever run into this city."

The air froze in shock.

"What?" croaked Krupper, his face reddening. "Why—how do you say this?"

Marsh shook his head. "The North Pacific will never bear the expense. Even now, they are barely able to pay their creditors. No, gentlemen, the railroad has stopped in Seacoma, and that is where it will stay."

"But a branch line, certainly…"

"Errant nonsense," Marsh rapped, in that smug tone that so infuriated his colleagues. "You may as well get it out of your minds."

The glistening faces glared apoplectically at Marsh but he continued, unruffled. "You—*we*—would do better to face the facts. That is why I am taking certain steps in my business to safeguard my interests for a long time to come, steps that I expect will redound well to our city. But I require that my time be free to concentrate my attention upon them."

The grumblings continued, but the businessmen of Port Landsend bowed to Unit Marsh's pronouncement. After all, if such a man desired to apply himself strictly to his business, that was his affair. It was also a certainty that the entire community would reap the benefit. Just look at the great house and the handsome wharf, which was by all appearances doing a brisk and growing trade in freight consignments. Look, too, at the new sanitary drainage system Mr. Marsh was taking in hand: was that not evidence of civic spirit? Look, finally, at the men employed, all good customers of misters Krupper, Clough, and Ash. No, it would not do to further antagonize Mr. Unit Marsh. He stood, surveyed the group with one dismissive sweep of his blue eyes, and left without another word.

For three years, James Swanson had watched those eyes. Watched, as they had overseen the ambitious constructions…watched, as their possessor became a prosperous man of business…and watched in Board of Trade meetings, where they betrayed not simply boredom but an almost palpable contempt for his fellow townsmen. Yes, for three years the venerable founder and perennial mayor of Port Landsend had watched those eyes. And hated them. For there was something beyond mere apathy or coldness about them:

something disturbingly alien. Swanson watched Marsh stride from the room, and frowned. What exactly were those "certain steps" he was taking?

In the dining room of the great house, the little family sat quietly. Mrs. Marsh and the boy knew better than to break the silence. Finally, Unit spoke: "Well, Lilian, it appears we shall be having company before long."

"Company, dear?" She swallowed, but took this potential bombshell with the placid reserve she had long since learned was the best way to handle her prickly spouse.

"Yes. I have heard lately from Uncle Asahel. He and Ida are coming to visit. From the tone of his letter, it seems he may settle here if Port Landsend agrees with him."

"Oh." She found the news vaguely unsettling, but kept her tone neutral. "What's he like?"

"I can't say. I've never met him, but he has been quite successful in the East."

"What is his business?"

"Like mine: shipping."

"How nice. We could use more like him out here."

Marsh reddened slightly. "What do you mean?"

Mrs. Marsh was surprised by his tone. "Well, I mean people with business success."

Marsh cleared his throat. "I don't know why you say that," he said, "as if we're wanting."

"Well, aren't we? If the railroad doesn't come, after all…I wonder if we'll be able to stand the next depression."

"The railroad was fool's talk. Those cretins downtown are too blinded by their own delusion to see it. And who says there's going to be another depression?"

"Honestly dear, there is certain to be one sooner or later."

"Oh, and now you're the authority on business conditions?"

Lilian Marsh reddened. She disliked this arrogant streak in her husband. Well, she too had a proud streak. "It's plain to see," she continued. "Declines always follow these booms, like the waves of the ocean."

"Well, I think we will let your picturesque little analogy pass, my dear. After all, it is I who is at the wharf every day."

"Very well," Lilian Marsh sighed. She knew when to leave off. "Incidentally, you've never said what city your uncle lives in."

"Haven't I? Well, I doubt you've heard of it. It was in decline for quite a long while, but Uncle Asahel has had a hand in its recent prosperity."

"Which city?"

"Innsmouth."

10

We Are Not Alone

Mist shrouded the road to Port Diablo, the few cars we met scuttled along as if anxious to escape the oppressive forest. Jeff played a Fats Waller tape, the jaunty swing of the Harlem piano master offering incongruous counterpoint to the glum landscape. Nestled in a cardboard box in the Volvo's trunk, our mysterious remains kept their own council.

"So, Jeff," I asked, "who's this guy we're seeing?"

"Edward Bishop Babson, marine biologist. He's done extensive work on marine mammals in the Northwest, including unusual and transient species. I checked out one of his articles: quite interesting. If anybody has some insight on these bones, it'd be him."

"Sounds like a deal," I said. Privately, I wasn't so sure. *Those bones are best let alone.* I stared out at the passing forest. What had the early settlers thought when they first confronted this dank, dark end of the earth? What fortitude they had, to carve out livelihoods and build a new civilization! What the hell had I done with my life? Right behind me, silent but accusing, sat the bones of something that had once lived, breathed, and possibly made love. *Might save yourselves trouble by leaving them lay.* What kind of trouble?

The dingy mill town of Port Diablo materialized against the azure backdrop of the Strait of Fury. We turned off the highway, passed through the white marble gates of Dungeness College, and slid to a stop in front of a modest brick building. A few twists and turns took us to the office of Dr. Babson. The professor was a youthful fifty, with silver-gray hair and a brown tweed jacket framing a pleasant, gray-bearded face. He rose smiling from behind his desk, shook our hands, and asked Jeff to place our curious parcel on a side table. He examined the bones for a moment then said, "An interesting find, a very interesting find indeed. How much do you know about them?"

"Not a thing," Jeff replied, "except to say they're like nothing I've ever seen. I'm a marine bio grad student, myself."

"A guy on the beach tried to stop us from taking them," Bradley interjected. "He told us it came there to die."

Dr. Babson eyed us curiously. "Did he?"

Jeff nodded. "He was rather, umm, mysterious."

"Ah. Well." The anthropologist removed his glasses and beckoned us into chairs around his government-issue metal desk. After an ominous silence he said, "There are many mysteries in this world, and that includes your bones. You see, they represent no known living species."

Jeff blinked. "But how can that be?"

Babson smiled tightly. "Oh, it can very well be. Yes, my young friends, we think we have discovered all there is to discover. We send probes into space and robots into the depths. Satellites scour the earth's surface. We beam radio signals to the far corners of the universe, hoping for an answer. Man's gaze is everywhere. Nothing, it seems, is impervious to detection. And yet, there is Sasquatch...the Loch Ness Monster...and this chap here."

"So," said Brad, "we've actually discovered a new species?"

The professor smiled gently. "Not quite, I'm afraid. No, we've known about him for some time. We just don't know what he is. Yes, as much as we like to tell ourselves otherwise, we far from know it all. We *do* know that your bones have turned up all over the world: the South Pacific,

Madagascar, the coast of New England, and in our own far Northwest. This fellow, whatever he is or was, did get around."

"So, no one's actually seen it," Jeff said.

"I wouldn't say that." The doctor swiveled toward a filing cabinet and extracted a folder. "Over the years I've amassed a dossier of mysterious events and sightings. Of course, most turn out to have ready explanations: tidal ripples, broaching whales, that sort of thing. But what about the others?" He slid a clipping across the desk, from the Seacoma *Sentinel* of March 27, 1899:

SEA SERPENT CAUGHT IN SNOOD CANAL

A large serpent-like beast was caught by two fishermen under Turtle Rock, two miles north of Stinking River. Mssrs. Brown and Jenkin, the captors, describe the creature as about eight feet in length and as big around as a man's thigh, with long dorsal, gills, large eyes, rows of sharp teeth, and a bulldog head. Its movement through the water is described as snakelike. They believe the creature is the sea serpent which has for some time puzzled locals on the Snood Canal. Jenkin had this to say: "The beast appeared suddenly as if out of nowhere, and its horrific features gave us quite a fright. It took some doing to finally subdue the monster." The remains have been placed in cold storage pending scientific examination.

Then another article, from June 8, 1904:

MONSTER OF THE SEA

Jos. Edmunds, owner of the Edmunds Wharf north of this city, this morning exhibited to reporters the remains of a

large sea creature. Edmonds explained that he discovered a
vertebrate and several other bones near his moorage on the
suburban beach. The articles are long, flexible, and oddly
textured. "I have seen a great many sea creatures," Edmunds
said, "but never a thing like this. These bones have a gelatinous,
or mucilaginous, texture. It beggars the imagination to
consider what sort of beast they came from." Scientists from
the University have stated their intention to visit the area near
the Edmunds Wharf in hopes of finding more material.

"Could this have been our boy?" Babson mused. "Possible, possible..."
He let out a bark of laughter. "Of course, they could've just made it all up,
to stimulate circulation. Newspapers did that in those days—still do, no
doubt. Nonetheless, these are intriguing tidbits."

He stood and smiled warmly. "So, the mystery remains: Are your bones
a variant of a known species, a mutation, or something else entirely? Thus far,
no link has been found. And until we can discover a live specimen, everything
about them must remain conjectural. I wish I could tell you more. But at any
rate, congratulations: you have entered a very small and fortunate fraternity.
If you happen to see a live one over in Port Landsend, give me a jingle." We
agreed that the bones should remain at Dungeness, and headed home.

"Well, what do you know," Bradley said, "our very own missing link."

Jeff was pensive. "Yeah. All we do now is sit and wait for one of these
babies to crawl up out of the bay and introduce himself. How could such
a species as this just go overlooked? It doesn't make sense. I mean, look at
those horns."

"Makes you wonder about how much we really see," said Bradley. "How
much we've missed."

"I'm glad to know man hasn't crowded everything else off the planet
yet," I said. "I hope we never find him."

"Not likely," said Jeff. "Sooner or later, we find everything."

Brad grinned wickedly. "Or it finds us."

11

Apparition

There was a lava lamp in my head. Everything was lime green and blobby, shadowy forms rubbed against me, flashes of emerald lightning ripped the darkness. I opened my eyes. What the hell— womb-memory? I pulled on jeans and staggered into the front room. Early Sunday afternoon after our third Saturday night the guys were heading back to the city. Brad grinned at me. "Morning, Erich, time to face reality. When are you going back?"

Reality—what was that? For Jeff, it was biology studies and for Bradley a nice job at a photo shop. For me, it was a dingy room and the lonely streets of Seacoma. I wandered over to the window and peered down at the Lamp Post Café and the water beyond. A sudden impulse grabbed me. "I don't know," I replied. "Maybe I'll hang out here awhile."

Jeff raised his eyebrows. "Okay, sure. Well, call if you find more bones." Their footsteps faded down the hall and all was still. I flopped down on the vinyl sofa and stared at the ceiling. *Reality, where are you?*

In school they called me "Zitface," out of school they ignored me completely, and I pretty much ignored myself. I lived at home, drove cab part-time, and spent the rest of the time daydreaming and hoping something would turn up. I was loafing in my room early one evening when Dad knocked on my door and entered holding a huge canvas-covered object. "This belonged to a guy at the office," he said. "Why don't you see what you can do with it?" He handed the thing to me and headed off to mix his first drink, leaving me too stunned to do anything but mumble a feeble thanks.

It was a bass viol. I stripped off the case and stared in disbelief. It was huge, rich weathered brown, scarred with age. A serious musical instrument. I'd never played a note in my life. I shrugged and saw in one of the holes a label bearing the name "Kay." I felt humbled, holding a piece of history. Whose fingers had traced out notes on the long ebony neck? Had it sawed away in a symphony orchestra, or thumped behind some long-forgotten dance band? *Boom.* I gently plucked the strings and my room filled with deep, mysterious sound. I plucked some more, this time stopping the strings and moving my fingers. *Zing.* I put on a record of blues and started picking out notes. I had no idea what I was actually playing, but I felt something new: excitement.

Kay and I became buddies. We were jamming to Miles Davis one night when Dad appeared in my door. "Erich," he said, crunching an ice cube, "I think you got it." With this encouragement I entered music studies at a community college and discovered that bass players were in short supply. After earning my blisters in the junior combo, I fell in with Jeff and his gang of trad-jazz cats who wore old clothes and idolized Armstrong and Biederbecke. Not exactly what I was used to, but we jammed and slipped into playing taverns and the odd private party. We thought we were the cat's meow.

Now here I was, in Port Landsend. Meow. We were grooving, and I liked the guys, but after the first couple of weekends the folks thinned out, leaving mostly the indifferent regulars at the bar. When I overheard one of them say, "They need a good country band in here," I felt like I'd been slugged. Well, the hell with it. It was too much to think about. I fell asleep.

Two hours later I awoke, lonely and hungry. I sauntered over to the Lamp Post, hoping the mean-looking guy with the smart mouth wouldn't be there. Hope smiled—there was only an old guy and a couple of giggly teens in the place. The waitress eyed me indifferently, took my order without comment, and left me with runny scrambled eggs and a view of empty beach and sleepy main drag. That the town was long sunk in senility was obvious. Still, the tranquility and antique atmosphere were unspoiled by yapping kids, bovine families, and all the bland banality of suburban American culture. I liked it. My eyes flicked to the waitress. Her clothes were neat and her glossy black hair flowed gracefully down her back. I liked the languid ease in her movements, her give-a-shit attitude. What was her story? I tossed her a smile and headed into the day.

The Harbor Street Victorians were old friends now, and as I moved through sunlight and shadow admiring the weathered brickwork, I felt like I was becoming part of the town. A plank sidewalk drew me down a side street, and halfway along the block I came to an open wooden sliding door, partially blocked by a battered green step van. Pinned to the door was a card lettered *Day's Magazines*. Inside, bare bulbs dimly lit an aisle filled of boxes and stretching away to a dusky vanishing point. "Hello?" I called.

"Huh?" A gangly, plaid-shirted man emerged from the shadows.

I waved my hand. "Hi—do you sell magazines?"

He regarded me curiously. "Yes, but we're not open to the public. We're strictly a mail order shop." His gray hair hung limply, his face looked worn but kind.

"Oh, okay." An imp grabbed my tongue: "Uh—do you think maybe you could use help?"

"Ho-ho-ho! Well, I might at that." He took his pipe from his mouth and waved it toward the stacks. "You can see what we've got here. We're getting a slug of orders lately and it's getting to be a bit more than I can keep up with, ever since the missus...Well, I can try you part-time, afternoons. Three dollars an hour?"

"That sounds good. My name's Erich Vann."

He shook my outstretched hand. "Jack Day. Do you live here in town?"

"I'm moving here. I play weekends in the jazz band down at the Star Chamber."

"Ho-ho-ho—a jazz band here? Well, well…"

Mr. Day gave me a brief explanation of his layout, and we agreed I'd work weekdays starting the following Monday. Walking back to Harbor Street, I felt the clammy hand of doubt. Was I really going to leave the city and move to a strange town for three dollars an hour and no visible social life? I caught a glimpse of the water and the distant mountains. Why not? I was ready for a change, and the change gods had plopped me down here in old PL. I liked Jack Day and his ho-ho-ho, and I liked the grub at the Lamp Post.

I passed the liquor store, then spun around and walked in to the pleasant aroma of distilled spirits. "Help you, young fellow?" said a round little man with blubbery lips and bulgy eyes. "Just looking." I had never been much of a drinker, and only my recent musical activity drew me to bars at all. Now, though, I thought I might use a little spine-stiffener. My gaze lit on a ceramic jug: *Old-Fashion Corn-Mash Whiskey.* I handed the clerk five dollars and left with my new friend. My boots thocked hollowly on the pavement, the air felt good on my face. I wondered if the waitress was still on duty. The Lamp Post was dark and the Star Chamber closed, so it was just me alone in the band room. I ate a cheese sandwich, stretched out on the couch, and lost myself in Kraftwerk and corn-mash.

Hours later I woke to a sound on the street below. It was people talking. I was set to doze off, but the voices rose to a weird garble that made me leap to the window—*shgllach-blaacchh-shlagl-grp.* Or something like. I thought it might be German, or Native American, but something about the sound made me doubt it. They moved out of earshot, then two figures materialized in the feeble yellow glow of the old incandescent street lamp at the corner. They hovered there an instant then turned the corner onto Harbor Street and vanished. It was a bare glimpse, but it was glimpse enough to make my scalp prickle. For the hunched figures could not have been more than four or five feet tall. Perhaps they were children. But what would children be doing out at that hour? And why were they *hopping?*

12

Partners

A bitter wind raked the dockhands and wharf rats watching the freighter *Molehaha* tie up at the United Wharf. Among them was white-bearded Mayor Swanson. The town elder had made it his custom to meet every vessel that called at Landsend, and not many years earlier such events would have been too frequent to permit the time. Lately, however, there was more than enough time—too much, in fact. This was the first ship of any size to call at Port Landsend in over a week. A temporary slump, opined the mayor's more sanguine associates. *Yes*, he told himself, *a temporary slump*. His gaze narrowed as it caught sight of a familiar carriage moving slowly toward the gangway: Unit Marsh's landau. Swanson eased behind a knot of onlookers. It would not do to give Marsh the idea he was being watched.

A small group of passengers filed ashore. Pulling their coats tight against the wind, some frowned, others smiled bravely. Following them came a large contingent of dark-skinned men, Pacific Islanders—more workers for the new drainage tunnel Marsh was curiously championing. They had already established a good-sized colony out at Point Judson—shanties, hardly a credit to the city! A short, stout man in a tall silk hat appeared at the top of the gangway, and beside him a shorter figure swathed in black bombazine, face concealed by a thick veil. As they walked slowly down the gangplank, a wave of muttering swept the spectators: *Some rare disease…bilious fever… hideous deformity…* Unit Marsh stepped from his carriage and nodded at the top-hatted man. "Uncle Asahel."

"Unit." The two exchanged a brusque handshake and the short man indicated his partner: "My wife, Ida." Unit bowed at the veiled woman, who returned the gesture with a barely-discernable nod. Mayor Swanson stroked his beard. So, he thought, Marsh has family. What brought them to Port Landsend? And why was Aunt Ida all covered up like that?

Marsh assisted his uncle and aunt into the landau and they clattered away, leaving a wake of buzzing speculation. Mayor Swanson offered perfunctory greeting to a few friends and walked slowly off toward Harbor Street, his gaze fixed on the receding vehicle. *Oh, Mr. Unit Marsh, you are a cute one.*

Unit Marsh would not have thought so. He was well-satisfied with the trend of business at the wharf and, for the most part, with life at home. Lilian had her usual woman's quibbles and she babied the boy overmuch, but she remained tractable. A few nights previous, though, she had asked how long Uncle Asahel and his mysterious wife would be staying.

"I am not altogether certain, Lilian," Unit replied. "Perhaps some weeks." He had not thought it necessary to inform her that it was in fact Uncle Asahel who had paid for the house and its furnishings, the wharf, the drainage tunnel, and now a new brick business building.

"What about Olin? I wonder how he will cope with this situation."

"Really, my dear, he must 'cope' whether he likes it or not."

"Unit, I wish you could be kinder toward him."

Her husband held up his hand. "Enough. Children require firmness and resolution from their parents. It is the best kind of love."

Lilian sighed and looked out the window. Black against the setting sun, the cypress kept its own counsel.

Some days later, late afternoon light filtered through the grimy clerestory of the United Wharf. In the dark-paneled office, Unit Marsh gathered a bundle of papers and locked them in a large safe. Then he and his uncle put on coats and stepped through a side door. The somber figures, one tall and erect, the other squat and dumpy, made a curious sight as they picked their way slowly across the muddy expanse of Harbor Street. No waterfront loiterer dared approach, however, and they continued along a boardwalk down Gribble Street then descended a precarious stairway. Unit unlocked an inconspicuous wooden door and lit a kerosene lantern. He closed the door behind them and the pair moved slowly down a dark corridor. The air was clammy, the walls melted into darkness beyond the cone of yellow light. Several yards further, the passage ended at an intersecting gallery of brick walls arched over a narrow waterway. "This tunnel is recently finished," said Unit, "and I am making extensions. The main tunnel will give access to our new building and the cistern."

"Most impressive," replied the squat man, "most impressive."

The men retraced their steps to the outside world, where the Marsh landau waited. It engulfed them and scuttled uphill like an oversized dung beetle. Inside, Unit turned toward Asahel. "How is Aunt Ida coming?"

"She is coming right along. She will soon be ready."

13

Hey, Ho, Nobody Home

The wind whistled through the tin ventilators and a wispy white cloud slid across the sky. I sat gazing into the circle of light vacated by the midnight lurchers until sleep overtook me. Morning banished nocturnal phantasms, and as gray light filtered in I pondered the strange apparition. They were probably just kids out late and fooling around, or folks with some kind of handicap, or maybe they'd just been hitting the old-fashioned corn-mash liquor. As Jeff said, most mysteries have mundane explanations. Anyway, I had a life to deal with.

I ate some cereal and called Rick, who okayed my staying in the room rent-free until I got on my feet, then fired up the Ford and drove to Seacoma to collect my scant belongings. In the milky light of day, the desolate valley was scarcely more welcoming than by night, and the stunted trees, fetid bogs, and moldering farmhouses made me feel like an alien and unwelcome presence, permitted to pass only by grudging sufferance. The city and the room that was once home now felt alien, too, and I kept my mind fixed on the future as I threw my stuff into a couple of boxes and phoned my regrets to the cab company and my landlord. Eyes on the horizon, I turned tail for PL.

Back on Harbor Street, I slid into the town's lone service station. The attendant shambled out to fill my tank; he was a tall, thin young man with oddly old-looking gray skin and a craggy face with a wide mouth and strands of wispy hair straggling from his otherwise bald head. He nodded curtly at my greeting and took ten dollars without comment. He reeked of fish. I was getting into the car when bulb-head came out of the station. He didn't look my way, but I didn't want him getting any ideas. I ducked low in the seat and watched him shamble off down the street, a sorry specimen who had dissed a total stranger. Maybe I should make nice and get him on my side. The again, you can't get along with every damn body, either. I'd just keep my eyes open and my mouth shut, and hope most folks observed my policy of live-and-let-live.

I dumped my stuff in the apartment and ate a cheese sandwich. The golden late-afternoon sunlight invited exploration, I hadn't seen beyond downtown, so I headed toward the bluff, where I figured there must be a way up the hill. Sure enough, a long stairway ascended the verdant hillside. I climbed briskly and at the summit turned to survey a magnificent view. Port Landsend Bay and Pilot Sound were a vast silver swath ringed by the snowy Cascadian and Olympian ranges. Closer in, the jumbled downtown roofs formed a picturesque urban tableau, and up the hill lay a neighborhood of elderly frame houses. A nimbus of yellow light drew my gaze westward, and saw several blocks away the jagged limbs of a giant tree and a congeries of crabbed gables rising in stark silhouette against the setting sun. I set off toward them along a clifftop street lined with small houses, many of them quaint Victorians in varying states of repair. I wondered how many eyes watched me furtively from behind lace curtains. An old folk song ran through my head—*Hey, ho, nobody home, meat nor drink nor money have I none.*

I arrived at the sunset vision and beheld a scene of awful majesty. The tree was a stupendous specimen of a cypress; almost obscenely, the trunk thrust titan roots deep into the earth, and with malevolent exuberance the gnarled branches pierced the soft winter sky. Even in direct sunlight the arboreal behemoth shone more black than green. It was the most magnificent tree I'd ever seen. A tall hedgerow and spiky iron fence kept the more intimate features of the house well-screened from prying eyes, and the front gateway was forbiddingly boarded and chained, but from the road I saw a concoction of witch-hatted turrets, ornate gables, and brick chimneys, all mimicking the monster tree in their insolent affront to the heavens. The visible siding was weathered a deep russet brown, and the whole assemblage seemed to suck the very light from the day.

I made a slow circle of the house, and as I came to the rear I saw a black wrought iron enclosure standing away from the building. I shifted my position a few feet and saw a thin slab of ghost-gray granite. A headstone. Something crunched behind me. I wheeled around and faced a pair of bulging eyes. "What are you doin' here?" said the man, in a mushy voice. He was ugly and bald and a lot shorter than me, and he stood too close for comfort.

I decided to play the innocent sightseer. "Just admiring the house."

"Thish's private prappity."

"Okaay…"

The dead fish eyes stared. "Better git out." He jerked his head.

I glared back. "It's a public street. Is that a gravestone in there?"

"None o' your bithneth." He came closer, puffing himself up like an angry grouse. I almost felt sorry for the little creep, but once you start letting people push you around, you're done for. "I can look all I want, pal," I growled in my most threatening voice. Then I turned and walked away. Why take chances getting into a scuffle with my bass-playing fingers? I left the house behind and turned up the hill, letting myself calm down. The area was a typical small-town neighborhood, but many of the houses were dilapidated and looked to be vacant. No kids played, no dogs barked, not even a bird chirped. *Hey, ho, nobody home.*

14

Queer Relations

Olin Marsh watched his father step from the carriage, then the other man in the big hat, then the shrouded woman. The afternoon was lit by a lowering sun and dark clouds, and there was a slice of yellow sky to the west that contrasted strikingly with the black-clad figures. He saw them disappear into the house, and watched from his cracked bedroom door as they traipsed up the creaking stairs to the third floor. His great-aunt and uncle, his father had told him, were coming to stay awhile. But why was she all covered up?

At ten, Olin was growing fast, but he was still afraid of his father and he knew that any inquisitive prowling upstairs could earn him unpleasant attention. It seemed to be the only kind his father was capable of. Lately, too, he seemed preoccupied, anxious. Perhaps, Olin thought, these new relations had him on edge. His father also seemed to know these people more intimately than he had let on.

Uncle Asahel was a short, stumpy man with big lips and wide eyes that never seemed to blink, but he was courteous and he joined the family for breakfast and dinner every day. "Please, call me 'Asahel'," he told Olin. His father forbade such familiarity, however, and under his stern surveillance conversation was stilted and strained.

48

His veiled wife was another matter. She took all her meals in her room and never appeared downstairs. "I hope Ida is comfortable, Asahel," Lilian asked shortly after their arrival.

"Yes, thank you," replied Asahel. "She is grateful, as are we both, for the comfort that you and Unit have so graciously afforded." He said no more, and Olin thought he detected a slight look of exasperation flit across his mother's face.

Impulsively, Olin asked, "May we meet her one day?"

"Hush," said his father.

"I'm afraid she must remain in seclusion, Olin," said Asahel in his soft, lisping voice, "Hers is an unusual—er, condition—you see, and we must consider her feelings. You understand, I'm sure." Olin nodded.

Often, the two men retired to the study, and when his mother was safely in her parlor chair, Olin quietly slipped into the corridor and listened at the study door. Fragments of muttered conversation only deepened the mystery: *Obed has done well…Innsmouth is building up…changeover…authorities have been dealt with…*

Olin eavesdropped as long as he dared, then returned to his room, his mind churning. Changeover? Authorities? What did it all mean? Despite warnings, Olin could not ignore the muffled paddings and mutterings, the clattering of the landau at odd hours, and his father's increasingly brusque manner. One day, he walked into the parlor in time to overhear Asahel say to Unit, "We will examine the book this evening."

"Book, father? What book?"

"Never mind, Olin. In time, you may see." With that, the two men left, leaving Olin with his mother. The young man retreated to his own books, with their pictures of birds and animals and antique cities.

His father paid little attention until one evening when he walked into the parlor and came upon his son, reading. Unit glanced at the picture book of jungle animals and scowled. "You waste your time with this twaddle," he said, in a voice as cold as the wind rustling in the cypress outside. "Why not direct your study more toward the practical side of things?"

Olin's heart raced. "I," he stammered, "I don't know, Father…"

The halting response only further exasperated Unit. Was the boy a complete ninny? "You don't know? Then why read them?" The way his father loomed overhead was terrifying. He had not struck him, ever, but Olin's instincts told him he well might. "I suggest," Unit continued, "that you pay stricter attention to things of importance. I want you prepared to enter business. As for this…" His father plucked the picture book from Olin's fingers and strode from the room, leaving his son to stare into a bleak and unrelenting future.

15

Tendrils

low wind, come wrack. I don't remember much high school Shakespeare, but I do remember that. Did it never stop blowing here? At last, the nagging moan in the vent drove me from my bed. I shuffled to the bathroom to wash the sour taste of whiskey from my mouth, then paced the deserted living room in frustration. I missed the guys and missed the restless hum and energy of the city. Why the hell had I come here, and why did I think I'd be any less lonely? I was down to my last ten dollars. Fool! Oh well, it was Friday—magical, mystical Friday. Brad and Jeff would arrive soon, full of noise and energy, and again we'd fling our brave, brazen music into the face of an indifferent world. Come Sunday I'd have some dough. And anyway, the Lamp Post was cheap.

I greeted the waitress with a cheery "'Morning!"

"Hey."

"How goes the battle of Port Landsend today?" Man, did I really say that? No matter, she wasn't biting.

"Coffee?" she asked. Standing close to me, she radiated a faint, musky scent. Her big eyes held a limpid, emerald glimmer, as if reflecting the sea, and her muscular thighs swished against her skirt as she walked over with my breakfast. She placed it gently before me and walked away to sit down

51

near the kitchen window. I took a bite of toast and caught the movement of dark eyes flicking away from me. *Getting curious?*

Yeah, right. I'd met exactly two women in the last five years, one I picked up in the cab and one a singer I occasionally gigged with. Both tried me on for size and found me a bum fit. Just now, though, things were looking interesting. I didn't want to get my hopes up—still…I ate slowly, enjoying the view outside and in, and when the waitress took my plate she brushed a stray hair from her face and gave me another eye flick—and, I definitely positively just about pretty nearly would swear to it, the faintest hint of a smile.

I looked out at the beach and saw three figures emerge from beneath the pilings under the neighboring building. The men were short and dark-skinned, and they carried large sacks slung over their shoulders.

"Fah!" exclaimed a man in the next booth. "Them guys."

I'd noticed him before, a pouch-faced old guy with petulant lips and gimlet eyes. I pegged him as the local rummy—I'd met plenty like him driving cab. "Indians?" I asked.

"Look like Indians. Ain't. These here's shore people."

"Shore people?"

"Live out to the point. Come over from the South Seas back in the old days, brung in as laborers, stayed on for fishing and such. You'll see 'um on the beach hereabouts if you've a mind to go wanderin'. Wouldn't advise it, though." His eyes darted nervously.

"No?" I said.

"I can see you ain't from around here," he continued, "and that's no worry of mine. Fact is, I like to see strangers in town. Only they's others ain't so happy."

"Don't like outsiders?"

"Don't like snoopers. Never cared for them shore folk, myself. Them and them sacks of theirs, all covered in fish guts, stink like rotten mack'rul. Worst thing is the talk—all slobberin'-like. Some South Sea dialec'. They stick to their own kind, I'll give 'um that. I keep clear of 'um and you'll do the same if you're smart, which it looks like you are."

All slobberin'-like. "Jeez," I exclaimed, "I heard them. The other night, right outside the window."

"That so? Well, steer clear of 'um, that's my advice to you." He coughed again and turned back to his coffee.

Two warnings now about "snooping"—three, counting the little creepy guy. A dog fed to the fishes. A dissing by a jerk who obviously hadn't looked in a mirror. What the hell kind of town had I fetched up in? Screw it. I was here to do a job, and I was going to do it. After all, this crap probably happened anywhere. I headed for the door, and as I turned the knob I said to the waitress, "We're playing across the street tonight and tomorrow. Drop in if you want."

Just after twelve my new boss greeted me with a ho-ho-ho and handed me a pencil diagram showing the locations of the major magazines. "It's very vital that each title get into its proper pew," he said, clenching his pipe in his teeth. "Leave go any you can't locate, and we'll revision them later." He advised me to lift with my legs and not my back, and for the next four hours I piled boxes on the hand truck and wheeled them down the dimly-lit aisles. The alcoves along the four aisles were stacked to the ceiling with magazines from every time period and sphere of interest, and I couldn't help but pause occasionally to flip through something that caught my eye. It was dusty drudgery at first, but as I got my rhythm my under-utilized muscles came awake and I felt good. It was good, too, hanging with all the old magazines and the faces peering from the covers of *Collier's* and *Look* and *Ladies Home Journal*. One more tendril had reached out to hold me to this odd little city.

Late in the afternoon I had just set down a pile of boxes at the far end of an aisle when I saw heavy timbers, cross-braces, and large metal runners suspended from a rusty track in the ceiling. A door. The upper works were shrouded in cobwebs and it looked like it hadn't been opened for decades. Cool air wafted from the edges, air tinged with the same pungent fetor that emanated from the mysterious aperture in Rick Weller's office. Then it hit me: the tunnel!

Jack was suddenly behind me. "Erich, have you seen my pipe?"

"No—haven't seen it. Big door here, huh?"

"Well, that's all closed up. Are you done here?"

I followed Jack to the front where he dismissed me with a smile, satisfied with my day's work. As I trudged slowly up the boardwalk and turned toward the Star Chamber, I could think only of the door. The tunnel—had to be. How could I get in there? A raucous blast from overhead broke the spell and I looked up to see hundreds of crows flapping westward, their cawing echoing through the deserted streets like sardonic laughter at us pitiful earth-bound humans. I walked to the beach, flopped down in a pile of driftwood, and watched the last black stragglers disappear. Where were they going? Crows, bones, doors. Women. So many mysteries.

Twilight settled in upon the quiet city. I needed to get back to the apartment and prepare for the evening, but nature held me in her heaving bosom. The water lapped, the breeze blew, and wisps of cirrus clouds glimmered high in the deepening dusk. Salt air filled me with primal energy and I felt a sudden hot jab of desire. I nestled into the driftwood and came alive spontaneously, letting fly a triumphant howl. Far away, a seal barked.

16

Shadow Of A Smile

The reflection made her tingle. She had never worn clothes like this. Most Port Landsend women wore jeans and sweaters and the men—forget it. "Dressing up" was not the PL way and not hers, either. Now, though, she stood happily in something she'd never worn before. Why? She hardly knew. She only knew the clothes felt and looked fantastic.

For Sara, childhood consciousness commenced with shadowy furniture and muffled mutterings. Then, a succession of unsmiling faces as she was passed among relations who fed and clothed her, at times just barely, but gave her little more. She was "different," the family ceaselessly reminded her: "No, Sara, you'll have to stay behind…No, Sara, you'll only be in the way…No, Sara, you're not ready…" No, no, no.

She suffered school in silence, hating the mechanical drone of the teachers, the casual cruelty of the other kids, and the joyless rote "learning" in the ugly cinder-block building miles from town. Sara had one friend, and for three happy years she and Judy played quiet games, walked by the beach, and shared secret dreams. Then, one sunny afternoon, Judy said, ever so softly, "You're weird." Sara still saw the glint of the sun off the windows that day, still felt the warmth, still felt sick to her stomach. She played with Judy only once more after that. She was sad for a little while, and then accepted it. Judy was just being a kid, and kids were creeps.

After graduation Sara settled into a fixed orbit. She took a tiny downtown apartment in a building her family owned, rose at seven six days a week, dressed in a black skirt and white blouse, and walked two blocks to her uncle's café where she dispensed bland food with a bland expression. Sunday was her day off, and that was enough. If an acquaintance or occasional face from school wandered in, she paid them no more mind than she would a fly on the counter.

She did have one passion: swimming. She first entered the water of the bay as a young girl, and marveled at the buoyancy of her body and how eagerly it took to this mysterious fluid. It was cold, but not that cold, and she never seemed to get tired. *Hey Judy,* she thought one night as she knifed through the cold water off Point Judson, *this weird enough for you?* For a long time, Sara was content to swim and walk and live alone. She liked thinking of herself as a loner; people were trouble (*You're weird*), always telling you their problems and what to do and what to be. Who needed them? Lately, however, strange thoughts crowded in: thoughts of men—young, handsome, smart, smiling men. Sara watched the local guys when they came in and sat joshing and cutting up, and studied the strangers as they roamed the town she took for granted. Where did they come from, what did they do? Sometimes, she saw a man who roused her desire, desperately, painfully. But they never seemed to see her.

Lately, though, one guy had been eyeing her in the café. She knew him only as a dropout who didn't seem to have any kind of life beyond taking up space and staring at her. "If you're not going to order anything," she told him, "you need to leave." He only grinned stupidly and asked her when she would go out with him. "Forget it," she replied. Next day, there he was again. Her cousin, the cook, shrugged off her complaints. It was such a drag.

But just now the guy was far from her thoughts. Sara turned and stretched languorously before the mirror, delighting in the tautness of her body in its new sheathing. She tossed her hair and smiled faintly. She'd never thought of herself as attractive. But now—now, there was another man hanging around, a good-looking young man with a gentle smile and cool clothes, who said cute things. She didn't mind him taking up space. Not one bit.

17

New Order

ames Swanson clutched his hickory walking stick and gazed out on the water. For more than twenty years the top of the bluff had been his observation post on the city the Father of Port Landsend considered his own. In those good early years, you could stand here and watch it grow, day by day, smoke puffing from chimneys, brick buildings rising into the sky, the bay bristling with ships. Sunup to sundown, the days dinned with hammering and sawing and the lusty shouts of laborers.

Not anymore. On this dank winter morning, the harbor was empty and all was quiet. Too quiet. The mayor, feeling the years but still ramrod straight, struggled to make sense of it all. He had tried, Lord how he had tried, feting the railroad, feting the prospective merchants and builders and shippers, feting the navy, feting the army. To be sure, a stout few had dug in and hung on, bless them. But they were the old guard now, and there was no new guard in sight. The railroad—well, that was dead and buried. Even the steamships shunned the Gate City, and the sight of them sweeping insolently by on their way to Seacoma, like society belles snubbing a former suitor, brought Swanson to the brink of tears. The Delmonico Hotel, which had opened to such fanfare only a few years previous, had closed its doors, and even Matt Krupper's once-thriving emporium was skating on thin ice. Swanson snuggled deeper into his Astrakhan coat and sighed. He was losing his city. But then, he was no longer mayor. In his place was a bland-faced youngster who had arrived recently from the East with oily promises of New York capital and Wall Street connections. The newspaper crowed lustily for a time, then lapsed into roaring silence amid rumors of unsavory assignations and drunken revels.

There were bright spots. The fishing fleet was having another banner season, its third in a row. Until recently, fishing had been of minor consequence, but lately the little smacks had been multiplying, as were the shanties on Point Judson. So, too, were slovenly saloons, where roistering song blasted late into the night. Swanson pursed his lips; fishing was not the kind of industry he had envisioned for his city, and fishermen—particularly *these* fishermen—not the kind of resident he had in mind, either. Oh, well, there was nothing else for it. Prosperity was prosperity, however it came.

Someone else was doing well: Unit Marsh. Well enough to raise a handsome three-story brick block in the center of town...well enough to push his "sanitary drainage tunnel" through the council (quite the champion of sanitation, Mr. Marsh)...well enough that yet another rust-streaked freighter was unloading at the United Wharf. Swanson scowled: What the devil was Marsh dealing in, anyway? Others wondered, too. Hardware dealer Bushrod Olds, for one, pestered the reclusive businessman with obnoxious frequency. "Here now, Marsh," he demanded, "what exactly is your business, that your wharf is so constantly busy?"

Marsh felt his face flush, but masked his annoyance under his customary opacity: "Dry goods, notions."

"Notions? Pah! What sort of notions?"

Unit Marsh did not like the man's tone. In fact, he detested him. Always braying sanctimonious bilge about how others ought to conduct their affairs and prying where he wasn't wanted. If Olds kept on, the man could become an annoyance. That would not do. Nonetheless, Marsh answered him civilly: "Articles that my clients find useful and that I find profitable.

Good day." He nodded curtly and walked away, leaving Mr. Bushrod Olds fuming in his wake.

Late one evening, Unit and Asahel Marsh drove to the wharf. A burly man in a brown derby emerged from the shadows, opened the gate for the landau, and closed it behind them. Entering the warehouse, Unit waved the two watchmen out, then pried open a large crate. "Yes," he said, "some appear to have expired. Regrettable."

"Still," replied Asahel, "the rest should be sufficient." He turned to another crate. "This material is to be shaped into stones of requisite shape and size, as ordered in the book. There can be no deviation; the stones are vitally essential if we are to maintain proper control."

"Is control possible?" Unit asked.

"It is essential," replied his uncle, "at least, at this point. Perhaps later, after humanity is subdued, it will no longer be necessary."

"Your man in San Francisco is in touch with the Ponpei contingent?"

"Yes, they're on their way. I imagine they will be here within the month."

"Excellent."

"The customs authorities have been taken care of?"

"Yes; Malone is quite thorough. We should have no trouble. I have arranged more housing at Point Judson." Unit grimaced and massaged his forehead.

"Are you feeling unwell?" his uncle queried.

"Not at all. A slight headache, nothing more." Unit walked into the adjoining office and pulled a lanyard behind his desk, ringing a bell in the outer shed. Asahel followed, frowning. "Your great-uncle Ralsa got headaches, too. Used to complain bitterly about 'em."

"Complained, did he?"

"Oh, yes. He was not a close-mouthed man like yourself."

"Yes, well…" Unit was not comfortable discussing his headaches or anything else about himself.

Answering the bell, the man in the brown derby entered and peered expectantly at the two. "Sir?"

Unit Marsh fixed him with a cool gaze. "You have alerted your men, Meek? Good. We want no attention here. Use rough methods if you must, but keep intruders out." Unit handed the big man an envelope. "Thankee, Mr. Marsh, sir," said the man. He touched his hat brim and exited.

Asahel peered darkly at Unit. "As to the other matter, Unit, it is liable to pose certain additional difficulties."

"Yes," said Unit. "However, Port Landsend has many transients passing through, as well as others of low class who may not be readily missed."

"Very well. Ida is ready."

Near midnight some days later, a tall figure watched the Marsh carriage enter the United Wharf. Two men, one stiffly upright, the other short and squat, got down and entered the warehouse. What were they doing in there? The tall man watched for a few more minutes, then walked slowly over to the water-side railing. It was a fine night, a night for remembering old friends and loved ones. Where had they all gone? Perhaps not so far as it seemed. He heard what sounded like seals barking, then a splash. Looking closely into the dark, he saw the wake of something swimming swiftly away from the wharf, something that appeared small and light in color. The swimmer made no sound except for one brief exhalation, soft, almost—human. S'kladog nodded to himself. *So, the whites, too.*

18

Man Is An Island

What was with bitches, anyways? They jerked your chain, they made you think they liked you, then they kicked you in the ass. All through high school they played with him, flirted with him, led him on, then dumped him. They acted like hot shit, but they were still just dumb bitches. Like this one at the Lamp Post, Sara what's-her-name. Stuck-up snoot. He'd show her.

Ron Crump was fed-up with the bullshit. Port Landsend sucked. It was too small, too rainy, too windy, and mostly too boring. Why the hell did they ever have to move there, anyways? His dad's "reasons" were so lame, when it was obvious that he was on the lam from certain homies in Evert. Oh, yeah, his old man was none too popular in that shithole. Crump gave him about a year in this new one. Then what?

At least his parents left him alone. They'd better; he showed that shrew-bitch step-mom of his where to get off after she ragged on him about fucking school. Bopped her one, and damn straight. After all, if his pathetic excuse for a father could get away with bopping her one, why the fuck couldn't he? As for his old man, he was never around, anyways. Come to think, it'd been a while since he saw him. Where had he gone off to? Fuck him.

Finally, Crump kissed school off. The teachers were lame and the other kids never accepted him. Fuck them, bunch of retards—some of them, what planet did they come from, anyways? Talk about stupid, half of them couldn't even hardly speak English. Who gave a fuck if he graduated? Better being out on your own and a real man and not a fucking pussy school kid.

No, what made Ronald Crump feel most like a real man was hurting people. He knew on some remote level that this was "wrong," but he couldn't help it. In fact, maybe it felt so good *because* it was wrong. Even now, the memory of the first time, the time when he discovered the absolute pure fucking joy of it, still raced through his mind and brought a grim smile to his thin lips. God it felt good, the fists impacting on that dumb fuck's fat face and fat belly. He couldn't even remember the guy's name, but he sure as fuck remembered the look on his face.

"I'm just trying to walk here," the guy simpered.

"You're such a whiner," Crump said, feeling oddly amused. He punched him in the gut once, and it felt good, so he punched him again. The kid yelped. Crump planted his feet wide and flexed his muscles and bashed him hard in the face.

"Leave me alone, asshole!" the guy yelped, and tried to run away.

Crump stared straight into the guy's eyes. They were jittering left and right, jittering with that sweet thing Crump recognized as *fear*. He felt all the blood in his body rush to his arms, his hands, and down below where it really mattered. "Asshole? You callin' me a asshole?" He hit him again. *Bam!*

"No!" the guy yelled, putting his hands up in front of his face. Crump drew back and slammed his fist into his stomach. He was surprised at how little his fist seemed hurt by hitting the guy. It almost seemed impervious to injury. The fat fuck didn't go down—this time—but he staggered and ran off crying. Crump watched him go, his body throbbing with pleasure.

Yes, hitting people felt good, but it didn't take care of everything. Crump had to find a woman, a woman to deal with the excess. Maybe he'd hit her while he was doing it. Yeah! There had to be one out there, one who would take him for who he was. Take him and *like* it. Or not. Same difference. Christ, his dad found one, didn't he? The old man treated his step-mom like crap and she still followed him around like a goddamn puppy.

Sara was the one. She was just playing hard to get, he knew that. Sure, she told him to get lost, that she wasn't interested in a "relationship." Well, he thought, I'm not asking you for one, bitch. At least she was honest. Okay, you could live with that. Only, he still wanted her. And plus, her eyes said something else. He was sure of it. That's the thing with bitches: Their voices said one thing, but their eyes and bodies said something else. Liars. As far as this one went, he'd show her lying ass, and it wouldn't be any stupid lame-ass "relationship," either. It would be a very simple, straightforward arrangement.

19

Portal

ack's van stood puttering outside the warehouse. "I've got to run up to the refuge," he announced, pipe in teeth. The county refuse facility was one of his main sources of used magazines, and I usually rode along to help. This time, though, he had other plans for me. "We've got a full regimen of orders to keep you busy," he said, handing me a thick sheaf of titles to ferret out. "You can lock up when you're done."

Groovy. I was digging my new life, hanging and practicing in the apartment, exploring the town, and working afternoons in the cool depths of the warehouse. Oh, and making eyes at a waitress in a dumpy café. Sometimes her wide lips seemed on the verge of smiling back, but they never quite got there. No matter, I'm a patient man. Good thing, too; I'd hoped that hanging out at the Star Chamber might open new social doors, but a few nights with the regulars cured me of that delusion. Aside from ever-smiling Ralph, they were broody, taciturn men with hard faces who drank harder, and they ignored me. I didn't get any smiles or nods walking around town, either. Women avoided my gaze and guys looked right through me. *Hey, ho, nobody home.* I chalked it up to wind, hard times, and natural aversion to strangers. I can dig it.

Touched by Jack's trust in me, I slid the outside door shut and set to shuttling boxes down the aisles. Afternoon was well on when my next load took me down to the mysterious door. Except in the one spot where a small portion of the crevice was visible, the boxes in front of the door were two and three stacks deep. Slumped in on themselves, caked with grime and mold, they had obviously been there for years. I stood staring at the upper door jam, thinking that if I moved some of the boxes, I might get a better look at the door. Might even get it open. What the hell. I moved the boxes away, trying to keep them in order, and the door stood clear. The thing was massive, a good ten feet tall and hewn from heavy timbers like something in a medieval castle. There didn't appear to be a latch of any kind, so I braced myself on the leading edge and pushed. It didn't budge. I pushed harder, it held fast.

I had just begun restacking the boxes when I heard something. I looked around and down the aisle. Nothing. It came again, louder. From the other side of the door. *Splash.* I leaned into the crevice and again the splash sounded, louder and louder and at regular intervals. A rowboat! I instinctively held my breath, knowing that mere inches separated me from an unseen oarsman. Something banged against the door. As the sounds faded, I raced to the front door and out to the side street, trying to get some bearings. Yes! The tunnel mouth the guys and I saw on our boat ride was in line with the warehouse, and the bore ran perpendicular to the aisles. How far in did the thing go? I thought of the weird stink in Rick's office, but if the tunnel did pass through the basement of his building, it had to make a ninety-degree bend. Well, okay. It was probably some guys doing repair work in the tunnel, or maybe somebody braver than me, exploring. What else could it be?

20

Worlds Collide

In the dark-paneled study, Unit Marsh gently closed the book and massaged his scalp. The headaches were getting worse, sometimes he felt like his skin was shrinking, like something was boring into his brain. Something off about the breathing apparatus, too. Now, at the worst possible moment. Why was this happening?

His uncle's scheme was hard to fathom. More material—"elementals," Asahel called it—had arrived, but Asahel said nothing more about it. All well and good, of course, as long as he was paying the bills. But how long would the money last? And what would happen when Asahel was no longer able? From the looks of him, that time was fast approaching. Forehead throbbing, Unit threw down his pen. Was he not getting enough rest? Rest—bah! There would be time enough for that. He shook his head and returned to the book. There was so much that yet needed deciphering.

In his bedroom, Olin stared at the ceiling. Even in the dark, he could see faces in the plaster, faces smiling, faces frowning, faces looking through him and beyond. What were they trying to tell him? He was fifteen and feeling a new kind of restlessness, strange and strangely exhilarating. For so long he had been content, even under the regime of his stern and unloving father. For so long he had enjoyed the after-school hours in the sunny parlor, doing his homework as his mother crocheted or read. He, too, loved to read, and loved reading at his mother's side.

But life was changing. In the past months Olin had grown tall, broad in shoulder, and deep in voice. He had also grown less shy, and where he never before looked anyone in the eye, he did now, steadily, unflinchingly. Now, too, he was no longer content to sit at home after school, shut away from the world. Now, he wanted to walk, to roam the neighborhood looking at trees and houses and sky. Pleasantly surprised when his mother did not object but actually encouraged his explorations, Olin steadily widened his range until it reached the waterfront. He instinctively avoided his father's wharf and found a place two blocks away, where he could gaze at the harbor and the rust-streaked ships riding at anchor. Were there any boys his age among the crews? He pictured them scrambling up masts and manning the wheel, plowing through the raging ocean. He thought he might like to be one of them, sailing the world, discovering its secrets. One thing he knew: He did not want to go into business with his father.

Olin was at his spot by the bay one warm October afternoon when a shadow fell over him. He turned and saw a man, tall and dark and wearing a raggedy overcoat despite the fine weather. From beneath a battered slouch hat, black stringy hair fell to his shoulders. Olin's heart jumped—it was the man at the pier, when they got off the ship. He sensed the man's eyes upon him and looked at him, eyebrows up. The man nodded slightly. His face was gaunt and craggy, but his mouth looked kind. After a moment the stranger said "Hello."

Olin looked him in his deep brown eyes. "Hello."

"I have seen you before," the stranger said.

"Yes," he replied, "on the dock, when we arrived."

The man nodded slowly. "Yes. You were a little boy. Now…You come here often."

"You've seen me?"

"Yes."

"I like the view."

"It is a good place." The man's voice was soft and deep. "I knew this place before you came. Before the whites came."

"You've lived here a long time."

"Yes, a long time. I have seen it come from one world into another—the white man's world. Now, I hear men talking about how Port Landsend is dying out. Not enough settlers coming in, not making enough money." He chuckled softly. "White men always talk about money."

"My father is probably one of them. He doesn't complain, though."

"No?"

"No. He owns the wharf. It seems to be doing all right." Olin wondered if should be saying all this. Then again, why shouldn't he?

The man's face grew stern again. "It is a busy place. Lots of coming and going, lots of men working. Bad men, some of them, I think."

Olin felt funny in his stomach. He had no idea what his father did, and felt ashamed of his ignorance. He looked up at the man's face. "I think my father's business is shipping. Maybe the men are guarding valuable cargoes."

"Yes, maybe so. Only, strange that a father would not tell his son his business. Or maybe not so strange. I did not know my father at all."

Olin smiled ruefully. "I might as well not know mine, either. He doesn't like me."

"Your father doesn't like you? A shame."

The stranger was mysterious, yet Olin sensed empathy. "Do you think my father is up to something bad."

"I do not know." His tone was unconvincing.

"I think he is. He and my uncle…I don't know what. My father is—hard."

"The little man is your uncle."

"You have been watching them."

"I watch everything."

"What have you seen?"

"Your father and uncle going about late at night."

Olin shook his head. "I don't like it."

"There is always uncertainty and mystery in the world. Many things beneath the surface. Some beings keep themselves hidden, and some men, too. Some of these people and beings are dangerous to us. I hope that your father and uncle are not mixing up in bad things." He smiled down at the young man and extended his hand. "My name is S'kladog."

"I'm Olin. Olin Marsh."

They fell quiet and watched the water. The sun dipped toward the western peaks, a cormorant flapped past. Suddenly, something snorted beneath them. A big creature swam broke the surface a then disappeared. Another thrust its snout toward the sky, and still more appeared in the stygian murk.

"Sea lions!" Olin cried.

S'kladog nodded. "Sea lions and others. They come here often these days."

"Others?"

"Water Beings."

Olin looked again at the man. Water Beings? What was he saying? Some obscure reticence kept him from prying further. *They are a doomed race.* And yet… Olin looked again at S'kladog. "The whites changed things," he said.

S'kladog grunted softly. "So they did."

"It must have been—strange."

S'kladog shrugged. "Life is often strange."

Another sea lion spouted and rolled over playfully. "They never used to come here in such numbers," S'kladog said. "So many of them…" He fell quiet again, remembering the things he swam with in the lagoon, long ago, and the things he had met since, things that took him a long time to see. He looked at the young man beside him and hoped they would meet again. Maybe then he would tell him more.

Several days later, Mrs. Kelly Carlson reported to the police that for three days her eldest son had failed to return home from work at the Marsh wharf.

21

A Rummy Tale

*A*t six I closed the warehouse and walked out into the purple early spring evening. I had eaten nothing more all day than cereal and some fruit, but I couldn't think of food. There was a tunnel behind Jack's warehouse and somebody was rowing through it. I didn't dare breathe a word of this to Bradley or he'd be all over us to go in. Then again, if someone else went in…I'd never been much into reckless daring-do, but now I was curious.

Still determined to discern the likely trajectory of the tunnel, I turned into Gribble Street and poked along, studying the old shopfronts. A few of the spaces held active businesses, but most were vacant, and in mid-block a steep iron staircase descended to a rusty metal door. An entrance to the tunnel! I was about to go down and try the door when a young man lurched from a recess. I nodded but he only grimaced at me and slouched away. I should say, he looked young at first glance, but on the second he looked strangely *old*, like the service station guy and others I'd seen in the Lamp Post. The parchment-like gray skin, the thinning hair, the shambling walk. What the hell—a bad case of inbreeding? Something in the water?

Heeding the accumulated anti-snooping admonishments, I turned away from the stair and continued down the narrow back street. I came to a faded wooden barber pole and a vignette frozen in time: two barber chairs with dusty leather cushions…an ancient brass cash register, empty tray open…a little group of porcelain animal figurines…a stuffed bobcat. My eyes roamed the quaint tableau, then froze on an object lurking almost out of view: a greenish barrel-shaped effigy with a fringe of tentacles around its middle and a star-shaped head topped with a glaring eye. As the lengthening shadows engulfed me, I stood rooted there in mute fascination. What fevered imagination crafted the bizarre idol—and how had it ended up in a barbershop window? I vowed to return during daytime and meet the proprietor.

Heading back to the room, I passed the Town Tavern, the sole saloon doing business downtown. The door was open and the beer-stink hit a nostalgic nerve. What the hell. A half-dozen guys peered vacantly at me, including a couple more with those queer eldritch features. There was no barroom joviality in this joint, just grim faces staring into stale beer. I ordered a schooner from the dour bartender and saw the old rummy from the café sitting alone in the corner. I sat down and said Hello.

He eyed me uncertainly. "Oh, hullo young feller."

"We met the other day at the Lamp Post."

"Huh."

"Been workin' for Jack Day. Do you know him?"

"Hmpf."

"Got loads of old magazines. Nice guy."

"That so?"

"Yep. I decided to move here."

"You don't say?"

I peered around the room and said quietly, "Do you know anything about the tunnel under the city?"

He looked at me warily. "Told you 'bout snoopin'."

Ah, you do remember. "I wasn't snooping. I was working down there this afternoon and I heard this weird noise from behind this big old door at the end of the aisle. Sounded like a rowboat."

He shot a glance at the bar but no one looked our way. He leaned toward me. "Ain't nothin' more than the old drainpipe."

"That's it?"

He made a shrewd face. "Can't positively say it hasn't been used for *other* purposes along the way."

"What other purposes?"

"Smugglin', maybe."

"Smuggling—what?"

"Bootleg booze, most likely. Back in Prohibition times, bootleggin' was big business."

"So, somebody could row a boat in there."

"Nah. All closed up. Prob'ly caved in."

"I don't think so. I definitely heard something in there."

Braacckk! He erupted in a violent coughing fit, and with a revolting *pop* his left eye burst from his face and landed on the floor with a vitreous clatter. I suddenly didn't feel so good.

"Fah! Damn thing gets away from me ever now and then. Lost it on the goddamn *Stickney*—gouged her out on a spar pole." I stared dumbly at the ugly hole in his face as he scooped up the errant orb and plugged it back in. "I tell you, young feller, don't ever go to sea."

"Sailor, eh?"

"Able-body seaman. Come off the *Wilford Stickney* in 1932. October. Ol' Stinky: called her a lumberman, but a sieve is what she was, a leaky goddamn sieve. Thirteen days outa Santa Rosita down to Enchenada, then twenty more beatin' back up this motherfuckin' coast. Damn lucky to make 'Landsend. Going to the bottom would've been pure pleasure compared to the joy ride that tub give us. Limped in here with the old three-banger done for, Cap paid us off in gold bullion and skedaddled. Think o' that—carrying a thousand dollars' gold on that damn scow. Holy bald-headed Christ! Anyhow, cap' and crew skipped, I stuck. To this day I couldn't exactly tell you why."

I introduced myself and he nodded. "Ivor Lumpkin." His eyes drifted to the door, mine followed them to two standing figures. Cops. One was young and blond-haired and gangly, the other older, craggy-faced, with hard eyes and a slit mouth. They hovered there a moment, scanning the room. Lumpkin pursed his lips, picked up his glass, and took a long pull, almost as if trying to hide his face. After a few more seconds, the cops left. "The law," Lumpkin muttered, "or what passes for it. The old guy, Earl, he thinks he's tough shit and sometimes tries to prove it. Larry, the kid, ain't bad. They don't bother me none, I will say that. Reckon they know better. Still, I keep clear of 'um and advise you to do the same."

Reckon they know better. What did he mean? I steered the conversation back to the tunnel. "Anyway, I definitely heard something behind that door."

Ivor's mouth set hard. "Probably just some noise from out yonder." He waved his arm vaguely. "Ears playin' tricks. Happens to me all the time."

"This was no trick. I definitely heard something in there, something moving."

He leaned in close and fixed his good eye on me. "You best steer clear o' them tunnels, an' them ol' buildin's an' houses, too. Them places that's all shuttered-up and empty-lookin'—well, they *ain't*. There's folks in there, some of 'um, as don't bear lookin' at. Run yuh right off if they catch yuh snoopin'."

"Like that big old house uptown? Guy tried to run me off…"

Ivor dug his hand into my arm. "That's the Marsh house. Marsh got eyes in back of his head, and what Marsh don't like, he *fixes*."

"Oh, come on! Just one guy?"

"It's the truth! In Landsend, what Marsh says, goes. It's Marshes that kept out the railroad back in the old days, and kept out the highway and the ferryboat, kept business down. That's how th' Marshes want it."

"That's crazy. You can't pull that stuff nowadays. I mean, people would complain, the press'd be all over the place."

Lumpkin shrugged. "Look here, friend, you might ask yourself just how deep you want to get, here. 'Cause I'm sayin' you're liable to run into things you ain't counted on. Like that gal, the one you been peekin' at over in the café."

I stared at him silently.

"Oh, don't think I ain't got eyes in my head."

Or one, least. "What about her?"

He jerked to his feet and started for the door. "Walll," he chuckled, "you let me know when you find out."

22

Faces In The Fire

The faces ringing the fire hung like masks in the smoky air. Seen through the acrid haze, puffing and chawing and farting, they seemed to shrink into the night and merge with faces from long ago. But hard-edged reality—scarce jobs, nasty bosses, disdainful shop keepers, jackass cops—dominated the conversation. Now, too, there was a sinister new topic.

"More folks disappearin'," said an old Indian. "That man Olds…kids…"

"White slavin'," said a man with sunken cheeks.

"Shanghaiin'," said a little fat man.

"Hell," said a grizzled sourdough, "shanghaiin' kids an' old men?"

"Them folks is behind it," said a gangly guy with overbite. Eyes flicked toward the far end of the point. "Them Kanakas."

The little fat man took a swig from a jug and passed it on. "Come from way down in the South Seas, don't they?"

"Ponapee or thereabouts, I heard," said the man with sunken cheeks. "Ain't normal, singin' them crazy songs late at night."

"Got some strange ways," said the grizzled sourdough, "no two ways about that."

Everyone agreed that, between the newcomers and the toughs at the United Wharf, Port Landsend was having a spell of bad medicine.

"Shit," said a young Indian with a partially severed ear, "I went to take a piss by their damn wharf and they run me off with my wanger still hangin' out."

Laughter rose and died. They knew what he was talking about.

"Levasser was workin' there," said the man with sunken cheeks, "he told me some stories. That's a bad crew."

"Whatever happened to him, anyways?" asked the grizzled sourdough. The two looked at each other silently. Smuggling of some kind was obviously taking place. And yet, some swore that they had seen boats laden with mysterious bundles rowing *away* from the Marsh wharf and certain other sheds late at night—and that they had seen the bundles heaved into the bay. One or two even claimed that people had jumped from the boats into the water, but did not come out.

"Aw, hell," said the little fat man, "just dumpin' shit."

"Dumpin' *what* shit's the damn question," said overbite.

"Bodies o' their dead," said the old Indian.

"Shit," said sunken cheeks, "that ain't decent."

"Just chummin'," said the fat man. "In case you bums hasn't noticed, fishin's got a lot better since them folks showed up."

"They're chummin' all right," said severed (partially) ear, "but what in hell are they usin' for bait?"

They shook their heads and nursed the jug. On the edge of the group, a tall, dark man puffed quietly on his pipe. He was more accustomed to listening than talking. Much foolishness came from idle talk, and men could quickly turn ugly, even among his own people. That, he knew all too well. He thought again of the young fellow he had encountered by the water. *My father owns the wharf.* "It may be nothing," he said. "Or it may be something else."

"Shoot," said sunken cheeks, "what does that mean?"

"Water Beings."

"What 'Water Bein's'?"

"Creatures who have lived here a long time."

"Aw, come on," said overbite, "that's hooey."

"Ain't hooey," said the old Indian, "the Water Beings are real."

Sourdough spat into the pit. "If it is these 'Water Beings,' as you call them, what are they doin' here?"

The tall man blew another smoke ring into the night. "Lured here, maybe."

"Lured—why?"

"Women!" said severed ear. "Gonna mate with 'em!"

"Do not laugh," said the tall man, "they are real. And they will want feeding."

"Don't they eat fish?" said sunken cheeks, suddenly nervous.

"Eat fish. And more."

"What more?" asked the little fat man.

"What they are offered." S'kladog turned away into the night.

23

Growing Pains

*A*t seventeen, Olin Marsh was still pale and slender, but his shoulders had broadened, his legs had shot out to a surprising length, and his muscles had become taut and strong. In bed early in the morning and later, as he roamed the city, Olin marveled at his body; it was as if a new being—a man—was trapped inside and straining to get out. Soon, he would. Good thing, too, for the last years had been miserable. A handful of friendships bloomed and died, curtailed by his father who insisted "You've better things to do than associate with persons of no consequence."

It was all ridiculously unfair. Olin took refuge in books, absorbing art and history and wildlife with insatiable curiosity. But as he long feared, when he turned sixteen his father made good his vow to initiate him into the family business. Saturday after tedious Saturday Olin sat in the cold, dusty wharf office staring at ledgers, account books, manifests, inventories, his father lecturing him about debits, credits, payables, and receivables. "Do you understand?" Unit demanded, tapping his finger for response. Olin did not understand. The ledgers full of crabbed figures made his head spin, he was disgusted by the lickspittle fawning of the men, and there was a nasty odor permeating the place. And his father never told him what was in the well-sealed crates delivered by dingy steamers. After three months Unit summoned him to his study. "Olin, I had hoped that our office visits might serve as a beginning of your involvement in the family business. And yet, you appear uninterested. Am I wrong?"

"No, Father."

"Your marks are good, and you read constantly. But what is the point of it?" Unit grimaced and massaged his head, something Olin had seen him do increasingly often.

"It's interesting, Father."

"Bah! 'Interesting' is all well enough, but can you not find business 'interesting' too?"

Olin felt his face grow hot. "I—I have no head for figures, Father."

"Well, then, what exactly *do* you have a 'head' for? A lot of frippery?"

"I—I..."

"You what, boy?" Unit snorted and strode to the window. "I see that I have raised a hothouse flower. Too much of your mother in you."

"I'm sorry I'm a disappointment to you," Olin said, surprised at a new note of determination in his voice, "but I have learned something in school. I've learned that the world is much bigger and more complex than simply 'business.' And I mean to learn more."

Olin's eyes turned to his father's desk, where an enormous book lay open. Something told him it was the same one his father had concealed from him years earlier. "What is that book?"

His father glowered at him. "Nothing to do with you."

"Why, Father? I'm just asking."

Unit winced again, the pain sharper this time. He placed a black cloth over the volume. "Never mind that. Of more pressing importance is your future. If not in the business, how do you propose to make a living?"

Stung by the rebuff, Olin studied the stiff and impenetrable figure who was his father. "I don't know, yet. Maybe I'll become a scientist."

Unit Marsh looked away, momentarily at a loss. At last, he sighed. "Well, never mind all that. What matters is that you have disappointed me. You have closed the door I had hoped you would enter. Well, so be it. You may continue in your mother's bower until next year, when you will be of age to go into the world. I advise you to determine what exactly that will mean for you." Unit Marsh opened a ledger. "You may leave."

Lying in bed, Olin pondered his strange and unhappy family. Why was his father so secretive about the book, and about the relatives upstairs? Uncle Asahel continued his polite greetings and queer comings and goings, sometimes with his nephew but often alone, and often in the small hours of the morning. And what of Aunt Ida? No one ever talked about her anymore.

One May evening, as his senior year neared its end, Olin closed his books and turned to his mother at the kitchen table. She looked tired— now, for the first time, he consciously acknowledged that she deserved better than the cold, hard man she had married. At that moment, Olin hated his father and he hated himself for what he was about to say. But he had no choice. "Mother, it will soon be time for me to go. Father has made it plain, and I need to get away. I need to get out in the world."

Her eyes filled, not with sadness but love. "Yes, Dear, I know." She stared out the window at the jagged branches of the cypress. "It cannot be any other way. Your father has been hard on you. He never knew love when he was a boy, so you have never known his. I did, once. I suppose for a woman it's different. Still…" She fixed her soft blue eyes upon her son. "I have money set aside for you."

"Money?"

"I've been saving it for years in a special account at the bank. There is enough to last at least a year, probably—longer if you scrimp a little."

Olin started to cry softly, but his mother stroked his hand and said in a firm voice, "Olin, you can only grow stronger and wiser from here. Get into the world, see things. You needn't take a job, at least for a while, but if you do, do it for the experience."

"I want to work."

"Do you have any idea what you might do?"

"Start in Seacoma and plunge right in, work, make friends, see things I haven't seen before."

Lilian felt like crying, but she couldn't suppress a laugh. "Lately, you've been sounding more and more like a man, and now I see a man sitting before me. All the things I…" She suppressed a sob. "I'm sorry you've not been able to have friends here. I'm sorry for so many things."

Olin touched her sleeve and looked into her eyes. The sudden intimacy jarred him with the realization that he was much more his mother's son than his father's. "That's all right, Mother. I guess things happen in their own time."

Lilian nodded briskly. "Olin, in spite of everything, you have grown into a strong young man. I know you will manage well. When you're ready, the money will be waiting. And I will always be here for you."

"Mother—what happened to Aunt Ida?"

Lilian shook her head sadly. "I don't know. I have heard nothing about her for several weeks. She doesn't appear to be taking meals. Your father and uncle tell me nothing. They seem to think I'm not worth bothering with." She smiled sardonically. "It's funny, isn't it? How they depend on me, and yet…Well, I don't know why, but I believe Ida has found a release of some kind."

"She died?"

"I don't think so. I think she's gone away, perhaps to live with some other relatives."

The front door clicked. Unit Marsh was home. Olin felt a sudden chill, as if the air had been sucked from the house.

24

Good Vibrations

Rain again. Rain spitting on the tin vent over the bathroom, rain beating on the windows, rain sluicing down Harbor Street, rain washing out one more day. The drizzly, pizzly Pilot Sound winter makes you want to do nothing but sleep. Not that there's anything much to get up for, anyway. Except maybe the waitress. *You let me know when you find out.*

What would the coming weekend bring? Maybe some Hollywood location scout would stumble into the Star Chamber and catapult us into fame. Yeah, right. Sure, we had good nights, with the odd locals seeking excitement and tourists escaping their dismal lodgings. The Grebe lady sat alone smiling enigmatically, fishing-hat Ralph crowed "you guys are great!", and Rick schmoozed and cackled and puffed his stogies. You had to love the guy, but his desperation was painful. Mostly, though, it was the same dreary knot of regulars camped at the bar staring into their drinks. Not that they were actually hostile, they were just so damn oblivious. It was all getting old.

So was the music. Not that I didn't love Jeff's jolly cornet and Danny's fat, old-school piano, but after three months I was getting my fill of thumping through the same moth-eaten tunes, one solo after another. I was ready for something new—but what? As we rambled through yet another

"Sweet Georgia Brown" and "All of Me," I heard other echoes inside Kay's big wooden chest, vibrations that made me spend more of my free time practicing, listening, and experimenting with scales and rhythms alien to the comfy confines of traditional jazz. With no one around to bother, I picked and bowed with Mingus and Miles, gypsy orchestras, and Indian raga. My mind, body, and instrument were creating a new sonic world.

I was always scared to take solos, but with practice I grew more confident, and one night it all bubbled over. Jeff called out an old piece of corn called "Lulu's Back in Town," charged into it like Custer's bugler, handed off to Brad's tenor sax, then raised his eyebrows at me. *Oh, Kaayyy.* I grabbed my bow and unleashed an ascending whine like a bird struggling to escape a cage. It swooped, beat its head against the bars in a string of repeated notes, soared to a long high G, then relaxed into a bluesy mantra-thing that hinted at another dimension. Old Lulu had wandered into a very strange part of town. Jeff grinned and nodded, but Rick's puzzled grin looked more like a grim. I fell back into steady thumping and for the rest of the evening kept things in the pocket, just as Rick liked. Still, I knew I'd crossed a musical divide.

"Wow," Jeff said, upstairs, "what was *that?*"

"Oh, just some stuff I've been working on." I pulled out my jug, poured a discrete thimbleful, and passed it around.

Brad took a healthy swig. "So," he beamed, "this is your secret."

"Not entirely but partly. Maybe."

"Well, hey, jeez," said Jeff, fumbling for the right words, "I dig what you're going for on the bass." His face darkened. "I'm not sure Rick does."

"Yeah, I kind of surprised myself. I'll keep it solid, for Rick's sake. I don't know, though—Something's coming out. I wonder if I can even control it, or if I want to."

Brad nodded. "You got to follow your inner voice. My saxophone talks to me. I don't always understand it, and lots of times I feel like I'm just along for the ride. But it sounds like you're on to something."

Lying in bed, I felt myself moving into a new plane, a star in my own mind. I even forgot that the waitress never showed up. Sometime later, I stood bare-chested in a vast, green-lit room. Pulsating tones, as if from some distant organ, throbbed in my ears. My hands held the bass and I struck it with the bow, unleashing unearthly tremors. The organ responded and I hit the strings again and again, *zam-zam-zam*. A figure appeared, black and fuzzy around the edge. It drew near and I let fly gobs of glorious sound as she leaned in close and kissed me.

25

Flight

Olin Marsh did not have long to wait for freedom. Though his father refused to have the newspaper in the house, Olin bought a nickel copy of the *Lector* every morning on his walk to school. He did not like what he read: strongarm robberies, disturbances of the peace, and a series of unexplained disappearances. Then, a headline stopped him cold:

> UNWHOLESOME ACTIVITY in the vicinity of the United Wharf has caused justifiable alarm among the sober and respectable element of our city. Tramps and other rough characters, frequently in an all-too visible state of inebriation, loiter about the wharf and seem almost to exist under its protection. Mr. Bushrod Olds, a longtime businessman of this city, has issued this statement: "There is a bad odor about the place. No one seems to know exactly what business is being transacted there. The management is secretive. All manner of rough individuals loiter about the premises, discouraging reputable persons from intruding in the vicinity. It is a deplorable situation,

one that is impeding business activity in Port Landsend at
a time when that business is sorely needed."

That evening, Olin took the paper to his father. "Have you seen this?"

Unit Marsh waved his hand contemptuously. "Rubbish."

"Rubbish, Father? This sounds serious."

"It's nothing. And I would advise you to forget about it."

"This is happening on your wharf."

"See here, I will thank you to mind your tongue."

"But one cannot ignore..."

"One *will* ignore foolishness!"

"Father, why do you conceal so much from Mother and me?"

His father shot to his feet. "Hold your tongue!"

"'Hold your tongue'. That's all you ever say: 'Hold your tongue.' You
never talk to us—you treat Mother like dirt and you obviously hate me.
Why did you even have me?"

"Olin!"

"What about Aunt Ida—what's happened to her?"

Unit Marsh was red with rage. "Boy, do you want a beating?"

"Oh, like your bully-men give out so freely?"

Unit Marsh moved to backhand his son, but Olin blocked his arm.
Surprised at his unleashed power, he sent his father stumbling backward.

"You—!" said Unit.

"You! *Dear* father! What did I ever do, for you to hate me?"

"Boy—!"

"Don't bother, I'm leaving!"

"Olin?" His mother stood in the doorway, pale and shaking. "Unit, what
have you done?"

"Lilian, stay out of this."

Lilian Marsh shook, her face red. "Out of this? Unit, I am in this!"

Olin put an arm around his mother. "I'm going. It's time."

Lilian stared from son to husband, suppressing a sob. "Unit…Our son—why couldn't you love him? Why has it come to this?"

Glaring straight ahead, Unit Marsh marched from the room.

Lilian took Olin in her arms, hugged him desperately, and let him go. "Dear Olin," she said, eyes streaming. "Always know I love you." She kissed him one last time, then Olin Marsh ran to his room, filled a valise with clothes, and walked out of the house.

Some days later, a pale young man in black stood at a pier in Seacoma, peering into the deep green water. He missed his mother sorely but felt no trepidation, only liberation. Around him swirled life and energy, hope. Olin looked up at the great buildings, down the broad, teeming avenues, and into hundreds of eyes. He was sometimes disturbed by what he saw, but more often he was energized by faces aglow with ambition and hope. Life could only get better, much better.

Several months later, Lilian Marsh gave birth to twins. The ordeal proved too much for her and she died shortly afterward. The infants were placed in the care of a nanny, and Lilian Marsh was buried in the small yard beneath the cypress. There was no funeral.

26

Water World

The silver slab of Pilot Sound became one with the sky and the sun in the east turned the mist into an opaque yellow veil. Far out on the fog-mantled Sound, a ship's funnel floated in mid-air, the rest of the vessel invisible. Scarecrow cormorants perched on pilings airing their raggedy wings. The air smelled like the fountainhead of all life.

On the beach near Point Judson, I let my thoughts wander to the mysterious horned thing, known only by its bones. *Are you out there watching me right now?* And wander to the enigmatic, oddly alluring waitress. *Where are you this Sunday morning?* I lay back and let the sun and fog caress me.

I awoke to a presence. She loomed darkly in the sun, seeming to flow up out of the ground. How long had she been there? Her limpid green eyes regarded me curiously.

"Hello," I said.

She didn't smile. But she did sit down. I barely recognized her in a black turtleneck, peacoat, and black boots. She was stunning.

"Day off?" I asked.

"Yeah."

"Good day for it."

"Mm. I like it here in the morning, especially when it's foggy."

I fumbled for words. "Live here long?" *Lame.*

"Born here." Her voice was gentle but slightly rough around the edges.

"I just moved here."

She cocked her head and looked quizzically at me. "You moved here?"

"Yep. Never thought of myself as the impulsive type, but here I am."

She stretched her long legs out in front of her. "Here you are."

Is that good or bad? "I hit a dead-end in Seacoma. Figured it was time for a change."

"Brave man."

Zing, went my spine.

"So, what kind of music do you play?"

Come see for yourself. "Jazz."

"I don't really know jazz."

"No?" I wrapped my arms around my knees and leaned toward her. "My dad listened to jazz every night, so I had it pounded into me from an early age."

"What instrument do you play?"

"Bass."

"Like one of those big violins?"

"Yep, it's my baby—though sometimes it feels more like a coffin."

She chuckled, soft but throaty, and flicked her eyes at me briefly before tossing her hair and looking back to the water. "Yeah, it's a decent gig and I like the guys in the band. Not sure how long it'll last, but there it is."

"When he opened, I was, like, Really? In PL?" She shot me a curious glance. "I would think Port Landsend would be too quiet for a music guy."

I nodded slowly.

"Or whatever you call yourself." Was that a smile?

"Mm." I turned to face her. "So, you're an old Pee-eller."

"'Fraid so." She eyed me sideways, running her fingers through her hair.

"Maybe you could show me the town sometime. Let me in on some of its secrets."

A hint of frown. "Well...PL is pretty boring."

"Oh, every town has its secrets." I looked into her eyes and held out my hand. "I'm Erich Vann."

She gently held her hand out to me: large, soft, surprisingly heavy, and very warm. The webbing between fingers was unusually deep. "Sara. Sara Marsh."

Something moved in the corner of my eye. In the brush a couple of hundred feet away, a guy in a hoodie stood staring at us.

Sara saw him too. "Goddamn it."

"Who is it?"

"Nobody."

My body tensed, I got halfway to my feet. She took my hand, restrained me. Her grip was firm and strong. "Crump. He's been kind of after me," she said. "I told him I'm not interested, several times. He's a total shit." She looked closely at me, as if measuring something. "Erich, this guy's got problems. He's violent. I don't want to be anywhere him, and you don't, either."

"I have a feeling you can take care of yourself."

She looked again at me and burst out laughing. "Oh, God, I hope so!" Her eyes bored into mine and I felt my head wobble. "Want to walk?"

"Sure."

We turned away from the man in the grass and headed slowly away down the beach.

27

An Angry Man Drinks His Own Poison

What the fuck? Ron Crump's blood rose as he watched her and the guy sitting there talking like old homies. And just the other day she said, "I'm not into *relationships*." Yeah, right. Lying bitches. They always lie. So, who the fuck was this dude? He itched to go over there and confront them. This asshole didn't look like anything he couldn't handle.

But something told him outright confrontation would backfire. It was all so fucked up. Why couldn't she just give in and keep things simple? He had one thing that would simplify things real quick. Then she'd know he was right for her. One way or the other, he'd have her.

The two in the distance looked right at him. Sara looked like she was saying something to the guy. They got up and walked away. Ooh, did I scare you, bitches? Crump thought about following but watched them disappear and kept doing what he was doing. Go on, bitches, walk away. I'll catch up soon enough. An electric wave swept his body as he pictured the treatment he would give them. Chuckling, Ronald Crump lost himself in the sweet reverie of retaliation, and moments later enjoyed the upshot of his imagining. Laughing raucously, he looked around but saw no one near. Not that it mattered. Who would stop him?

28

Reunion

The smoke curled toward the ceiling, curled and coiled like her words. *You will see the Hidden Ones.* So much smoke those words seemed to him as a young man. Only later did they make sense. Later, when at last he did see.

So long, the time. Working on the railroad, the hop yards, the canneries…the white kids yelling insults…the kindly doctor who helped him back on his feet…the women…the darkness of some men's souls, and the light surrounding others. Now, he was happy on the beach at Port Landsend. Some of the people were Humans like himself, some were whites, and some were from far across the water. Everyone spoke in different languages and had different customs, but nonetheless they were able to come together and communicate and get along. Sometimes there were fights (men were still men), but mostly the men worked together. It was good to sit at the fire, and good to lie in a small, warm house and feel the earth hold you.

S'kladog was dying. He accepted it without fear or complaint, only with wonder at what the next world would be like. Perhaps he would see *them* again. He slept a while, then as the shadows lengthened he rose and walked. He had been waiting for the right time to return, and now that time had come. His good old legs took him steadily along the bluffs and out onto the flats. The white man's road was a new intrusion, but beyond it the prairie looked much the same. Passing through thick stands of cottonwood and poplar, he came to the place. He found only a few rotting house poles, but it was enough. Great white clouds piled high in the azure sky, like spirit beings watching with approval. He raised his arms and began to sing. S'kladog was home.

After a while, he stopped singing and walked slowly to the lagoon. For long he had feared the pain of returning. But time was surely a strange thing: The little sheltered place had hardly changed at all, and if one looked in the right direction, it might even be just as it was. And now, thanks to time and the magic of Tahmanous, the Spirit Power, he felt warm and strong being here once again. He felt their love coming back to him and filling him, he saw their heads nodding in approval, their smiles, undimmed. He was the last man of the S'klalth village.

A kingfisher rattled past, making him think again of M'katl. Where had she gone? Most likely she had changed shapes, changed worlds. But how? Had she herself joined the Hidden Ones? He sighed deeply: Yes, he was still alone, and still strange. Near tears, he sat down on a large log. Some time went by before S'kladog noticed the other man sitting in the shadows: one of the young men from the sandspit, whom S'kladog liked for his quiet dignity and for the wry sense of humor he detected in his blue eyes.

The stranger raised his hand. "Hello."

S'kladog nodded and said, "Come and have a smoke." The man came over and S'kladog held his pipe out to him. "I am S'kladog."

"Ka'atah'teh."

They smoked, and after a moment Ka'atah'teh spoke. "The guys at the spit are an interesting group, don't you think?"

"Yes," replied S'kladog. "I like them, mostly. There are a few I don't trust. Their eyes are empty. But I guess you get those anywhere."

"Those folks from the point," said Ka'atah'teh,

"Mm. From far away over the ocean."

"They pray to gods by the water, and they take things out and dump them."

"Sacrifices."

"I think so. The fish swarm around, and sea beasts have been seen."

"Water Beings…"

Ka'atah'teh knitted his brow. "Ah! Where did you learn about them?"

S'kladog savored a big draft of weed. "A friend."

"They're real, then."

"Quite real."

"Well, that keeps things interesting."

"Oh, hell yeah," said S'kladog. They both laughed.

S'kladog grew somber. "There may be others. Those outside people, I think they're up to something."

"You have heard their songs."

"Yes, I have listened. They don't like me coming around there and have tried to scare me off, but I don't run away. This is my place. But I hear words that make me afraid, words that I was told once, long ago: names of black spirits who once ruled Earth and who want to take it back again."

"Take it back from the white man, now."

"From us as well."

Ka'atah'teh took his turn on the pipe and said, "Well, we've taken our share of shit before—and given it. Look out, white man!"

"Look out, white man!"

The sky deepened, the moon was a ghostly disc. The men retreated into their own thoughts. A ripple creased the water, then another.

Ka'atah'teh raised his eyebrows. "A fish?"

"Yes," said S'kladog, "there's an underground passage out to the bay."

"I guess all sorts of creatures might come in here."

"Oh, yeah, as a boy I swam here with seals."

Ka'atah'teh looked closely at S'kladog. "Here, you say?"

"Yes. This was my home. My village."

The young man's eyes widened. "My mother lived here."

S'kladog's heart skipped. "Your mother?"

"Yes."

S'kladog's head went light. "What was her name?"

"M'katl."

S'kladog felt like he was floating into the clouds. Tears welling, he gazed into Ka'atah'teh's blue eyes. "Then you are my son."

29

Burrower In Time

Something was sucking me, sucking me into a dim green void. I was drowning—no, I was swimming, deep in the ocean. Towering fronds of seaweed waved in weird synchronicity and close by rose a domed temple ringed with columns. Fish and squid and other things rubbed against me and we swam gracefully around the dome and through the great green tendrils. Something moved inside the temple and emerged: tentacles…a star-shaped head…an eye….

Sara drove it from my mind. I lay revisiting every second of our meeting on the beach, walking and looking and laughing at nothing in particular… going to her little apartment and the smell of the tea she made us…how, as the light dimmed, she looked into my eyes and said, "Erich, I'd like to do this again." Reluctantly, I pulled my coat on. "Me too." As I opened the door, she kissed me lightly on the cheek. I forced myself to walk away, back to my empty apartment, where I paced the room trying to clear my head. The girl from the café…Sara Marsh…Sara…she kissed me…she actually, really, truly, in fact kissed me! So, was she my "girlfriend" now? I turned the word around and around in my mind as I turned circles on the carpet. Is there a more glorious word in the universe?

I shook my head and told myself to cool it. Either it would happen or it wouldn't.

Meantime, I had a life to live. And a question: What was Port Landsend's story? Remembering what the book store lady said, I called the Port Diablo Public Library and found out that they had a complete run of the Port Landsend *Lector* on microfilm. I got Jack's okay to take the next day off, and bright and early I was on the Peninsula highway with a banana and a cheese sandwich. I reached the library moments after opening and spooled up the *Lector*. I was glad to see that it was a weekly paper and a thin one at that. Even so, slogging through decades of newsprint would be a grind.

I took a deep breath and dug in. Amid the ads for carbolic smoke-balls and Miracle Electric Belts ("Guaranteed to Restore Full Manhood"), the little paper reflected the concerns and prejudices of a dominant but anxious white elite: vice and intemperance among the "lower classes," the Chinese and Indian "problems," and of course, the constant striving for economic betterment. Mayor James Swanson was front and center preaching civic unity, and the struggle to attract the railroad and impress eastern capital dominated the early editions. The final, crushing decision of the magnates to terminate their transcontinental line at Seacoma sent residents packing and businesses shuttering. A small 1886 item about the impending construction of a "sanitary sewerage and water catchment system" piqued my intrigue, but this was eclipsed in 1888, when the town's grandest mansion and a large wharf were "thrown up by the eminent local capitalist," one Unit Marsh.

Marsh! Heart racing, I moved on and was rewarded by notice of the "New Drainage Tunnel" initiated by none other than Unit Marsh, intended to flush storm runoff and "other material" from the city. Marsh was even quoted: "This network, along the lines of those of large eastern cities, will promote sanitation and be a boon to our city." I smiled in anticipation of Rick's cackle when I assured him that the tunnel under his building was sanitary. Just a few months later came another piece: "New Marsh Block Opens." Unit Marsh was quite the mover and shaker. Then came a letter from one Bushrod Olds complaining about "unwholesome activity" around the Marsh wharf. I scanned closely but found no follow-ups on any of this, and items of an increasingly trivial and sometimes sordid nature reflected the sad slump of the erstwhile boomtown. There was a brief stir when the army established a garrison of fortified bunkers to guard the entrance to Pilot Sound, but the editors seemed to give pride of place to the rise of public drunkenness and disorderly behavior along the waterfront. Then, from March 1896, came this:

LOCAL BUSINESSMAN VANISHES

Mr. Bushrod B. Olds, businessman, has been reported missing for several days. Associates are concerned that Mr. Olds, merchant, long prominent in the affairs of this city, may have met with criminal circumstances. However, none acknowledge the existence of any rivalries or antagonisms.

Poor Bushrod, he complained, he disappeared. Was that a coincidence or what? A few editions later, I found this, and this time felt a chill:

MISSING

Two children are lately reported missing. John Jonsrud, aged ten, and Andrew Potter, twelve, both failed to return home after school-hours Thursday last. Following the mysterious vanishing of Jon Carlson, last December, and prominent businessman Mr. Bushrod B. Olds, this new occurrence must certainly raise fresh alarm. It is to be lamented that our city has lately become a stopping-place for a peculiarly undesirable element, and the Police Department would be well-advised to make this group the first object of their search for explanation as to the disappearances. The editors call upon our citizenry to exercise heightened vigilance, and to take note of unfamiliar individuals and loiterers.

Four disappearances in less than six months, and one which apparently did not even merit earlier notice. I read on, hoping for more developments, but—nothing. Crap! My disdain for small-town journalism grew as subsequent editions were increasingly dominated by "news" of the most trivial nature. Then, an item from 1903 jerked me bolt-upright:

FOUL AIR

Mr. C. Detels, 517B Water Street, has complained repeatedly to the Sanitation Dept. of foul stenches in his basement. His is not the only complaint of strange odors emanating from the drains along Port Landsend's main thoroughfare. Last week Mr. L. Grobe, 424 Falmouth St., filed a similar complaint. Supt. Post promised to investigate.

Well, what did they expect, running a "sanitary drainage" system under the city? The guys would love this! I took some coins from my pocket, made copies, then broke off to massage my eyes and eat my sandwich. Pondering the vicissitudes of my adoptive home, I felt an odd, almost proprietary affection for the proud little Gate City. The finale of boom times was symbolized by the death of Mayor Swanson in 1902, and thereafter the shrinking editions of the *Lector* reflected only dreary decline in the many notices of store closures and homes for sale. Then came one last bit of interest, dated October 30, 1933:

A QUEER PHENOMENON

Odd sounds and lights were observed over the city last evening. "It appeared to me to be a freak storm," said a witness who was walking along the beachfront just before midnight. "The clouds roiled up considerably and turned a peculiar shade of purple, and a strangely-smelling wind whipped up." Drawn by the odd meteorological conditions, a small crowd gathered on the beach north of Point Judson, and some later reported that a few individuals appeared overcome by hysteria and claimed to have seen an "eye in the sky." The claim may doubtless be attributed to over-proof stimulants.

A raft of missing pages followed, then the *Lector* vanished into newspaper oblivion, leaving me with more questions than when I began. At the information desk I told the librarian of my search. "Ah, Port Landsend," she responded. "There isn't much out there. No history of the town that I'm aware of. One of our volunteers used to live there, Dee Brice. She was always big on local history, I'll bet she'd be happy to talk to you. Shall I give her a ring?"

Moments later I pulled up at a tidy white bungalow. A little lady in a gray sweat suit with pink hearts on it greeted me at the screen door. "I just got back from my exercise class," she said. "Would you like something to drink?" Inside the little room, her voice was loud and peppery. We settled down with some tea, I got out pen and paper, and Miss Brice ("not *Mizz*, please!") fixed me with a bright-eyed gaze. "So, you're interested in Port Landsend."

"Yes, I just moved there. I'm playing in a band there, weekends."

"A band, in Port Landsend? I'm surprised they have a place for music. Hah! The town's been dead on its feet for years. It was dead even when I was a girl. We left there in 1939. So, you're interested in Port Landsend history. Well, they called PL the 'Gate City', on account of its location, right at the foot of Pilot Sound. They thought it would be the big seaport, and there was a lot of shipping for a while, and a sawmill and boat builders and the like, but they all just petered out. There was the army post, too, but it closed down, oh, sometime in the twenties, when I was just a little girl."

"I saw some of this in the old newspaper."

"That paper—it had a funny name..."

"The *Lector.*

"Yes, the *Lector!* I remember the editor, an old fellow, been around forever. I was working as a waitress in a café and he used to come in for coffee. Nervous—always seemed to be looking over his shoulder. Can't remember his name."

"You worked in a café? Which one?"

"The Apex. 'Apex'—hah! It was a hash house!" She laughed heartily.

"Whereabouts was it?"

"Right downtown on Harbor Street."

My heart jumped. "There's one now called the Lamp Post. Don't know if it's the same place or not..."

"Good heavens! Well, if it is the same place, I'm sure it's changed hands more than once. Oh, the characters that used to come in..."

"What kind of characters?"

"Well, that was the Depression, you know, so nobody had any money. There were a lot of down-and-outers, but then PL had already been going to the bad. Folks would come in to eat in their good clothes, only you'd see that they were old and frayed. I felt sorry for them. But there were some very queer-looking people, or at least what *I* considered to be queer-looking. Mind you, I'm not prejudiced in that way, but there were some dark-skinned people with strange features and wearing the most rag-bag clothing. Somebody said they came from the South Pacific and that they lived out at Point Judson in sort of a shanty town. Of course, I was just a naïve girl who hadn't seen anything of the world, so I suppose anything would have looked odd to me. But they *were* odd-looking, with wide mouths and weird, bulging eyes that never seemed to blink. Talked funny, too, kind of mush-mouthed. You could hardly understand them. I remember that very clearly. But when you're serving the public, you serve 'em all. They never made any trouble, I will say that."

"Shore people!"

"Who's that?"

"That's what the old rummy guy at the café called them. Said they came from the South Pacific. I think I heard a couple of them the other night—weird, mushy-sounding…"

"Yes, mushy-sounding! Seemed like English mixed up with some other language. But we have to realize that the world is made up of many different cultures. Only fools try to deny that." She paused to sip her tea. "Well, I've been rambling. What else would you like to know?"

"Do you remember anything about the Marsh family?"

"Oh, they were one of the big families, right back to the early days. They lived in a big old house surrounded by hawthorns. Nasty, prickly things. We kids were warned not to go near the place. Some folks said it was empty and that old man Marsh had gone insane and died years ago. But other people said he was still in there, and if he heard you he'd come out and *git* ya! But I was brave: I sneaked up and peeked through that hedge. I could only see a little bit, and it looked like lot of the windows were boarded up. Couldn't tell if anyone lived there or not. Then I ran like the dickens.

"They had a carriage and a horse. Most everybody had automobiles by then, so I thought that was really something, that old-time black carriage with the window curtains drawn tight so you couldn't see in. It looked like a hearse! I saw it a number of times. Some people said it was the old man, but there was also supposedly a son and maybe a daughter. It may have been one of them in that buggy. I suppose we'll never know. My mother also said once that they had relations from back east come out here from someplace in New England."

She leaned in close, eyes glittering. "Now, here's something: I remember one of them, a young man, who had a face like a frog. Hah! Now that I think about it, I wonder if they weren't in some way related to those folks that came into the restaurant. You get that in small towns, you know. But I'll never forget that fellow. It was during the Dahlia parade, which was a big deal in those days, and that frog-faced young fellow crossed right in front of Gunnar Olsen's beer wagon and scared the horses crazy. They reared up in a panic, but the boy just kept right on his way, and he was smiling in a way that gave me the willies. Almost like he scared those horses on purpose. I remember somebody behind me saying, in a scary-sounding whisper—'Marsh'."

"I know a Marsh, now. At least, her name is Marsh."

"Well, of course, it's not an uncommon name. Do you think she's one of those Marshes?"

I nodded. "I think so." I couldn't say exactly *why* I thought so, except… "Miss Brice, do you remember any unusual occurrences? Like mysterious disappearances?"

Without a beat, she replied, "I remember when little Susan Atwood went missing."

A name I hadn't seen in the paper. How many had there been? "How about Bushrod Olds?"

"Bushrod?" She frowned and shook her head. "I don't recall the name, and you'd think I would remember one like that. But I do remember the Atwood girl, probably because I was a girl, myself. I remember being scared. I don't know if they ever found her or not. You'd think it would have been all over town if they had, at least in the paper. But who knows what all goes on? So often, these things end up being a family matter, or something they'd just rather hush up."

Miss Brice spread her hands as if in apology. "I was just a young girl, and when you're that age, life moves on quickly. And we moved on, too, up here to Port Diablo, in 1939. You know, I've never been back to Port Landsend since."

I could see she was tiring. As I stood to leave, she gave me a searching look and said, "I wouldn't think a place like Port Landsend would have much to offer a young man like you."

"Yeah—we'll see how it goes. So far, it's been a nice change from the city." I thanked her and headed into the purple evening, my mind only on Sara Marsh. *You let me know when you find out.*

30

Destiny Deals A Hand

Bowsprits speared the sky, locomotives snorted, draymen jostled, stevedores cursed. The air stank of salt water and horse dung. And in the midst of it all, incongruous yet strangely at home, elegant ladies and gentlemen strolled, their faces aglow with excitement. Nothing had prepared Olin Marsh for the energy of Seacoma in the summer of 1899. Gazing at the soaring masts and quaint figureheads of the sailing ships, he felt invincible. Perhaps he would go to sea, himself. Now, though, he would live in a city! He missed his mother sorely, but he was eager for a new life in the thick of things. Knowing that this was what his mother wanted for him gave him courage

The young man took a room in a dingy dockside hotel and spent his first days walking the streets. The vitality of the city was overwhelming, as were the eyes and figures of the young women. Olin was shocked, too, at the contrast between glittering wealth and squalid poverty. Drunkards staggered and fell in the mud, ragged urchins hawked newspapers, and on one corner an elderly Indian woman sold curios. He recalled how his father once called the Indians a 'dying race'—yet this woman and the many other Indians he saw along the harbor were very much alive.

It was physical work Olin wanted, and the Haglund Wharf was happy to oblige. He trundled carts, hefted bales, and soaked in the wonders of life on the waterfront, rubbing shoulders with grunting, sweating men of all ages, ethnicities, and demeanors. A pair of genial young Irishmen soon latched onto him, and after work they made for the nearby Central Saloon, where the piano was lively and the conversation jolly. No one asked Olin his age, and over rich Seacoma lager he and his mates debated politics, the growing labor union movement, and women. Especially women. Over the long months, Olin learned that many women (and some men) had eyes for fresh-faced young fellows, and that many of those women were nothing like his mother. He learned also about avoiding the police, recognizing a rigged card game, and the wisdom of drinking slowly.

But lessons are often forgotten. It had been an arduous week and the beer tasted good—too good. Olin had just finished his second when a flash dude proposed a game of cards. He was a novice, but eagerly pitched in. The mood was jolly, the banter humorous and, after all, what were a few paltry coins? The sharp-dressed man placed a third beer before Olin; well-fortified, he lost a few coins but won more, and the evening came to a happy conclusion. Olin parted from his mates and wended his wobbly way toward his lodgings. He never made it.

He awoke in a small, dark space. Olin's head throbbed—and the room was swaying unpleasantly. A distant voice yelled, "Let go aft!" Olin opened his eyes, shook his head, and saw another man, older and weary-looking, sitting nearby.

A man appeared in the companionway, a belaying pin in his hand. "All right, you maggots," he yelled, "turn to!"

The older man looked mournfully at Olin. "Well, kid, looks like we're Shanghai-bound."

31

Regeneration

S'kladog gazed at his son. The likeness was unmistakable: the cheeks, the mouth, the eyes—they were M'katl's. Father and son released each other and stood trembling with joy and disbelief.

S'kladog asked, "Where were you born? Where did M'katl live?"

"Down Snood Canal," replied Ka'atah'teh.

S'kladog felt anger boil up. "Tcha! You know, she just left one day. Said nothing, just up and left. We loved each other—at least, I loved her. Oh, yeah, I pined for her! She was much older than me, you know, but that didn't matter to us. Not one bit. Shit…"

He sat silent for a moment then continued, feeling warm and alive as he hadn't in a long time. "Oh, your mother—she was a woman! She seduced me, an innocent young boy. Hah! I used to swim in this lagoon here, and she would stand and watch me with her blue eyes, eyes just like yours." He almost started crying. "Man, to see those eyes again…" S'kladog looked away into the woods, then asked, "Did she ever talk about me?"

"All the time. She loved you. But she said if she stayed it would not have been good for you. You would have never left the village and would have died there. She didn't want that. She wanted you to get out and be in the world and become strong. She hated to leave you."

"Women," S'kladog said, shaking his head. M'katl had made a great sacrifice—she had loved him as much as he had loved her.

"Did the rest of your family live here?" Ka'atah'teh asked.

"Yes, my mother. She was a beautiful woman, too. I guess I realized that, once I came to appreciate the beauty of M'katl. Older women, they have much to teach us young cubs, eh?" They both laughed, then let several minutes pass in silence. Then S'kladog asked: "How did your mother die?"

His son shook his head sadly. "The sickness. So many did. She said, 'Son, leave here and be strong and you will live to keep our family going. Take care of yourself and live.' I refused to leave. She died in my arms. Then I left. I walked all night and all next day, and I went to Seacoma and worked and got drunk and sober and drunk again."

"Yeah." The sun dipped low, another kingfisher sailed over, something rippled the water in front of them. A seal poked its head out, snorted, and disappeared. Perhaps spirits had not abandoned the place after all.

"The Hidden Ones," said Ka'atah'teh.

S'kladog chuckled. "A seal."

"I saw them on the Snood Canal."

"Your mother first told me about them."

"On Snood Canal there is a place where they come ashore and hold communion with the people. It was something frightening, yet awesome. Truly a change of worlds."

"The sacrifice—people accepted voluntarily?"

"Yes, people went into the water with them."

"I think they have been coming here, too," said S'kladog. "And there are others, men with odd features. Young men, but with skin like old men. And I have seen one or two that look almost like frogs."

Ka'atah'teh frowned. "I do not much like them."

"Well, then," said S'kladog, "we may be in for something."

The younger man pulled something from his pocket. "What do you think of this?" It was a carved figurine with a starfish-like head and tentacles. "M'katl gave me this."

S'kladog started from his seat. "Whoa, that thing!"

"You know it?"

"Yes, she showed it to me! Told me she got it from her grandmother. Some guys from up north came in their canoes and took slaves, and left this behind to scare us."

"Scares me plenty."

"I get a bad feeling, seeing this again." S'kladog shook his head. "A bad feeling."

32

Night Shades

Pit of night. Tattered clouds, ink-black sky, blood-red walls, gaping windows. *Hi, guys, any fresh bodies this evening?* Walking again, just as I'd walked in the city when sleep wouldn't come and something drew me out into the night, the night of brooding houses and sullen shadows. Now here I was, lost in a strange and enigmatic new world, slouching down a dead-end street in a dead-end town, population one. A cigarette glowed in an alcove, a door banged somewhere, I ghosted on, invisible, my mind humming with random thoughts: the guys...Rick Weller's cigars...a brass band blaring *Ta-ra-ra-boom-de-ay*...a guy in 1950 thumping my bass at a dance in one of those same old buildings...Sara.

I passed the dark Town Tavern and Grebe Bookstore and crossed the street to look out on the bay. Far to the south, the reflected lights of Seacoma cast a weird glow in the sky, my old world now light-years away. I thought of my schoolmates, the student bands playing on without me, the streets swirling on without me, the whole shebang doing just fine without me, thanks very much. Now, I was here, in this strange little old town, and here I would stand. Life was an open door.

As if answering my thoughts, a faint chanting came across the water from the houses on the point:

Ya! Ya! Yog-Soth! Yog-Soth!
Ya! Ya! Coolie-oo Fatagan!

I listened hard—it sounded like the voices I heard from the apartment. I felt a shiver, eavesdropping on music that was probably sacred to a small group attempting to preserve its traditional ways.

I moved on and was nearing the beach when I heard running footsteps. A man burst off the nearby side street and passed close by. He was balding and scrawny and—it was the bulb-headed guy from the café! Only, he wasn't being an asshole now, he was running scared. "Fuck you!" he screamed, "I ain't goin'!" I shrank into an alcove as he stopped and looked around. More feet came running, and three men hot on his trail caught him as he tried to escape down Harbor Street. I watched dumbly as they pummeled him into submission. "Hey!" I croaked, halfheartedly, "you can't…"

But they did. I remained frozen as they dragged him away toward the marina. Heart racing, I emerged from my shadow and stared after the vanished figures. I heard and saw nothing, so I walked to the beach and peered into the night. I saw only water and the scattered yellow lights from the cabins on the point. The chanting had stopped, all was silent. I felt like shit, a craven little chickenshit.

Whoosh! The water erupted in an explosive snort, a pale form surfaced. An albino sea lion—or? Another head popped up, then another. One of the heads swiveled around and I could see its bulging yellow eyes clearly as they scanned the horizon and came to rest on me. Another pair of eyes found me, and another. Did one of them have horns? I couldn't be sure. Abruptly, they slipped beneath the surface. Then I realized: I was standing just yards from the entrance of Unit Marsh's sanitary drainage tunnel. Could one of these things have been what I heard splashing behind the big door?

No! Far out in the bay, a faint voice yelled. I watched and listened for long minutes more, but nothing more came, nothing but a sickening feeling I had witnessed the latest Port Landsend disappearance. I thought about going to the nearby police station. But what would I tell them? I shuffled back to the apartment and flopped onto my bed, too tired to undress. *It was probably nothing,* I told myself. *Nothing.* Yeah, chickenshit.

Later. Blobby white things, crawling, inching, boring, eyes burning, ears buzzing…ugly colored balloons growing, pop, pop, pop…stench…*No!*

33

Naked In The Dark, Dreaming

Light never penetrated here, only rankness and cold. Nevertheless, in a dank niche beneath the city, it clung to the side of the slimy brick wall, and to life. Fungus-like, its amethystine carapace shining dully, it strained at its casing, but the casing did not give. Not yet.

Those who had brought it here and tended it had not come for a long time. Sustenance had been scarce but not wholly absent. And so it lived, barely, but barely is sufficient. Well it should be, for it was a life form tempered by many adversities, not least of which was a terrible war with the great elder beings that had, long before, created its forebears. The elders won that match, but victory is never absolute and the victors—beings of vast intelligence and power—could possibly be said to have made a strategic retreat. The balance continued uneasy, and in the vast, vertiginous depths encompassing unfathomable eons, all life mingled into one.

Far from the little city, fathoms deep in the ocean, in another city immeasurably older than anything on land, another being stirred. Something impinged on its sensitive consciousness and vibrated its multiple appendages. Earth had shaken again. It did that now and then, no big deal.

There had been many shakes, many upheavals in the timeless void of existence. The heat, the cold, the infinite depths, the blasted orbs and

113

gaseous clouds—all had nurtured the things and spawned more things, things that coalesced into something like a galaxy, a confabulation of consciousness teeming with electrical impulses that propelled them onward through space, through the very confines of time itself, and that, through strange eons, rendered them into the consciousness of other beings—small, weak beings, but beings of great sensitivity, who gave them names and worshipped them as elder gods of surpassing power. Beings who learned to communicate with them.

And now it came once again: a faint, feeble hint of words, garbled and indistinct. Them: those pesky, puny two-legs. The elder one sighed; well, if they were serious, and worthy, a response might be warranted. It was, after all, not entirely unpleasant being thought of as a god and receiving various *offerings*. Until then…The great, lumpen entity stretched its wings, fluttered its tentacles, and sank back into blissful catatonia.

34

That Old House

You heard the damnedest things. Police chief resigning...mayor departing under sordid circumstances...library padlocked...The Depression had everyone on edge, so many businesses failing, so many folks moving on, leaving behind empty houses and shops. What was left was hardly a city at all. No one dared say it, but Port Landsend was now all but a ghost town.

Some things did not change. The old Marsh house had been there forever, or so it seemed. Some said it was empty, and some said "old man Marsh" was in there. Never mind that he had not been seen in years, they knew because they heard him. Or heard *something*, moving around inside, talking and sometimes even singing. Well, *sort of* singing, as far as you could tell. Sometimes, they heard other sounds, sounds more difficult to pin down, but rather like a dog barking. Well, *maybe* a dog. What else could it be?

Some remembered the disappearances, the vanishings never solved save for persistent rumors that a number of the lost ones had returned in strangely altered states. Most discounted these as kid stories—even as they continued to shun the old dark house under the cypress. Around dinner tables, in the Town Tavern, and over cups of watery coffee at the Apex Café, they shook their heads and muttered: *They were behind it…Stay away from that place…up to something nasty…face like a frog!*

Rumors faded to legend, and for a time all was quiet. Then, in October 1931, the kid grapevine buzzed with a strange tale. The Lott boy was pedaling his bicycle past the Marsh mansion on his way home at dusk when a figure darted into the road and tried to force him into an opening in the hedge. Young Lott, thought by some to be simple-minded, said that it was too dark to get a good look at the figure, but not so dark that he did not see another being behind the hedge—a being that made a terrible gibbering noise. Lott thrust his bicycle away from his assailant and rode furiously away. For years after, the deranged young man would recount the story to all who would listen, his thin voice rising to an eerie wail as it described the frightful, toadlike face and horrible stench of the lurker in the hedge.

Next day at Swanson Elementary, ten-year-old Ralph Donald listened in fascination as Lott told his tale. That night at dinner, he told his parents. "Yeah, a monster ran out into the road and tried to grab him!"

"Oh, really, Ralph," his mother protested.

"I don't know," said his father, "there's always been stories about that place."

"Those Marshes are an odd lot, I will say," said his mother. "I see one of the women in the store: sad, pasty-faced thing. Never smiles. There was talk of disappearances and…"

Her husband shook his head slowly, cutting his wife off mid-sentence. He turned a stern gaze on young Ralph. "Just stay away from there, son,"

Ralph Donald nodded. "Yes, Dad. I will. I promise." He said nothing about his appointment with a couple of schoolmates. One of them said he'd heard rumors of weird noises coming from the old tunnel. On Saturday they would meet downtown, rent a rowboat, and go inside.

35

Threads

I drove toward Port Diablo on auto pilot, staring down an empty highway into the black hole of dream memory. Something had crept into my overheated imagination—or had it always been there? I remembered the rainbow-colored worm-beings I drew at age nine, striped crawly things living in futuristic dream-cities, and how I made worm sleeve-puppets with my sweater and chased girls with them through the playground, shrieking worm-cries. My baffled parents sent me to a shrink, a nice guy who fed me cookies and tried to make sense of my fantasies. Exactly what was gleaned from that investment remains a mystery, but I knew I wasn't crazy and I proved it by becoming a musician. But now, some weird shit was creeping into my brain.

Doctor Babson welcomed me warmly, then stroked his short gray beard as I described the white, possibly horned seal-things I'd seen near the United Wharf. The professor kept silent for a moment, then spoke softly. "Erich, what do we really know of our world? What do we know of the strange giants of Easter Island and the secrets of Machu Picchu? What of strange survivals—the persistence of myth-legend into our own time? I think there are common threads running through human civilization that cannot be dismissed as mere fantasy. Stop to ponder the similarities between, say,

Mayan gods and Greek, Native American, and Celtic. Did you know that certain totem carvings found in Micronesia bear an uncanny resemblance to ones on Vancooder's Island? Or that cultures all around the world share a 'sunken city' tradition? Brittany, Atlantis, Lyonesse, Tirnanog..."

The doctor swiveled toward the window, where the looming Olympian Range hinted at vast and alien dimensions far beyond man's grasp. "The similarities are legion," he continued. "As for evidence—the world is littered with ancient and enigmatic ruins, some of them barely more than rumored, hidden beneath Antarctic glaciers and remote Asian deserts. And who is to say but that there aren't even now, other remnants—certain *survivals*. What about the Loch Ness Monster, or the T'lingkit legend of 'water people'? There are other phenomena much closer to home. Take the small earthen mounds that dot the western portion of our state: We have long been content to dismiss them as nothing more than either tailings left by the retreating glaciers of the Ice Age, or the work of gophers. Gophers—hah! Gophers working in a damnable and unnatural *symmetry*."

He turned to his desk and extracted a sheaf of papers and photographs. "English chalk carvings: giant figures carved into chalk hills in ancient times, scattered throughout the British Isles." He tapped his finger on one. "This chap is known as the Wilbury White Horse. Like so many oddities on that curious island kingdom, we don't have the slightest inkling of its true age, who created it, or why—the 'why' being the most confounding question of all. We do know that the horse figure as it exists now, roughly one hundred feet in length, is a relatively new carving dating only from the eighteenth century. It had long been rumored that a much earlier carving lies concealed under the horse. Now, modern infra-red scanning proves it."

He lifted one print. "Here's our eighteenth-century carving—a nice, friendly white horse. And here's an infra-red image. It's faint, probably effaced long before the eighteenth century, but readily discernable nonetheless." The second picture revealed superimposed upon the white horse the ghostly outline of something very un-horse-like. Something long and slender, with legs more like flippers. And horns.

"What do you make of that? Consider, if you will, the old British legend of the 'White Worm' and the Celtic 'Selky': half human, half seal."

I could only shake my head. "I've never heard of them."

"Legends, centuries-old." Babson leaned back, savoring the mystery. "But yes, fairly well forgotten nowadays. And, of course, the origins of these tales are, if you will pardon the cliché, shrouded in mystery. Still, the question haunts us: What did those people, our ancestors, *see?*"

I knew what I saw, in the water at Port Landsend, and in my head: something that looked a lot like this white worm-horse thingie. "I've been having these dreams," I said. "I know it sounds flaky, but I never used to remember my dreams, and I never used to have dreams like *this*. Now, I remember every detail: a dull throbbing sound and vague, blurry images... swimming deep in the ocean...the water a glowing bright green...Also, I see the bones. At least, I think it's the bones, and it's like they come together and form into living creatures, and they swim beside me: seal-things with sort of dog-like faces and golden eyes staring at me. I know it's only a dream, but..."

"I wouldn't discount it, Erich. Not something so vivid and persistent. If it's a dream, movement and details can be interpreted in numerous ways. When did the dreams begin?"

"When I moved to Port Landsend. Exactly then." I stopped and blew out my cheeks. "Crazy, huh?"

Babson sat quietly, not objecting, not shaking his head, but looking like he believed me.

"The thing is," I continued, "the dream is getting more *real*. At first, the swimming things were just blobs. Then, last night, I saw them more clearly. Them, and some other things: weird-shaped things with tentacles. Long, waving tentacles."

The professor stood and turned to the window. For several minutes he stared out upon the peaceful campus. Then, he spoke: "A fellow I know back east has done extensive research into obscure legends and what one might call suppressed folk-memory. I believe we must consider the possibility that you possess some kind of subconscious sympathetic mental acuity—and that this acuity has allowed you to break through the mental barriers that normally suppress ancient memories, and to receive a faint glimmer of that memory."

"Subconscious sympathetic mental acuity—me?"

He looked sternly at me. "Indeed. And, from what you say, you may well be in for a progressively *clearer* picture."

"Oh, great."

Dr. Babson smiled sympathetically. "It's a lot to take in. But our world is vaster and more impenetrable than most of us humans, smug in our technological bubble, can fathom. The ocean realm covers billions of cubic miles. All our electronic eyes and sensors are puny toys in comparison. There remains so much that we have never seen, and may never see. It's probably just as well we treat such phenomena as Bigfoot and 'Nessie' like the old 'missing link' or the bearded lady at the carnival. Lord knows how we'd fare if we could tie all the threads together. Perhaps something primal within us—some psychic lock—keeps us from connecting them up."

"We couldn't handle it."

"Precisely. The consequences might be devastating to our spiritual and cosmological constructs, our fundamental sense of reality." Babson offered me a soda from his small refrigerator. "I'm glad you've made the brave decision to share your dreams with me, Erich, and that I can share some of these thoughts with you. Perhaps, being young, you are more open-minded."

"With dreams like these, I guess I don't have much choice."

Setting a ginger ale in front of me, Babson laughed heartily. "That's the ticket—embrace the mystery! Ah, what wonders await us, if only we open our minds to them." He rubbed his hands and beamed at me. "Erich, how would you like to take a little trip? I think we should pay a visit to that man back east."

I was stunned. Doctor Edward Babson, someone I barely knew and a professor no less, wanted to take me on a trip? Hell yes! I told him I could get away for two or three days during the week, but I didn't want to leave the band in the lurch. Only one thing: I had no money for traveling.

He smiled warmly. "I think we can manage expenses; I've got a little slush fund set aside for just this purpose."

I didn't need any more convincing. I barely knew Dr. Babson but I liked him, I liked the way he talked and what he said, and I had a feeling he'd make a good traveling companion. Plus, I'd never been on an airplane before.

"So, where are we going?"

"We'll fly east," Babson said, rubbing his hands, "and see Victor Lewis. He has a chair at Miskatonic University, in the little city of Arkham, Mass."

36

Emergence

Mist swirled thickly over the lagoon. The Water Beings were out there, he knew it. Others in the little settlement had spoken of them lately, even white men. Usually, the beings avoided human settlements, but they were no different from anything else in responding to those who offered them favors. What would happen if more whites learned of the beings? He thought often of this—of fate and the changing world. What is now and what will be.

Ka'atah'teh thought again of his father. S'kladog had not lived long after their meeting, but he had lived long enough that father and son could hold each other in their arms and feel strong even in a world that was changing from day to day. Now, with his father's memories and strength inside him, Ka'atah'teh would walk his path and keep alive his memories, his wisdom, and his warnings. Ka'atah'teh closed his eyes and opened himself to the spirit of the place. A soft wind stroked his face—yes, spirits were all around. Spirits good and bad. That thing with the starfish head: it was making him increasingly uneasy. Black energy lurked within. He must get rid of it. Maybe someone would buy it from him.

He rested another moment, then opened his eyes. A cormorant winged by, chickadees chirped in the poplars, the sky darkened, and a slice of sunlight lit the lagoon. He felt his father beside him. He stood and began to sing the song his father taught him, the song for the old village. He let his voice carry across the little lake and beyond, into the mist.

Ka'atah'teh felt a shiver race up his spine. The water rippled and from the smooth, gray surface emerged—a head, the head of a being, black and shiny with golden yellow eyes, eyes fixed on him. Fear lanced through Ka'atah'teh but quickly left him, and his song did not falter. Another head, lighter in color, appeared beside the first, then a third, and the creatures watched quietly as Ka'atah'teh moved deeper into his voice. He sang louder now, and the Water Beings began swaying gently. New tones, strange and eerie, joined his song, and beautiful figures moved slowly behind his eyes—she among them. The vibrating dark continued for a long time, and Ka'atah'teh felt like he was lying in a lover's arms. Awhile later he heard the water lap softly. He dropped his arms, stopped singing, and opened his eyes. He was alone. The still waters of the lagoon gleamed black and silver in the setting sun.

37

Doubtful Lodgings

ew people stayed at the Bayview Hotel more than one night. Some didn't last that long, and it was not uncommon for a prospective lodger to give the dismal inn a quick once-over and flee into the dusk. The decrepit Harbor Street hostelry was among the last holdovers from the salad days, erstwhile pride of the Gate City boosters who would have been appalled at its Depression-era decrepitude. Respectable locals had long regarded the Bayview as beyond the pale, the haunt of bootleggers, loose women, and other shady characters. The brickwork was weathered black by the elements, and the stench of mold pervaded the musty rooms and doubtful bedclothes. A bare, low-wattage bulb lit the lobby, casting an eerie glow over proprietor Josiah Sargent as he slouched at the front desk, his dour and oddly toadlike countenance offering dubious welcome to new arrivals. Those who persevered and signed the book often quickly regretted that the lateness of the hour precluded searching for other accommodation. Regret was not unwarranted, and muffled mutterings and furtive creaks often roused guests to uneasy wakefulness and sent them scurrying to their automobiles at first light.

Ivor Lumpkin had no auto nor much of anything else, but he did have a job, which was more than many men had in the depression year 1932.

He landed in Port Landsend that September, when the tramp steamer *Wilford Stickney*, thirty-five days out of Santa Rosita by way of Enchenada, limped into town, her ancient steam engine gasping its death rattle. Even non-believers among the crew called desperately upon higher powers as the vessel struggled through mountainous seas off the Strait of Fury. Providence heeded the appeal, and a grateful Lumpkin joined his mates in whispering thanks as the *Stickney* made port.

The young deckhand with a patch over one eye stuffed his pay into an inner pocket, hocked a farewell loogie at his former place of employment, and tramped down Harbor Street. Lumpkin grimaced; the wind in town was almost as bad as out on the strait. He looked at the old buildings and scraggly streets largely empty of foot and auto traffic, and felt his heart sag. Still, it was terra firma. He came to the Bayview Hotel and saw a paper in the window saying *Hlep wantd*. Hotel work might be a nice change, especially if there happened to be any pleasant young women around. Ivor opened the door and walked in.

Sargent speared him with a gimlet eye. "Want the job, huh?"

Lumpkin nodded respectfully. "Yes, sir."

"Need a janitor," lisped the desk clerk. "Lash man quit."

Ivor affirmed his abilities in the custodial line, and Sargent nodded toward a back room. "Go find Carney, down th' hall, he'll tell ya what to do. An' don't go snoopin'." Lumpkin peered around at the dingy lobby; by the look of things, he reckoned his duties would not be onerous. The Bayview's new janitorial assistant was given a cot in a back room, and he settled in to swabbing toilets, sweeping halls, and running errands.

Ivor Lumpkin was glad to have work on solid ground, but he had not been long in Landsend before he realized he had fetched up in a dead end. By the onset of the Great Depression, the town was deep in senility. Mayor Swanson was long in his grave and only a dwindling handful still clung to the images and dreams of the glory years. As the city shrank, municipal amenities—police, fire, library—contracted or ceased altogether. Behind shuttered windows, the remaining old-timers muttered of decline and shattered hopes.

Lumpkin was all ears. Loafing in the Bayview lobby and at the Apex Café, he eavesdropped on grim prognostications: *Moving on...Town's done for...Lord, not another one...*He did not like the sound of that. Nor did he much like the small but nasty gang of toughs hanging around the dilapidated United Wharf. Still, Ivor liked the lack of city hurry and the absence of hard-eyed cops ordering him to move on. He'd had enough of that in Santa Rosita.

He was loafing outside the hotel one afternoon enjoying a chaw of tobacco when he heard a clatter. A gray landau rolled into view behind a slim black horse. As the carriage passed, Ivor saw movement in a side window. A hand pulled aside the lace curtain, revealing a face: a face sickly gray, with fat, droopy lips and bulging eyes. It was a mere seconds' glimpse, but it made Ivor shiver. Half a block down, the carriage swept through the gate to the United Wharf and vanished inside. "Marsh!" exclaimed a nearby woman. "Thought he was dead." She cackled raucously, threw a boozy wink at Ivor, and tottered away. Lumpkin grunted and hocked his quid. Whoever was in that carriage certainly looked like death warmed-over. But he apparently had business at the wharf. A couple of rough-looking men pulled the gate shut and stood guard in front. What kind of business did a man presumed dead have in there?

Questions swarmed, but Ivor had learned that questions often caused trouble. He kept his head down, his mouth shut, and did his work. His immediate supervisor, gangly, gray-faced Ed Carney, a stooped man of uncertain age who stank of fish and cheap liquor, mostly left him to his own devices, which suited Ivor fine. He had developed some definite notions of cleanliness during his sea time, and he now set about applying them to the decrepit lodging house. Nobody could accuse Ivor Lumpkin of being a freeloader.

But Ivor could not avoid noticing things. Things like an occasional faint moan from upstairs, odd shuffling footsteps and muffled gruntings, and a weird odor permeating the corridors that seemed to emanate from somewhere deep inside the building. Yes, Port Landsend was truly the bitter end. Still, it beat hell out of the *Wilford Stickney*

38

A Nasty Scrape

nother flying fish whirred into the setting sun. Amazing creatures, flying fish, but then, the Pacific was an amazing place. He wanted to see the world and he had: Hong Kong, Japan, the Celebes…Komodo dragons, birds of paradise, macaques. And never did he imagine such men, often crude in their manners yet formidable in wisdom and history. What stories they told, of ancient legends, forgotten cities, and lost empires!

For Olin Marsh, late of Seacoma by way of Shanghai, Ponpei was a serene and pleasant oasis in the middle of the Pacific. The affront of being kidnapped and dragooned into sailoring had long-since passed to joy at his new berth on a trading schooner manned by a kindly Scot and as jolly a gang of seamen as could be. Visits to remote islands had been welcome breaks, and now, walking the beaches of Ponpei, young Marsh felt the very soil beneath his bare feet pregnant with legend. And legends were legion. Over a mug of particularly foul grog one night, a wizened Irishman whispered of mysterious ruins in the interior. They were within walking distance—but best avoided. "Some old heathen temple, t'is said," rasped the sailor. "The natives shun the place and ye'd be wise to sheer off your own self." He winked evilly. "'Course, you bein' a young and strappin' lad, ye'll steer your own course."

Earl the next morning Olin set out on the narrow trail into the jungle, thankful that large snakes had apparently never populated the island. Hanging vines and creepers made it slow going, but within an hour he rounded a sharp bend and beheld a looming apparition. Thickly mantled with vegetation, the edifice was a cube about thirty feet tall and perhaps forty wide, constructed of massive and snugly-fitted ashlar stone. Arrayed along the upper margin of the structure was a frieze of carven figures; though the overgrowth obscured many of them, some were clearly human, wearing distinctive cone-shaped headgear. But others, where visible, appeared to be nothing less than grotesque parodies of the human physique—topped with the heads of reptiles and other, less definable forms. The monument was stained black with age but well-preserved overall. Marsh could scarcely pry his eyes from the frieze and its hideous cartoons; something in their nature made his blood run cold as they marched in grim grandeur high on the weathered black rectangle. Who had the artists been—and from what *models* had they worked?

A light rain began to fall and Olin turned toward a small rectangular aperture at the center of the monument. As the drops became a torrential tropical downpour, Olin retreated inside. He cursed his failure to bring a torch, for beyond the small vestibule a low, flat-roofed corridor stretched away into darkness. A dank odor filled his nostrils and a cold, clammy breeze wafted gently from the depths of the temple. He coughed at the dust in the confined space, sending an echo into the blackness. The delay of the reverberations suggested that the chamber was of prodigious extent, and Olin was pondering this when he heard a faint rustling. A footstep? Olin shivered but held his ground, listening. Nothing more sounded, only the pounding rain reverberating in the small chamber. He wished it would let up—wished he could leave the dusty vestibule, and more especially put behind him that stygian hallway and its fetid vaporings.

He was peering out at what he hoped was diminishing rainfall when another sound came from behind him: a sound like slow, labored breathing. Skin prickling, eyes straining into the dark, Olin backed toward the light. A vague, smoky wisp of something twined lazily from the darkness and crept along the near wall, and the eerie sibilance sounded once more, this time more distinctly—this time, he would later tell disbelieving shipmates, like nothing so much as a loathsome and sinister *slithering*. Dogged curiosity held him by one foot, even as the other poised to run for daylight. He thought of the procession of grotesques on the outside of the temple, the carven array of hideous *composite* creatures. The vaporous emanations waxed thicker, the ominous echoes grew louder. Olin bolted from the chamber and down the path back to town.

A belt of good grog, supper, and the laughter of his shipmates banished the eerie echoes, the sensation of something—or things—lurking in the dark, waiting. Still, Olin Marsh couldn't could not shake the feeling he'd had a close shave, and with something he dared not imagine. Now, though, the *Oriole* was making ready to sail and he was eager to leave this haunted rock in the far Pacific. As Olin stood on the beach gazing at the sunset, well-fortified against unwelcome thoughts, he felt a presence. A small old man with bright green eyes came and stood beside him, peering at him intently. He had noticed the man before—and that he seemed to be watching him. "Hmmm," the little man purred—"hmmm…"

"What is it?" Olin asked, more curious than annoyed.

The elder gestured toward the sea. "Out in water, old god. Bad god! Live in big house. R'lyeh!"

"A god lives in the sea?"

"Bad god! Very bad."

"What god?

"No say. Bad to say! You know, I think."

The young man knit his brow in puzzlement. "I know? How?"

The elder stared at him and whispered, "You. Marsh."

39

The Thing In The Bookcase

With an exultant roar, the jet pierced the clouds. My heart pounded at the rush of power, the skyward leap, and the final, glorious emergence from leaden opacity into dazzling blue. Professor Babson, who had shed his jacket and insisted I call him Edward, smiled at my astonishment and let me enjoy the moment in silence.

"I'm glad we could make this trip," he said after several minutes. "Your dreams are significant. Disturbing, perhaps, but I hope we may glean some insight into what they might represent. Perhaps they are a glimpse into another world, a world you have somehow been privileged to see. Put the dreams together with your other observations, and the bones, and it all seems to point at something."

I could only nod dumbly. I hoped I wasn't getting in over my head. "Hmm," I said, "tell me more about this man we're seeing."

"Doctor Victor Lewis. His field is—well, I guess it's best described as anthropology, with an emphasis on ritual survival and folk memory. He's got some interesting theories, and what sounds like even more interesting things to show us." Babson sighed happily. "Now, let's forget about all that and enjoy this little getaway. I believe I'll have a cocktail."

I savored my first airborne meal and a movie about a couple of guys traveling through time. I could relate. Then I closed my eyes and pondered my circumstances. Here I was, a part-time musician and full-time ne'er-do-well, flying thousands of miles through the stratosphere or whatever the hell it was, in the company of a distinguished professor, to meet an eminent man of science. Swell. I was flattered to think that I was the cause of this expedition—but what could I say that would impress these academic types? My doubts were shoved aside by a persistent mental musical mantra (does everybody have those?), and I drifted off to the sensation of impending revelation.

Early that evening Edward drove our rented sedan through the lonely landscape of northeastern Massachusetts. Patches of late winter snow littered the hills, and the isolated farmsteads looked older and more squalid than even those outside Port Landsend. Livestock seemed curiously absent, too. "Creepy old places," I muttered. "Must be a hard life out here."

"It is that," said Edward. "I grew up here, just over the hill, in Aylesbury. Spent almost twenty years here, then I headed west, like a lot of folks before me. Those who remained behind—well…" The pallid sun slunk behind the bald hills and presently a river glimmered through the trees. "The Miskatonic," Edward announced. We followed it for several miles, and at last beheld the gables and spires of Arkham. We checked into the Arkham House, ate dinner in the frowzy coffee shop next door, and fell into sound sleep to the distant rush of the Miskatonic.

Next morning we rose early, returned to the café for a hearty breakfast, and walked to the leafy little campus of Miskatonic University. We found the Anthropology Department easily and were greeted by black-suited Dr. Victor Lewis. "Ah," he beamed, extending a hand, "the Western contingent. Welcome! Edward, how are you?" Dr. Lewis was a short, stout Black man with close-cropped gray hair and an engaging smile. He eyed me warmly. "Professor Babson has informed me of your experiences. Interesting, most interesting. I think, gentlemen, that we have in our collection certain objects which may shed some light on this little mystery."

Tottering stolidly, he led us down a series of narrow corridors before turning into a dimly-lit room full of wooden cabinets. He unlocked one and slid out a tray to reveal a familiar sight. "Remains," he said, "unless I am mistaken, very much like the ones you found in—Port Landsend, is it? These were found in the Miskatonic River, near the village of Dunwich, after a flood in the nineteen-twenties." He smiled enigmatically. "A curious place, Dunwich."

The bones did indeed resemble ours, but were smaller and brown with age. We viewed them silently for another moment, then Dr. Lewis led us outside and across the quadrangle to the library, where we slipped quietly down two floors to a darkened vestibule. He unlocked an innocuous-looking door, showed us into a low-ceilinged room, and switched on lights to reveal metal shelves lined with books. Many were of great size and in worn leather bindings that bespoke antiquity. "Few people now living have seen these books," Lewis said. "They came to us from the personal collection of one of my predecessors at this institution, Dr. Henry Armitage. See here: *De Vermis Mysteriis*, by Ludvig Prinn. Fifteenth century Dusseldorf. Poor fellow—burned by the Inquisition. And here is the *Fournier Register*, published by Bishop Jacques Fournier, who later became Pope Benedict the Twelfth. When he wrote it, he was investigating a revival of the Albigensian heresy in fourteenth century France. It chronicles the testimony of no fewer than fifteen people, who testified before the Bishop of Tours that horned demons were seen flying from a cave near the village of Montaillou." Lewis turned and regarded us with raised eyebrows: "Horned demons. Hmm… what does one make of that?"

I nodded soberly, feeling more out of my league than ever.

"And now, gentlemen." Dr. Lewis crossed the room, opened a small door, and carefully removed a volume which he set on the table before us. The thing was massive, bound in black leather hoary with age, its cover inscribed faintly with cryptic lettering. Even from where I stood, several feet away, the titan tome smelled faintly of stale breath trapped within its desiccated leaves. The doctor rubbed his hands together. "Here is the gem of our collection. Few are aware of this book's existence, fewer still are privileged to lay eyes upon it. I think it appropriate that you do now. There are only four other known copies in the world. This, my friends, is the work of the enigmatic Abdul Al-hazred, in its Greek translation: *Necronomicon*. Book of Dead Names. This particular edition is an early Byzantine edition dating, we believe, from the tenth century. The Al-hazred manuscript has been dated as far back as the eighth century." He shrugged and smiled tightly. "Perhaps. I, however, am among those who suspect that the Arab's work was itself a translation of something far older."

He turned the cover open, revealing a florid and well-faded epigraph, and translated with evident fluency:

"Man must not believe that the Earth belongs only to him. Nor is it to be believed that Man is the oldest and last of earth's masters, or that earthly beings walk alone. The Old Ones walk unseen between the spaces where Man now walks. Yog-Sothoth was, is, and will be the Keeper of the Gate. Man rules now where they ruled once. Soon shall they rule once more."

Lewis looked up with an odd gleam in his eye. "'between the spaces where Man now walks'… 'Keeper of the Gate': what could that mean?"

"Evidently a proto-legend," said Edward. "Most certainly a significant departure from other Greek legends. Passed down, perhaps, from Assyria or the Philistines. Of course, many cultures have 'Old Ones' in their pantheons of deities. But this…" He shook his head.

"'Soon shall they rule once more,'" said Lewis. "One wonders about this 'soon.'"

"And 'Yog-Sothoth'.

I suddenly felt weak. "Yog-Sothoth," I whispered—"that's what I heard. The shore people in Port Landsend—I heard them chanting 'Yog-Soth, Yog-Soth'!"

"Ah," said Lewis, clapping his hands together. "A cult, in your town? Most intriguing! This certainly demands investigation."

"Well," said Edward, "consider us your point-men."

"I shall, indeed. You will note that this incantation refers to 'Old Ones,' plural. Suggesting a pantheon: Yog-Sothoth is a name that appears often, as do others: Azathoth, Nyarlathotep..."

"A pantheon, indeed," exclaimed Edward. "I wonder what parallels might be found with the Bible and other known texts."

"Gods succeeding gods," I ventured.

Lewis nodded somberly. "Very likely."

"Incredible," said Edward, "but frightening. The implications here could pose a severe challenge to conventional wisdom."

"Bah," Lewis snorted, "'conventional wisdom'! To think of what we are missing, in our slavish obeisance to 'conventional wisdom'. This discovery of Erich's may possibly overturn 'conventional wisdom'."

Aw, shucks. Well, hey, I was the reason we were here, right? I still felt unworthy as hell.

"Most of the remainder of the *Necronomicon* appears to consist of various formulae," continued Dr. Lewis. "Spells and incantations. For example: Ya! Yaa! Nyarlathotep n'gah gah fthagn phn'glui!"

Edward frowned. "Nyarlathotep: sounds vaguely Nilotic."

"Yes," said Lewis, "there is a certain Egyptian evocation, but I do not believe there is any connection with ancient Egypt."

"Extra-terrestrial?" I ventured, feeling even more weirded out after hearing those eerily familiar syllables.

"Possibly, although, as I am sure you realize, one must take care making such pronouncements. And yet, I am convinced the origins of this document must be more profoundly alien than we can imagine."

"Well," Edward sighed, "hell of a job tracking it down, I should think."

"Perhaps not so difficult. Earth, after all, is a finite globe. And from what Erich tells us, there may be clues right within our grasp. This cult, for one, offers a most tantalizing prospect."

I was beginning to feel like I belonged.

Lewis gently closed the great book. "Yes, a bottomless mystery, the *Necronomicon*. Do you know, the Library of Congress refuses to admit to its very existence." He smiled that enigmatic smile again. "I think perhaps this is for the best. I strongly suspect that to bring it into the harsh light of ignorant society would open chasms beyond our means to bridge. Even serious students of this work must tread lightly. There are reports of some who delved too deeply and suffered, mmm, *unpleasant* consequences." Lewis stroked the cover in a way I did not quite like. "There is an old rumor that one of these volumes was bound in human skin. Makes one think, doesn't it? But visiting these chronicles reminds us of how little we know. How little we *see*. Perhaps there is so little seen of these beings because we have not *wished* to see. Perhaps, too, what is represented here did not wish to be seen."

"Perhaps it simply evolved," I blurted. Well, I might as well throw something out.

"Precisely," smiled Lewis.

"Yes," said Babson—"but evolved into *what?*"

The doctor placed the book back in the safe. "What, indeed," he said. He moved to a cabinet and took out a small velveteen satchel. "What does our 'conventional wisdom' think of this, eh?" He extracted an object and set it on the table. "This object came to us many years ago under circumstances which, I am pained to admit, are now forgotten. It was on exhibit in our museum here for some time, but we felt it advisable to withdraw it from public view."

The room tilted. The object was a figurine, about three or four inches tall and made of a dull green-gray material. It was a creature, sort of like an octopus, only one with a head like a starfish, with a big eye in the middle. "That's—" I croaked. "That's like the one in the barbershop!"

Edward's jaw dropped. "You saw this in a *barber shop?*"

"In Port Landsend. Yes, same color, same tentacles, same head…" I had another flash, and pieces fell together. "I've seen something like this in my dreams, too." I told them both about the ghostly music, the green depths, the strange figures. "I'm swimming with them, deep down." I shook my head in amazement. "Yeah—things that look like this."

"Indeed!" Lewis exclaimed. "Such a dream as yours must bear profound significance. You are not alone, my friend. I have heard others report similar sightings. The implications are sobering."

Babson frowned. "And yet," he objected, "we find nothing like this effigy in ancient hieroglyphs or petroglyphs…nothing in the annals of Greece or Rome. At least, nothing I've ever heard of."

"Suppressed, maybe?" I said.

Lewis nodded emphatically. "Very likely." I liked him more and more.

"Survivals," said Edward. "Evolutions. The implications are boggling. And this…"

"Exactly, Edward," said Lewis. "We stand at a threshold. Do we dare to plunge ahead, to perhaps discover the line of evolution and its possible survival in our own time? Or do we do as many throughout history have done, and suppress and deny?"

"Is it all merely legend?" Edward mused, "or perhaps scare stories to keep primitive societies in line."

"Like the Christian devil, perhaps," said Lewis. "Indeed, religion has its uses, even for the non-observant. It offers windows on events and a means of perpetuating ways of thinking that might otherwise be lost to us. I also believe that religion serves to make the universe more comprehensible, and perhaps veils certain phenomena whose exposure might threaten the foundations of civilization. Perhaps even our very sanity."

Edward, who had made the same point to me, puffed his cheeks. "Well, gents, we're in some deep waters, here. Thank you, Victor, for a very fascinating and stimulating day. Will you be our guest for dinner tonight?"

Dr. Lewis smiled broadly. "I would be most delighted. May I recommend the Old Colony? It is an Arkham institution." We agreed to meet at eight, and took our leave of the good Doctor Lewis.

Walking back to the Arkham House, Edward asked, "Well, Erich, what did you think of our friend?

I hesitated. I didn't want to be flippant with a respected colleague. "Don't hold back," he said, as if reading my mind. "I respect your impressions. After all, you're the main reason we're here."

"He's very interesting," I replied. "I like him."

"There's something curious about the man, don't you think?"

"He seemed like he was about to explode. Maybe he's gotten too wrapped up in his own perspective?"

"Yes. It's a failing all too prevalent among us academics. We dig ourselves in, develop our pet theories, and hoist the drawbridge. This can be a serious obstacle to true knowledge. Still, I like Victor and do believe he's on to something, or perhaps many things. He's done research in Tibet and the South Pacific, and has published one quite intriguing paper. But I think he's got more up his sleeve and I'm going to try to weasel it out of him. Fellows like Dr. Lewis require a certain delicacy of handling."

We laughed, but inwardly I felt small again. Expeditions, discoveries, publishing—it was overwhelming. "Edward," I said, "this is all new territory to me. That *Necro*-thing: to hear that 'Yog-Sothoth' from it, after hearing those people actually singing it on the beach at Port Landsend? Very weird."

Edward shook his head. "Weird is right. And yet…Well, let us continue to cultivate the good doctor and see what we may see."

We walked slowly through the afternoon sun, savoring the crooked streets and antique architecture of old Arkham. Awkward as I felt, I also felt a vast new world opening to me. I felt Edward's excitement, too, and knew that, unworthy or not, I had made this all happen. Only, what the hell was happening in my dreams?

40

Freak

Too bad about the old man going insane. All that work, all those reams of notes, all those maddening formulas—drive anyone insane! Still, it was up to him. He would not go insane, he would not fail. Of course, others could bungle it up. Like that bunch at the wharf, dumb as posts. Well, that's all right; being dumb, they could be led. A few were bound to object, but throw enough money at them and they would fall in line. In the depths of the Depression, money talked. Trouble was, money was getting low. Well, there were other methods of keeping people in line. Micah Marsh had learned that much.

It was good to remember the nights when he sat with Asahel and his father studying the great book. At first he had been frightened by some of the pictures, but he soon came to regard them as friends, and was keen to know more about them. His great-uncle's scheme to transmute certain elementals into—well, God-knows what—had until recently baffled him. But with the assistance of two elderly men from a small Pacific island, it began making sense. Many of the formulas remained a mystery. Still, he knew he was up to the task. He had read about Napoleon and others, men who had overcome great obstacles to accomplish great things. He, too, could do something great. He would change the world in ways no one could possibly imagine. Everyone else—what did they matter? If they refused to see, so much the worse for them. Not that anyone paid much attention. They would now, though. Oh, yes, they most certainly would pay attention!

Late that evening Rauf phoned from the dock. "The material is ready, sir," he reported. Rauf was a drunkard, but loyal. He called for his carriage and wrapped up well in top hat and shawl. The landau moved slowly into the street. Through the heavy chintz curtain he saw no one, but there were few people around, and so many of the houses were empty. All well and good, all well and good, to be sure. Now and then some dumb kid stopped to gape, as if they expected to see something. Micah Marsh's thick lips curled in a tight grin. *Gape away, brats. You might just get more than you bargained for.*

41

Wheels Within Wheels

There was mystery here. He could taste it in the dank air, in the leaden silence of the old buildings, and in the musty corridors of the Bayview Hotel. There was something else, too, something organic, a dimension hidden but nonetheless perceptible to one who could look, listen, and keep quiet in the shadows. Ivor Lumpkin could do that, easily.

Lying under his stained quilt or sitting out in front of the hotel on warm days, he took stock. Work was boring but easy, and for now, easy was good. His overseers were gruff but drunk or absent much of the time. Better yet, the town cops—all two of them—hadn't rousted him, not once. Port Landsend was dead on its feet, but he liked it that way. And lately, there was a girl with raven-black hair and thighs that hit him right where he lived.

Off duty one Saturday afternoon, Ivor was poking around town and came to a line of shopfronts. In front of one stood a sandwich board bearing the quaintly-lettered legend, *Percy's Barber Shoppe*. A haircut and head-massage sounded good, and Ivor had been hoarding his modest earnings. He opened the door to the tinkling of a bell. A counter along one wall held a curious assortment of curios and oddities: Chinese temple blocks… porcelain animal figurines…some dog-eared Technocracy pamphlets…a stuffed bobcat.

"Well, hello, young fellow!" A plump little man burst from behind the curtain at the rear of the shop and bustled forward. "Looking for a tonsorial?"

"Uh—"

"A haircut?" The barber was bald, round-faced, and wore a white coat and rimless glasses. He smiled hopefully and rubbed his hands ingratiatingly. Ivor liked him at once. "Yes, sir."

"Well, well, now," said the barber in a high, asthmatic voice, "that's fine. Make yourself comfortable." He snatched up a rumpled blue smock and gave it a crisp snap. "Yes, sir, you've come to the right place. Shelton's the name, Percival Shelton. Most folks just call me 'Percy.'" He offered his hand.

Ivor took it. "Ivor Lumpkin," he said, in his best grownup voice.

"Well, well, good to know you, Ivor—mind if I call you 'Ivor'?"

"No, no sir."

"Well, now, splendid, splendid!" As barber Shelton lay the smock over him, Ivor settled into the wooden swivel chair and looked around at the curios and the two worn captain's chairs for waiting customers, customers he reckoned were few and far between. In the cracked mirror across the aisle he saw an unfamiliar face, a face with a black patch over one eye, a face somehow older than he expected.

Shelton took a scissors from a glass of cloudy blue water and clacked the sheaves twice. "You must excuse my little word play there," he said. "Don't get many opportunities to exercise my diction these days." Almost imperceptibly, he began clipping the fringes of Ivor's head. "Yessir, a 'tonsorialist', that's me—heh-heh! Fancy word for a barber. That's what they called us, long before your time." His words rose and fell like waves. "Well, sir, if you don't mind my asking, what brings you to our fair metropolis?"

Ivor cleared his throat. He had barely spoken to anyone since his arrival. "Well, sir—I come off the *Wilford Stickney*. Tramp steamer. Just barely made it into port."

"Ah, yes, the *Stickney*! Remember when she came in. Still docked, I see."

"Yes, sir, Cap and crew beat it. Probably sit there and rot, and that's fine by me." Ivor chuckled weakly.

"Well, well, castaway on our little island, eh?"

"Yes, sir, we were about done-for, I'll say. Engine like to quit on us."

"Oh, that must've been quite the thing!"

"That's one word for it---but we made it in."

"Pretty relieved, eh?"

"Oh, yes, sir, relieved as hell—heck!"

"Pardon me for asking, but is that where you lost your eye?"

"Yes, sir."

"Can't be any much fun, losing an eye."

"No…They gave me some pretty strong grog." Lumpkin left out the bits about screaming and puking his guts out and fainting dead away.

"Oh, the grog'll do it every time."

They both enjoyed a hearty laugh and Ivor felt a sudden expansiveness, talking like a seasoned man of the world.

"You know," Shelton continued, "I can fix you up with a nice glass eye."

"Say—uh, that'd be swell. 'Course, I don't have a lot of dough."

"Oh, don't you worry about that. A good tonsorialist keeps at least one glass eye around for customers like yourself. You come see me when you're ready and we'll get you fixed up."

Lumpkin agreed, liking Percival Shelton more and more. The barber made a thoughtful face. "Well—Ivor—I'm afraid there's not much doing here for a young fella. No, sir, I'd say you're about fifty years too late."

"That so? I work down at the Bayview Hotel. Queer sort of place. But I like it here in Port Landsend."

"Bayview, eh?" Shelton smiled tightly as he snipped ever so gently around an ear. "Well, that's fine, fine."

Ivor's eye drifted to the curios then into a corner, and stopped on something that looked like an octopus—only this octopus had a big, bulging eye on top of its head. Lumpkin felt a shiver in his spine. He opened his mouth: "So, what—" Something caught him— "do folks do around here?"

"Well," said Shelton, "mostly boat work and fishing and such. But so many's moved on, you see, on account of conditions not being very good."

"A lot of the buildings look empty."

Shelton stopped again and waved his scissors. "Yessir, the old 'boom and bust.' We had our boom, and now it's bust. But you know, that's mankind for you, animals, too, everybody eking out their little niches, scheming and plotting. Heh-heh—the lower orders are no different from the higher, not one bit. We're all jockeying for position in this world, aren't we? 'Wheels within wheels', I like to say."

"That United Wharf seems to be pretty busy," said Ivor. "What sort of business do they do there?"

Shelton stood back from Ivor and gave him a curious look. "Well, sir, it's a funny thing. I used to wonder that, myself. Oh, yes, in my younger days I was full of questions!" He took off his glasses and jabbed them at Ivor. "But, do you know something? I looked around and made a simple discovery: Most of the time I had no one to ask for answers. Yes, indeed. Such is the predicament of a man alone, a man with more questions than he knows what to do with. Well, sir, at that point I made another simple discovery: I figured it was none of my business. Heh-heh, simple as that! Yessir, I made up my mind to mind my own business. And do you know, I haven't had a lick of trouble." Boykin put his glasses back on and smiled primly. "So, my friend, what does that tell you?"

Ivor got the message. He'd forgotten how wary of outsiders townies could be. "Just curious," he said, shrugging.

Shelton resumed snipping. "Yes, of course. Don't mean to put you off. The fact is, there are things about this town that—well, not to put too fine a point upon it, but you know how it is. Some folks are suspicious of strangers. Suspicious of friends too, for that matter. Folks here in PL, well, they tend to be on the reclusive side." *Snip, snip.*

"Reclusive."

"You see, Ivor, we have a lot of what you might call shut-ins. Folks obliged to remain indoors for one reason or another. Disease, disfigurement, emotional trouble. Oh yes, the human psyche is full of complexities. Those wheels, again. I imagine you saw your share of 'em on shipboard."

Ivor remembered the carriage, the woman's hysterical laughter—*Marsh! Thought he was dead!*

The scissors snipped and the sun filtered in through the dusty plate glass, casting a yellow glow over the room. The stuffed bobcat bared its teeth in a frozen rictus. Shelton said in an odd, soft tone, "Ivor, you're a wide-awake young fellow with all youth's natural curiosity about life. Got no kick against that, no, sir. Let me just say, though, if you go roaming, as I'm sure you must, you might just keep this in mind. As I say, folks here are suspicious of strangers." Pointing with his shears, he cautioned, "Take those shanties out around Point Judson: I would steer clear of 'em. They fit 'suspicious' to a 'T'. Yes, my young friend, there are some in this old town who—well, never mind, heh-heh, I'm sure you get the point." Shelton regarded his client with approval. "Yes, sir, I think that will do very nicely." He swept the smock from Ivor's lap and gave it a final snap.

Lumpkin paid the barber and headed outside. The sun was gone, a thick raft of charcoal clouds fanned out overhead, clouding Ivor's own mood. He headed slowly downhill, looking into the distance. Funny little fellow, that barber. Ivor liked him. But his words—*Things about this town…mind my own business…wheels within wheels*: what did they mean? Every mystery had an explanation, and Ivor Lumpkin was growing into a man who liked explanations.

Reaching Harbor Street, he walked toward the United Wharf. All was quiet, and the few idlers in the vicinity paid him scant notice. Reaching the wharf, Ivor slipped innocuously into an open alcove near one of the side windows and peered in.

42

Picking Bones

fter a welcome siesta Edward and I enjoyed a brisk evening walk through Arkham's quaint city center to the Old Colony. The town was quiet, and the scant traffic scarcely shattered the illusion of timelessness. Crows cawed in the darkening sky as they flew to their nighttime rookeries, and two blocks away the Miskatonic whispered. We came to an arched stone doorway, entered a paneled foyer, and were greeted by beaming Victor Lewis. With a proprietorial manner he ushered us to a secluded table.

Edward spoke first: "Well, Victor, I found our meeting this afternoon edifying, if not yet fully graspable."

"Quite understandable, Edward," Dr. Lewis said, "quite understandable. There is, after all, much to grasp, as you say."

We made small talk until an elderly waiter served a supper I imagined was enjoyed by diners a century before: medallions of pork with cranberry dressing, green beans, and succotash. It was superb. At Lewis's strong recommendation we ordered a bottle of red wine with a bouquet alien not just to my ignorant palate but to Professor Babson's as well.

"Victor," Edward purred, "this is a most unusual grape."

Lewis grinned impishly. "A local variety, quite overlooked, I believe, by our more august friends across the water." He smacked his lips daintily. "I find it most invigorating."

It certainly invigorated our tongues. Edward and the doctor traded tales of academic obtuseness, and even my normally reticent self waded in with my recent musical experiences, including the extraterrestrial flight on "Lulu's Back in Town."

Lewis laughed warmly. "Oh, I know that old chestnut well. Danced to it many a time in my younger days. And as I am a native-born New Orleanian, I find the development of jazz improvisation always fascinating. How did the ancients discover harmony and develop intricate rhythms? How did Beethoven and Louis Armstrong become titans of western culture? By doing exactly as you." He looked warmly into my eyes and said, "If I may be presumptuous, I advise you to keep on exactly as you are. I believe you may well find a new form of musical expression."

Lumping me with Beethoven and Armstrong? Hey, presume away!

He took another swallow and said, "When I was in Tibet, I heard Monks singing in tones so low as to defy human capability. What was it that inspired the monks, centuries earlier, to express themselves in such a manner? Was it something they discovered, themselves—or the influence of some outside agency?"

Edward gazed into his wine glass and said, "An agency, perhaps, akin to some of these other phenomena we've been puzzling over."

"Quite so," replied Lewis. As the plates were cleared he leaned back and said, "Now, gentlemen, speaking of that. Your bones: what are they, really?"

"I've read newspaper clippings going back a hundred years about sightings and findings of bones like these," Edward replied. "We know that the record of such things is extensive. What does this record suggest?"

"Common links," I said.

"Indeed," said Lewis. He took another drink and sighed happily. "I believe, Erich, that you have a real affinity for this work."

Edward continued: "Victor, you have written of 'whispered legends' and 'aberrations' among certain tribal groups, and you have followed their trail to Tibet, Machu Picchu, Pacific islands, perhaps even our own doorstep..."

"More than 'perhaps'," the doctor replied. "We are offered tantalizing glimpses, such as we examined today, but in our modern age, we scarce know what to make of them. Are they mere allegory, the vaporings of a superstitious, myth-obsessed age? Or are they in fact reflections of reality?"

"My dream..." I murmured.

"Yes: a phenomenon which may yet be merely a dream—or perhaps a vision from *memory*. I believe we must look beneath the surface of material reality in all things. Are you aware of a certain old Pennacook Indian legend which tells of winged beings from the Great Bear Nebula taking up residence on earth?"

"No," Edward replied.

Lewis shrugged and poured himself more wine. "Ah, well, it's not important. Such legends—if legend they be—are perhaps too, um, *outré* for most people. And after all, where does such knowledge get us? No, my friends, for the sake of human well-being, some things are best relegated to the shadows."

Edward frowned. "But who is to say what knowledge should be 'relegated'? From many seemingly insignificant nuggets come great discoveries, new understanding."

"Exactly," said Lewis. "I am pleased to hear you share my feelings." He leaned in close, an odd glint in his slit eyes. "I mentioned today that some had probed the mysteries of the *Necronomicon*. One of those individuals was our very own Doctor Henry Armitage. During the early twentieth century he was the head librarian here at Miskatonic. As I believe I mentioned, our *Necronomicon* and many other volumes came from Armitage's own collection, gathered over many years, to be sure. But you have seen some of his collection and will agree that such volumes beg the question: How did

Dr. Armitage become interested in such things? I believe a partial answer may be found in his diary. It contains a tale to strain the credulity—if not the sanity—of most people." Lewis grinned coyly. "But then, we here are not 'most people'. Please allow me to tell you a little story."

43

Conjuring Congeries

Micah Marsh bent again over the massive volume. He was getting close, he could feel it. How proud his father and great uncle Asahel would be! And if some individuals happened to intrude, and perhaps happened to abruptly "move on"—well, so much the better. Let others think twice before poking their noses into things that were none of their affair.

His no-account sister had been one of them. "Crazy," she'd said. "You and your old books." He'd show her crazy. He stood and stared out on the bay. Lately, he had purchased the old Kliemann Block, and in the corner cupola high above Harbor Street he set up an office from where he could gaze down on the puny men and women scuttling along like ants. That's what they were: ants, who would one day be crushed.

His elders had been wise indeed to come to a place where the human tide had receded. All that rubbish of "humanity," with its machines and filth and corruption and chaos. Fah! There was another order waiting, a better order, and he would open the door to it. Port Landsend would be *theirs*. And after that…

But the Necro book was a damned puzzle. Lately he had pieced together the eighth and twelfth stanzas and recognized his earlier errors. Certain sections remained opaque, but key sequences were falling into place, and the words his great uncle had so patiently taught him echoed in his head, sometimes even to the point of causing him headaches. Well, he would not overdo it, the way his father had. He knew better. Micah Marsh shivered with excitement—he truly stood at the threshold! He stared again at the ancient script and chanted softly, "Fang looey miglaf arleea waggle-naggle ftaggan Cthu—kach-OO!"

Goddammit! He shook his head in disgust. Something was missing. If only he could shake the exasperating tremor in his limbs, the feeling that they were about to fall off and become something else. He remembered his father: how he ran shrieking into the twilight and collapsed in the street, his brains running from his nose and mouth. That would not—could not!— happen to him. Micah Marsh smiled to himself; he was already on the verge of at least one success: *It* was ready.

Late that night, he stood alone beside a dim subterranean canal. He heard a splash and saw a rowboat approach. The skiff pulled up beside Marsh and two men got out and handed him a large object covered with dirty canvas. He set the bundle down on the dry walkway and pulled away the canvas, revealing a lump of dark brown substance. He unfolded a sheet of paper and extracted a flask from his coat pocket and sniffed the contents. They had been hand-carried from back east and painstakingly distilled through many months. If he was correct in his estimation of the text... Marsh poured a stream of brown liquid from the flask onto the lump and began reciting words from the paper. He read slowly and haltingly at first, then faster, faster. He had only a vague idea of what the words signified, but they should—yes, there! *Pop!* The two men standing nearby recoiled in horror as the object expanded into a frothing mass of bubbles of a darkly iridescent purplish hue. The frothing mass trembled and gave a vigorous heave, then with a sulfurous belch collapsed into a foaming green ooze.

"Damn," Micah Marsh grumbled, "something is not right." He dismissed the others and remained, staring at the smoking object. "No matter," he whispered, "we will continue until we get it right." Around the far corner, unknown to him or anyone else, another object stirred.

44

Weird Tales

Quiet settled over the Old Colony dining room. The wood paneling, the velvet cushions, and the ancient waiter seemed to hold time itself in check. We were the only ones left. Victor Lewis gave a genteel belch and began:

"In 1912 Professor Henry Armitage, of this university, heard rumors of strange behavior among rural people living around the village of Dunwich, about fifteen miles northeast of here. In his notes he described a circle of stones on the top of Round Mountain, just outside of town. I have been to the top of Round Mountain and have seen these stones, or what's left of them. They appear to have been greatly damaged, perhaps by Dr. Armitage himself. At any rate, I am not convinced that they were placed there by men for ritualistic purposes, but they do appear to constitute something of a geological anomaly. There are other such stones scattered throughout the region, even right here in Arkham, on the island in the river.

"So: Armitage reported that, at or near the stones, certain individuals had been seen and heard conducting what appeared to have been ritual exercises. At this time, too, reports began coming out of the back country of thunder-like rumbling in the hills, with no storm in the area...noxious stenches emanating from deep ravines...cattle suffering bizarre mutilations.

Armitage continued to observe and record these reports over a period of years, without coming to any conclusions. However, in 1928 he discovered the identity of one of the individuals reportedly seen on Round Mountain, a man named Wilbur Whateley, a local resident from a degenerate family and allegedly subject to violent delusions. Apparently, this Whateley managed to possess himself of certain ritual knowledge and fell victim to a nightmarish sorcery." Lewis leaned in close and whispered portentously. "In fact, gentlemen, he attempted to steal the *Necronomicon* from this very library. The same volume you yourselves saw this afternoon."

"Incredible!" exclaimed Edward.

"More than incredible. It seems that as this poor soul grew older, he underwent a terrible metamorphosis far beyond all—umm—*normal* parameters. We know this because Whateley himself kept a journal of his activities, which the authorities gave to Armitage after the incident. Professor Armitage later claimed to have destroyed this diary. A pity, I suppose, from an academic viewpoint, but perhaps prudent. In any case, Whateley came to a bad end: a guard dog attacked him, with fatal results."

"Tragic," muttered Edward.

"Yes," nodded Lewis, "most unfortunate. But in this case for the best." He leaned across the table, a strange glint in his eye. "I say this because, according to Armitage, Whateley's journal recorded in a shocking and intimate detail the process by which this poor soul was subsumed by an alien entity, and how under that entity's influence he attempted to unlock a passage to another dimension—the entity's 'home' dimension—by reciting certain formulae from the *Necronomicon*."

"My god," Edward whispered. I could only stare, bug-eyed. What the hell had we stumbled into?

"But this is not all," said Lewis. "It seems poor Whateley had a brother who fell prey to an even more drastic mutation and was transformed into a monstrous globular *thing* that ravaged the countryside, killing people and destroying houses. Armitage watched as this being climbed Round

Mountain, and he later described it in his diary. Fortunately, Henry Armitage was more than a good observer; in fact, it seems he took the *Necronomicon*, followed that trans-dimensional abomination to the summit of the mountain and there read out the formulae that sent the thing back to its own world."

Edward stared at Lewis bug-eyed. I hoped he wasn't losing patience. "Trans-dimensional!" he exclaimed. "You mean, some entity from another dimension actually materialized *here?*"

Lewis nodded soberly. "Yes. In Armitage's own words, the thing appeared for brief seconds as a tremendous, pulsating globe. Then, Armitage read the lines and the monster was expelled—shrieking the name Yog-Sothoth."

The room went cold. "Him again," I murmured.

Edward raised his hands. "Victor, all this seems to be a bit over the line."

Lewis grunted. "Line, Edward? There is no 'line' and there is no certainty, only an account, written by a reputable scholar like yourself, of something fantastic, something beyond all lines and certainties. Unless, of course, the Whateley diary and Ainsworth's own experience were nothing more than some bizarre hallucination, or even a work of fiction."

Edward shrugged in bewilderment and Lewis kept on, as if determined to goad him. "We scientists: always so eager to make one more entry in the Cartesian ledger." He shook his head violently. "No, my dear Edward, I am afraid it will not do. Nature and history itself abhor straight lines, and this case is a perfect example.

"I will tell you more. In our archives are a few blackened sheets from the notebooks of one Captain Ebenezer Holt, who brought back from extended explorations physical specimens that could not be catalogued—not even named. As he recorded, when exposed to air they dissolved in a fog of fetid smoke, leaving no trace. And then there are the enigmatic chronicles of our own Prof. Nathaniel Wingate Peaslee, who early in the twentieth century suffered a five-year spell of amnesia and, when he emerged, ranted of cone-shaped monsters and enormous basalt ruins deep in the ocean. For his pains,

Professor Peaslee was eased into part-time status, but he did not knuckle under. No, in 1935 he led an expedition into the Australian interior and reported the existence of vast ruins and evidence of unspeakable survivals."

"What became of him? Did he publish his findings?"

"Who would publish such things? Our so-called 'academic establishment' shunned him, just as it has shunned all who would upset its accepted orthodoxies, myself among them." Lewis drank the last dregs of his glass and glowered, as if saddened by the inability of the modern world and even his own colleague to accept things beyond the pale of conventional understanding. Then he smiled wistfully. "I remember years ago an associate told me of a man in Providence, whose name escapes me, who was apparently quite the authority on arcane lore. He was something of a recluse, as I understand, and I've found that such individuals often possess sensitivities beyond the usual, enabling them to see into other dimensions."

Lewis turned his now thoroughly gimlet gaze on me. "Perhaps, Erich, you may find yourself among their number. Such a possibility is not to be dismissed. At any rate, it seems that this fellow was privy to many fantastic events and had written his own accounts of them—accounts I have not been able to track down. Ah, why the devil can't I remember his name? Well, it's a pity he's no longer with us."

Edward tapped his fingertips together pensively. "A fascinating and provocative story, Doctor. It appears we have much work to do. But, as always, resources are limited."

Lewis smiled ruefully. "Money, you mean. Yes, always the deciding factor, is it not? Money, and the limitations of our own minds. Still, we must persevere."

"Semper persevero," Edward chuckled. "Indeed, we must."

We parted with Dr. Lewis and walked back to the Arkham House in silence, digesting a wonderful meal and a profoundly perplexing conversation. The night was warm and soft, the air drier and somehow older feeling than what I was used to out west. I liked Arkham and was a bit sorry we couldn't spend more time in the cozy and legend-haunted little city. But what had we just heard? Could those things really have happened, just a few miles away? I looked at Edward, he looked at me, and we could only shrug.

Back at the inn, I told Edward I wanted to take a walk. We shook hands and I headed down Depot Street admiring weathered brick commercial fronts like those in Port Landsend, and was pleased to see on many corners the old-fashioned incandescent streetlights, long-gone from Seacoma, which always seemed to shed more darkness than light. The rush of water drew me down a side street, and I arrived at a stone parapet overlooking the Miskatonic. The river flowed cool and fresh in its ravine, a benign force of nature. And yet, bones of some strange horned beast—bones like ours— had been found in this river. And upstream lay the enigmatic valley of the Whateleys. What other mysteries lurked in the depths of this innocuous stream and the surrounding hills? The Miskatonic flowed on, revealing nothing.

I walked slowly along River Street past abandoned brick factory buildings and antique frame shopfronts, encountering only occasional walkers. The town seemed to be folding in on itself, and folding me in with it. Maybe I'd been in Port Landsend too long, but I had a weird sensation that my ties to the modern world were getting looser and looser. Funny, too, how both Lewis and Babson talked about connecting threads, and the limits of our sanity. Was my tentacled dream-apparition a relic, a buried memory of what had been? Or was it a ghastly *precursor*?

The loamy aroma of cottonwoods hung over the stream, and something more obscure, almost nostalgic. Burning leaves, perhaps. A full moon had risen, casting a silvery light over the ancient walls. I emerged from a brick-and-stone defile and came to another overlook. Just downstream, an island smudged the shining waters, and on it was a barren patch studded with oddly regular shapes: the stones Dr. Lewis had mentioned, standing like Druids in the moonlight. I felt a strange kinship with them, these stolid survivors of an ancient age. I wanted to touch them, to know them! *Come,* they whispered—*come...see*. I wished I could, but there was no bridge and I could only commune with their strange, silent forms at a distance. I closed my eyes and thought again of the Whateley brothers' monstrous mutations, of Peaslee's cone-thing, and of the little effigy in the barber shop. "Connecting threads"—I could feel them vibrating in the cool air and tightening around me.

A raucous sibilance shattered my reverie. I peered into the trees and saw black forms fluttering among the branches—birds, thousands of them, shrieking into the night. I'd never heard birds like that, probably some variety not found out west. As long as I stood by the river, they kept up their song, calling—for what? The sound grew until it became one vast cacophony, unlike anything I'd ever heard, a sonic shroud settling over the valley and enveloping everyone beneath. I looked around, expecting people to flood the street in startled wonder, yet I remained alone. Gradually, the avian symphony diminished into an eerie silence. It's said we live in a shrinking world, but mine seemed to be growing larger by the minute.

45

Truth Or Dare

"Hey, you!" Hands pulled Ivor Lumpkin away from the window and whirled him around into the faces of two young toughs. At least, they looked young, despite balding heads and scabby gray skin. "Better take him to the boss," one said, his voice thick and mushy.

"Shaid not to d'shturb 'um."

"Yeah, okay," said the first guy. He shook his fist in Ivor's face and growled, "Stay away from here, boy, or next time you won't be so lucky." They marched him away from the pier and shoved him into the street.

Lumpkin lay in his bunk that night and thought again about his encounter. *I made up my mind to mind my own business.* Sure, snooping got you into trouble. But rats! Life was for living and mysteries were for solving. He had fetched up in a city of mystery, he would damn well sniff it out, just like he'd sniffed out the berth on the *Wilford Stickney* and he'd sniffed out a nice easy berth at the Bayview. As for the dark-haired woman…Ivor smiled slyly. Yes, he was damn good at sniffing.

Ivor went back to work, and in the squalid Bayview lobby and along Harbor Street he kept his eyes and ears peeled. He was loafing at the front door one evening when a business coupe pulled up at the curb. A big, oily-faced man got out, dropped a case down in front of Ivor and ordered,

"You, boy, carry this in." Lumpkin reddened but did his duty, hoping for a good tip. The man checked in and Lumpkin lugged his case to his second-floor room, only to have the guy slam the door on him. Late the next morning the car was still parked at the curb. Odd—the room was vacant, its occupant nowhere to be seen. Maybe he was off at the nearby café. Late that afternoon, however, the car was still there, and next day, too. Had its owner fallen afoul of bootleggers?

Lumpkin tried to steal a peek at the register to see if the man had checked out, but hawk-eyed old Sargent gave him no opening so he slouched downstairs to feed the furnace. "Don't use too much coal," the clerk grumbled. He gave the furnace its daily dose of bituminous, followed by a vigorous kick, and peered around the dingy cellar. Dimly lit by a single bare bulb, the musty hole seemed to swallow light. The strange smell that was a constant presence around the hotel tugged at his nostrils. The most nagging thing was the big door in the corner, a door he knew must lead to the sub-basement. He wanted desperately to investigate, but dared not disobey the stern injunctions of both Sargent and Carney against venturing beyond his appointed rounds.

But idleness did not suit Ivor Lumpkin. That night, Moses Waite, Sargent's cousin, 80 years old and nearly blind, was at the front desk. Heart racing, Ivor slipped on his overalls and crept into the hall. The wind rattled through the ventilators, no one stirred. He padded quietly down to the front desk. Old Waite was snoring heavily, head propped against the wall. What about Carney? By midnight he was usually passed out in his room.

On cat's feet Lumpkin descended to the furnace room and eased the big door open. A light breeze blew in, laden with an odd pungency. Ivor stepped through the doorway and down a flimsy wooden stair. At its foot, a dimly-lit brick corridor stretched into the distance, and far down the way stood a man. Carney. He appeared to be busy with something, so Ivor waited until he looked away, then slipped to the concealment of a nearby buttress. He saw a narrow ditch of water beside the walkway, leading to a dark portal in the further distance. A sewer of some kind—that would account for the smell. Near Carney was a wheelbarrow. *Ah-ha!* Carney had so adamantly warned him away from the sub-basement for a good reason: The sly dog was a bootlegger!

Ivor considered the situation. Would he slink away and leave Carney to his booty, or stay and catch him out? Lumpkin snorted softly; he was no slinker—he would catch his boss red-handed and demand his cut. You can talk about your wheels-within-wheels and minding your own business, but when you got right down to it, life was about percentages, and Ivor Lumpkin wanted his. Crouching deep in the darkness, he held his breath and waited.

46

Dark Spirits

Mount Kulshan squatted in the dusk like a great stone idol. Around the fire, voices spoke softly. At moments like this, when the peaks gleamed and the embers flew, it was almost like old times. Now, though, the clammy hand of depression gripped the old city and a strange unease enveloped the point, an unease that whispered of old Percy, the barber, and how he'd disappeared…whispered over young Asha Armstrong and how she'd taken to swimming alone late at night—naked…whispered about strange sounds and smells—smells as of something rotting—emanating from the United Wharf.

Now, too, there were more cabins in the shanty town at Point Judson, most occupied by newcomers from Polynesia joining generations of predecessors. Like their forebears they did not care to learn English or join the larger community, but kept to themselves and worked as laborers at the wharf or fished, with singular success. And late at night, they gathered at the far point and, as they and theirs before them had for decades, sang loudly and lustily into the darkness.

The new generation of campfire sitters didn't like it any more than their forebears had. "Them Kanakas is up to no good," said a man with a withered hand.

"Devil's work," muttered a man with a cauliflower nose.

"Gives me the willies," said a big man in a battered brown derby. "Movin' their arms up and down and facin' out to the bay, almost like they was sayin' prayers to somethin' out there in the water."

"What about them sacks they're always packin' around?" said the man with the withered hand.

"Folks been complainin' about their dogs goin' missin'," said a young stripling.

"I ate dog once," said a slope-backed Indian, "it ain't so bad."

"Not if you're hungry enough," said the man with the cauliflower nose.

The men laughed lustily. The bottle made another round, the pipes were relit.

The big man in the brown derby jerked his head toward the cabins. "I know damn well they're bootleggin'." He took a long swig and studied the bottle filled with ugly brown liquid. "Stuff ain't half bad, neither. 'Leastwise not after you drunk enough of it."

"Nah, it's somethin' eltse," said the man with the cauliflower nose. "I'm just an old bindlestiff, but I tell you, I been around enough to know there's some strange doin's—*hic!*—I can tell you that."

The slope-backed Indian shrugged. "Hey, live an' let live, I say."

"I'm for that," nodded the stripling, "but man, them songs they're singin'…"

"Urrrr," said a man the others said was three cents short of a dollar.

The man in the derby hat hawked a quid into the flames. "Heard Old Man Marsh's been runnin' around in that buggy of his."

"I seen it," said the man with the withered hand. "Just the other night I was downtown, and here come this horse an' buggy, clop-clop-clop. Looked like a goddamn hearse. Scared me silly."

"You see Marsh in it?"

"Nah, rig's all curtained up."

"S'posed to got some disease or other and can't show his face."

"Off his nut, more like it. They say his old man went loco."

Brown derby spat again into the flames. "All's I know is them Kanakas give me the willies."

"Ain't all Kanakas," said the slope-backed Indian. "Some's from back East—white men."

"See 'em down at the Apex," said cauliflower-nose. "Damn peculiar-lookin', and their talk—all garbled an' slobbery."

"Shit," replied the stripling (who everyone else thought talked too much), "I was goin' by the wharf the other night and I coulda swore I heard noises, like there was some kinda animal in there."

"Seals, prob'ly."

"Shit, seals—*inside* the place?"

On the fringe of the group, a quiet, craggy-faced man studied his roasted marshmallow. White man's food was full of surprises. "Water Beings," he said. "Lived around here for a long time."

"I heard of 'em," said the slope-backed Indian, "but I never seen 'em."

"They are quiet beings," said the craggy-faced man, whose name was Ka'atah'teh. He looked much like his father, but these men did not know that. "They do not wish to be seen. But they are here."

From down the point, voices keened.

"There they go again," said derby hat. He cleared his throat. "Now, don't get me wrong, I'm as Christian as the next one o' you bums, but I'll tell you, I heard some strange things in my time shipboard. Back around 19-and-15 I was mate on the *Halloween*, and we had us a feller from the island o' Ponape, away out Micronesia. This feller worshipped some bunch of gods I never heard of before. Said one of 'em lived in a big old stone house down at the bottom of the sea! Give me the willies an' then some, he did. Damn if that jibber-jabber of his didn't sound a lot like these folks right here."

"Aw, sheepdip," said the stripling (who was getting fed up with it all).

Brown derby shrugged. "I know what I heard then, and I know what I'm hearin' now."

"Dark Spirits," said Ka'atah'teh. "Those guys are calling to them."

"Jesus," said the stripling, "this truck is givin' *me* the willies. I'm turnin' in."

"Me too," said cauliflower nose. "You boys's been hittin' the hooch too hard."

The man others called three cents short of a dollar said, "Urrrrr…"

The sound of a whining pipe drifted over.

"There's that idiot flute player," said the man with the withered hand, taking a pull from the bottle. "Damn racket'd wake the dead."

The voices shrilled, louder and more distinct.

"That's it!" exclaimed derby hat. "The Yog-Soth call."

"Yog-*who?*"

"That's what the Ponapee called him. 'Yog-Soth' Never forget a name like that."

"Then you know," said Ka'atah'teh.

The distant voices altered their cadence with a new word.

"I've heard that one somewhere before," whispered the slope-backed Indian. "God who lives in the sea."

"Blas-pheemeous paganistic hooey," cried the man with the cauliflower nose.

"Must be that bug juice you're drinkin'," said the slope-backed Indian.

The guttural mantra rose to a fevered crescendo. Derby hat sat up and listened closely. "My god," he muttered, his face ashen. "Cthu—" He erupted in a fit of coughing.

47

Seaweed Bungalow

lorp! A tentacle flopped, a wing stretched, the great form shuddered and lay still. All was quiet at the bottom of the sea. Quiet, deep, and dark. Far away, something echoed and faded. Yes, them again. Little buggers, never knew what they wanted, one moment they're falling all over you, the next you're out on your arse. Still, good to have a bit of fun once in a while, like the time not long ago when they actually got it right and called it out, and it flew from its house out over the sea and came upon that ship, and the ship went right through it. Oh, the looks on their faces! And in a pinch, they weren't bad tasting. So many pages in the book of happy memories.

Well, one couldn't have fun every day. One day, it would all be theirs again, no more loafing. But until then…It sighed and dozed off, woke again. Something was bothering it, but it couldn't put its finger (actually, two-dozen fingers) on it. Again, the faint words pinged. It listened awhile but heard nothing more. Probably nothing. In its house at sunken R'lyeh, the monster dozed, green water ruffling its fluted carapace and producing a subsonic rumble that fanned out through the cold, crushing depths. *Blorp.* It opened its eye for a moment. Must be getting hungry.

48

Dreamscapes

Tumbled ruins lay in awful splendor. Shafts of green light lanced through a milky haze. The bow swept back and forth, deep tones throbbed, dark shapes swirled around me as the rumbling *basso* oscillated in and out of consciousness. Far away, another sub-bass note hummed. Out of the inky void a figure appeared, growing larger, coming closer, closer. Its lips parted, a bright green tentacle snaked toward me.

I burst awake, heart pounding. That green again, that radiant, unearthly green. Some kind of womb-memory. Sure, why not? Victor Lewis's strange narrative didn't help; winged beings from outer space, the Whateley guy, Yog-whoever. Well, what can you do? Ride with it, brothers and sisters, ride with it. Hmm, sounds like a song.

In the lobby that morning, Dr. Lewis looked none the worse for his bibulous evening. "I hope this visit has proven worthwhile to you both," he said. "There are many strands connecting things—mostly hidden and undetectable by normal methods." Turning to me, he said, "Perhaps, Erich, you will have the good fortune to discover one of them. Perhaps more. Keep in mind what you have seen and heard here, and what others have dared to explore."

We shook hands and Lewis said, "Gentlemen, I would like to leave you with one last quotation from the *Necronomicon*, something that has lodged in my mind ever since I first laid eyes on it." He cleared his throat and intoned,

"That which was dead shall once more live
That which was old shall become young
The universe will tremble at their touch.

"Most evocative, isn't it? Something to think about on your travels home." He grinned widely. "Or wherever they may take you."

We had all day to drive back to Boston, so Edward suggested we take back roads and head east toward the Atlantic—"There's a place I want to see." The bald hills looked peaceful, even benign in the midday sun, and the desolate farms quaintly picturesque. I wondered again at the lives of rural folk, the ancient backbone of America. How did they survive? What cunning tactics did they devise to maintain their dignity—and their sanity?

As if reading my mind, Edward said, "Ah, the secrets lurking in these hills. Some of these folks, inbred for generations. One can only imagine."

"Strange mutations, like that Whateley."

"Hah! I'm still digesting that whole scenario, or trying to."

"And there's really no documentation left of all that? It's all just in Dr. Lewis's head?"

"Seems so. Pity, isn't it? Part of me wants to believe him, but sheesh!"

We threaded through groves of gnarled oaks and tumbledown rail fences, a ruined barn, a fallen rock wall, tattered remnants of shattered dreams. "This rural life is tough," Edward mused, "tough and isolated. Beneath the surface tranquility and the 'quaint charm' of these old colonial backwaters, what strange genes perpetuate themselves? What *about* this Whateley character? I can't swallow it, but I don't believe Professor Ainsworth wouldn't make something like that up, or that Victor Lewis would give credence to it lightly. And that ritual, those incantations—some remnant of local superstition? After all, in the 1920s the modern era had barely penetrated these parts. Most folks didn't have electricity or automobiles. Probably seldom left home or venture further than just a few miles. Yes, there are centuries of human substrate here, layers of legend, myth, folk-memory, and God-knows what more. I almost shudder to think."

I told Edward about the stones on the island, and the screaming birds.

"Ah, the whippoorwills! There's an old Native American legend that says whippoorwills capture the souls of the dead, and how when they catch one, they shriek to high heaven."

"They were certainly loud."

"The ancient Greeks called them 'psychopomps'—soul-guides to the afterlife. Curious, isn't it, how widespread some of these things are. And like Victor said, how can we know that some legends don't have some basis in reality, or at least, in *perception* of reality?"

"So, it all comes down to perception?"

Edward sighed ruefully. "Well, partly. And that, my friend, is one big can of worms."

"Leaving us no closer to solving the riddle of the bones."

"Probably not yet. Oh, Victor has some intriguing ideas. The odd thing is, as fantastic as what he said was, I don't think told us everything."

"Oh?"

"You noticed how he was barely containing himself. I think he knows more than he told us, much more."

"Maybe he was watching to see how we'd react."

"Maybe."

"The Whateley papers: If they *were* destroyed, how does he know so much about the episode, and why has he never published anything on it?"

Edward nodded. "Quite so." Our eyes met, and I felt a rush of warmth at Edward's confidence in me.

"Yes," he continued, "I think Victor is holding back. Then again, what difference does it make? Like he said, it all comes down to money." Edward laughed heartily. "Oh, poor Victor would be laughed out of every grant committee in the country for telling them what he told us. Then again, as he said—and I believe I've said, once or twice, if you're not thoroughly sick of hearing it—I'm not sure if we have it in us to connect the threads. What would happen if we found out that 'Yog-Sothoth' was a remote predecessor of the Biblical God? Such a discovery could upend all our ideas of history, religion, even God himself. As an academic, I hate to say it, but it's possible that some things are best left alone, at least as far as keeping any reputation for sanity is concerned."

"Let sleeping bones lie."

"Mm—or be darn careful who you tell about 'em."

We forsook the hills for the coastal plain and entered a region of scrubby hillocks and dunes. The desiccated dreariness of the country induced an unpleasant lassitude in me. Edward snapped me out of it: "Tell me, Erich, what brought you to Landsend?"

"Jeff's phone call, to play in the band."

"The finger of fate."

"Yes."

He looked out the window a moment, then said, "You may as well know, I've had my eye on Port Landsend for some time."

"Really? Even before the bones?"

"Yes. And I apologize for not being more forthcoming. But being a scientist, and a cautious one at that, I don't like shooting my mouth off before I know what I'm talking about."

"Sure, I get that. Talk is cheap."

He laughed heartily. "You're too young to be a cynic, Erich. But yes, I agree. Talk can too often spoil hard work—and stir up resentment. But like I said, I've been interested in Landsend for a while. I discovered that picturesque little backwater when I came to Dungeness over ten years ago. I thought I'd take a side trip one nice summer morning, and when I got to Port Landsend I was smitten by its air of decaying Victorian charm and its resemblance to certain coastal towns of my native New England. I've spent several weekends there over the years, and what I've seen has convinced me that there is more to old PL than meets the eye. As you yourself have discovered."

He looked at me, an odd gleam in his normally gray eyes. "Erich, how would you like to be my man in Port Landsend? Keep me apprised of things: the chantings and other activities."

"And horny sea-beasts, of course."

"Definitely horny sea-beasts."

We headed up a long rise toward an empty sky. "Yes," Edward said, "should be coming up soon." We tipped over the summit and beheld a stunning panorama of Atlantic surf arcing in a vast, frothy crescent far away toward the south. But close in lay something even more interesting: a congeries of roofs and chimneys looking like an older and more decrepit version of Port Landsend.

"Ahh," said Edward, "here we are."

We turned off the highway, passed a ruined covered bridge, and drove slowly down an old-fashioned main street. We passed a moldering church with a curiously leaning steeple, a few frame business blocks, and scattered small houses. The center of town was desolate, and most of the buildings appeared derelict, with few cars and even fewer pedestrians. A stage set for a bad dream. "Man," I said, "I thought Port Landsend was dead."

Edward made a wry face. "Erich, welcome to Innsmouth."

We came to the waterfront and sat a moment taking in the sagging remnants of wharves and warehouses, then drove on through a residential neighborhood of slouching frame houses. Isolated figures glared at us with unconcealed suspicion and I got a tingly feeling that I'd missed something, something that had happened here years ago, and that the town was only just recovering—barely. "I may have had family here," Edward said. "A great-aunt or something, or so I was told. Never found out any more than that. I told you we lived in Aylesbury; well, I was in the store one day when I was about ten years old, and I overheard some fellows talking. One of them said, 'Innsmouth,' and another said, 'You'll never catch me goin' within ten miles of that place. Devil's doin's there.' That's exactly what he said: *'devil's doin's.'* I've never forgotten it."

"Did you find out what those doings were?"

"Accounts are very sketchy, but seems to have been some big smuggling operation. Bootlegging, probably, common enough back then. Those 'Roaring Twenties' were really pretty desperate times for many folks. I understand the government had to come in and put the kibosh on it." Edward was quiet for a moment, then said, "But 'devil's doin's': does that sound like bootlegging to you?"

49

A Loathsome Luncheon

ost in the shadows, Ivor Lumpkin watched and waited. He knew he shouldn't have defied his boss and ventured into the cellar, but he had to see it for himself. How would he get out without Carney noticing? He made a tentative move toward the stair, but a muffled hissing sound stopped him. White mist swirled around the far tunnel mouth and that now-familiar malodorous breeze wafted down the gallery. Beneath a bare lightbulb, Carney coughed and shuffled his feet. Ivor squinted toward the portal. The hissing sound grew louder, and to Ivor Lumpkin it could only be one thing: a rumrunner's boat.

But no boat emerged from the black tunnel mouth. The water erupted in a loud splash that sent shivers down Ivor's back, followed by gouts of white foam and glimpses of something that looked like flippers. Seals! Carney bent over the wheelbarrow and began throwing things into the water. Whitish things, like—fish parts? Was he feeding seals? Ivor snuck forward a few feet until he could move no more without being spotted. Carney flung another object toward the water, and the light caught it in mid-fling. It splashed into the water, and then came the sound of a loathsome chomping and grunting. Choking down nausea, Ivor pressed himself back into the shadows, trembling. For the white thing was no kitchen scraps, no fish guts—it was an *arm*! Christ, no—the *salesman?*

The water churned and slopped over the lip of the walk, and a foul stench filled Ivor's nostrils. He doubled over and heaved, his retching echoing in the close space. "Hey!" Carney yelled. An ugly scowl on his face, he sprinted toward Ivor, who began running back down the corridor, only to catch his toe on an uneven stone and fall sprawling on the pavement. Carney pulled a blackjack from his pocket and smashed it squarely down on Ivor's head. Ivor flailed his arms and tried to fight him off, but Carney sapped Ivor again and began dragging him back toward the water, grunting hatefully. Ivor felt himself weaken and let himself go limp. But as Carney jerked him toward the water he gave a mighty heave and jerked away from Carney's clawlike grasp.

"God damn you!" Carney rasped, his breath sour with alcohol. He raised the blackjack again, but Ivor's push threw him off balance on the slimy pavement. His raised hand banged the overhead light, swinging it wildly back and forth and throwing the hellish scene into a nightmare vision of alternating light and shadow. And into those awful oscillations came not seals or sea lions, but a thing that defied all reference. Ivor stood frozen, trying to make sense of the monstrosity now creeping toward him—a blobby, oozy, misshapen lump of purple and green globules, seemingly expanding and shrinking, hissing, grunting, and stinking to hell and back.

"Holy bald-headed Christ," he yelled as the thing lunged forward. Carney staggered and struggled to regain his footing, then fell backward into the pulsating blob. The man's shrieks blasted down the tunnel and Lumpkin looked on in horror as the crazily-swinging light fell on his suddenly ex-supervisor being engulfed and, with a sickening slurp, not so much devoured as *absorbed*.

50

Convergence

The crooked finger of the wharf cupola jabbed the sky, the water shimmered, the creosoted pilings exhaled a resinous stink. The day felt old, like 1910 or 1930, and the waterfront was bleached in metallic light that made the buildings look like cardboard cutouts. I threw my mind back in time to a dance-band musician waking up in a small upstairs room and peering into a gray day and an uncertain future. Time was unknowable, a series of nested hatboxes. I stood at the railing, waiting. Done plenty of waiting in my time, but this was good waiting: waiting for someone I knew would show up.

We were plowing through "China Boy" the night before and there she was, all legs and shoulders and hair. She walked in slowly, almost regally, and sat in a corner booth. My pulse redlined, I felt my face flush. I decided to play it cool and ignore her. It almost worked. Break came and I sat down beside her. It felt—natural. "Hey," I said.

"Hey."

"May I join you?"

"Looks like you already have." We both laughed. "Your fingers on the bass—they're very nimble." Her voice was soft, almost sultry.

"Been practicing."

"Is it hard to play?"

"Hard enough. Very physical."

"That was nice, what you did with that stroke-thing."

I'd taken a short bow solo on a blues, no big deal, but it came out all right. Rick gave me the biggest smile I'd seen from him yet. "Yeah, my stroke thing. Thanks." I looked at her hand, noticed again the deep webbing between her fingers. "You must like to swim…" Jeff and Bradley walked by, said hi to her, grinned at me, and headed for the back room. *Good boys.*

"Why?" she asked.

"Your hands: they look made for swimming."

She gazed thoughtfully at her hands. "It's true, I do love to swim. Always have."

"Where—in the Sound?"

"Yep."

"Isn't it cold?"

"Doesn't really bother me."

Hmm. "How was work today?"

"More of the same only the same."

We laughed again. I got the feeling that was something she didn't do very often, and that she liked doing it.

Her eyes flicked over the room. "Nice place. I suppose the food's expensive."

"Not bad, actually, I think Rick's trying to keep the prices down." I offered to get us drinks, she said she didn't drink, so I went to the bar and got us two Cokes.

"So, you like playing old music?" she asked, after I sat back down.

"Yeah. At least for now."

"I say the same thing about working in the Lamp Post. Only, 'for now' is getting to be a pretty long time."

I nodded understandingly. "Any exciting customers today? Oh, wait—I didn't come in today."

175

"No, you didn't," she said. "Was it something I didn't say?"

We laughed some more. Her mouth was broad and shapely, her teeth shiny white but oddly pointy. It felt good, laughing with her. Really good.

"Yeah," she added, "probably not much danger of that. It's not like I get into any great conversations at work."

"I've never been a great talker, myself," I said.

"I don't know if I am or not," she said, "I've never had much opportunity. Probably not having many friends doesn't help."

"Yeah, I've had my share of 'space,' myself. So, do you know any other musicians in town?"

Sara shrugged. "Not really." She got a distant look in her eye. "In case you hadn't noticed, PL isn't exactly an artistic kind of place."

"Oh, I don't know—seems to me it's the perfect place for an artistic type. Wouldn't mind meeting some local players, jamming a bit on different stuff."

"Yeah, maybe..." She trailed off. I studied her dark eyes, the way they surveyed the room. Jeff headed for the stage and Dick climbed behind his drums. Why couldn't this be one of those half-hour-break bands?

"Time to start. Gonna stick around?"

"For a couple of songs." She was as good as her word, and as she vanished into the night she shot me one last flick of a glance.

Suddenly, Sara. Striding toward me, vibrating the air between us, cleaving the day neatly in two. I became somebody else, somebody better. Her smile stopped my breath. "So," she said, her voice low and warm, "you made it through last night."

"Yep." I looked into her eyes. "Made it. A good night."

"Mm." It was sweet, the way she puckered her lips together. "I enjoyed it. I don't go out much. At all, actually." She brushed her hair back and looked away across the water.

"Lonely life."

"I'm used to being alone. It works, mostly. Maybe."

"Yeah, it works. Until it doesn't."

She cocked her head and looked me up and down. We edged closer to each other. I said, "You've lived here all your life?"

She did that slanty leg-thing again. She had to know how sexy it was. "All my life."

Before I could stop it, my mouth blurted, "Your family was quite prominent here."

Her eyebrows clenched. "How do you know about my family?"

"I went on a little fact-finding mission."

"A fact-finding mission."

"Yeah, facts on Port Landsend. Drove up to Port Diablo library, read the old newspapers—the *Lector*. Couldn't help running into the Marshes. Talked to a lady who may even have worked in your restaurant in the 1930s. She said the Marshes were pretty big."

"Well, there are Marshes and there are Marshes…"

"How 'bout Unit Marsh?"

She looked steadily at me a few seconds and said, "Unit was my great-uncle. He died way before I was born, and my family never talked much about him. That was the other branch, anyway." She sighed a deep, delicious sigh. I wished my head were on her chest. "We're not close, me and my family. Except for running the café, we pretty much don't speak."

"My folks were always kind of remote, too."

"Mine are more than remote, they're non-existent." Elbows on the railing, she rested her head on her hands and stared out at the water. "So, what did the paper have to say about us?"

"Oh—that Unit Marsh built that big house up on the hill." I thumbed toward the wharf—"And that."

"Uncle Rule owns it now. And the café, and other places."

"Suspicious things in the paper—'Unwholesome activities'…"

She laughed heartily. "'Unwholesome'! Wouldn't be surprised. I remember them talking about how Unit went crazy, and how his children had to be cared for by somebody else. Kind of like me."

"Ah."

"Families are weird—at least, mine is. All I really know is that 'my' branch came here a long time ago from Massachusetts. Maybe you already know that."

"No, I didn't. Funny, though: I just got back from Massachusetts."

She raised her head. "Really?"

"Arkham. Nice little town. On the Miskatonic River, up in the hills."

"Never heard of it. What took you back there?"

"One Edward Babson, an anthropology professor at Dungeness College in Port Diablo."

"How did you meet him?"

"The guys and I were on the beach downtown, and we found some bones."

Her voice went flat. "Bones."

"Yeah. Long, stringy bones."

"Hmm."

"And a skull. With horns."

"A cow."

"Nope."

"Goat."

"Uhn-uhn."

"So—what?"

"A thing."

"A thing."

"Yup. Unknown. And the thing is, after we found them, I started having these weird dreams, where I saw the bones, or rather, the things that *were* the bones. I told Edward Babson, and he asked me to go to Arkham with him. So, we went and we met Doctor Victor Lewis at Miskatonic University. Interesting guy, seems to know a lot about strange phenomenals."

"Erich…" I looked at her, she looked at me. "Nothing."

A couple of guys walked slowly by, with that queer "Landsend look" of leathery gray faces and balding heads, drooping lips, and unblinking eyes. One of them nodded slightly at Sara. They ignored me.

"I've noticed that lots of young guys here look—old. Are they all from one family or...?"

"I think there's people like that everywhere," Sara murmured.

I'm not sure about that. Not sure about that at all. The sun blazed forth. "Let's walk," I said. Our eyes met, then our hands. *Zap!* A bolt of electricity surged through me. We strolled to the end of Harbor Street and turned down a dirt lane through dense bushes. I stepped on a giant puffball, collapsing it with a sticky pop and releasing a cloud of brown dust. It looked like a rotting skull. "Those things are so gross," Sara giggled. More puffballs clotted the underbrush, and shelf mushrooms gripped the mossy cedar snags like some marauding fungus army. We circled around to a meadow where a tall tin funnel rose out of the grass. "The old cistern's under here," Sara said. "Big water reservoir from the old days."

"I read about it in the *Lector*! I wonder if it connects with the tunnel."

She turned and stared at me.

"The tunnel behind Jack's warehouse, where I work. According to the *Lector*, Unit Marsh built it. You can hear water lapping around in there behind this big old door. Other things, too."

"Other things."

"Seals, rowboats, other things. Sometimes, when I'm down one of the aisles in there, I get the feeling I'm standing between dimensions."

Sara looked into my eyes and placed both hands on my shoulders. "You're a very curious man, Erich," she whispered. "Very observant. Just—be careful." Then she wrapped me in a vise-like embrace and blew everything away in a mind-erasing, soul-blasting kiss.

51

A Wise Man Plays The Fool

Holy bald-headed Christ! The old mate's favorite oath circled Ivor Lumpkin's brain like a crazed bat. He heaved again into the bowl and flopped down on his cot, rubbing his head where Carney had sapped him. Rotten bastard—got what he deserved. But what the hell was that thing? He had to warn somebody! The cops? He hated cops ever since that bastard in Santa Rosita smacked him for not "moving along" fast enough. He'd only seen but two uniformed officers in Port Landsend, but instinctively hated their hard faces and their nasty-looking nightsticks. Hell, they were probably in on this racket, themselves—whatever it was. What he needed most was a good belt of that turpentine the first mate doled out on the *Stickney*, but Prohibition bollixed that all to hell.

"A wise man plays the fool," he'd once heard said. Ivor Lumpkin could do that—oh, he chuckled to himself, he could play the fool and how! He would bide his time, see what played out, and not let anyone get the jump on him. Clearing the demons from his head, he fell into righteous and dreamless slumber. Next morning he was pushing a broom down the back hall when the cops entered the lobby. They barely glanced at him as they approached the desk where Sargent squatted—exactly what Ivor wanted. He ducked around the corner and bent his ear.

The voices were low and ominous: *Got 'im put away…call it an accident… see what Mister Marsh says…*What did they mean, "put away"? And who was this Marsh that everyone seemed so afraid of? That afternoon Joe Sargent promoted Ivor to custodian. "Carney's quit," he said in his froggy voice. "You take over. Just keep things clean around here, and keep out of that damn sub-basement. Ceiling's comin' loose, probl'y cave in anytime."

"Yes, sir," Lumpkin nodded. He would have no trouble following this particular order.

Two afternoons later he sat on Percy Shelton's well-worn bench. The shop was empty and the genial barber prattled happily about hard times, olden days, and bygone customers. Ivor's heart pounded. Old Shelton was his only friend in town—should he tell him? No, not yet. His eye flicked to the little octopus figurine. "Say, uh, Percy, what is that thing, if you don't mind me asking?"

Shelton picked up the effigy and gazed at it affectionately. "Funny little jigger, ain't he? Bought him off an Indian feller. Nice man, used to come by now and again. Seemed glad to get rid of the thing." He handed it to Ivor. It felt slimy, unlike anything he'd ever touched. Ivor quickly handed it back.

"That's something, isn't it" said Shelton, putting the figure back on the shelf. "Yessir," he chuckled, "it takes all kinds, as we say."

Ivor felt queasy, and something stopped him from saying anything about the horror in the tunnel. *I made up my mind to mind my own business.* He needed a drink. "Say," he asked, "you wouldn't know where to get a little whiskey?"

Percy pursed his lips, then smiled tightly. "You know, Ivor, they used to call us 'barber-surgeons' way back when. Now me, I don't do any doctoring myself, of course, but I can offer directions to a little establishment downtown where they will attend to your particular requirements."

The bell dinged, a stooped old man entered. "Hello, Hiram," Shelton said.

"Percy."

"Ivor Lumpkin," said the barber, "meet Mr. Hiram Higginbotham, esteemed editor of our local news organ. Ivor here's a seaman, able-bodied."

Higginbotham waved his hand. "Bahhh—'esteemed'! Perce, you do so like to exaggerate."

"Oh, eh, not at all, not at all! You *are* esteemed, by me."

The old man smiled wearily. "Well, then, that'll have to do."

"H'lo," Ivor mumbled. He'd never met a newspaper man before.

Higginbotham looked at him with red-lined eyes. A rummy, Ivor thought. "You're a seaman, eh?"

"Yes, sir. Off the *Wilford Stickney*."

"*Stickney*, eh...In port long?"

"Guess so. Cap and crew skipped."

"That so? Well, good luck to you." Higginbotham nodded curtly at Lumpkin and turned toward the chair. "All right, Perce, do your worst."

Ivor said his goodbyes and headed down the street, then stopped. Newspaper man? Maybe...He slipped into a disused doorway and waited. The sun winked out and a sharp wind whipped up from the bay. The few pedestrians paid Lumpkin scant attention. At last, Higginbotham emerged from the barbershop and Ivor made his move. "Excuse me, Mr. Higginbotham?"

"Eh?" The newpaperman eyed him warily. "Oh, it's you, young fellow."

"Yes, sir. I've only been here in Port Landsend, and I'm—well, sir, I've got some things on my mind that I need to talk about. Serious things."

Higginbotham frowned. "What do you think I am, a psychiatrist?" A small glob of spittle sparkled on his lip.

"Oh, no, but—well, it's about something I saw."

"Something you saw." The boy was bright-eyed, wide-awake, eager: the sort of young fellow he'd been himself, once upon a day. He moved into the shade of a nearby entryway, away from prying eyes. "What'd you see—or think you saw?"

"Well, I don't know what it was, but it was terrible. Some kind of monster."

Higginbotham's lip trembled, his eyes darted up and down the street. "Where'd you see this 'monster'?"

"Down the cellar in the Bayview Hotel. It got Carney—it ate him!" Ivor felt himself tearing up. Just uttering the words was too much.

"It *ate* Carney? Uhhh…" The old editor felt weak. *Goddamn them!* He coughed violently then stared hard at Ivor. "Look here," he said in a soft, tremulous rasp, "I don't know what you think you saw, but you forget it. Sea lions, that's what you saw. Awful things, bite a man in two. Put it out of your mind. And look here: Don't be getting down in the sewers, it's not healthy. Falling down…lot of filth and disease down there. You understand me?"

"Yes, sir," replied Lumpkin, "but, I know sea lions, and this…"

"Sea lions! That's what you saw." The old man waved in dismissal and walked stiffly away, leaving Ivor more troubled than ever. Oh, well, who said life was simple? At least tonight, thanks to old Percy, he would end his dry spell.

52

Love In The Ruins

Time passed, eddying around us, caressing our hair, our cheeks, our bodies as they swayed gently together like young elms. We didn't want the kiss—*the* kiss—to end. Kissing—*this* kiss—was all there was. Nothing else mattered.

The kiss did end, but there were more, many more, and from then on, we seldom stopped kissing. We kissed at the Lamp Post, we kissed at the beach, we kissed in the Star Chamber on Friday and Saturday nights. Sara seemed to like the music, but didn't really dig the whole bar scene, so she usually ducked out after one set. Later, I'd climb the stairs to her little upstairs apartment and we'd kiss the rest of the night away. I still liked hanging with the guys, so I split my time between places. Sara never minded; she wasn't the clingy type and neither was I. We liked our space, and that only made us want each other more.

Sundays were ours, ours for waking in each other's arms, sitting at her kitchen table and eating breakfast as the light flooded in, her little hanging crystals shooting tiny rainbows on the walls. Then we'd walk the beach or jump in the Torino and drive around town. I couldn't resist a look at the Marsh mansion. As we slowly passed, I told Sara about my run-in with the little creep. "Oh, God," she snorted, "you met one of the cousins—my uncle Rule's kids."

"What's Rule like?"

"A jerk."

"Does he live there?"

"Yeah."

"Have you ever been inside?"

She shook her head emphatically. "Not for ages. I don't keep up with that side of the family, okay?"

"Sure, babe. Only…" The black look changed the subject.

One green and springy Sunday we got in the car, Sara snuggled close, and said, "There's a place I want to show you." She directed me through narrow back streets up the hill behind town and at a weedy parking lot told me to stop. "Come," she said. She took my hand and led me into the woods. I gazed at the shoulders beside me, the hair brushing back and forth with each thrust of her thighs. She gazed back, smiling. The sweet, loamy aroma of naked earth hovered in the middle air. Sara looked like she'd been born here, as much a part of the forest as the moss and trees, her magnificent legs only moving extensions of the roots bulging from the earth. I ached to hold her again.

We emerged in a clearing, and before us loomed a colossal concrete structure, overgrown with ivy and moss. "The old army bunkers," Sara said. "They used to have big guns here." She led me gently toward a black hole in the cracked gray wall and guided me deep into the shadows. We entered a ghostly realm of dangling wires and rusting beams and discarded beer bottles. Our boots thocking hollowly, we passed through an aperture into near total-darkness. I felt her soft breath on my face as she kissed me, so softly I hardly knew what was happening. She kissed me again, more strongly, and only then did I take her to me.

You'd think the novelty might have eased off a little by now. But no: Sara tore into me like a ripe melon, our lips met each other like ravenous wiggle-worms, and our bodies writhed and shook in the heat of ecstasy. The briny smell of Sara's hair kicked my desire deep into the red zone, and her mouth enfolded me like the soul of woman. She kissed my face, my eyes, my neck, and slipped her big, warm hands under my clothes to claw at the skin of my back. I wrapped a leg around her and let her feel my full, majestic manhood. Hungrily, she yanked at my coat, I ripped it off, then my sweater, and took her tightly in my arms again—it was torture having her away from me even an instant! She curled a leg around mine and we sank to the cold, clammy pavement, our lips locked in desperate, feverish passion. "Mmmm," she purred, "so sweet...so smooth..." Her fingers tightened, she grasped me in her always amazingly strong embrace, and I stroked her firm, black-sheathed thighs all the way to the tops of her tall, shiny boots. I kissed her lips again and again, my long-festering anger and the touch of her skin driving me harder to her. We frantically ripped our remaining clothes off then lay back on the floor, lips locked. "Erich," she whispered hotly, "please...Uh! Yes! *Uhhhh*..." Clenched together as one, we rolled and heaved and slithered and slurped until time forgot our existence.

Hours later, we walked in the gloom, arms tight about each other. I wondered at my night vision—the floor and the walls were dim, but nonetheless visible. I also realized something else: I didn't feel the least bit afraid or vulnerable, even though both of us were naked.

Obviously, Sara didn't, either. "I come here often," she said. "It's one of my favorite places." She kissed my shoulder. "Now, it's our place."

I kissed her hair. "Always and forever."

She stopped. "Erich," she whispered.

"Hmm?"

"'Always and forever' sounds good. Really good. But do you think you'll stay in PL? I mean, you play music. What about when this job ends?"

I didn't like thinking about that, but I had been. But now there was something—someone—else to consider. I took her in my arms. "Yeah, I know. I mean, I don't see how Rick can keep his place going. I should be thinking about moving on. That's what musicians do. But the thing is, I like it here, especially now. I like being here with you. I want to stay here with you."

She shook her head. Were those tears in her eyes? "Shit, Erich, there's nothing for you here. You're a musician, you're—normal. I shouldn't even be loving you, dammit."

"Normal? God, I hope not!" I pulled her close. "But why shouldn't you be loving me?"

She shook her head and pulled away. "Forget it—I don't mean it. I only mean, there's so much for you out in the world, not here. It's not fair for me to keep you from that."

I felt empty inside. She was right. If I really wanted to make a living as a musician, I would have to move on, or stay and get awfully damn lucky. "Okay," I said, "sure, a musician can't depend on having nice places to play. It's a feast or famine business. And anyway, the kind of music I want to play doesn't *have* a place. Not yet. But it's mine and I want to make it into something. But there's got to be some other players around town. Maybe there's somebody like me, looking to do something new. And I can always work at my 'real' job—I like working with the magazine man." Part of me believed it.

She shrugged. "Maybe." With a deep, delicious sigh, she snuggled closer. "You feel good to me, Erich. You feel *right*. But—you must feel it. My skin."

"I do," I breathed, planting my lips on her shoulder. Her skin was smooth yet curiously leathery. And on her neck were faint ridges, like some old scar. Had I noticed them before? I couldn't remember. And I didn't care. "I feel all of you," I murmured, "and I like it."

"But be honest: do I feel 'normal' to you?"

"Sweetie," I replied, "I don't have a whole lot of experience with 'normal', so I'm really no judge. And in this case, I'm prejudiced."

"I love you, Erich Vann. I love your smile—that smile I saw the second time you came to the Lamp Post…standing there in the doorway, all alone.

You looked like a lost little boy and a hero-man in the same body, those boots. And then you sat down and actually smiled at me, looked at me with that kind of little-boy hope in your eyes. Shining…"

"Was I so obvious?"

"Mmm. I didn't think I'd ever love anybody. But that's only a small part of it. I think you know things. You don't know you know them, yet, but you know them. I see it in your eyes. You understand things."

"Well, that'd be a first."

"Come on!" She gave me an exasperated look that made me feel invincible. "Give yourself some credit. You *do* see things, and I think you see them with more than your eyes." She caressed my chest with her finger. "I think you see with your whole body."

I shot a glance at the entrance and saw darkness edged with deepening orange. The air grew danker, fanning my desire, and our breathing filled the little chamber. She moaned softly, panting desperately, as I moved and became part of her. Later, much later, we fell asleep in each other's arms.

Pitch-dark. Silent. Far away, a crow. I woke, alive, animal. Still inside her. I hissed gently in her ear, "Sssss…"

"Hmmm?"

"Hungry?"

"See? You *do* understand things."

"I could go for a nice piece of fish."

"It's about all I eat."

"No meat, huh?"

"No, meat." She giggled, her chest heaved. "I mean, I eat meat. I guess I only really don't eat sweets. You know, candy, ice cream. Makes me gag."

"Pity. I've always had a terrible sweet tooth."

We stood and strolled to the doorway and peered into the twilight. The trees were black against the sky, great swarms of crows flapped cawing overhead.

"Wonder where they go."

"Home."

"But where's home?"

"Secret."

"She hugged me tightly to her and said, "Crows are tricky. Did you know they wait for someone to die, then when their soul leaves their body they try to catch it."

"Seems I've heard that story before."

"Crows are tricksters."

"Birds are creatures of mystery," I whispered, burying my lips in her hair. "Like you. My raven-haired beauty."

"Ummm," she purred. "So, what'll we do the rest of the evening?"

"This." I put my around arm her and we ghosted back into the dark and let the dank air of the ancient place of war come alive with the sounds of love.

53

If Only

Hiram Higginbotham had seen it all. Or so he thought. The editor of the *Lector* was still proud to have been present at the creation of the Gate City, the moniker he boasted of coining. As a wide-awake young scout with ten dollars and a secondhand linotype machine, he made himself a force to be reckoned with in a time when smiles were bright on Harbor Street.

But how those smiles vanished. Vanished with all the eager suitors who had once so cravenly courted his favor. Hiram Higginbotham never vanished. He held fast, he never forsook his city, and he never forsook old Mayor Swanson as Port Landsend began its long slide into senility. "Well, Hiram," the mayor said, not long before taking his last, ragged breath in 1902, "We gave it a good fight, didn't we?" Yes, James," replied Higginbotham, "we certainly did." Higginbotham would never forget the haunted look in those dimming eyes.

Thirty-three years later, there were few left to talk to. Higginbotham tended his cantankerous linotype machine as ever, but the once-proud *Lector* was down to nickel-and-dime ads and insipid man-bites-dog stories—on good days. By noon, with nothing left to do, the editor locked up, spat ceremoniously on the pavement, and retired to his little uptown house where he passed the remainder of the day in communion with illicit spirits.

Higginbotham did not commune in silence. As the acrid distillations warmed his brittle bones, they also loosened his tongue. How he missed those nights when he held forth at the Delmonico bar, fawned and fossicked over by merchants, bankers, boosters, pushers, and grifters! "Rats, all of 'em," he muttered. "Rats deserting the ship." Hell and damnation, why must a man be cursed to live alone? Yes, the bottle was good company, but even that was about gone. "Have to see Perce for another," he mumbled. "Good man, Perce, real friend...Perce, he understood. But those others—I warned 'em! Certain things do not belong on this earth."

He took another pull, and as the shadows deepened he felt them gathering: Kelly...Potter... Olds...The missing ones. They crowded in and pointed their skeletal fingers at him. *You were silent. You did nothing. NOTHING!* "W-wha'd want me to do, dammit all? I tried, I tried..." But had he, really? He shook his head violently. "Goddamn my worthless hide! Olds, why'd you have to be such a damned windbag? Own goddamn fault... follow the goddamn lead...din' follow my own goddamn advice—*hic!*"

Tick-tock mocked the Regulator. Higginbotham shook a bony fist at the blank, mechanical face, which so reminded him of police chief Shull, that pickle-brained bag of bones. "Cowards!" he muttered. "Where the hell were you and your brave boys in blue, hah? I know full well where—warming your backsides and drinking Unit Marsh's liquor, that's where!" Even Swanson wanted it hushed-up. That hurt the most. Higginbotham swigged again and puffed his cheeks out in disgust. "Dammit, James..."

It all went back to that damned Marsh: those eyes, so damned cold... that voice, dripping with disdain—*Now, Higginbotham, we mustn't cause upset...This business about so-called 'disappearances': I am sure there is some perfectly ordinary explanation. These are simple people.* Marsh had gulled him for fair, gulled the whole damn town, and no mistake. Well, at least the man got what he deserved. Apoplexy, some said; fright, others said. But then, people said all kinds of things. And now there was the son. Micah. Another Biblical name—and you never saw a Marsh anywhere near a church. Fah! No telling what kind of man he was, he'd never laid eyes on him. Damnedest thing. Damnedest thing, too, what some folks were saying about the sounds coming from the old Marsh place, and about seeing that old buggy out on the streets late at night. Sure as shin plaster *this* Marsh was up to something.

Well, what could you do? There was no going back, no finding those poor lost kids or that blockhead Olds, and no reeling back the years and finding his own better self, the young, clear-eyed self who had almost refused to go along, almost refused to hush-up. "Almost": there was a word for you. Higginbotham got to his feet and stared hard into the dark corner where the accusing shades of the vanished lingered. The press, the almighty press, guardian of the truth—that was rich. "Truth," he snorted. "Now, what might that be? 'Truth'...fah! If I'd been any kind of newspaper man—Hell, any kind of man at all—would have stuck to my guns. Stuck with the story! Dug, dammit all, dug, like a fox terrier. *I* was editor, not Swanson...Was up to *me*!"

And now: what about now? What about these odd reports filtering in: strange sounds in the old sewer...the racket from the Point Judson folks...and now, new disappearances. Something was up, for damn sure. Bootlegging, probably, or even white slavery. If only he could get a couple of wide-awake young reporters with grit—why, he'd get stories for damn sure! "If only"—hell, "if only" was worse than "almost"! Hiram Higginbotham may have been a cowardly journalist, but he was no fool.

Now, there was that kid. *Some kind of monster...it ate Carney...!* Crazy. No, not crazy—a witness. To what? The old man shook his head, trying to clear the fog. It would not clear. Damn booze, if only he didn't like it so much. Besides, it helped. Helped with the damned rotten-egg stinking foul-stenched *reality* of it. Higginbotham took another pull. He knew damn well what the kid had seen.

54

Be Careful What You Wish For

Ivor Lumpkin walked into the alley and looked for the blue light. The "little establishment" Percy had directed him to was a speakeasy, and he had learned enough in his short career as a seaman to avoid seaport dives. Still, he wanted a taste, and how bad could a Port Landsend joint be? After all, he'd survived the *Wilford Stickney*.

Lately, he had been feeling like a new man, stronger and more confident. He also noticed something curious: the horror in the cellar had not left him fearful but curious, even energized. He had to penetrate the mystery! But what he wanted most of all was to meet a woman, in particular the black-haired beauty he saw often on Harbor Street. Well, perhaps she was not exactly a beauty in the normal sense, like a movie star, but she was a beauty to him. And just yesterday he passed her on the street and got the distinct impression that she had given him the eye. Maybe, just maybe…

There it was: a door with a blue light burning overhead. He sauntered up and knocked. The door opened a crack and a soft voice asked, "Yeah?" Ivor tried, without complete success, to pitch his voice lower. "Percy Shelton sent me." A large man opened the door and stood aside, and Ivor walked in. Four or five guys hunched over the bar and a handful of others dotted the dim, smoke-filled room. Ivor ordered a whiskey from the pan-faced bartender and peered around the room. She was sitting alone in the corner with a glass of brown liquid. He gathered his courage, walked confidently over, and sat down next to her. "Good evening," he said. His voice held steady, he was pleased to hear. He lifted the glass without inspection and took a tentative sip of something that burned going down. It settled in warm and cozy. "Ahhh," he purred, "that's better."

She eyed him coolly, then flashed a smile that made his head swim. "It usually is."

"Live here in PL?"

"Who wants to know?"

"Ivor Lumpkin. Late of the good ship *Wilford Stickney*, may barnacles rot her backside."

She chuckled softly. "Ah...When do you ship out?"

"Never. Tub's gonners, we barely made port." Ivor was partly amused and partly excited to hear this new man speaking from deep in his chest.

"That so?"

"Yep. Miserable old scow. Heavy weather, I can stand. It's when you start takin' water through your rotten, patched up excuse for a hull, and the old three-banger decides to quit—that's when I started wishin' I was somewheres else."

"You got a way about you, mister—Lumpkin. What kind of name is that, anyway?"

"Dunno. Ma's Norwegian, don't know my pa, so I guess Norwegian's good enough for me if it's good enough for you."

She laughed, a full, husky, deep-chested laugh that pitched him ass-over-teakettle into a new and slightly terrifying state of mind. "It's fine with me, Ivor Lumpkin, I got nothing against Norwegians. My mother was—well, never mind what my mother was. She was woman enough to bring me into this world, that's all that matters."

"I like that, sister." He smiled shyly. "So, what's your name, anyway?"

"Rebecca. Rebecca Rains." She edged closer.

"It's very good to know you, Miss Rebecca Rains."

She gave Ivor the brightest smile he'd seen in months, then leveled a feline gaze at him. "So, Ivor Lumpkin, what've you got in mind?" What Ivor Lumpkin had in mind was what she had in mind, and they both knew it. He lit her cigarette, a trick he'd seen in the movies, she looked him in the eye, he looked her back, and they became a couple.

Thereafter, they were seen every night walking arm-in-arm on Harbor Street and snuggled in "their" booth behind the door with the blue light. And as they stood gazing out at the harbor one evening, Ivor told Rebecca what he had seen in the cellar. It felt good, getting it out. But her response was baffling. After staring silently at him for a long minute, she said, coolly, "Sweetie, you're letting your imagination get away from you."

"No, honey, I'm not. I know exactly what I saw, right there almost directly under our feet."

"Look, sugar, Port Landsend is—it just is what it is."

"'It is what it is'? What's *that* mean?"

She held him in a half-lidded stare. "Ivor, I like you. I think you and me could go somewhere. I just don't want you to go getting mixed up in something."

"What thing?"

"Things in this world that's beyond folks like us."

"Jeez, now you're really gettin' me curious."

"Sugar, there are some bad men in this town. Don't go nosing around too much and get on their bad side, okay?"

"You're the second person who's told me that."

"Who was the first?"

"Percy, the barber."

She nodded. "Good man, Percy. Good advice, too. I'd take it."

Ivor knew when to let go. What she said was true: The world was full of bad men, and he had no desire to mix it up with any of them. He looked into her eyes. "I'll watch it, honey. I promise. Only, you got to believe what I saw down there."

"I do."

Ivor went all funny inside, and a smile broke his lips. "Hmm," he said, kissing her. "I like the sound of that." He kissed her passionately, she moaned softly, and he kissed her some more. He wanted to kiss her neck, but she was wearing one of those high-neck blouses she always wore, even now, with the weather getting warm.

"Say, baby," he said, "let Uncle Ivor kiss your pretty neck."

"No, honey." She raised her hands around her throat.

"Jeez, what's the big secret?"

She gazed at him an instant then smiled slyly. "Ah, what the hell." She pulled down her collar and revealed her throat.

For a fraction of an instant he thought it was some crazy tattoo. God knows he'd seen some on the *Stickney*. But then, his stomach gave a lurch as he realized that this was no tattoo. "Jesus Hosephat," he said, "what is that?"

"Ivor, honey, it's just a little something to help me breathe."

"You mean—?"

Gills fluttering, she swallowed his lips with hers.

55

Regulators

The tall, rangy man in brown riding breeches and black boots sighted down the barrel of his hunting rifle. *Click!* He smiled grimly and turned his barrel toward the window. Six other men watched him uneasily, yet all agreed that the proposed action was necessary. They knew enough of Micah Marsh and his gang, or thought they did, to be nervous. They also knew what the tall man had in mind. This made them even more nervous.

"They took my boy," muttered a slight man with gray eyes, as if to reinforce their resolve. "I know damn well they did."

"Damn right," said another, heavy and hawk-faced. "Them heathen bastards is behind all this. They got to go."

"Took the Atwood girl," said another.

"That goddamn Point Judson gang…"

"Opium…"

"It ain't opium. It's a whole lot worse. A body-snatchin' cult is what it is."

"Exactly," said the tall man, turning from the window and striding into their midst. "If we don't act, it will only get worse." They did not like the chilly glint in his blue eyes, the hard smile on his thin lips. But they did like his certainty. "I've had reports that they'll be meeting tonight down around north cove. We must confront them, and if it comes to that, impress upon them the error of their ways. Show no mercy. We know who's behind this deviltry, and if they try to pull what I think they will, we must stop them by any and all means."

"What about the law?"

He snorted. "Law? What law?" He looked around the room, smiling his cold smile. "Anybody see any *law* here?"

The men were silent.

"Me neither," he said, nodding. "And we know well enough they're in Marsh's pocket. No, gentlemen, *We* are the law. Now, anybody who is not one-hundred percent ready to go ahead is free to leave, with nothing said. No hard feelings."

No one moved. The tall man nodded. "All right. Tonight, then. We'll meet here at 11:30 and proceed."

The men relaxed and began talking among themselves. "I saw 'em myself," said one. "I was fishin' off the wharf there and I saw 'em throw somebody in the bay. Broad daylight—you could see him squirming and trying to get away. Those *things* got him!"

"Ain't even human."

"That bunch has wrecked Port Landsend."

"Need done with the lot of 'em."

"Take our city back!"

The tall man, whose name was Randolph Olds, nodded grimly. "We will put an end to them and their devil's work once and for all." He sighted once again down his rifle barrel and—*click*.

56

A Typical American Town

swim, swim, whispered a voice, *faster, faster.* I was a projectile, a serpent-necked projectile shooting through a realm of electric green. My eyes darted from side to side, my hands burned, and I almost pitied the one destined to satisfy my raging desire. Around me swam thousands of beings like myself, twirling and writhing in ecstasy, lost in some proto-lithic submarine rite of fathomless antiquity. Before loomed the great fluted temple, with pipes belching great gobbets of sub-bass sound. Something emerged from the distant murk, something long and lithe, with powerful arms and a strangely feminine torso. It beckoned to me, flipped around, and faded back into the dark. I followed.

I felt something cold and hard. I opened my eyes and saw ceiling and sloping white walls. I was in the bathtub, wearing pants and coat and boots, but no shirt. My coat was damp and splotched with mud. I hoisted myself out and looked in the mirror. My cheeks and forehead were streaked with ugly brown stuff. Mud. I looked closer: *blood.* I felt myself all over but found no wounds. Somebody else's blood! I'd gone sleepwalking!

Well, first time for everything. And last, I hoped. I pulled myself together and sloped over to the Lamp Post. "She ain't here," said the cook, his usual gruff self. Back on the street, I glanced up and saw something in the high cupola of the Kliemann Block: a figure, moving in and out of view. Long dark hair—a woman. Sara? *There's some things I have to deal with.* I stared hard, but the figure did not reappear. Had she spotted me?

The sky blazed, the air shimmered with salty emanations, and a raft of clashing emotions rustled through my brain. A gull yelped and I thought again of the Indians who lived here; was I feeling their spirits, their energy? I guessed that the seaweedy air gave the Indians good sex lives. I walked on, feeling part of all time and part of all people. I wanted Sara desperately.

I got old marble-eye. Ivor Lumpkin lay in a drunken stupor amid a tangle of driftwood and old cardboard boxes, a brown bottle beside him. He sat up with a start when he saw me, then relaxed. "Well, hullo, young fella."

"'Morning."

Ivor peered blearily at me. "Still here, eh?"

"Yep," I replied, "You too, I see."

"They ain't run me out yet."

"Who hasn't run you out?"

He ignored the question. "Have a drink?"

I took the bottle. "It's funny," I said, "before I came to Port Landsend, I was never a drinker. Now…"

Ivor chuckled. "Oh, PL'll make a drinker outa you, you can count on it."

"Why is that, do you think?"

He regarded me coolly. "Wind…rain…isolation. Most folks don't much care to live under them conditions. And folks that do—walll, you live long enough in the wind and rain and isolation, the mind gets to playin' tricks. Sees what it wants to see, b'lieves what it wants to b'lieve…"

"Interesting point of view."

"Humph." He pointed the bottle at a rusty basement door across the way. "You see that cellar door? Some folks might just look at that and say, 'Oh, that's just a old cellar door'. Me, on the other hand, I see a whole lot differ'nt. I see what might just be *behind* that cellar door."

"Like what I heard in the warehouse."

He looked warily at me.

"I told you I work for Jack Day. He has a warehouse in one of these cellars, and the other day I heard something down there, behind this big old door. Sounded like a rowboat, and maybe something more."

He nodded slowly. "I learned long ago that if you keep your mouth shut and your mind open an' you learn to become part of the woodwork, you'll be surprised at how much you can pick up. And brother, I picked up plenty. Oh, yes, folks is always a darn sight better at blabbin' than listenin'. I remember folks blabbin' about them kids that went missing back in '34-'36. Remember folks blabbing about doin's at the wharf. Oh, I remember when this town was full of blabbermouths. Most of 'um moved on. Some was scared off."

"Scared? By what?"

He went quiet for a moment, then asked in a soft whisper, "Ever hear of a 'shut-in'?"

"Sure."

"Well, we got a lot of shut-ins here in Landsend. Folks keepin' outa sight on account of havin' certain *conditions*. Some of 'um for years."

"I have noticed some odd types around town."

Ivor gripped my wrist. "Steer clear of 'um! And steer clear o' them shore folk shacks out to the point. Set the dogs on you. An' if you go pokin' around uptown you'll be seein' houses that's all shuttered-up and empty-lookin.' Well, they ain't—there's folks inside. Some of them is folks that s'posably went missin', only they come *back*. And their kin. Some's been shut in for years." He took a long draft, belched, and looked around before continuing. "Some of 'um get to where they don't hardly bear lookin' at. Can't be seen out of doors no more."

"I read in the old newspapers about people disappearing."

"Yuh. Knew one or two of 'um."

He swigged again and leaned back on his hands. "I come here in 'thirty-two, and bein's as I was a wide-awake young fella I saw certain things

going on and I put two and two together. Oh, I done my share of snoopin'
too—snoopin' just enough to learn when to quit. That's the trick. Like that
goddamn United Wharf they keep all boarded up. I went pokin' around
there and almost didn't live to tell about it. But I did. Haven't bothered me
since. They's others went snoopin' wasn't so lucky."

"I've seen some things, too," I said. "The other guys and I were out near
Point Judson one day and we saw those people—those 'shore people'—
singing there by the water. And then we found some bones."

Ivor looked suddenly sober. "You found bones? Where?"

"Just lying on the beach out near the point. We took them up to
Dungeness College to get them analyzed."

"Anala-sized, huh?" He spat a long one and shrugged. "Heh-heh. You
see this guff on the television about bein's from outer space and you think,
'Now, ain't that a lot of eyewash'."

I nodded slowly.

"So's you might think. So's most folks might think. Only, maybe they
oughtn't to be so damn sure. Old Percy, he knew better. The barber, a good
man—'tonsorialist' he called himself. He damn well knew. Newspaper man
knew, too. Higginbotham, another good man but scared of his own shadow.
Not that I blame him any. Liquor got him. But he damn well knew all about
them Marshes and their doin's. Didn't want to talk about it first-off, but I
kept bumpin' into him here and there, and after a while he loosed up. Had
me up to his house and told me some stories as'd curl your insides. Poured
the liquor, too. Old Hiram, he wised me up to a lot of things."

Ivor edged in close and clenched my arm. "Him an' me, we made us a
kinda deal whereby I promised I would keep an eye out. Make sure them
devil-worshippin' bastards didn't go too far." He let out a belch on one end
and a fart on the other. "Yessir, forty years I been hearin' them sounds and
smellin' them stinks and seein' things that would drive any man to drink.
And I got it all right up here." He tapped his head and chuckled softly.
"Other 'n that, I'd say PL is just your typical American town."

"Crazy," I muttered.

"Maybe. But there's lots of things would have been considered crazy once, and here they are—jet planes, rocket ships, TV. What I'm sayin' is, there's things in this world, and there's things out of this world, and there's things *in-between*. And there's folks who keep tryin' to mix 'em up."

I thought of Lewis and the Whateleys, I thought of the star-headed things in my dream and in the Miskatonic library and in the barbershop window. "Christ!" I exclaimed. "The barber, you say? That little shop down off Gribble Street?"

"Yump, ol' Perce. Left me in charge, so to speak. Been takin' care of it all these years."

"He's not around anymore?"

"Nope. Changed—moved away, years ago."

"There's a weird doll in there."

Ivor spat into the bushes. "You seen it, then."

"I seen it. And back east, too, in the college library."

"Bald-headed Jesus! How many of them things are there?"

I wished I had my little jug with me. "So—is there actually a cult of this—thing—in Port Landsend."

"Can't say no more. Said too much as it is." His head sagged, his eyes dimmed. He was fading. But he fixed me with one final gimlet glare: "You might ask yourself just how deep in you want to get. 'Cause I'm saying you're liable to run into things you ain't counted on. Like that Marsh gal o' yours." He chuckled ominously.

I suddenly didn't feel so good. "What about her?"

"You just let me know when you find out, and we can swap notes, so to speak. Bein's how I married one of 'um."

57

Nothing To See Here

Spring reared its musky head with promises of warmth and fecundity. The tourist grapevine was warming up and even the locals seemed to be thawing. We still had our gig, and in truth we'd been having some good nights. Fishing-hat Ralph remained our staunchest fan, but a couple of the old-young Lamp Post regulars had taken to hanging around, too. One of them even told me he liked my playing and bought me a drink. "I play a little guitar," he said—"want to jam sometime?" Well, so much for snap judgement. "Sure," I said, properly humbled.

The guys and I continued snacking and sipping sour mash into the wee hours, debating the nature of music and horned beasts, and hanging out at the Lamp Post with Ralph and Sara. I introduced them to my little star-headed friend in the barbershop window, and revealed my Arkham journey.

Jeff was intrigued by Victor Lewis. "So, he had bones like ours?"

"Yep. And other goodies." I told them about the ancient books and the twin to the barbershop grotesque, and I attempted to convey the Whateley story—"Okay, so, this guy is actually a sort of hybrid monster, and his brother is taken over by an even worse monster from another dimension, and this professor chases it and says a spell and sends it back to where it belongs—well, you get the idea." Brad and Jeff stared at me like I had rickets. "Hey, I only know what Dr. Lewis told me. He thinks there may be some kind of cult right here, worshipping the same gods or monsters or whatever the hell they are."

"Maybe they'll try to recruit us," said Brad, chewing a stick of jerky. Brad loved his jerk-sticks.

"Whew!" said Jeff, laughing. "You guys can do what you want, but I'll give them a wide berth."

One Saturday we walked up to the bunkers. "Amazing," Jeff said, gaping at the crumbling concrete battlements, "how fast stuff not even a hundred years old becomes ruins." We shuffled through the moldy galleries and up a long, inclined tunnel that sounded a weird, continuous echo—the voices of long-departed soldiers and the screams of frolicking kids, trapped forever.

We headed back to town down a narrow trail, dodging giant puffballs and blackberry stickers. A hawk glided silently over, glaring balefully down on the intruders. At the edge of downtown we descended to the little meadow where the cistern vent funnel stood like some Stone Age idol. A faint humming sound hung in the air. Insects—no, it seemed to be coming out of the funnel. We listened close: it was not insects, it was voices, voices chanting.

"What the hell," I said, "somebody's *singing* down there!"

Guttural syllables rose through the echoing tube in a demonic diapason. "Jesus," I yelped, "that sounds like—Yog-Sothoth…Cthul….Shit!"

"Those god-things you heard about in Massachusetts?" asked Jeff.

"Yeah," I replied, "nasty god-things. Whose names are now being chanted right underneath us."

"What do you suppose they're up to?" Brad said.

"Having a little Saturday afternoon devil-worship," I shrugged. I put my ear on the pipe, and in a moment picked up fragments of recognizable English: "Wait…You can't!"

"Jeez, guys," I muttered, "something's going on here."

The frantic voice sounded one more: "No!"

"Shit! It sounds like someone's in trouble."

"We better go to the cops," said Jeff.

We race-walked two blocks to the little cop shop on Harbor Street and found the young officer at the desk. "S'cuse me," I said, "but there may be some trouble down in the old cistern. Sounds like somebody's in trouble in there—voices, somebody yelling 'Stop!'"

The sallow-faced cop looked up blandly. "When was this?"

"Just now. They might be in danger."

The older sheriff emerged from the back office and slapped a hard stare on us. "What's the trouble, Hill?"

"Uh, chief, these guys are reporting hearing voices around the cistern, there. Somebody shouting, maybe in trouble."

The sheriff chuckled grimly. "Well, it's probably nothing. Kids, they go in the old tank there and make all kinds of racket. Not s'posed to, but they're not doing any harm." He walked slowly to the door and opened it. "I wouldn't worry about it." If he recognized me from the tavern or the bandstand, he didn't show it. His gray eyes revealed only cold indifference.

Okay. "He didn't seem too concerned," said Jeff.

"Well, we tried," said Brad. I looked back to see the sheriff's face turn away from the window.

A man lounging nearby leered at us. "You're wastin' your time with them guys," he said, "'less you get on their bad side. Don't wanna get on their bad side."

We did not ask him to elaborate.

"Probably nothing, hell," I muttered. "I know what I heard."

58

Meet Me 'Round The Corner

The sun was bright and the mood at the Lamp Post was torpid. On the way to work that Monday I sloped in for pie and a moment with Sara. Ivor Lumpkin nursed a coffee and pretended I wasn't there, and sitting across from him in the same booth was Ralph. He too was oddly distant. Well, guess the bloom's off that particular rose.

And there was him. Squatting sullenly in the corner, staring at us and being a shit and knowing it: Crump. Sara told him to get lost, he ignored her, her cousin the cook did nothing. Finally, I had it. I got up and stood before him: "You. You sit there, not buying anything, not doing anything, just staring at us. Why?"

"Staring at you? Why would I want to do that?"

"Uh-huh. Sara's not interested in you. Never will be. You're wasting your time. Why don't you go do something with your life?"

He grinned contemptuously. "Oh, okay, dude, I'll do that."

"Sad," I said, and walked back to my booth.

Sara took it in coolly. "Waste of time, right?" she said.

"Yeah," I shrugged, "figured it would be." Inside, I was less cool. I'd never been in a fight in my life, and being as my hands were my livelihood, I wasn't keen on starting now. But sure as shit it was coming. Well, to hell with it; you can't live in constant worry. I kept my eyes and ears open, stepped up my pushups and calisthenics, and waited.

Two days later, Fat white clouds piled high over the eastern peaks and a soft, warm breeze wafted down Harbor Street. Even the habitually sullen kids at the pizza shop laughed. Sara seemed strangely distant; I chalked it up to her time, but I still felt weird. I stared out at the water awhile then wandered aimlessly. Life suddenly seemed nebulous. It was as if the city was shrinking toward an ever-nearer vanishing point and taking me with it.

Mulling the vicissitudes of fortune, I turned down Gribble Street toward work and there he stood, with empty eyes and an ugly sneer. I went to Defcon 1, considered various blocking and kicking moves, then considered running. But there was no escape. He closed in on me and whispered, "She's mine, asshole. And this is for you." He rammed a fist toward my face. I say toward, because it never got there. My reflexes were sharper than I realized, for I not only blocked his punch but shoved it right back into him. He staggered, a hint of surprise on his face, then rebounded. I looked around frantically for something to use as a weapon. "You're crazy!" I yelled, "Sara doesn't want you!" He came at me again. I sidestepped him at the last microsecond, then tripped him, at the same time slammed my fist hard into his temple. He wobbled again, but he was too damn tough. He came right back up at me, and I did the only thing I could do: I ran. Bok-bok-bok! Okay, so what? Fighting is stupid, especially when you are deficient in experience and inbred nastiness, the curse of too much Mister Nice Guy. I could hear him breathing hard on my heels. "Fucking chickenshit," he rasped. "I'll kill you."

"You're still not gonna have her, Crump," I laughed mockingly. "You're never gonna have her, might as well get over it. Go home."

His hand grabbed my shoulder and spun me around. He was strong, but I was surprised to find my own strength not flagging at all, but boiling with adrenaline. I pulled away and crouched in a fighting stance. "You fucking trash," I snarled, "you're pathetic." He said nothing, just charged. I met him with an upward lunge into his windpipe that threw him off balance. I went back low, ready for his next charge, and when it came, I blocked him hard and struck out with my fist. After which he kicked my ass.

59

You Make Me Feel Brand-New

Bzzzz. I sat up and rubbed my head. *Bastardbastardbastard.* No gaping wounds, teeth intact. Great. Where was Crump? I struggled to my feet and looked around, bracing myself for more. He was gone. A man stood nearby with a shovel in his hand. "You okay, mister?" he asked. "I saw that guy beatin' on you so I run him off. Crump, he's a sonofabitch, all right. Glad I had my shovel with me." I shook my head groggily, thanked him, and went to Jack's to explain that I had been suddenly rendered unfit for duty that day. Then I headed for Sara's place, eyes darting, heart racing.

"Oh God, Erich!" I guess I was banged-up worse than I thought. She gripped my arms and gazed at me, shaking her head. "That scumbag! Did you hurt him?"

"A little—maybe."

"I hope so." Eyes lighting up, she kissed my bruises, then ever so slyly began unbuttoning my pants. Hours later, a yellow moon peered in at Sara as she stood at the counter. A pleasant aroma filled the little room and a moment later she placed a large bowl in front of me. "Eat."

I took a slurp and a spicy tang flooded my senses. "Mmmm, what is this?"

"Oh," she said, hair falling over her eyes, "just some scraps."

"Hmmf! Scraps of what, I won't ask."

She giggled sweetly, and it was all I could do to stay in my seat. "I'm glad you're okay," she said, "but I want you to promise to behave."

"But it was Crump…"

"Ah-ah." She put her lips on my head. "Just promise."

What could I do? "I promise." Then I resumed slurping. "But he will come after me again," I said. "Don't know why he didn't finish me off then and there. Playing cat-and-mouse, maybe."

"Shit. What can we do?"

"Fight. He might try to kill me—I think he's crazy enough. But I'm not backing down and I'm not running. Maybe I'll go to the cops and file a complaint, get a restraining order or something."

She gave me a look. "These cops, Erich? No."

"Why?"

"I know them. They're lazy and they can't be trusted."

"Well then, babe, it's you and me against the world. Funny: I should be worried, but I'm not. I feel fantastic, like a new man. Must be the soup." Dessert was mighty nice, too.

The morning sun winked over the far peaks just visible through the narrow window.

She snuggled in close. "Erich?"

"Mmm?"

"Do you think you'll stay here?"

She sounded so small. I kissed her and said, "Yes. I want to stay here, with you. Even if I go away to work or whatever, I'll always come back. Or, maybe…"

"Maybe?"

I didn't want to overplay my hand. But I had to. "Maybe you could come with me. At least, some of the time."

"Maybe. There's some things I have to deal with."

I had brains enough not to push it. Stroking her hair, I said, "Tell me about your family. Your folks…"

"I never knew them. I lived with my uncle, Rule, and his wife, Roslin. They would only tell me I was an orphan, nothing else. I think I must look like my mom, though: all mouth."

"Hey," I laughed, "works for me."

"They were okay, I guess," she said, "but there was no affection. They fed me and clothed me and got me to school, for all the good *that* did. All so I could work in their crummy café."

"I don't think it's crummy."

"Yeah, well…At least they pretty much leave me alone. Rule is acting weird lately, distracted, like he's got some scheme he's cooking up. Ros is just kind of pathetic, does whatever Rule says."

"So, you pretty much run the place."

"My cousin, the cook, and me."

I thought that was enough for the moment, but she went to her dresser and pulled out a tattered scrap of paper. "Since you're so interested in my family, here's something." She laid it before me. It was from the Los Angeles *Times* of January 12, 1936:

ACTRESS VANISHES

Actress Arlene Marsh is reported missing and presumed drowned after disappearing in heavy swells off Bay City. Miss Marsh, aged 28, appeared as the Panther Princess in "The Perils of Jungle Jillian" and other RJO pictures. Associates describe Miss Marsh as an exceptionally strong swimmer, but say that the ocean where she was last seen was running very high, and hold out little hope for her survival. Miss Marsh was born in Port Landsend, Washington, and moved to Los Angeles to pursue her acting career. She has no known relations.

Sara arched an eyebrow at me. "Ros gave me this. She said Arlene was my aunt. It's funny: the way she said it, it was like didn't want Rule to hear. I think about Arlene a lot. I wish I could have known her."

"'No known relations,'" it says. 'Strong swimmer'—like you?"

"Yeah...weird, huh? Maybe the family didn't want any publicity. Or disowned her or something."

"Happens. Newspapers only scratch the surface of things like this." I wondered if this had run in the missing pages of the *Lector* I'd seen in Port Diablo.

"Mm. Well, anyway, what's 'family,' anyway? I mean, yours, mine— after a while, we're left to ourselves."

"Or..."

She shot me her magic ray that burned right through me. "Yeah, 'or'." She smiled and took me gently by the arm.

Later, as sunlight flooded the room, I gazed at her, my girlfriend, my love. How did I get so damn lucky? I could only shrug. Then, I again noticed the weird ridges on her neck. Now, they were darker and more prominent. "Sweetie," I asked softly, "what's this?"

She looked away. "It's—nothing..."

"Honey, it's not nothing. You should get it looked at."

She looked at me sadly and shook her head. "No. I know what it is."

60

Crack In The Sky

The Marsh landau squatted beside the secluded cove like a grim gray carbuncle. A small knot of men milled about, and fifty feet away, a stooped, stumpy man stood alone. One of the group walked slowly over to him and asked, "Boss, are you sure you want to go through with this? That Olds has been stirring folks up—could be trouble."

Yes, he was sure. He was damned sure. He knew the formulas, he knew the chants, he knew it was time. Hell, he had made a shoggoth, hadn't he? And soon, there would be more. Soon, too, he would be where he belonged. He was one of a special breed, a breed destined to transform the earth. It was only minor errors and mis-translations that had thwarted his ancestors. He would not make their mistakes. As for Olds and all others who would stand in his way—they would be taken care soon enough. Micah Marsh raised his hand. "The book."

The assistant fetched a wooden podium from the carriage and set it down in front of Marsh, then retrieved a large book and set it gently on the podium. "Turn it open," Marsh ordered. He leaned over the open volume, turned several pages, and began to speak. Softly at first, then steadily louder, his sepulchral voice rose in unbreathing crescendo, pushing out words—strange, unearthly words, words that seemed to turn the night darker. The idling men looked at one another nervously, the horse snorted.

Abruptly, Marsh broke off and barked, "The formula." His assistant handed him a vial containing a thick orange-brown fluid, a concoction of pepper root, hibiscus bark, St. John's wort, and other, less innocuous elements. Marsh drank a few drops then slowly poured the rest in a wide circle in the sand. He stepped into the circle and began reciting:

"Ya! Ya! Gh'rnn fnglui fthagan! Ya! Ya! Cthulhu Fthagan!"

The stertorious voice strained to a rabid howl. A breeze blew up from the dark waters and sighed along the sandy verge, the clouds writhed and roiled into globular lumps that sagged from the sky.

"Marsh!" A tall man carrying a rifle stepped from the trees, followed by others. "You all can cease and desist, or die," he yelled, his voice thin in the rising wind. Micah Marsh did not look at the men, did not seem even to hear them. Randolph Olds raised his gun and shouted, "I'm warning you for the last time! Go home, and take your gang with you." Oblivious, Marsh continued his unearthly threnody. Olds aimed his rifle, but the wind whipped up whorls of sand, throwing him and his companions off balance and making them lower their guns to shield their eyes.

Out of the seething clouds, a funnel spiraled down above the shrieking Marsh and a hideous rasp rent the air.

"Twister!" yelled one of the men. He and two others ran frantically into the trees.

"Marsh, for the last time!" Olds again raised his rifle, only to be buffeted by the funnel-cloud as it jittered lower and threw off waves of hot wind. The men stood transfixed as the funnel writhed and shot out sparks of acrid green phosphorescence. "What the hell!" Olds yelled. He staggered and fired wildly into the sky.

Oscillating back and forth like a hideous Hoover, the whirling funnel whirred and roared, then suddenly coalesced into a monstrous, pulsating blob. Tentacle-like things drooped toward Earth. Micah Marsh saw—saw and shrieked with maniacal laughter, even as he continued his chant in a frenzied roar.

Olds fired again at Marsh and at the quavering apparition, then ran as a spray of sickly green liquid cascaded to earth and upon the head of the bellowing Micah Marsh and his attendants. The hunched figure staggered and dropped his arms, even as the monster rasped furiously and flared up in a blaze of violet-green light. The onlookers stood paralyzed, their wills sucked from them, clenching their ears against the thing's frightful sub-tonal emanations. The flailing tentacles twisted in a furious spasm, the cloud-thing gibbered and flickered, and with a sulfurous belch disappeared.

Marsh shook, his throat tightened, his vision blurred. *No!* He pressed a hand to his stomach, saw blood, and as his vision blurred and darkened, he looked again to the sky. Yes! He had succeeded! He had opened the gate. With a last hysterical laugh, he collapsed on the sand.

Randolph Olds advanced toward the supine form. "Goddamn you, Marsh! That's for what you people did to my father. And all the others."

But Micah Marsh was beyond hearing or caring. His twisted body shook violently, his mouth spewed green bile. "Father," he croaked—"Father, we did it! They'll never stop us! Cthulhu…fthagan!" With a shuddering heave, the thing that was Micah Marsh imploded into a reeking husk, pinkish-green ichor foaming from its every orifice.

Hiram Higginbotham was dozing in his armchair when heard a rippling thunderclap. He shuffled to the window and saw an ugly purple glow in the east. Faint voices yelled as if in drunken revelry, a strange pulsating roar swelled and faded. "Damn fools," he muttered, "what are they up to now?" The wizened newsman opened the door and listened, but heard nothing more. Whatever the foolishness was, it was over. Still, Higginbotham was a journalist, and he felt the journalist's tingle in his soul. Something had happened—what? Once, he would have raced toward the sound and the light. Now, however, he was old and tired. You couldn't cover every damn thing, and anyway, it was probably nothing more than the usual drunken carryings-on of that Point Judson crowd. The editor of the Port Landsend *Lector* slumped back into his chair and passed out.

People drifted off the beach, unsure of what they'd just seen. Next day, some were blandly dismissive. "Freak storm," they said—"tornado...couldn't really tell what it was...didn't see nothin'." But others were adamant: What they had seen was no natural occurrence but a visitation of a hellish *thing*, a thing summoned by the evil Micah Marsh, who stood there on the shore screaming out spells from a big book—spells that called the thing by name.

Someone else saw it all from beneath an overturned skiff. Coughing the stench from his lungs, Ivor Lumpkin had no doubt about what it had been. "Tornado, my aunt Fanny," he muttered to himself. "Not with that great goddamn staring *eye*."

61

Touched By A Strangeness

Monday morning I stuffed some cottage cheese down my throat and rattled my bones downstairs. After an hour's practice, I felt good, even with another afternoon of warehouse dust ahead. It was my life, and no apologies. In the Grebe Bookstore window, the little brown cat looked out at me and yawned. I opened the door.

The owner stood in puffy purple pants and black boots, offered her hand and a luminous smile. "Hello! You're one of the musicians down at Rick's place."

"That's me." I offered my hand, which she took in a surprisingly firm grip. "So, I took your advice and checked out the *Lector* up at Dungeness College."

"Ah." She looked at me frankly. She was a tall, handsome woman with faintly Asian features and a coppery complexion. "Find anything interesting?"

"I did. Odd doings in our little town, back when."

She raised her eyebrows.

"Maybe now, too."

"Hmm. I've seen you during the week. Are you living here?"

218

"Yep, moved here."

"Did you? Any particular reason?"

"Got tired of the city, and I just kind of like this place."

"Not much doing here during the week…"

"I got a job working for Jack Day. He sells used magazines."

"Oh, yes, I know Jack. We do some dealing now and then. I've known him for years, him and his wife…" She moved closer, green eyes intently at me. "So," she said, "what 'doings' have you uncovered?"

"Oh, nothing much. Disappearances…a possible cult…stories of mysterious shut-ins…bones…" I raised my eyebrows back at her.

She nodded soberly. "So, you see things." She wandered to the window and looked out toward the bay. "Yes. I guess you might say Port Landsend has been touched by a strangeness." She twisted a strand of hair and looked down at the floor. "I'm not sure how much I should say. It's not that this is a sensitive matter, just that—well, you know how small towns can be."

"'Strangeness,' you say. Like, why a lot of the young men look so *old*?"

Her lips formed a chilly smile. "Oh, they're not bad people. But—yes, some have, shall we say, diverse backgrounds. I think we'd best leave it at that. You come from Seacoma?"

"Yes. I was going nowhere—felt stuck."

"And you think you'll do better here?"

I nodded slowly. "I have positive feelings."

"Hmm. You are a positive young man." She eased closer, put her hand on my shoulder, and gave it a gentle stroke. "You're a very smart young man, I think," she said, moving close. "Why don't you come by some evening and we can talk more."

I smelled something spicy mingled with—with something that made me forget books and head for the door. "Sure," I nodded.

A shadow flickered across her face, then she smiled brightly. "Well, thanks for stopping by, Erich. I'll be in this weekend, I love your music."

She watched him walk away, the young man with the pointed questions. She had been starved of youthful beauty too long, and it was good to have live music in town, too, even if it was old-fashioned. She sat down at her desk and gently caressed her breasts as she thought once more of her youth, her mother, wan and weary in their little old house, a gray house beneath a gray sky. "You have a gift," her mother had said, in a voice soft and tremulous. A gift—that would be nice. But why did the word sound scary? Years filed by, filled with boys, longing, and a strange growing unease. Then came that warm summer evening when a slice of magenta ripped the heavens, her mother bade her farewell, and she knew at last what she really was.

62

The Walls Have Mouths

By all odds it should have been long dead. The ones who had said the words and brought sustenance had not returned. And yet, clinging to a wall deep beneath the city, it lived. There had been meager food at first, nothing but a few fish and other things that strayed into the nether tunnel. Some of the sustenance was bigger and better than others, but however it came, it had been sufficient. In the perpetual night of the underworld, all was dark, damp, and still. And so, it waited patiently for the day it would move into the next stage. Down the nighted corridor a cold wind blew, vague pricks of light winked and faded. The black water rippled, stilled. Now—faint movement. Perhaps…Yes. More sustenance.

63

Cool, Cool Water

Her hand was gorgeous. Gorgeous but *big*. And that pronounced webbing, almost like—well, what, I couldn't say. Not that it mattered. I took it in mine. "You have big hands," I said. "Big and beautiful." I kissed it and said, "Oh, I went sleepwalking the other night."

Her eyes bulged. "What?"

"Woke up in the tub, clothes on, mud on them. And blood, on my face. Someone else's blood."

Sara shook her head. "God, Erich, leave you alone for one night..."

"I'm thinking I've got some kind of mental disturbance going on. Some kind of overload. My first night here, I see these guys, short little guys, hopping around the streets at midnight. Then I hear sounds in the warehouse. And now I'm having strange dreams of swimming way down in the ocean with all these dinosaur things, and there's this weird singing. And it sounds very *real*."

She narrowed her eyes at me. "Well, maybe you have some hidden sensitivity..."

"Sensitivity to *what*, is the question. Babson and Lewis—the guy in Arkham—say it might be repressed memory, or something deeper. Whatever it is, I'm getting creeped-out."

"Well," she said, smiling brightly, "we'll just have to see, won't we?" She took my hand and studied it. "You have beautiful hands, yourself. Musician's hands."

I looked again at hers. "You said you like to swim."

She nodded.

"So, let's swim."

"Are you a good swimmer?"

"I don't know—average, I guess. It's been a while. Let's do it."

"Seriously? Erich, do you know how cold that water is?"

"Yes. But I need to feel it. With you. Even if it's just for thirty seconds."

She stuck her fingernail in her mouth and smiled impishly. "Okay. I'll get us some towels—no, blankets. You're going to need them. Do you have anything to swim in? Or..."

"Or."

She laughed. "Gotta admire the guy's bravery. Okay, frog-man, let's go."

The afternoon was waning but still warm when we arrived at the little cove just north of Point Judson, a sheltered place scooping in from the expanse of Pilot Sound. A sandspit created a sheltered embayment perfect for an exploratory plunge. I had no idea how I'd hold up in the frigid waters, but I had to try. And after all, it had been a hot summer.

We shucked our clothes and stood poised. "Erich," Sara asked, looking worried, "are you sure?"

"Sure." *No, not really.* But I am sure my face wore that mask of self-delusion men all through history have put on before doing something very stupid. She kissed me hard on the lips, gave me a gratifying overall glance, and dove in. Not wanting to be a pussy, I followed. I plunged in over my head—then pawed frantically for the surface. "CHEE-RIST!" I screamed, gasping for air and thrashing like mad, hoping to somehow warm up the water around me. "Wow!" I felt a zap of electrical energy and swam some strokes. I felt stronger than I expected.

Sara swam in close. "How you doing, honey?"

"F-fine," I said, plowing further out.

She flipped over and speared away into the depths. Just as I felt like I was getting used to the water, I felt an ominous numbness grip my extremities. I staggered from the water, shook myself vigorously, and wrapped up in a thick blanket. After a moment's rest I felt a new wave of energy and waded back in, now more confidently. My body slipped through the water surprisingly easily, my feet and legs working with exhilarating strength. The water wasn't quite as cold this time. "Hey, this feels pretty good!"

"Erich, be careful." She'd been saying that a lot lately, and it was starting to ever so slightly bug me.

"Yes, dear," I joshed. "Come on!" I dove beneath the surface and cleaved the water, my crawl stroke strong and sure. I opened my eyes underwater and saw nothing at first, but the water was translucent, almost iridescent in its blackness, and I felt like I was peeling back the top layer of something and that more layers could be peeled back, to reveal—what? I shot to the surface and Sara wrapped me in her arms. "Erich, are you sure you're okay?" We were farther from shore than I realized.

Something brushed my leg. Sara was right in front of me, so this—I felt it again. A snorting head broke the surface. A seal, small and cute. Another head popped up. We saw them, laughed, and dove again, this time for what seemed like at least a minute. Underwater, I could see their long, sleek forms darting with us. I swam as long as I could, then surfaced. Sara kissed me and said, "Let's head for shore, babe." I didn't need convincing. I'd had a nice burst of energy, but now I was getting seriously cold. Fast.

The far peaks stood orange in the fading sun, the air was turning cool. We snuggled together in our blanket, kissing and laughing and shivering—me, anyway—like mad. Down the beach, dark forms squatted before scattered fires. "Ah," I said, "the mysterious shore people."

"Not so mysterious," Sara said. "I know some of them. They're all right. They just keep to themselves."

A shadow crossed the sun, someone stood over us, a man, tall and black against the dusk. Crump! No—the guy who caught us with the bones.

A faint smile creased his face. "You have been in the water?"

"Yes," I answered.

"Cold?"

"Yep."

The stranger chuckled. "Brave man. I used to swim, myself, but now I'm too old. I like my comforts."

I got to my feet, offered my hand. "I'm Erich, this is Sara."

"I am Ka'atah'teh." He looked more closely at me. "I remember you. You and your friends took the bones."

"Yes. Seems they're rather unusual."

His face remained impassive. "Who is to say what is usual and what is not?"

"Not me. I—we—probably let our curiosity get the better of us. Maybe some things should just be left alone…"

Ka'atah'teh shrugged. "I've let my curiosity get away from me once or twice, myself."

"Sit with us for a while," Sara said. "I'm Sara. I've seen you around a long time, but for some reason we've never met."

"Passing shadows," he replied, sinking stiffly to the ground. His clothes were somber and dirty, contrasting strikingly with his luminous blue eyes.

"You live nearby?" I asked.

"This is my home," he said, "my people's home." He gazed at us a moment then said, "You say the bones are unusual."

"Yes. Seems scientists don't know what they are."

"I can tell you what they are. Have you seen the Hidden Ones?"

My heart skipped. Should I tell him about the other bones in the drawers? "I don't think—I'm not sure…"

"You seem like a thoughtful young man. I got mad when you and your friends took the bones, but I think maybe you weren't acting badly. I'm glad to meet you now and to talk about these things. What else can old people like me do except trust young people?" He looked over the water, then back at us, smiling. "You swim here, in this place where my people gathered and fished, long years ago. That makes me feel glad."

"I have thought of them often," I said. "Wondered about those who lived here. Those folks out at the point…"

His face clouded. "Different people from us, mostly. Strangers, with strange ways. They are up to something—saying spells. Dark spells, I think. I have been watching them for a long time. And now, the Water Beings are returning. Maybe others, too. Be ready." He stood, nodded curtly, and disappeared into the brush.

64

About A Mover

He hated school. Or, rather, hated *the* school. Squatting on the verge of downtown like a piece of unwanted furniture, it was an ancient and lugubrious pile—"Victorian," his mother called it—that smelled of mold and stale memories. But in 1936 Swanson High was the only one in town. Sophomore Ralph Donald made the best of it, and what he loved best was band. Mister Adamovich was a jovial young instructor who preferred jazz to marches and threw in the odd light classic to keep his young charges on their toes. Among them, Ralph was a star on the saxophone. He only hoped band could keep going; the school was shrinking, families were moving away and there was talk of replacing it with a new consolidated school way out on the peninsula highway. At dinner, his folks talked about the old giving way to the new, and about having to "move with the times."

Ralph liked to move. After school and on weekends he walked the town studying things. Old things, like the United Wharf and the frowzy storefronts (the old barber shop window with its collection of curios was especially keen). The Marsh mansion was a special favorite, and he often stopped by on his way home from school and stared up at the jagged gables and tried to imagine what went on inside. He wasn't sure but that once

227

or twice he didn't hear voices inside. And maybe other sounds, too. A sensitive boy, young Donald liked to look at people, too, and he saw in many a haggard face the blight of frustration and failure, both worldly and physical. He often encountered a stern-looking Indian man near the beach; he wanted to ask him how old he was—he had to be at least a hundred—but could never get up the nerve.

One day on Harbor Street he discovered faded letters etched in the sidewalk in front of a shuttered building: *Bayview Hotel.* Surveying the old place, which was brick in front but plain wood on the sides, he rounded the near corner and found a metal stair descending to a dark cellar. He knew he shouldn't, but he couldn't help it. He crept quietly down into the alcove and found a partly-opened door. He peered in on ghostly shrouded furniture and an old overcoat lying on the ground like a dead man. Something like rotten eggs hit his nose, and he heard a scraping sound from somewhere deep in the shadows. He had one foot in the open door when a hand took his arm and led him gently back outside. "Don't want to be pokin' around here, my friend," said the man. He was young and had a friendly face. "Good thing I came along," the man said when they were back outside, "them guys ain't too friendly." He looked again at the man's face and saw that one of his eyes looked like a marble.

Twenty years later, sitting in the rowboat he and his father had made, Ralph Donald considered his life. He considered that some might— *would!*—consider him a failure. He didn't. Fishing and loafing were good enough for him, and Port Landsend in the 1950s was the ideal place to do both. Ralph had his fishing rod and his saxophone, and when he wasn't doing odd jobs and working on boats, he could fish. And late at night, in the house his parents left him, he played along with records of jazz greats and let music take him far away. So much changed, yet so much stayed the same. Like the calm gray waters of the bay, and the mysterious movements of fish and squid and other water creatures. He loved floating among them, fishing pole lolling off the transom, lost to everything but the wind and current.

The currents of the mind being similarly restless, Ralph considered again his days at the dismal old high school, and the band class, and things his classmates said after school. Things like what Jem Summers said about a "monster" under the town—"I know somebody who saw it," Jemmy insisted. "You're full of horse-pucky," said Egleston, making everybody laugh. "Am not!" Jem shot back. "You can smell it if you go down by the old tunnel, stinks like hell!" The kids laughed again, but their laughter had a nervous tinge to it. None of them felt like going to the tunnel. Ralph had been to the tunnel and had seen the thick blueberry vines that overhung the portal, and he had smelled that weird, nasty smell that seemed to issue from within the overgrowth. Then, one Saturday, three of the older kids did go into the tunnel. Only two came out.

Ralph Donald thought of them often, even now. Thought of how the two kids who came out seemed so different, and about how nothing was ever said about the kid who did *not* come out. He thought too of his friend Ivor Lumpkin, who formerly had liked to accompany him fishing, but had more recently been stubbornly adamant in his refusal to set foot in a boat of any kind. "You ain't seen what's down there," he had said. "If you had, you wouldn't go out in that damn little skiff o' yours." Ivor took to the bottle, and there was no talking him out of it.

The boat gave a sudden lurch. Ralph tensed and looked into the water. Something long and white shot from beneath, then another. A horn—a narwhal! Impossible. But what—? Ralph stared at the water—and into eyes, yellow eyes that sent a blast of cold fear through him. The ripples distorted things, but no—the face! Was it—human? Something bumped the bottom of the boat and Ralph grabbed the gunwale. The damn thing was trying to poke through the hull! Ralph rowed for all he was worth, but it wasn't enough to make shore before he was holed through. They bumped and shoved at the boat until Ralph feared he'd be swamped. Desperately, he grabbed his biggest fish and threw it over. The being caught it—in something that looked a lot like a *hand*—and Ralph could have sworn it smiled at him. He threw another fish over, and the swimmers dove. The last one vanished into the depths and Ralph Donald pulled for shore. That horn—that face. That face that smiled back at him.

65

A Shot In The Dark

Sun, shadow, heat, cool, light, dark. Solitude—for so long, solitude—now contrasted starkly with holding Sara in my arms. Was it real? I stretched and moved against her, eking a soft moan from her parted lips. We walked slowly through the bunkers to our place. All was silent and redolent of ancient ages. It was Sunday, it was warm, we were young. "So," I said, "what do you think of our new friend?"

"The Indian guy? Funny: I never knew his name until now, and I've seen him around since I was a kid."

"I like him. I hope we see him again. I feel kind of lousy about taking the bones against his advice, but…Hey, you know the old guy in the café?"

"Ivor?"

"Yeah. He's got some interesting things to say about good old Port Landsend. Things including a certain Marsh family." I hoped I hadn't gone too far, but I couldn't resist probing a mystery.

She only shrugged. "Yeah, well, Ivor's the town gossip. And every family has its issues."

"He said the Marshes controlled the whole town. Had some kind of smuggling operation, scared folks off…"

"Honestly, Erich, I don't think any of my family's smart enough to do anything like that. Maybe a long time ago. Nobody ever told me much, not Rule or anybody. Wouldn't even tell me who my mom and dad were."

"He also talked about kids disappearing—which I read about in the old newspaper—and 'shut-ins' with 'peculiar conditions', and 'devil-worshippers' who tried some weird shit back-when and are trying to do it again. And then he said something that really freaked me out. He said, 'There's things in this world and there's things out of this world, and there's things in-between. And some folks are going to try to let those things in.'"

"And you believe him?"

"Well, considering what I've seen and heard lately—yep."

"Oh, shit, I love you, Erich, but look, there are people with too much time on their hands and not enough brains."

"Sure, okay. But it's still weird."

Sara sighed and smiled at me. I didn't tell her what else Ivor said: *You just let me know when you find out…Bein's how I married one of 'um.* No matter; by now I was getting an idea. Not that it mattered.

Scrape. I jerked upright. Footsteps: slow, measured ones. I coughed loudly to make the newcomer aware of our presence, and we got silently to our feet. The footsteps got louder and a man stood silhouetted in the square of light. "Well, well," he said, "don't you two look cute."

Ron Crump. Crump holding something that froze me solid. A gun.

"Okay, bitches, who wants it first?" He stepped toward us, waving that ugly pistol and a sneer on his even uglier mug. I felt my innards freeze solid.

"Ron," Sara growled in a deep tone I'd never heard before, "have you lost it completely? I never did anything to you."

"Yeah, well, tough shit, bitch. You're mine anyways."

"I'm not, though."

He came closer. "I'm gonna show you. I'm gonna give it to you till it hurts. And you…" He pointed the thing at me, oscillating it slowly, savoring his power. We edged back, deeper into the dark. Close behind us was the tunnel to the next chamber, and beyond that, more tunnels leading who-knows where.

Pock. A faint noise down the passage made Crump flick his eyes away from us for an instant and I shoved him hard, knocking him off balance. He fired blind and the shot went wide. We ran into the darkness and Crump fired again, hitting concrete with a nasty ping. "Straight ahead, Erich!" Sara panted. "Okay, go left." She shoved me into a black void, and we plunged down a shallow incline. I saw a pinpoint of light ahead. Crump's footsteps scuffled somewhere behind us, then stopped. Thankfully, he didn't have a flashlight. Still, he had a gun. Again, he fired, again, he missed. How many more times could that happen?

"We have to kill him," I whispered. "We need to surprise him. Get the gun away. Shoot him or bash his brains in."

"Trip him up as he goes by, get him by surprise."

His footsteps crunched close, closer.

Now. Sara kicked out savagely and connected hard. "Uhh!" he grunted, staggering. Sara kicked him in the knees, and as he buckled, I kicked his face and tried to pin his gun hand to the floor. In the darkness, though, we were all flailing.

"Fuck you," he rasped, struggling to get up, but he couldn't handle both of us, and I kicked him hard on the temple. He fell with a grunt, dropping the gun with a metallic clatter. Got it! It felt hard and evil and strangely warm from Crump's hand. I'd never fired a gun before, but how hard could it be? I held it in both hands, cocked the trigger, and pulled. *Blam!* The damn thing jumped, shooting way wide.

Crump scuffled to his feet and ran back into the blackness. I fired again, and missed again. His footsteps faded into silence.

"Fucking piece of shit," I breathed, chest heaving.

"Totally," Sara nodded. As we came to the entrance of the bunker, a car started and roared away. We got into the Ford, drove to her apartment, and flopped. "Well," I said, "that was fun."

"He'll try to kill you again," Sara whispered grimly.

"I have to go to the cops."

She made a scornful face. "Pff! There's only two guys on the police, both worthless."

"Still, I have…"

"We'll have to kill *him*."

Someone knocked softly at the door.

We jerked to our feet. "Yeah?" Sara demanded loudly.

A faint voice responded. "Hello? I'm looking for Miss Sara Marsh."

"Could be Crump," I whispered.

"I don't think so," Sara said. She cracked the door, then opened it to a tall, elderly man. He looked at Sara and bowed slightly. "Hello. Are you Sara?"

"Yes, I'm Sara Marsh."

The man smiled and took off his hat. "Sara, I'm your great-uncle, Olin Marsh."

66

Visitation

He glided into Sara's apartment, an apparition in gray: gray-skinned, gray-haired, shrouded in a faded gray topcoat, a gray muffler wrapped tightly about his throat, a gray homburg pulled low over his eyes. His mouth was wide and thick-lipped, his ears small and oddly sunken, as if withdrawing into the skull.

Sara looked stunned. "Do you—would you like to sit down?" She pulled the other kitchen chair from beneath the table.

"Thank you." He sat heavily, breathing through his mouth.

"Can I take your coat?" I offered.

"No, thank you. A man my age feels every little chill. I am now one hundred and four years old, and I feel every minute of it. But I had to see Port Landsend again."

Sara smiled uneasily. "Well—Uncle—Shall I call you that?"

"You may, or you may call me Olin. Olin Marsh, son of Lilian and Unit Marsh."

"Unit Marsh!" I exclaimed.

"You know the name?" he asked.

"Yes. I've seen it in old newspapers."

"Ah, indeed." He cleared his throat, accepted a glass of water, then continued. "I left here in 1897. Hated like hell to leave Mother." He eyed Sara somberly. "Your great-aunt, Lilian Marsh. A real lady." He shook his head and appeared on the verge of tears. "She made it possible for me to live my life, to work, to learn, to see." His face darkened. "As for my father, I will simply say that Mr. Unit Marsh was not a sterling specimen of humanity." He smiled at me. "Excuse me if I'm speaking out of turn, but are you by chance Sara's young man?"

I tingled all over. "I am, sir." Introducing myself, I held my hand out. He kept his in his pocket. "Please forgive me," he explained, "but I have a condition that precludes me shaking hands. Do you live here in Port Landsend—Erich?"

"Yes, I just moved here from Seacoma. Got a job here during the week and play in the band across the street on weekends."

"A musician—splendid! Oh, there were some crackerjack bands around Seacoma in my youthful days. They'd play 'Hot Time in the Old Town Tonight' and make your hair stand on end."

"You got it," I said, pointing a finger, "we'll play it for you."

"I'd love it. Yes, I've heard some music in my day: Georgian Cossacks, Romanian gypsies, the throat-song of the Tibetan monks—positively unearthly."

"Sounds like you've traveled a lot, Mr. Marsh," I queried.

"*Olin*, please. Oh, I've poked my nose into more than a few nooks and crannies in pursuit of things left behind in civilization's mad march forward. I never went to college, had no interest in the stuffy academic environment. I wanted to get out and see things and meet people. That's what comes from being raised in that damned old mausoleum."

Sara grinned. "The house is still there, you know. My uncle Rule lives in it. At least, I think he does."

"Always hated the place," muttered Olin. "Cold and arrogant, just like Father. And that godawful tree—is it still standing?"

I nodded. "Yes. Very impressive, too."

"Oh, it's impressive enough, in a wicked sort of way. Must be huge by now. I always felt like the damn thing was *watching* me. The branches used to bang on my window at night, as if it was trying to reach in and grab me. Don't know if I could stand seeing the place now. Too many memories."

Olin took another sip of water and asked Sara, "You say your uncle—what's his name?"

"Rule."

"Yes, Rule—he lives there now?"

"Yes," she said. "I don't have much contact with him, I only see him at the café. He owns it, I work there. He's not really what you'd call friendly."

I wondered how Olin had found Sara. He cleared his throat. "Sara, please stop me if I'm being presumptuous, but may I ask who your parents were?"

"I don't know. Rule and Roslin brought me up till I was eighteen. They would only tell me that my mom and dad 'went away.' They never talked about 'family' things, ever."

"Yes, well, it seems our family is at least consistent in its taciturnity." He sighed and looked out the window.

It was my turn to be presumptuous. "What brings you back to Port Landsend after all these years, Olin?"

"Morbid curiosity, I reckon, and—well, a certain field of interest, you might say. My field is difficult to explain. One might call it 'esoterica': the study of ancient rites and cult survivals in modern times."

I felt my spine tingle, but I held my tongue.

"I've been in seaports all over the world," he continued, "and I've been in remotest deserts, where strange customs enjoy prolonged survival. And now…here I am, home again." Olin looked at us both and smiled. "Well, where shall I begin?"

67

Old Friends

Damn rotgut. Riled the innards all to hell, made you jittery. Aged you, for damn sure. Had to cut back. Well, thank God for beer. Now, he was hearing things—creeping, slithering, hissing things. Was it only his imagination, feeding its morbid hunger? Hell, no: that goddamn monster in the tunnel was real enough, and so was that eye in the sky.

Port Landsend put her clammy hand on Ivor Lumpkin, and he never shook it off. But the horrors from below and above did not return, and life slipped softly into that which Ivor was happy to call normalcy. The cursed Prohibition ended and the dirty thirties gave way to the wartime forties. The army stationed a small unit at the moribund Point Filson outpost, but distant hostilities made no greater ripples. The United Wharf was abandoned, at least to all appearances, the Bayview Hotel long defunct, and Ivor Lumpkin—exempted from wartime service by his monocular status— drifted along working odd jobs. For him and Rebecca, life was quiet, and quiet was good. The fifties brought new businesses—a hardware store, an A&P grocery, the Lamp Post Café—and ever more garish automobiles laden with tourists enough to warrant a small clump of hopeful shops and two new "motor hotels." Something like genteel contentment settled over the Gate City.

In other ways, though, the fifties were less kind. Barber Percy Shelton, Lumpkin's only man friend, contracted a sudden disfiguring ailment, asked Ivor to look after his shop, and disappeared. And then, one rainy morning, Rebecca went. She had long since counseled him that the change was inevitable and indeed, certain *conditions* ended their more intimate moments years before, somewhat cushioning the blow of her final departure. Still, when she kissed him goodbye and slipped into the water, where others waited in welcome, Ivor missed her fiercely. But time passes, and with it hurt, and by the 1960s Ivor Lumpkin found, if not happiness, peace. He found some of that peace at the Town Tavern, where he could ease through the plentiful non-working hours in the company of passable beer and barmates who knew enough to live and let live.

Nonetheless, Ivor Lumpkin remained a haunted man: haunted by the loss of his lover, and haunted still by a vision of an arm, chalk-white in the light of a swinging lightbulb as it flew into a—a *thing*. Haunted, too, by the question: Was *it* still down there? Were there *others*? Possibly. You smelled the air, you read the signs. True, things had been quiet for years; no disappearances, no rumors, no unsettling smells near the old drain entrance, where he habitually stood staring out at the water into which his erstwhile spouse had delivered herself. But one rainy October evening, he was at the railing when he heard a snort. In the water below, dirty white forms darted in and out of the tunnel. Rebecca? No—her coloring was different; darker. The real clincher came later, when he was helping renovate the cellar of a downtown building, and from a chink in a brick wall he smelled something that transported him back thirty years. He retched onto the dirt floor and leaned back against the wall, shuddering. *It's still here.*

He scuttled into the Town Tavern, took his usual stool, and halfway through his third beer he could hold back no longer. "It's still down there," he muttered.

239

"Huh?" said the ruddy-faced man on the next stool

"That goddamn thing," Ivor said, louder. "Dunno what the hell it is, but I saw it, plain as my one eye can see."

The bartender raised his eyebrows. "Prob'ly a octopus."

"Pfff! That was no goddamn octopus. I know damn well what I saw with my one good eye, and it was a big lump of some kind of purple globes, sweatin' an' stinkin' to high heaven. Come outa the tunnel an' ate Carney. Saw the whole goddamn thing, back in '33"

"Shit you say," said the ruddy man.

"Shit I do! Sucked ol' Carney in like a sponge. That thing oughtn't to exist—but it does exist, right under this city—hell, under our barstool-settin' asses. I know it's down there—smelt it. Never forget that damn stink."

The bartender frowned. "You know, friend, the walls have ears."

"Ahhh—don't have to tell me 'bout any stinkin' walls. I seen what come out o' them walls with my own good eye. Seen other things, too." Lumpkin belched loudly and slumped slowly toward his beer. The barman shook his head and walked to the far end of the bar, where he shared some private words with a small gray-faced man in a watch cap. "You think I'm bats, don't you?" Ivor muttered. "Maybe you weren't there when that goddamn thing came down outa the clouds—hic! Then again, maybe you *were*." Ivor drained his glass and wobbled out the front door and down Harbor Street. As he neared the small rooms he had once shared with now-aquatic wife, a man stepped from the shadows. "Lumpkin, someone wants to see you." Ivor peered groggily at him, the same gray-faced man who'd been at the bar. Well, there it was, he'd said too much. Now, he was in for it. Oh, well, it had been a good life. But Ivor was more curious than afraid. "Okay, friend, lead the way."

The man ushered him into a narrow door, down a flight of stairs, and onto a walkway along the drainage tunnel. The harbor portal was a blinding oblong, tantalizingly close. Ivor shivered: the man was leading him to the monster, the monster that ate Carney! He gave a piercing whistle—he was summoning the beast! Ivor got ready to run for it when the water roiled and something flopped out of the water onto the walkway. It was not the monster, but a plump, man-sized, oddly familiar form. Rebecca?

The creature looked at him with penetrating yellow eyes and croaked, "Ibor."

No. He knew that voice, even now. "Percy?"

"Ish me, Ibor."

The creature moved into the light. Ivor felt his stomach lurch, but he held his ground. "Percy! Well, you—you changed, too, eh?"

"Changed" was an epic understatement. Ivor's old friend was now something—well, something very hard to categorize: part-man, part-seal, and part-frog. His lumpy yet oddly streamlined form was covered in hair of mottled gray and black. The arms which had once clipped his hair were now long, powerful appendages ending in thickly-webbed hands, and his bulging legs terminated in massive, flipper-like feet. But most shocking was the face: Percy Shelton was always odd-looking, but any past oddity was eclipsed by the streamlined head with unblinking eyes, wide and gaping mouth, and pulsating gill slits along his neck. Ivor scratched his head. "Well, uh, Perce, ah…"

"Yuh, Ibor…I changed"—*snort!*—"better now. In my drue element… millions of us—cities, far in the ocean…a better world."

Lumpkin could hardly make out the words, but the tone was warm, even gentle. Percy sounded—happy! "Well, Perce, I'm glad—glad it's worked out okay…" Ivor stifled a sob and forced himself to look at his old friend. After all, Rebecca had prepared him. "The shop is just the way you left it, Perce."

"Thanks, Ibor. I wan' you to have it. I fixed it up for you, before."

"Aw, Percy…"

The Percy Shelton thing snorted and heaved. "Can't stay too long outa wadder, probly won't see you again. You been a real frien', Ibor, jush you watch yershelf, Look out for the bad ones." The barber-turned-batrachian flopped toward the water, then shot his young friend a parting wink. "Remember, Ibor: eyes open, mouth shut." The creature once known as Percy Shelton gave his friend a last grin and slipped smoothly into the water. A faint wake speared away toward the light.

Ivor leaned against the nearby wall. "Okay, Perce," he whispered. "I won't let you down."

68

Strange Eons

A scowl creased the placid dignity of Olin Marsh's face. "My father—your great-great-uncle, Unit—was not a pleasant man. He was a bully, a greedy, selfish bully. Bullied my mother and he bullied me until I got fed up and left. That was in 1897.

"Wow," I said in slack-jawed inanity, "1897!"

Olin chuckled warmly. "A few seasons ago, eh? Well, as for your great-aunt Lilian, she was a fine, gentle woman, and far wiser than her husband. She gave me my nest egg, set money aside for my future. Let me live life." The old man's eyes teared up. "Well, at any rate, we led a quiet and unassuming existence there in that damned house. Then, in the fall of 1888, Asahel showed up."

Sara looked at him questioningly.

"Your great-great uncle, from Massachusetts. Moved in, with his wife, Ida. I never knew how this all came about. Father kept Mother and me completely in the dark. Asahel was pleasant enough, at least until my dear father put a stop to it, but it was aunt Ida who was the real oddity. I saw her only once, when they arrived from the steamer. She got down from that carriage, a strange little thing all shrouded in black. Couldn't see her face. She lived with us as a complete recluse, never appeared once. Asahel explained it away as a rare, disfiguring disease. Their rooms were upstairs at the far end of the house. I surmised later that Father probably had that part of the house set aside for them all along. He ordered me never to go into that wing of the house, but being a young boy, I naturally did a little 'exploring' from time to time, and one day when he was away at the wharf I snuck upstairs. I heard voices; one of them Asahel's and the other—to my young and inexperienced ears it was hardly speech at all, but weird *slobbering* jibberish. Heh-heh, of course, all languages sound like 'jibberish' to those unfamiliar with them. I like to say that one man's jibberish is another man's poetry."

The midnight hoppers! I opened my mouth to speak, but Olin kept on.

"It wasn't too long that Aunt Ida vanished. No explanation—just gone. And Asahel himself underwent a strange metamorphosis; his face aged visibly, the skin seemed to *tighten* around him, he had more and more trouble breathing. Then he, too, disappeared. Father forbade all questions. He tried to induct me into the business at the wharf, but I had no interest. I knew he and I could never get along. Never did find out what he did down at the wharf, but I began to have suspicions. I knew there was violence done there. But I was coming of age, and I knew I had to get out, and get away from Unit Marsh.

"I left home and headed to Seacoma to seek my fortune. I tramped the streets and went stevedoring in a waterfront warehouse—became a regular wharf rat, in and out of saloons and gambling houses. The so-called 'liquor' they served would kill you if you weren't careful—almost killed *me*! One of my mates from the warehouse told me, "Olin, never let anybody know you're drunk. You're liable to get a free trip to Shanghai—if you take my meaning.' Well, sir, I took his meaning and took it the hard way. One night I went into the Tenderloin, ordered a beer, and woke up on a ship bound for Shanghai." He smiled impishly. "Yokohama, actually, but you get the idea."

"Shanghaied," I whispered, "my god…"

"Indeed," Olin murmured, "though I don't think God had much use for the good ship *Congolia Breckenridge*."

Sara looked horrified. "Uncle! What did you do?"

"I worked! It was work or else. Had to work to keep from freezing to death. But then we darn near froze anyway, up on the shrouds, working sail. After several weeks on this little excursion, my charming hosts chucked me off at Yokohama, no money, just the clothes on my back. I went to the American embassy hoping they might help, but no such luck. Told me without papers they could do nothing for me. There's your government for you. Well, the funny thing is, you'd think my ordeal would have soured me on the sea, but it actually left me wanting more. My experience on the *Breckenridge* was not all terrible—it put me into shape and I liked my fellow crewmen. Not so much the officers, but I stayed clear of them, did my work, and they left me alone.

"So, we got to Yokohama and I was up the crick. I thought, 'Oh, I've got to get home.' But then I had another thought: Where was 'home,' anyway? I was young and ready for anything—the world was my home! I roamed the docks and found a lovely two-master, so I went aboard, met the captain, looked him in the eye, and signed on right then and there. For the next three years I was an able-bodied seaman on the schooner *Oriole* plying the western Pacific. A happier ship you couldn't imagine: flying fish, dazzling sunsets, warm winds, and a crew of lovable ruffians from all over the world. God, I miss 'em yet!"

An odd look flashed across Olin's face. "I guess if you're at sea long enough, you'll run into some strange things. We were beating across the horse latitudes east of the Marianas when we sighted a queer-looking object in the distance. Some of the crew were afraid, and warned the captain not to go near, but the wind took us close enough to see that it was a black column sticking straight up out of the sea maybe fifty feet or so. Damnedest thing—gave me chills. And those scared men—they looked away and made the sign of the cross! No idea what it was: some sort of geographic anomaly, or perhaps a ruin from some unknown Atlantis. I never did find out.

"A few weeks later, we stopped at the island of Ponpei. The captain decided to lay over there for several days, and we crew scattered to take advantage of the island's many pleasures. Some of the women and men were very odd-looking, and only later would I understand why. But at the time I took it as a matter of course. Who am I to say what's 'odd' and what isn't? I was standing on shore looking out at the water one evening when an old man came and stood beside me. He was short and scrawny and had a weird sort of copper-colored skin. He looked at me closely for several minutes without saying anything. Finally, he whispered, *You Marsh.*

"I froze. How would he know who I was? *Marsh Cap-i-tan,* he said—*here Ponpei. Same you.* I was speechless. The old man hunted up a young fellow who spoke English, and between them they claimed that one of our forebears, Captain Obed Marsh, was on Ponape around 1850, and he and some of his crew fell in with some native women, married them, and returned with them to New England. But the oddest part of all this is, Obed apparently entered into some sort of arrangement with the priests of a small sect, of which this elderly man who accosted me was one.

"What sort of arrangement?" Sara asked.

"Something involving human trafficking, marital—or other—relations between certain island women and Obed and his men. I also ferreted out a strange hint at some sort of deal involving the raising of certain rare life forms. Naturally, that set me to wonder if my father and uncle were up to the same thing—which I have decided they were."

I felt queasy. "Life forms? What kind?"

"I'm still not certain, but something rare, something that Obed and Asahel and Unit valued. To this day I don't know why. Too many loose pieces, yet. But I suspect it was something sinister. There was a feeling on Ponpei—an atmosphere—of dark doings far in the past, but lurking just beneath the surface. We were there long enough to do some exploring, and one day I went hiking inland to some ruins I'd heard about. Ah, you should see it! A glorious old haunted place, covered with hideous vegetation and looking like a house of evil spirits. There was a frieze of hideous monsters carved around the buildings, and when I ventured inside, I heard sounds I did not like. Like something slithering. I scrammed out of there fast!

"But the weirdest thing of all was, that old fellow who told me—'You Marsh'—also told me about an ancient legend of a great god who lived deep in the ocean offshore. "Very old god," he said, his voice barely a whisper. "Very bad god." He refused to so much as utter the god's name. He said, 'No say name—no! Say name, bad god come out!'"

Olin brooded silently for a long minute. Then he said, "Well, it was all eons ago and I think I've bored you long enough. But I'll say this: I believe Obed and kin were involved in some dark business, a business that began in the far Pacific and made its way to this country."

My spine tingled. "Where?"

"A little town called Innsmouth."

Shit oh dear. "I've been there."

Sara and Olin stared at me marble-eyed.

"Yeah. Edward and I passed through there on the way back to Boston."

"Edward?" Olin asked.

"An anthropologist. Interested in the same things you've been describing."

"Ah! Well, when I visited Innsmouth it was pretty much a ghost town. Very few people about—that I could see. I did stop at a small store not far out of town, and the old storekeeper told me that there had been strange doings in Innsmouth several years earlier. He said, and I remember this very clearly, 'Them folks went too far—got tangled-up with them devil-gods. Some of 'em *changed over.*' Then he said this: 'The government men come and took a bunch of them Innsmouth folks away. Put 'em in the insane asylum!'"

"My God," I said, "Babson said something about that! Some kind of smuggling operation."

Olin puffed his cheeks. "So the official line reads. In fact, this was something much deeper and much more malign: a 'smuggling' operation of vast, even cosmic, implications. With Obed, Asahel, and my father at the center. Now, I fear others in our benighted family are involved. Others here in Port Landsend."

Sara was ghostly pale. "Rule."

Olin looked at her sadly. "Yes. You see—and please forgive me my earlier prevarication—this is not my first visit to PL. No, I've been back here a number of times and have done some discrete investigating, and what I have discovered falls in line with other things I have pieced together in my travels. I'm sorry to say I think Rule is playing the same dangerous game, led to it by his uncle, Micah."

"Micah!" Sara exclaimed. "I wondered about him."

Suddenly, the dots aligned. "Cosmic implications?" I said. "You mean opening a gate and letting in…" My throat felt dry, my head dizzy. I could barely croak the word: "*Necronomicon.*"

Olin nodded grimly. "Quite so. There's a shadow over our family. A deep, dark shadow."

69

Into The Bleak

Olin disappeared into the night and Sara and I went to bed nursing weird thoughts. Next morning she rose early, and when I joined her at the table she took my hands and said, "Sweetie, I need space." Space. Okay, swell. I can dig it. We all need space, right? Wrong. I was pretty much done with space. I wanted Sara. I tried to embrace her but she turned away. She looked scared. "I think I need a rest. We've been going heavy, maybe too heavy. I need to—I don't know—catch up."

"Does this have something to do with Crump?"

"No."

"Olin."

She looked away. "I don't know—maybe. Don't ask me what, I don't know."

"Has Rule got you mixed up in this thing?"

"I can't say any more. Trust me."

I looked into her eyes. I could either be selfish and blow it, or be adult. "I do."

"I know you do," she said, folding herself into me. "Dammit, Erich, I just want this to be over." She pulled away and walked to the window.

"Okay...okay." I tried to sound "reasonable," but I sure wasn't feeling it. I wanted to say that now was exactly when we needed each other. But hey, I can be noble with the best of them. "Sweetie, you do what you need to do. I'll be here for you, when you're ready." I kissed her on the forehead and walked away, leaving her staring glumly into the morning. I didn't want her to see the tears welling up in my eyes.

But life goes on. I hate that stupid banality, but still. Jack had to make a run to the "refuge" and he needed me on time. It actually felt kind of good to be needed by *somebody*. Jack, bless him, seemed to catch my mood, and he gently steered me into a good day's routine. The hours flew, I went into the zone and forgot everything but the tasks before me, and I was almost sorry when the workday was over. Walking home, trying to keep her out of my head, I felt a sudden chill. Would I go sleepwalking again, this time outside—this time *naked*? I picked at some leftovers, put on Kraftwerk, flopped down on the sofa, and flipped through a water-stained 1927 copy of *Astonishing Stories* that I'd rescued from our damaged magazine bin. The twenties: a turbulent time—Al Capone, lynchings, dazzling wealth alongside squalid poverty—but also a time of great art, architecture, and music. Not to mention pulp fiction full of half-naked women and bug-eyed aliens, the beginnings of modern sci-fi. I lingered over a bizarre image of a burrowing mole-man and thought of the tunnel just three floors beneath me. But my mind was full of enough weirdness of its own. I dropped the magazine, gave the jug another kiss, and let Sara and the band and everything else fade to black.

Robotically I moved, dividing the dark, going nowhere, thinking nothing, doing the Landsend shuffle, eyes wide shut. Around me, a dead city, a flashing yellow light, and ahead a blob—no, two blobs. *Blorp*, said one blob. *Blorp*, said the other blob. They stood motionless, waiting for me to pass, and as I drew close I felt them and smelled the Landsend stench. One of them blorped softly again, but they did nothing as I moved past them and on into the darkness. I felt them behind me, following me as I descended a familiar incline and came to a large, wooden door. Jack's place. The door was shut and bolted, of course. I stood a moment, smelling them behind me, aware subconsciously that they were those midnight hoppers I had seen from the apartment. I felt it was good to finally meet them and be included in whatever night revels they were pursuing. I walked on down the side street, my new friends moving along behind me, not speaking.

My mind saw loose planking over a doorway and brought me close in. A dream-face flashed in a crack, a gaping mouth, bulging eyes, eyes staring into a space far beyond me. Voices behind the planking muttered softly, my two companions and I moved—floated, in an odd, lurching motion—into a dark, dank place. The muttering stopped. Hands took me and guided me deeper into the blackness.

70

The All-Seeing Night

He was tired, eternally tired, but something kept sleep from him, kept him walking, watching, listening. Just as his father had done. There was no doubt: He was here for a reason. The distant campfires blazed, the voices chanted, louder now and more frenzied. They were calling out to black spirits. That much he knew. He knew because he had watched from the darkness as they stabbed and sliced and threw into the water victims, some calm and accepting, some not. He knew because he had seen what responded to their chants and guzzled the dark, red, unclean water. And he heard the voices of others, calling from places no man could see.

This old white man's city, this city of his people, still: he must love it, he thought ruefully, he certainly could not leave it. Not even when the young ones yelled "Hey, Indian!" Not even when the shop keepers—what few there were, now—eyed him coldly. Well, he'd seen worse and he'd seen better. Like this young man with the bushy hair who took the bones: He was humble, respectful, and after all, they were only bones. He was glad the man was friends with young Sara. He had watched her for a long time, and admired her. Did she carry some of his people's blood? It was very possible, and the thought gave him hope. At any rate, she was a hard-working woman with strength and dignity, like others he had known and loved. She and the young man could be trusted. He could see it in their eyes.

They had better. They most likely did not see what he had seen recently: the boat with the large bundle, a bundle that moved and made sounds of fear and issued a muffled scream as the men heaved it over the side. They would not have seen—at least, he hoped they would not have seen—the things in the old tunnel, things that looked and smelled like nothing else of Earth. What seed of black spirits was it that gave off such a smell?

Someone was coming. The bushy-headed young man—Erich. He walked oddly, staggering, stumbling, like he was drunk. From the shadowy doorway, he watched as Erich continued down the street. Two men stood in his way; did they speak? Erich passed them and kept walking. The two followed, lurching, almost hopping. Yes, the strange ones. He watched Erich turn the corner and disappear, then he watched the others follow him. Silently, invisibly, he followed them. He peered around the edge of the building—they were gone. He looked into the doorway, crept softly forward. Inside, he heard voices: those words again, words not of men. Silent as an owl, unfettered by years, Ka'atah'teh moved closer.

71

Heir Aberrant

Why the hell did it have to be in Greek, anyway? Well, at least there were pictures. But pictures of *what?* Rule Marsh stared at the insectile eyes, the snake-like appendages, the queerly small wings. Those guys had been into some serious shit. But shit that might just get him somewhere.

That would be a nice change. The long, dry years of the sixties meant only poverty and hunger and loneliness and smacking by parents who didn't want him around. *Freak!* shrieked the other kids as they laughed and threw rocks at him. More bitter years working boats and fishing and—well, the less said of some of the other means of getting by, the better. Life was shit, going nowhere fast, but where the fuck was there to go in Port Landsend, anyway?

One gray and aimless day, Rule was poking around the basement of the old house, which now belonged to him. Far in a dark back corner, he found a chest, and inside it he found a mass of old papers and a book, a very big book. And a name: Micah. Micah! They would never talk about his uncle, who had died long before Rule was born, and they told him not to ask "stupid questions." Now, they were gone, and Rule Marsh could ask all the questions he wanted. Such as, what exactly were those bizarre beings in that huge book? Where did they live? The book looked to have some answers. He carried it upstairs, and in the cobweb-clotted study pored over it day and night, as if something held him in the chair forcing his eyes upon the hideous images and enigmatic cryptograms. The pages were gnarled by time and the inscriptions barely discernable in many places, but Marsh was confident he could piece the sequences together properly, even if sections of the book seemed to be missing. He knew that it was mostly in Greek, and he didn't know anyone who knew that language. There were other words, too—not Greek, he surmised. He stared again at the page, mouthing the short line over and over:

"Gwath flui g'harn fangoolie…Zarafinga fthagan ar-lee-a Cthu…Cthu…"

Damn crazy stuff. Thankfully, though, there were loose pages of notes throughout the book—notes written in English, like this one:

Form the stars with the (unreadable) powder to hold Them beyond the Gate.

Them. Gate. Formula. The words were a jumble, but the pictures that came with the notes—well, anyone with brains could see. And you couldn't tell Rule Marsh he didn't have any brains. After several days, he began to see a pattern. Just say the words and—holy shit! He found something else, too. One of Micah's old maps had led him to a dark chamber deep beneath the city. And in that chamber was exactly what his uncle had said would be.

And it was probably getting hungry.

72

On The Brink

Tenebrous light filtered into the low-arched room. A doorway gaped blackly at the far end. Shadowy forms stood, making a weird *glub-glub-glub* sound. They stank like fuck-all, but they did not seem threatening. My body was at ease, my eyes closed tight, my mind open wide to a new and limitless world.

A voice said something like *Gwoth flooey garn shoggoth,* hands led me into the dark doorway, I smelled seaweed, water lapped. I was adrift, far from the world and its trivial hassles, free of its restrictions and expectations. Nothing mattered. Sleep: the highest form of existence.

All my life had been a sleepwalk, always this feeling of waiting, expecting, thinking I was destined for something more, dreaming. Driving cab in the city, hauling strangers who were but shades and shadows of life-force, wavering on the edge of unreality, figments alien, unreachable. Playing bass in a jazz band, faces talking, laughing, coming, going in a cosmic kaleidoscope, never stilled, never settling. Was I real?

I had a mother, a father, I had been a little boy with a train set, a bike, he waved at me and receded into yesterday and I walked on, a man with a bass viol and a girlfriend. Where was she? She should be here, she should be here with me, now...

The *glub-glub* sounded closer, more agitated. A splash, a smell—rank, familiar. Jeff's words crossed my mind—*most mysteries turn out to have mundane explanations*—on their way to somewhere else, Sara reached for me, pulled me strongly toward blackness. Shapes moved, green, purple, gray…voices muttered words I could not understand…a hissing sound…

From behind me came new words—strong, sharp, yet strangely melodic. Hands grabbed me and yanked me backward. The blobby figures raised their arms and blorped loudly, moved in slow-motion. A voice yelled in alarm, feet scuffled, I flailed my arms blindly, my hands slapped skin. Stronger hands steered me toward the door and into the night. We walked, my eyes opened on a mocking moon and a face, grim and gaunt, glaring at me.

73

Star Gazing

One hour before downbeat the following Saturday desultory figures sat scattered around the Star Chamber lounge. I did not recognize a one of them. In the dining room Rick schmoozed up a table of acquaintances in the dining room, and in a quiet corner Danny Phipps nursed his customary cup of tea. He was a veteran working musician who had long since learned how to pace himself.

I plopped down next to him. "Funny old town we got here," I said.

Danny smiled at me. "Why do you say that?"

"Oh, just a feeling..." Let's see: dog fed to sea lions...mysterious cult singing on the point...dreams of being a sea monster...sleep-walking into near-oblivion...I just looked at Danny and smiled stupidly.

The pianist stared into his cup, then at me. "I've worked jobs here now and then, and I could never get it out of my head that there was something queer about this place. I hesitate to call it a ghost town, but more like a backwater. Kind of died on the vine. Personally, I'm glad; I rather like backwaters." He chuckled impishly. "Don't tell Rick I said that."

"Yeah," I smiled, "he's quite the booster type, only maybe he's about a hundred years too late."

"Oh, I hope not. I like this room, and Rick's a good man. But these old places…" He shook his head sadly. "I worked the Elks here about twenty years ago. The club was dead on its feet, just a handful of customers staring into their beer. The only reason I worked here at all was because of Larry Wells, the manager. I knew him from when he had the Bremerville lodge, and he liked my playing and was good enough to throw me a gig now and then. Only, in this particular instance I don't know if he was doing me any favors."

Danny grimaced. "There were some *odd* types who used to come in. Larry said they were Polynesians. How they wound up in PL I don't know, but I do know that the whites and these Polys did not mix well. Ho-ho—not well at all!"

"Really? Could be the ones Ivor calls 'shore people'."

Danny raised his eyebrows.

"Ivor Lumpkin," I said. "Another old rummy, but a good guy. I think there's more to him than he lets on. He's been here since the thirties and has definite opinions of them. Folks that live out on the point, supposedly from the South Pacific."

Danny's eyes glittered behind his glasses. "'Shore people', eh? Well, whatever they were, those Elks didn't like the Polys, not one *bit*. I don't think they were Elks members, but by that time Larry wasn't particular about who he let in. Not to flatter myself, mind you, but I think they came in to listen to me. Didn't speak to anybody, just sat there and listened. I think I probably said hello to them, but I don't remember if they said anything or not. See, I've learned over the years that it's the best policy on these barroom jobs to be non-committal: not stuck-up or anything, just be cordial, keep quiet, and do your job. Too much palling around with the locals can sometimes get you into situations you'd rather stay out of. But those Polys didn't bother me any—shoot, next to Larry they were my best audience here. Sometimes they were my *only* audience.

"Well, one night, this one Poly was sitting there listening and minding his own business, when one of the older white guys got nasty with him. Got off his barstool and made some crack. Well, the Poly started barking back at him in his dialect—weird, slobbery-sounding! Made my hair stand straight up. The Poly made a nasty face, grimaced like something you'd see on a totem pole. Well, the guy who started it all just turned and slunk right out of there like a whipped dog. I've seen worse barroom mixups, but this kind of left me with a sour taste for PL." He sipped his tea and smiled tightly. "Yes sir, I thought I'd seen the last of the place, now here I am again."

"So, where does the name 'Star Chamber' come from?"

The piano player licked his thin lips. "I asked Rick the same thing. Do you know about the old Star Chamber back in England? Secret law court, hush-hush and not always very nice. Let me show you something." Danny drained his tea and led me to the back office, where he pointed out an odd frieze of gray stars running around the entire room. "Well," he said, "That's one thing. But what do you make of this?" He pulled a section of paneling away from the wall to reveal a solid mass of the same five-pointed stars. Each star was about four inches across and looked to be fashioned from plaster or something like. They felt chalky to the touch.

"What the heck?" I said.

"What the heck indeed! Some kind of ceramic or stone. Never seen anything like it. Rick thinks the whole place might be covered in them."

Rick bustled by on the way to the kitchen and saw us looking at the queer stars. "Star gazing, fellas?" he said, puffing his cigar. "I've thought about strippin' off all the paneling and seeing how far these things go. Guy who did my drywall says they been here for ages. Same family's owned the building a hundred years."

I felt my back tingle. "What family's that, Rick?"

"Marsh. Own half the damn town, from what folks say."

74

Botheration

There was no escaping the little bastards. They with their dancing and singing and puny attempts at extending their power with tin gadgets. They were not to be taken seriously and they certainly could not be trusted. And yet, here there were, again, and every waking eon more and more of them, chattering and begging like young birds, always expecting you to be tricked out in some outrageous costume or other. Silk, velvet, denim—how much store they put in appearances! All those places they had summoned it, from the kingdom of the pointed temples to the time of machines. Yes, a bothersome lot. Still, they had the book, and the book was law. This one particular cell seemed to be quite insistent lately. Bah!

Well, let them call, let them nag, let them worry themselves, preferably to death. For death would one day sweep them all away, and the Great Old Ones would once again rule the universe. No more being jerked this way and that by spells and nonsense, no more being prisoners of some book. Oh, yes, the little two-legged joker would have his comeuppance, and no mistake!

The thing some called Chaos and some called Nyarlathotep flexed its diaphanous extremities. The others must be notified. Time for a little exercise. And nourishment.

Now then, what to wear?

75

Killing Time

The sun was veiled by a cold gray scrim. Pigeons wheeled in the sky. A good day to die. Stupid morbid me. But hey, I seemed to be a marked man: marked for bizarre dreams and sleep-walking and now, possible ritual sacrifice. I needed air.

The cat was lolling in the window at the Grebe Bookstore. I overcame my trepidations and walked in.

"Hello again," said the Grebe lady, eyeing me cooly. My previous abrupt departure probably still fresh in her mind. "Looking for anything special?"

"Just killing time."

"Killing time," she said, smiling. "Isn't that an odd expression—killing something that can't be killed. Unless, perhaps, it can."

"Do you know something I don't?"

"Just being metaphysical. An old habit."

"Sometimes I try to feel time moving—sometimes, I try to make it stand still. See how much I can slow it down." I couldn't help staring at her copper-bronze face and her eyes, which appeared to be more Asian than I had seen before.

"I embrace time and let it carry me." She smiled sweetly. "Can I offer you some tea? It's a special brew."

Paranoid me pictured a Mickey Finn. But—"Sure." I took a breath. "Do you know anything about the people out at the point?"

She cocked her head. "Why do you ask?"

"I've heard them singing. Some people think they might have a cult."

She smiled tightly. "Oh, some might call us a 'cult,' but I prefer to think of us as a society."

"You…?"

"Oh, yes. Ours is a group that goes back quite some time here." She moved to a small table, poured us both tea, and handed me a cup.

"And the disappearances—human sacrifice?"

"I know some who have 'disappeared,' but not really. They are still very much here, just in different form."

"How different?" I wanted to hear it from her.

"Let's just say more comfortable in water than on land."

Ah-ha! "So—amphibious."

"Something like."

"But, there are some who don't exactly volunteer."

"In the past—the early days—there were excesses, I'm sorry to say."

"And now?"

She only shrugged. The light hit her like one of those old black and white movies, half sun, half shadow. Her intriguing bronze complexion glowed. How much did she know about what went on in town?

"You see, Erich, our little coterie is not the only one. Far from it. We are everywhere. For us, time is not an adversary to be 'killed', but an ally—an ally in the natural progression of evolution."

"So, we're all going to turn into frogs."

"I wouldn't put it quite so simply. But in time, man will inevitably evolve. And as you seem to be aware, he is already evolving in that direction. We are everywhere, you see."

"We."

"Those who follow an order older and higher than outdated Earth-bound religions. Some might call us a dangerous cult. In our view, it is the modern world that has become dangerous. Hard, mechanized, lost to the sensations of nature—the true reality of the cosmos. And why? Christianity. The church has denied nature and made us deny our natures. A history of violence, persecution, corruption, abuse of the foulest kind—all attributable to the institution bearing Christ's name. Inquisitions, crusades, holy wars: is this 'Christ-like'? That's why some of us turn to something deeper and far older."

"Like Yog-Sothoth?"

Her eyes blazed. "Ah, you know of him. Yes, Yog-Sothoth, the all-in-one…Nyarlathotep, the great messenger…Cthulhu, master of the depths."

Nyarlathotep…Nyarlathotep! "Nyarlathotep—in the *Necronomicon!*"

"You know the *Necronomicon?*" She smiled and nodded. "You *are* a clever boy!" She moved closer, I could feel heat pulsing from her radiant body. "Well, then, you know that our gods are timeless, masters of all dimensions—primal elementals that will ascend as our so-called Christian order declines. As I believe it is, even now."

She was in on it! "Jesus Christ, the other night I sleepwalked right into the arms of some guys—I think they were going to make me a sacrifice."

"I am sorry," she sighed. "There are some among us who harbor darker motivations. I cannot excuse them. It is something many of us fight against, but I fear cannot win. You must be careful. Those you encountered are not numerous, but they are dangerous."

"So, why shouldn't I report them to the cops?"

"I understand your anger. The police can do only so much. And in any case, they know enough about us—well, you understand."

I did. Thanks Ivor, you tried to tell me. Something in her voice soothed me, made me almost want to understand. "So, this—society is serious about bringing in god-things from another dimension."

"Many dimensions. Yes, it will happen, and soon. It already has here, once, long ago. But enough of all that. You are a good and honest young man, and I want you to take care. After all, we could use more like you." She came around the desk, stood before me, and opened her blouse.

There in the middle of her chest was a tattoo, an anemone or medicine wheel of purple rays encircling a denser circle of radiating starfish arms. I stared, speechless.

"Like it?" she asked, moving close. My breath caught in my throat, my mouth tasted metallic.

The tattoo moved.

76

What's A Girl To Do?

ara turned to face the wall and let the wave of self-loathing wash over her. *I'm crazy. I am fucking crazy.* Erich was all she had wanted, all these too many years alone. And now, when she had him—*No, no, no!* She flung the blanket off and rolled onto her back. Tears dripped down her round, glistening cheek. Right about now, his arm would be holding her. A cry burst from her lips, she jerked from the bed and pounded the wall. She strode around the little room, stomping the floor and cursing her body, cursing her skin, cursing the blood that churned around inside her and made new demands on her that she was not anywhere near sure she wanted to heed. She wanted Erich, she ached with wanting him. Did he understand? Yes. She knew he did—Erich was that kind of man. She could not lose him.

Even if it meant not changing. She asked herself again and again, and again she found the same answer: *Fuck changing. I don't want to change. I want Erich. I want to be a woman!*

Late that night she walked down Harbor Street, entered the Kliemann Block, and climbed the stairs to the cupola. Her uncle Rule sat at his desk. Beside him stood Aunt Ros and two of the cousins.

"What do you want from me, Rule?" she asked.

"You know what. We got to do this."

"Why?"

"Got to. Family'll fall apart if we don't."

There was no penetrating her uncle's dull gray eyes or the thick skull behind them. She knew only that she must neutralize the danger they posed. Bastards, threatening Erich. What could she do—fight? Leave?

"Shit, Rule, it's already fallen apart."

"Not yet, it hasn't." His black eyes bored into her, she felt violated. Fucking Rule and this fucking weird-ass family, those creepy "cousins." Cousins of *what*, she wondered. Lately they were getting so odd-looking, like the change was hitting them in unexpected ways. Such as their skin flaking off onto the floor in front of her. Was she really one of *them*? They all seemed to think so. Sure, she loved swimming with the seals and sea lions and the salmon and the other creatures that rubbed against her when she ploughed the dark waters of the Sound. She still felt part of them. But she knew better: she was too much of land, and too much of humanity. Erich was a landsman, and she loved him for it. Loved him all the more for his brave plunge into the bay beside her. God, how cold he must have been! He did it for her, for them. The very thought made her shiver with love—and desire. Her life: it had been so small, so closed-in, so sheltered, even if her family was indifferent if not cold. She had her little job and her little place and her little—everything, little. And then Erich came along. Erich, who was not little at all, despite his attempts at modesty. He was trying to do things, to live more, to discover, to grow. Fuck it; she would find him and make up. Oh, how she would make up!

Rule pulled a small black book from his desk and thrust it at Sara. "Your mother left you this." Then he handed her a folded piece of paper. "This come with it."

Oh, now you tell me? She opened the paper and read:

> If any of my relation's or my children see this book they
> should no that the things writen in is meant to be folowed

and obayed as the survival of the Marsh famly depend's
on it. Your father and your gran-father and his father befor
him all wished it to be done.

Sara read the lines once, twice, then looked away. Was this really written by her mother—whoever she was? She looked her uncle straight in the eye. "Dammit, Rule, I don't know what you think I'm supposed to be capable of, but, I'm *not* capable of some weird sorcery shit like you expect. I'm not like that."

"Don't matter," he grunted, "you know what you got to do."

"What I 'got to do' does not include killing, got it?"

Then Roslin butted in. Pathetic, airhead Ros. "Sara," she simpered, spewing out cigarette smoke, "this is family."

Right. When had the goddamn "family" ever cared about her? Only now, when they thought she could do something for them. They seemed to think it was so simple. "Yeah, Sara," said the younger cousin, Enoch, "just go with the flow."

"Then why don't you do it?" He could only grin stupidly and shrug.

"You know why," Rule growled in that ugly voice of his. She thought again of Erich, his eyes, his lips, his soft, musical voice. "It's got to be you," Rule said. "And if you don't, I will, and you and your friend will be sorry."

"Rule, you leave him out of this."

"He's already in, girl. You brung him in, so you best cooperate if you know what's good for you—and him."

They stared at her with their unblinking eyes, the cousins *blub-blubbing* and sloughing more skin onto the floor. Falling apart right in front of her. She saw now how much Rule had changed in the last few days; he looked ten years older and his breath stank. It was all too crazy. She shook her head and turned away. She knew she damn well shouldn't. But they raised her. Fed her. Kept her warm, safe.

And now, they threatened. Threatened *him*.

So she did.

77

Enchantress

Nothing made sense. Kay played herself. I couldn't meet Jeff's eyes. I smiled perfunctorily at Rick. He'd gotten used to me by now, and as long as I kept the beat, he was happy. This, I could do. Ta-ra-ra-boom-boom-boom-de-ay. I, robot.

The shock of the Grebe lady and the cellar incident had not worn off. I couldn't see it wearing off any time soon. I mean, I'm as tolerant as the next dope, but that…Maybe she was one of the things Sara and Ivor had tried to warn me about. Maybe she—oh, God, maybe nothing. She was a freak, a monster, one of those who wanted to feed me to—something.

Sara knew. She had to. *Just be careful, Erich, okay?* Okay, babe, I dig. I am now standing on the edge of an abyss, a threshold of something nameless, something cosmic. Oh, and there's a woman down the street with tentacles growing out of her chest. But hey, I'll be careful. Yup, "careful" will be my watchword.

But life drags you on, kicking and screaming. I don't know exactly when I noticed the woman sitting there in the club all by herself, watching us. Actually, watching me. That was obvious, almost painfully so. A shiver ran up my spine. I glanced only briefly at her, trying to keep cool, but her icy blue eyes were vastly cooler than anything I might bounce back at her. And then, she was gone.

Next night, she was back, back in her sheer black dress, back with her twin cobalt lasers boring in on me. And this time she was still there when we took our first break. What else could I do? "I'm Erich."

"Yes."

"Do I know you?"

She smiled coolly. "It is possible we may have met at some point."

Cryptic. I liked that. I also liked her thick, black hair, blacker even than Sara's, and her long, long neck, and that killer dress. Why was she watching me?

I tried to maintain my cool. "Passing through?"

"Yes." She tilted her head enigmatically. "Passing through." She flashed a jawful of immaculate whites and held out a long, delicate hand. "You may call me Arla. Please, sit."

I felt myself slip into a whole new dimension as I fumbled with the chair. "So, Arla, what brings you to our little hideaway?" Around her hovered a suggestion of sea air and incense. Her nails were long and brilliant red, her lips were full and beautifully shaped, she wore high heeled black boots and sheer black hose. The kind of woman I'd dreamed of often, but never dared hope to meet.

She regarded me coolly. "I was in the neighborhood."

"Ah. Are you a jazz lover?"

"I don't know much about music. But your fingers are very nimble on that big instrument. May I?" She took my right hand in hers and studied it, eyebrows knit. *Sara. Shit.* She leaned toward me. "You put a lot of expression into your playing." She squeezed my hand and smiled. "A lot of passion."

I am so fucked. I shrugged casually, my heart doing its best to climb up my throat. *Yes, ma'am, passion is my middle name.*

Abruptly, she pulled her hand back and, with a soft, silky rustle, stood. Her voice was a scirocco. "Come out with me sometime. We can walk by the water."

I stood, struggling to stay cool, and aimed a tepid gaze into her eyes. "I'd like that—Arla. It's been a pleasure." I kissed her hand. *I kissed her hand.*

She gave me her Mona Lisa smile once more and turned toward the door. For the rest of the evening and beyond, I was a palpitating wreck. *Come out with me sometime.*

78

By Their Smell Shall You Know Them

He felt like he had lived forever. "Old Indian," people called him, never asking his name, never thinking twice about him. Decade upon decade of the white man's years passed and still he walked the streets of his home town to the taunts of the young and the indifference of the old. In the house of his father, a little lean-to behind the old Chinese laundry, Ka'atah'teh relished the company of friends who brought him food and news.

Lately, the news had been bad. Ralph and Ivor had seen and heard what he had: the strange chanting increasing…crouching figures loitering around the old wharf late at night—some going into the water…ominous utterances: *Soon, we will call them out…The time is coming…Great Cthulhu will hear us.* He gazed often at the doll his mother gave him: God, *no!*

Yes. The nameless ones, alien and malign, were growing under the city. At certain drains and openings their charnel odor rose like ugly black smoke—smoke calling to others. Soon, they would have to show themselves. Perhaps then, called by the smoke and the smell and the words of the foolish ones, the black spirits would come.

The Water Beings were another matter. He them saw often, when he returned to the old village and communed with the spirits of his father and his mother, and out along the water. When they appeared, he was not afraid; they listened when he sang, they gave good energy. Friends. Man could learn from them, if only he would listen. Could *they* stop the black spirits?

It had been a close one, getting that young man, Erich, away from the ones who lurked in the shadows and made foul noises and emitted even fouler stinks. What might have happened if he hadn't been there, he hated to think. As it was, he'd had a hell of a time getting him back out onto the street. Good thing he remembered the words his father taught him, and his grandmother before that. Erich was only half-conscious, his eyes rolling back in his head, moving as if drunk. "Uhhh…." he moaned, "something in the tunnel…weird shit…" Erich's eyes snapped open, looked into his. "You," he said, "how did you…?"

Ka'atah'teh said nothing and helped him back to the Star Chamber. "Sleepwalking again," Erich said. "Damn…."

Ka'atah'teh nodded. "And you walked into them?"

"They were out there—on the sidewalk…Like they were waiting. Weird, I didn't feel in danger…"

Ka'atah'teh peered up and down the street, then looked grimly at Erich. "Bad ones, those guys. Dangerous. You need to keep away from them."

"Guess I better tie myself to the bed." Erich looked into Ka'atah'teh's eyes. "Thank you."

The tall man nodded curtly, then smiled. "I'll be watching out for them *and* you."

As the last crows flocked to their roosts, Ka'atah'teh walked to his place on the beach. Some of the point gang were there; lately they had been getting bolder and more open, swilling from bottles and bragging about how they would take back the world with the help of "new gods," gods who would give them better lives. And money. Always money. And if they thought for one minute those black gods would do anything in their favor, they were fools indeed.

The shore guys looked at him and through him, a familiar sight, just an "old Indian," harmless, one foot in the grave. Maybe they hadn't heard about the rescue. As night fell, he crept quietly closer to the group and slipped into the shelter of an upturned skiff. Just within earshot he heard rough voices: *Gettin' time…who we gonna git next?…how 'bout that old Innian?*

He felt a shiver lance up his spine. A moment later he heard footsteps. Two men passed the skiff and one saw him. "Hey, old Indian," he said, "maybe you'd like to offer yourself."

The other one grunted. "Yeah, we can use volunteers."

Ka'atah'teh stared blankly through them, willing them to disappear. They stared insolently for a moment, then shambled away toward town. Chickenshit.

Ka'atah'teh had no illusions; this time, they had done nothing. Maybe next time would not go so well. And if what they had in mind was what he had saved Erich from, he had better make damn sure he was ready. Ka'atah'teh smiled grimly, gripped the handle of the stout old knife. It had served his father well, it would do as much for him.

79

Break On Through

A black tower loomed, figures gyrated in ecstasy, as if performing some proto-lithic submarine rite of eldritch antiquity. An insistent two-note riff, like something plucked on an ancient lyre, rang through the depths. A shadow emerged from the tower, long and lithe, with webbed hands and a strangely feminine torso. It beckoned to me—it grinned and receded into the dark beneath me, and as it vanished, I caught a glimpse of black hair streaming back from its head. I swam after her, swam into her, and she opened her arms, her mouth. The harp droned, *lyre, lyre, pants on fire.*

I woke up on the stairs wearing only my shorts and coat. My feet were filthy and bleeding. Another night in Morpheus. God, had I really been out there again, walking, vulnerable, unconscious—where had I gone and what had I witnessed? Got off lucky, damn lucky. I stripped and showered and crashed. Hours later, sunlight poured through the windows and I was glad I had a job of mindless work waiting. I ate slowly, letting my head air out. Then, I remembered: Arla. Christ. *I kissed her hand.* I'd never kissed Sara's hand. Arla…Sara…the Grebe lady, whose name I didn't even know. Sheesh, three months earlier, I couldn't get a date.

Jack handed me his search list and I lost myself in images from a lost age—hip chicks on *Mademoiselle,* young eyes still glowing after all these years, eyes concealing anxiety over paychecks and wavering boyfriends...the art deco wonders of *Fortune,* with its almost poetic faith in capitalism and American industry...Norman Rockwell's America on the covers of *Saturday Evening Post,* revealing not just the sunny surface of American life but the darker things beneath.

I was in back near the big door when I heard something. I listened at the crack, hoping to hear more, and a rank smell hit my nose. I heard a faint splash, then nothing. I had to see behind the door. I had to go in. The sudden resolution gave me a jolt of energy, and I rushed through work, my head formulating plans. I'd have to be quick and stealthy, slip into the tunnel when no one was looking. I needed a light, one I could wear on my head, leaving my hands free, and certain other supplies.

After work I stopped at the hardware store down the street, and lucked out finding an old-fashioned miner's light. I also had the bright idea to pick up a cheap fishing pole—out on the water, I'd just be another harmless fisherman. I paid the young clerk, who had none of the "Landsend look" about him, and headed for the apartment.

Early next morning I stuffed headlight, water, and a banana into my backpack, put on warm work clothes, picked up my fishing rod, and headed for the dock. It was one of those dreamy fall mornings, quiet and timeless, and the lightly-veiled sun cast a watercolor light over the moldering buildings. I covered up and slouched along down Harbor Street like a local. There were only a few people on the streets, and no cops. I arrived at the "merina" to find the shed empty. I waited a few minutes, debating whether to just take a rowboat, but getting arrested for theft was not on my list, and after a few more minutes the attendant showed up. I paid him, slipped a boat into the bay, and rowed slowly toward the tunnel mouth. I dangled the pole over the gunnel; a casual observer would see only a fisherman in a rowboat.

I reached the portal, peered around furtively and quickly nosed in. I slipped the miner's light on over my stocking cap, turned around on the bench to face forward, and pushed into the darkness. Slightly awkward, but I damn well wanted to see where I was going and not where I'd been. The light was gratifyingly bright, but less reassuring was the crumbly look of the roof. I scanned for fissures and was relieved to see only a few mossy seeps. The tight space stank of salt water and mold, and the plop-plop of dripping water echoed faintly through the tube. Dark recesses in the tunnel roof suggested manholes or waste chutes from the buildings, and I hoped they were not still in use. A few more yards and my light picked out vertical lines. Jack's door! A shallow landing stage shelved out beneath the woodwork, and I sat still a moment, savoring the feeling of discovery. I really had broken through to the other side! I imagined what the door and warehouse were used for back in olden times, the days when all Jack's moldering magazines were fresh and new, and decades before that. Back, back, they years stretched, back into an inaccessible tunnel, back, back. I relaxed on my oars, feeling adrift in time.

Snort! A small geyser sprayed from the water and a face stared at me with bulging black eyes. A seal. Cute little thing—then I remembered the dog. Had this guy been among the feeders? He snorted again and vanished. Onward I bored on through my cone of light, hearing only occasional dripping of leaks on the oily black water. The tunnel smelled rather pleasantly of salt water and moss—where was that weird stench? A moment later I came to a fork: now, there were two tunnels. I spun my mental compass and concluded that the left fork probably ran under Harbor Street and toward the Star Chamber. The other was anybody's guess. It did, however, offer one attraction: light, faint but definite. I went right. I heard no noise, saw no movement.

Pushing on, the light gradually grew brighter, I saw the outline of a portal, and emerged into a vast circular space. The water was smooth and silvery-black, and slivers of bright light creased the darkness overhead. I was in the cistern that Sara and I had walked over. I flashed my beam along the walls, picking up a moss-covered ledge encircling the chamber and a large metal door that could be lowered over the tunnel entrance I had come through. On the far side was a small arched doorway, and near it on the narrow ledge sat a rectangular object. I rowed closer and saw that it was a table with two candles on it. Some kind of altar? Probably kids smoking pot and indulging their adolescent ideas of Satanic ritual, *Dude, we're all getting together for, like, a black mass.* I chuckled softly—the towns and suburbs of America seethe with juvenile doings parents can scarce imagine. Then I remembered the voice screaming up the funnel—"You can't!...Stop!" Like the voice out in the bay that night—the screaming, then the silence.

Probably nothing—Why was the sheriff so quick to dismiss what we'd heard? Damn.

Feeling a growing unease, I rowed back toward the tunnel mouth. I was almost to the junction of the two passages when I heard a *pock*. I doused my light and peered around the corner toward the entrance. Silhouetted in the bright oval of the tunnel mouth was a rowboat with two men in it, coming toward me. One of them had a flashlight. I backed down the side-tunnel into the cistern and prayed the intruders would keep going straight. They did, and after a moment I eased back into the main tunnel. My gut told me to get out, fast, but the imp of curiosity had other ideas. *Follow 'em, dummy, or you'll never know.* No arguing with an imp. It was dark, but a faint light shone from further ahead and I could see rusty doors and obscure holes in the brickwork. Then I heard faint voices. I kept going, I knew I had to be getting close, probably close to the Star Chamber. There: a landing—a landing and a wooden stairway, and at the top of the stair, a door.

I edged the boat up to the landing. There was an iron cleat on the curb, with a rope attached, so I tied up and stepped gingerly onto the pavement. I saw a hole in the drywall just under the stairway to the door, and an odd bend in the wall, and patchy spots, as if hastily covered. I smelled that rank stench, my light fell on a globular cluster of blackish purple. Some kind of mineral deposit, I thought, and moved on. Voices muttered again, faint, muffled. I froze as I heard their weird slurping, slobbering speech, the same speech I heard beneath the apartment. Then, footsteps, and getting louder. I raced to the boat and began untying the line. A faint voice yelled, "Hey you guys!" It almost sounded like—*Rick?*

Out went the lights.

80

Thin Blue Line

Deputy sheriff Hill did not like trouble. Trouble meant work: paperwork, mostly, but also the other, nastier kind of work: subduing and cuffing and bringing them in and holding them. Drunks, mostly, but now and then druggies and mayhemmers. And trouble-makers. Thankfully, none of these were in abundance in Port Landsend. Of course, "troublemaker" was an all-too handy handle to hang on someone you didn't like, or whose looks you didn't like, or when you had some quota of arrests to fill, usually self-imposed. Sheriff Hammers was an old-school imposer, and a "troublemaker" was whoever he said was one.

Thankfully, he hadn't had to say it often lately. It had been a good summer, with a brisk tourist trade and stores and businesses happy. A summer of good vibes, as the hippies used to say. Hill smiled at the thought; his father had been a hippy and he—well, best live in the here and now. Here and now, it was late September and raining. The tourists had fled with the sun, and now there was one more missing-persons report on his desk. There had been two others in the past three weeks: the Strogach boy and old man Rauf. "Harry didn't come home from school," sobbed Mrs. Strogach, "and it's not like him." He nodded somberly and had her fill out the form. He wished he could do or at least say more, but he knew the uselessness of that. Ninety-nine percent of all "missing" persons turned out to be simple runaways, anyway. He did, however, promise to "do our best."

"What do you think, Boss," he'd asked Hammers later. "Maybe I could look into these a bit harder."

"We're doin' what we can, Hill," the sheriff replied, "c'mmenserate with the resources. Can't do any much more." That was that.

The 32-year-old deputy had been in the department—if you wanted to call two uniforms and a desk man a "department"—not quite a year. Not long enough to get even a modest toehold of authority. The boss was the boss, and there it lay. Didn't mean he had to like it, though. Nor did it mean he could not make some discrete inquiries. His job was his job. He would protect and serve.

Now, it was near midnight and nothing was moving. Hill thought again of Hammers's response to his missing persons follow-up and other suggestions lately. Being, in so many words, NO. Deputy Hill sighed and checked his mirror again. No, the sheriff was not a likable man, and there were other things he did not like: those gray-faced young men who looked old close up and who seemed to scuttle into the shadows like hermit crabs when they saw him coming…the folks at Point Judson carrying on… those missing persons. Yes, there was something in the air—almost as if the city was expecting something.

Then there was Rule Marsh, whose very name made his boss stand to attention. "Do not interfere with Mr. Marsh," Hammers had warned him. Almost like the sheriff was afraid of the guy. And those certain few individuals who had taken to hassling tourists near the old United Wharf? "Let 'em be," said his boss, "ain't worth the hassle." Well, weren't they being paid to "hassle"?

Nevertheless. Hammers's gray eyes bored into him. "Got it?"

"Got it."

And after all, crime *was* scarce and PL was, for the most part, quiet. He liked his small apartment uptown. And the owner of the Grebe Bookstore had a nice smile. Still, it was no place to advance a career in law enforcement. He'd move on soon enough.

But there was something wrong, somewhere. He could feel it. He was young and green, but his instincts for cop work were sound, and those instincts told him something was funny. Down the way, he saw a familiar pair at the harbor railing. Tweedledum and Tweedledee—Lumpkin and Donald. Old Ralph was all right, but Lumpkin—lately he'd been on his case about the missing persons. "It's them shore folk," the old soak insisted. "They're kidnappin' folks and usin' 'um for sacrifices."

Deputy Hill balked at that. "Oh, come on, Ivor!"

The old man was adamant. "Don't 'come on Ivor' me! I've seen things you couldn't even imagine, right here in this town. I'm telling you, them folks is up to evil doin's! Don't you have eyes in your head?"

Yes, he did, and they had taken due note. Note, especially, of the increasing late-night activity at the point, with torches and dancing and screaming of weird jibberish. Who the hell were "Nilethotep" and "Yoggasoth" and "Kalulu"? Some crazy cult, from the sound of it. He did not like the furtive, even sly way they eyed him as he drove by. And those gunny sacks: what was in them? Old Ivor's last warning was just as cryptic: "There's bad things underground and bad things in the sky, and folks is stirrin' 'um up."

Was it beer talking—or was there really something to it? He could imagine what the boss would say to any notions of poking around down in the old sewer. Hill shrugged, turned his car around, and cruised slowly south on Harbor Street. He threw Lumpkin and Donald a lazy wave, noted all quiet at Hot 'n' Crusty Pizza, and all dark at the Star Chamber. This Rick Weller—what made him set up shop here? Well, it was his nickel. As he neared the old Apex Mill site, Hill saw some men with sacks standing by the water. One of them, then another threw their sacks into the water. What the hell? The deputy turned on his spotlight and rolled down his window. "What's going on, guys?"

They only glared sullenly.

"You throwin' things in the water?" He got out and turned his flashlight on the group.

One of them stepped forward, a thick, slouchy man with a bullet head and blubbery lips, an individual Hill had always instinctively avoided. Rule Marsh. "We done nothin'," he said, a nasty burr in his voice.

Deputy Hill bristled. "What's in the sacks?"

"Trash."

Crunching gravel, the other patrol car pulled up. Hammers. The sheriff got out and looked Hill sternly in the eye. "What's goin' on here, Deputy?"

"Caught these men dumping things into the bay. Says it's trash."

Sheriff Hammers scowled. "All right. Well, I'm sure Mr. Marsh has a proper explanation."

Rule Marsh grinned nastily at Hill. "Yuh. We was kinda caught short…"

"All right, then," Hammers nodded. "I'll handle this, Hill. You can get on with your rounds."

Hill got into the squad car, heart racing, head shaking. Dumping trash into the bay and these guys walk? It stank. *Mister* Marsh! Hammers came over and leaned in close. "Deputy," he rasped, "I'm gonna tell you again: Lay off the penny-ante stuff. We ain't got the staff or the facilities to run in every damn misdemeanor. Okay?"

He nodded stiffly. "Sir."

Rule Marsh threw him a last, contemptuous leer.

81

Eye To Eye

Rick Weller was pissed. The band was sounding great, summer had brought plenty of tourists in for dinner and jazz, the take had been fat. But now it was September and things were going slack. Now, the complaints came back to haunt him: dingy motels…gas station closed…hooligans on the streets. Damn hick-town yokels, didn't have a pot to piss in and didn't want anyone else to, either. The till wasn't keeping up and he wasn't sure he could pay the band next weekend. He stared again at the numbers. *Shit on a shingle.*

He knew PL would be a tough nut, and so it was. No organized town council, no chamber of commerce, the whole place was just—slippery. Well, he'd seen slippery before. That smell in the office, and other places, now: it was positively evil. And the damn landlord, Marsh, doing nothing but shining him on—"Naw, that's nothin'." Something very *off* about the guy, how on earth did someone like him come to own the building, anyway? The smell was probably mold, a health time bomb ready to explode. He would have to take it to the authorities if he didn't soon get satisfaction. But what would that do to his business?

Weller wanted to succeed, and he wanted his town to succeed. He liked the place, for all its slowness, and loved his home in the woods. He had brought his reluctant wife from the city, be hell to cut and run now.

But there they were, selfish bastards like Marsh, always ready to frustrate anything that might do Port Landsend some good. He remembered something Ralph Donald said. "Sure like to see you succeed, Rick, but this town's got too many secrets, and too many folks who don't like any kind of change, even a place like yours." Good guy, Ralph, and a great jazz fan. Too bad PL didn't have a few more like him. But what did he mean by "secrets?"

Then there were the weird stories coming in: one of the kitchen guys saw boats entering the Chinese tunnel on Harbor Street... screaming fits from the locals involved in some kind of cult-play...and now, of all things, a "creature" living under the city. Weller shook his head. How nuts could you get? No wonder the town was dead on its feet. But he wasn't about to pack it in. Rick Weller was no quitter.

Something scratched the back wall. Weller looked up from his desk. Lately he'd been hearing noises coming from the cellar. Must be working down there—doing what, exactly? Rule Marsh and his bunch...He glimpsed a flicker of movement in the chink between the plywood sheet and the wall. Someone was back there! Weller slipped quietly around his desk, sidled up to the crevice, and peered in. Faint voices muttered.

"Hey!" he yelled. "What's goin' on?"

He heard heavy breathing, the movement of a large body. A gut-churning smell puffed through the crack and something brushed the other side. A cold yellow eye filled the crack and glared at Weller. His heart bucked, once, twice, he jerked back and banged hard on the panel. The eye vanished. Weller took another quick look into the crack, strode to his desk, poured himself three fingers of bourbon, and fished Rule Marsh's number from the drawer.

82

The Hidden Midden

Drip…drip…drip…water fell from the ceiling, a cold wind blew through the tunnel. A flashlight speared the darkness, two figures followed its radiance as they splashed through the shallow water. The water lapped blackly, the slimy walls reeked with an acrid stench, a benighted Acheron. Rule Marsh smiled grimly; it was an odor he savored, knowing what made it, and how he was the one responsible for its existence.

That Weller was pestering him again about it. Damn the man—Marsh had no idea anyone would actually open a nightclub. The place was attracting attention and new people, the last thing he needed, but he had little choice. His uncle's legacy was gone and he needed the money. Well, soon enough there would be no more use for money or other tedious human rubbish. Soon enough, the world would belong to others. As for those stupid enough to come to Port Landsend: maybe some of them would prove useful.

Rule Marsh held the thought and trudged on. He and his nephew came to a chamber and Rule stopped abruptly. "Here," he barked. He pulled a sheaf of crumpled papers from his pocket, and began chanting in guttural dissonance,

"Ya! Ya! Shoggoth! Shoggoth!
Ya! Ya! Shoggoth flanglui!"

He had only a vague idea of what he was saying, but he knew the words carried power—potentially limitless power—and in the stone-girt tunnel his voice was loud and strong. Inhumanly strong. He pulled a short wand from his coat, examined it closely, and dipped it into the liquid then splashed it at the wall. He felt himself getting hard. A good sign, had to be! A dark purple stain on the wall began to jiggle and vibrate. One, two, three quivering lumps of quivering goo separated themselves from the stain and dripped toward the ground. As Marsh chanted louder and more insistently, one of the lumps gave a flatulent pop and began to expand. Within minutes, it was as large as a dog. There was no other resemblance, and even Rule felt a twinge of fear at the rapid, almost obscene increase of the thing. Still, he continued his rasping chant, and the lump jerked and heaved as it pushed against its dull purple skin. Rule burst out in a high, eerie laugh. Where his uncle and great-uncle and grandfather had failed, he would not. This would be a triumph!

Now for a little experiment. His nephew stared dumbly at the lump, and Rule glanced slyly at him. What would Ros say? An accident: she'd gone for that before. The kid had never been worth a shit, anyways. "Look here," Rule barked. The boy shuffled closer and Rule shoved him hard against the throbbing excrescence and held him. "Wha' th' fuck, Rule!" his nephew yelled. He tried to break loose, but the purple blob puffed up and with a rasping hiss burst outward and engulfed his face. "Ahhhh!" he screamed, his voice muffled by the loathsome *material*. The screams died abruptly, and Rule Marsh watched with clinical interest as the thing engulfed the boy's head and shoulders. After a moment, the body of his late nephew gave a final jitter and went limp, and with a nasty squelching sound, the ravening entity released its motionless victim. Two bleeding holes gaped where the eyes had been, only a mass of quivering cartilage left of nose and mouth. *Interesting*, thought Marsh. *Damn interesting*. Yes, his little brood was coming along nicely. He laughed, quietly at first, then in a rising, triumphant howl that echoed far down the cold, black tube.

83

Chained Melody

O*w!* My head throbbed, I was lying on a cold, hard surface, my hands were pinned behind me. I heard faint, muffled mutterings…a scraping sound. This time I was not in the bathtub and I had not been sleep-walking. I almost wished I had, I might have taken care of my assailant. This time, I was wide-awake. I saw objects in the half-light. Boxes. Was that Rick Weller I heard—was I in his basement? Something brown and long-tailed skittered across the floor. I was in the shit.

Distant sounds ebbed and flowed. I figured the muttering was the furtive frog-men pondering my fate. Maybe the Grebe lady was trying to intercede in my favor. Or maybe—Rick? Sure seemed like his voice I heard, just before they whacked me. I thought of him, cackling behind his drums…Ivor's glass eye…Sara's boots…my bass, alone and waiting in the apartment, possibly right above me. Even Lulu got into the act, shoving her insipid melody into my brain. I shook my head, tried to move my hands and get some play in the damn rope. I heard footsteps. The door scraped open and a man stood silhouetted in the doorway. "Well, well," he said, "if it isn't my favorite cocksucker." Crump.

Shirtless and disgustingly obvious, he sauntered over and kicked me hard in the thigh. "So, bitch, what are we gonna do with you?"

I gritted my teeth and considered my options. The bindings were tight but I knew from movies that they could be loosened, given enough time. And time, I also knew from movies, could be bought with talk. "What do you want, Crump?" I growled.

"Want? Nothin' you got." I forced myself to look at his eyes, and saw only dull gray holes.

"Look, Crump," I said, "you're wasting your time over her. There's lots of chicks who'd go for a man like you."

"Fuck you. Think 'cause you're some kind of fucking hotshot musician..."

"That's a laugh! I don't make shit. You probably got more dough than I do..."

Hate is an interesting emotion. We're taught that hate is bad, that we must not hate. Only, at this moment, I hated Crump like I'd never hated anyone. He was a rat bastard bully, a curse on humanity. The world has too many like him. Nevertheless, I had to connect somehow or I was dead. And I wasn't up for that just yet.

"Listen to me, seriously—there's lots of women who'd go for you. You're not bad looking..."

He leaned down close, his breath reeking like he'd been living on candy bars and beer.

"Goin' faggy now, bitch?" He punched me, sucking my wind out. I totally hated him now. *I suppose you know this means war.*

He moved in close. "Okay, asshole, got any last words?"

No comment.

He jerked me to my feet and marched me out the door.

84

Sacrifice—Moi?

Funny, how curiosity can overtake fear. The mind, in denial of clear and present danger, just keeps rolling along. *Isn't this wall texture interesting?* Yeah, good old mind, always there with obscure and irrelevant goodies when you need only to GET THE HELL OUT OF HERE. So far, though, the old noggin wasn't exactly setting the world on fire. No, sir, in this time of crisis, my little gray cells were stuck on "Lulu's Back in Town." Thank you very much.

Where the mind fails, the mouth stands ready. I had to keep Crump distracted, prolong the fun of toying with me. "Quite the setup you got down here, Crump."

No response, he kept propelling me down narrow corridors lit sparsely by bare bulbs. Here and there, mysterious doors broke the brickwork, probably access to the shops along Harbor Street. We turned into a side tunnel and marched up an incline. My mouth tasted like metal, I wanted to puke. He was going to kill me. I would have to fight, fight with all I had, at the right instant. We rounded a corner. "So, fuck-face," Crump croaked, "ever been sacrificed before?"

My guts churned, my head burned at the soul-searing insanity, and I focused my mind on breaking free. "Is this a life, Crump? Living down here like a rat? It's not too late, you can still get a life. Still get a girl who actually wants you. Must be plenty around here…" I kept working the ropes around my hands.

"Too late for you, asshole," he said, punching my head. I coughed and stumbled, he laughed. I strained at the ropes, desperate to catch him off balance and trip him and bash him with my locked hands. He yanked me around a sharp bend and into a small round room lit with a single Coleman lantern. Good old Coleman, for all your camping and torture needs. The Landsend stench hit me full-force, and there they slouched in the far entrance portal: my blorp-blorp buddies, three hunched, gray-skinned, dome-headed beings with dangling web-hands and huge flat feet. They glub-glubbed through drooping lumpy-lipped mouths, dribbling gray-green spit onto the ground. They looked like they were falling apart—had they *deteriorated* since our last encounter? "Okay, guys," Crump growled, "here's your bait."

Come on, rope, give a little, already.

And you know, it did.

Crump came in close and with a nasty glint in his gray eyes slugged me in the gut. My wind exploded and I doubled over. "Like it, cunt?" He and the three others shuffled over to the water and Crump said, "Now, all's I have to do is make a little noise. Hey! Hey-ay-ay-AYYY!" A gray mist wafted from the tunnel mouth, and I heard a faint, sibilant scraping, as of something dragging over a cement floor. Then, splashing. *Cool,* whispered my friend, curiosity, *you're about to see the thing in the tunnel.* Great. *Probably do more than just see it, though, pal.*

The frog-guys glubbed and blorped, Crump gripped me hard, and I dug in, straining at my bindings, getting ready to shove him with my shoulder. The vapors thickened and with an eerie crescendo something appeared in the black aperture. It was—bubbles. Blackish-purple bubbles. A chemical phenomenon, a hallucination—no, a *being,* moving steadily toward us as we stood staring like wax dummies. Even Crump seemed to forget I was there. It crept slowly, squish, squish, and I thought idly that maybe one of the white horned things would come along and pop this sucker. I almost laughed.

"Okay, asshole," Crump giggled—nervously, it sounded like—"here's where you get yours." He grabbed me by the shoulders and shoved me toward the thing. I jerked my arms upward, the rope gave way, and I whirled around and grabbed his wrists with my super-strong bass-playing hands. "Huh!" he grunted—"Fuck you, bitch!" He tried to pull away and I dug in and used his own frantic energy against him, then I kicked out hard and nailed him in the nuts. Crump bellowed in agony and doubled over. We twisted and turned, I let his wrists go, then slipped on the slimy flooring and fell into the channel. By now, though, the blob was no longer in the water. It was on the ledge and slithering and sloshing—toward Crump. Even as he scrabbled frantically, trying to stand, something shot out from the creature and grabbed his leg. "What the fuck!" he shrieked—"NOO!!" That weirdly high, desperate shriek will forever keep Lulu company in my turbulent brain. Crump fell and the thing dragged him relentlessly toward it and—well, how do you like them apples, *bitch?* He didn't, not one bit. White-faced, shrieking in terror, Crump looked at me plaintively, suddenly a new and very different man. "Help me!" he screamed. "HELP ME!"

Well, shit. I clawed up from the trough, grabbed Crump's wrist, and pulled hard. I hope it hurt. "Okay, Crump," I bellowed, "pull free!" I pulled, Crump yanked, and with a loathsome squelch he tumbled away from the beast. He scrambled to his feet, ran back into the side tunnel, and disappeared. "You're welcome!" I yelled after him.

Leaving me to—it. *Interesting shade of purple* was my thought as it narrowed the distance between us. The frog-face guys still stood there gaping like they were watching "Jeopardy," and the grotesque globoid sloshed onward. I shook myself out of my trance and said sayonara to my erstwhile blubbery buddies—"I don't know about you guys, but I'm gone." I followed Crump out the side tunnel, up a steep stairway, and burst through an open door into a sullen twilight. I pushed through tangled underbrush, onto a trail, and ran headlong into Ivor Lumpkin.

85

Dirty Little Secret

rraacckk!! I'd heard of projectile vomiting, but so clinical a term does faint justice to the reality of hurling every atom of a week's stomach contents fifteen feet, and to hell with whatever might lie in its path.

Fortunately, old Ivor knew enough to stand aside. He looked at me intently and soberly. "What'd you see?"

"Gaaacckk!" I gasped, panting and retching. "That thing!"

His eyes widened. "What thing?"

"That big crawling purple blobby thing!"

His eyes narrowed. "Shit. Yuh saw it."

"You've seen it, too?"

"C'mon down here." He led me down a steep trail to a ledge overlooking Point Judson beach, and into a cozy den of driftwood and cardboard.

"Just set down right here and get your breath." He spoke softly, calmly, like a man in control.

"It almost ate Crump…"

"So that's why he was runnin' like all git-out."

"That thing had him! I pulled him out…fucker…"

"Yuh saved Crump's life?"

"I guess…So—what the hell is that thing?"

"Shoggoth," he whispered. "Saw one once, back in '33. Found out later what it was. Didn't make the sight of it any easier. Ol' Carney, he was feedin' the thing. Carney ended up *feedin'* it, all right. God-damnedest thing I ever hope to see."

"Shoggoth? Where—how…?"

"Devil's work! Somethin' from the nether worlds. Them bastards is tryin' to breed 'em."

"Breed them? Why?"

"To use in their devil's work! Bring that thing down again, join forces with 'im."

"Again."

"Tried it once before that I know of, maybe more. Back in '33—oh, they tried, and they almost succeeded."

Shit. Shit, shit, shit. Olin was right. Obed, Unit, Micah—now Rule. And Sara. I slumped down on a log. "The Marshes," I croaked.

"Yup. Been at it 'least as long's I've been here, prob'ly a lot longer. Brung in them shore folk from Polynesia to do their biddin' and make offerings to the devil-gods. I don't mind tellin' you, when I first figured out what they was carryin' inside them sacks, I was plenty scared. Even more scared when I figured out what they was *doin'* with 'em." He gripped my arm hard and rasped unpleasantly into my face. "They was makin' *sacrifices*."

"The dog! Almost fell right on top of us."

"Dogs ain't the least of it. There's folks gone missin' over the years, too, and I got a pretty good idea where they went."

"Human sacrifice."

He nodded grimly.

"And the rest of the town—they don't know?"

Ivor's glass eye skittered weirdly in its socket. "Heh-heh! I reckon most folks *do* know. Truth is, you can't hardly keep anything much secret in a place like Landsend. Fact o' the matter is, most folks go on about their business, don't hardly pay any attention to a little bunch of 'crazies,' as they call 'um. Say they're bats an' be done with it."

"And so, they get away with it…"

"Prob'ly the same the world over. Them as got no family or nothin' here, and some as do, but who ain't all that well-liked, if you get my meanin'." Ivor gave a shrug. "After all, who's gonna miss 'um?"

"How do you know all this?"

"Heh! I may have just the one good eye, but it was good enough to see Carney get et up by that shoggoth. Seen lots more, too. Seen them shut-ins late at night, when nobody else is out—seen 'um go a slouchin' an' a-hoppin'…seen 'um go slippin' into the bay an' not comin' out. Yessir, add 'er all up and…" He gave me an ugly leer, as if daring me to call him crazy.

"Them! They're down there with that--shoggoth. Those little fuckers, they tried to sacrifice me to that goddamn thing!"

His glass eye glinted weirdly. "Well, sir, now you know our dirty little secret."

There are certain things you just don't want to be involved in… Some things I have to do. "Shit! Sara…We've got to do something!"

Ivor leaned in close, clenching my wrist, his good eye terrible in its intensity. "Them folks is lookin' to bring in that very same devil-god they tried back in '33. Damn well pulled 'er off, too. I was watchin' from underneath a skiff and I saw old man Marsh there on the beach screamin' out the gibberish o' Satan—*Ya-ya! Calulu*-something-or-other—and then what come out of a crack in the sky but the devil himself, just like that statue in Percy's shop, a monster abomination sproutin' all over with tennacles, and right smack in the middle the biggest goddamn bulgin' *eye* you could ever imagine."

"Shit, didn't anybody see? How could all this go unnoticed?"

"Hushed it up is what they did! Hushed it up good. Put out that it was a storm—a 'tornado'. Hah! A tornado with a great starin' bloodshod eye and black *tennacles* reachin' down outa the clouds! Old man Marsh, he was fallin' to pieces from all the yellin' an' screechin' tryin' to keep the spell goin', and then Olds come along and shot 'im—shot Marsh down, though to tell the truth, I think he was done for by then. He was startin' to wobble and pitch like demons was in him, which I guess they was. Then that Olds, he shot into that thing and damn if he didn't draw blood! Green blood spurted outa the thing right down on old man Marsh. Must've been terrible acid-like—he started foamin' at the mouth and collapsed into mush. Then the sky closed right up and that damn monsterosity went back where it come from."

Lumpkin caught his breath and shook his head. "Now, we got this Rule Marsh and his kin fixin' to try it again." His eyes glinted darkly. "And holy bald-headed Christ, if that bastard says his prayers right, we're in for one hell of a time."

86

Should I Stay Or Should I Go?

She hated how they all stared at her. Stared like they knew. Which, she guessed, they did. Bastards. As if they knew what they were doing—and what they were getting into. Why, why, why did she let herself get involved? Rule and the cousins were insane, and yet here she was, going right along, la-de-da. Then there was the change. Alone in her room now, staring into the mirror, she knew what her body had been trying to tell her: that strong currents were at war within her, forces that could either lead her to follow Rule and the others, or let her live as she had been living, as a woman of earth, a woman with a man, a woman she loved and felt right with.

She did not want to have to choose between one or the other part of herself. "Why the fuck should I?" she cried, moving to the window and staring out at the bay. "Maybe I don't have to. Who says it's only one or the other? Why can't I be *both*!" She could, she damn well felt it. But not with this other weird bullshit. Spells, gods, monsters—fuck, who needed that? She had to break free of Rule and "family."

She must do it without putting Erich in danger. *You do as I say, or that boyfriend of yours'll be sorry.*

Okay, Rule, I'll do what you say.

I'll also do some other things.

What, exactly, she would have to figure out. She changed into her grubbies and walked to the Kliemann Block, where Rule and the two remaining cousins waited. Without a word, they filed down the narrow spiral staircase to the cellar and continued down a dark passage. God, that smell!

87

Call To Arms

Edward sounded excited to hear from me. Even more excited a moment later, after I'd filled him in on my run-in with the thing in the tunnel. "Edward, I saw it! I mean—I don't know what the hell it was. Not the horned thing, the bones, but something very weird and very dangerous. Ivor Lumpkin called it a 'shoggoth', says the Marsh family have been involved in strange trafficking for years, and they're going to try to call down some kind of cosmic monster-god."

"Wow! Well, I guess things are on the move. Listen, Erich, Victor Lewis has uncovered some new and very disturbing material from someone called Thurston, which describe in disturbing detail encounters with an entity called Cthulhu."

Cthulhu, master of the depths...Ya-ya-Calulu..."Cthulhu! Edward, that's the name Lumpkin said. He said they actually brought him over, in 1933. Ivor Lumpkin saw it happen. And the woman at the bookstore, she knows about him too—says the old gods are going to re-take the Earth. She belongs to the cult!"

"Erich, this is cosmic—and potentially disastrous for mankind. We've got to stop them. We've got to go in there and find that shoggoth-thing."

"Ahh..."

"I know it sounds risky…"

You think?

"…but there's no alternative. If not stopped, God knows what harm it'll do."

"Stop it how?"

"We've got to find it, see what we're up against."

I know what we're up against. "Okay…So, how 'bout you and I and the guys all go in?"

"Now you're talking. I'll get some things together that should protect us. Our safety is paramount, but we'll have to try to get a tissue sample of this thing."

I hung up, tense with excitement. Me and my big mouth. But hell, who doesn't love an adventure, especially when a city is being endangered by a giant purple slug? I popped open a beer and flopped down on the sofa. All too soon, the excitement waned, the beer took hold, and a queasy feeling begin to rile my gut. *Tissue sample?*

88

Belly Of The Beast

"You say it tried to *eat* somebody?" Jeff and Brad stared slack-jawed as I told them about the purple menace lurking beneath Port Landsend.

"Tried and failed."

Brad shrugged. "Oh, well, then..."

"What did you say it was called?" asked Jeff.

"Shoggoth."

"That has a distinctly creepy sound to it."

"The whole thing sounds creepy."

"Which is why we have to go in."

"Your logic escapes me," said Brad, "but logic often does. Let's do it."

"Okay," Jeff nodded, bursting into laughter. "Don't know how I'm gonna write it up in my resume."

I told them about my journey into the tunnel and sleepwalking and hanging out with the frog-guys, and Ivor Lumpkin's tales of sacrifices and bizarre mutations.

"So, the dog was a sacrifice," said Brad.

"Jeez," said Jeff, "to what?"

"I dunno. To Cthulhu, I guess: the 'devil-god' they're going to try to call out, by spells."

They looked at me like I had bats flying out of my mouth.

"And stuff. They did it once before."

"I *thought* this place was haunted!" grinned Brad. "Geez, Jeff, nice gig you found us."

"So," Jeff said, "some people have made some kind of evolutionary jump into a new biological state of—what, frog-people?"

I could only shrug.

Jeff laughed. "Cripes, I'm open to new developments and all that, but, man!"

"Some development," said Brad. "And this shoggoth-thing sounds evil."

"Very," I said. "But hey, Edward says he's got some stuff that will protect us—well, *might* protect us, anyway. But we've got to do this."

They stared at me, looked at each other, and puffed out their cheeks. "Let's do it."

Sunday broke dull and gray, matching our trepidation at what lay ahead. Still groggy, we sat staring into space. No one felt much like eating. The ghostly echoes of last night's "My Honey's Lovin' Arms" still rattled around in head. It all seemed unreal and far away. It even seemed like there were more of the old-young men hanging around the bar, too. Things were closing in.

And now we were going shoggoth-hunting.

Edward rang just after ten, shaking us from our lethargy. We munched and crunched and tromped downstairs. On the trailer behind his well-worn Volvo sat a liberally dented but stout-looking aluminum rowboat. He pulled back a stained canvas tarp to reveal a confidence-inspiring pile of supplies. "I tried to foresee circumstances. We've got grappling hooks, rope, sample box, and fishing poles, to make us look like simple fishermen. I tried to keep things to a minimum." I noticed a thick knife-sheath on his belt, something

I suddenly wished I had. Mister Nice Guy was shit for self-defense. That situation would have to change.

"What if there's more than one?" asked Bradley.

"I've thought of that," said Edward, smiling. He lifted a corner of the tarp, revealing the butt of a shotgun. "And, something else, too." He pulled back the tarp some more, uncovering a stout silver canister with a black rubber hose and nozzle. "A mixture of iron-phosphate and ammonia. Slug-killer and then some. Do *not* get any on you. I have no idea whether it will be effective on this thing or not, but it's one more arrow in the quiver."

Edward drove us slowly to the marina as I described the creature and its movements. We would just be four guys out fishing, row casually up to the tunnel, and slide on in. If someone happened to see us—well, so be it. We pulled into the marina parking lot and I was glad to see two other cars and trailers. We slid the boat into the water and shoved off, I manned the oars while the guys got out the fishing rods and dropped the lines. We drifted slowly along the waterfront toward the tunnel mouth, eyes studying the waterfront and Point Judson. I thought I saw a couple of distant figures looking our way, but maybe I was just being paranoid.

"So," muttered Jeff, "how could we miss these shoggoths? It's crazy—or it's a much bigger world than we realize…"

"It's probably a small and tenuous local phenomenon," Edward replied. I hoped he was right.

"I wonder," said Brad. "Maybe we're entering the next phase of evolution."

"Why not," said Jeff. "It happens, doesn't it? Why shouldn't we expect to see it?" He laughed. "Could actually be kind of exciting."

"Yeah," said Brad, "I've always wanted to be eaten by a shoggoth."

We approached the hole in the seawall, saw no nearby watchers. "Ready, gentlemen?" Edward said quietly. We nodded somberly, hunched down into the boat, and with a few firm strokes I rowed us into darkness. We put on our headlights and Edward pulled out a large flashlight and played it on the arching walls. The water was black and calm, the tunnel silent as a tomb.

We passed the familiar rectangular recess—"Jack's door," I said quietly—and arrived at the junction. "Here's where the tunnels branch," I said. "The one on the right goes into the cistern, where I saw the altar-thing."

Hmmm. From somewhere in the murky blackness came a faint hint of tone. Four pairs of eyes peered intently ahead. Again, louder. Voices, melded with something more obscure. "The shore people chant," I whispered. "Must be in the cistern, at the altar."

"Fascinating," whispered Edward.

"That's what we heard that day," said Brad.

Away down the side tunnel, light flickered dimly beyond the portal to the cistern. "All right, my friends," Edward said in a low voice, "I suggest we move in slowly. Erich, you might swing us around in case we need to make a fast getaway."

I oared us about and Edward peeled back the tarp, picked up the two grappling hooks and set them on the floor of the boat. He extracted a roll of duct tape and fastened a small cylinder to the longer shaft, just behind the hook. "Specimen tube," he said, with a brief smile. He removed the shotgun, cracked open the magazine, inserted two shells, closed the barrel, and slung it over his shoulder. Then he hefted the slug-killer canister astern. "I'll take the hose," he said. "Jeff and Bradley, would you mind manning the hooks? Let's hope a good jab or two will hold it off and give us our tissue sample at the same time." Edward asked me to push the boat slowly and silently back toward the wan light. I could almost hear our hearts beating in the tight bore.

Far down the tube something made a hissing sound. A dark form emerged from the murk; it looked like a bundle of black balloons and stank like a dead whale. "Shit," I whispered, "there it is." I yarded back hard on the oars. The thing wobbled and grew steadily larger, a black but eerily iridescent lump.

Brad grabbed the long pole with the specimen tube on the end, Jeff gripped the shorter one and crouched, catlike. We gagged at the sight and the stench of the pustulant horror bearing down on us. "Hold up, Erich," Edward said, his voice coolly reassuring, "let it get closer." Staring grimly at the thing, he clenched the hose, ready to spray his toxic potion. The creature didn't swim so much as heave itself awkwardly through the water, as if partly pushing itself on the bottom. The globular protrusions seemed to throb independently of one another, and a low hissing sound emanated from the beast. "Amazing," said Jeff, "it almost looks…" *Bang*, it was on us! Edward fired off a succession of flash photos, giving us micro-second visions of a nightmarish congeries of purple blobs. "Now, Brad!" he yelled.

Bradley jabbed hard and the hook and specimen tube went into the thing with a sickening *plorp*! The hissing increased and a nasty green pus spewed from the wound, I pulled the oars for all I was worth, but the monster pushed harder. Then my stomach lurched as I saw a thick, slimy tentacle twining up from the black water. "Look out!" I yelled, pointing. I watched in slow-motion horror as it reached into the boat and wrapped itself around Edward's foot.

"Damn!" he yelled. He handed me the camera then turned the spray can nozzle at the beast and released a jet of green foam. The shoggoth hissed sharply but held fast. Edward kept spraying, but with startling swiftness the monster yanked him to the side of the boat and sucked his foot into its shuddering mass.

"Quick, Erich," he gasped, "the rope!" I slipped the noose over Edward's head and around his waist, even as the shoggoth began drawing him in. I stood up and beat the goddamn thing with my oar, but it only bounced off the rubbery globules. "Okay, Erich," Edward yelled, "pull back, hard. Jeff, Brad, keep hold of this rope. Don't panic, just pull and get me out of this thing."

I yarded desperately on the oars, Edward kicked and kicked, all the while spraying. "You're getting it, I feel it weakening! I think the solution's working. Pull!" With a loathsome *Pwack!* Edward's foot wrenched free. He tumbled back on us and I rowed with mindless fury. The thing gave a sharp rasping grunt—had yanking Edward out actually hurt it? Leaving the monster sizzling and stewing, we shot from the tunnel panting and high on adrenaline. Spent, I yelled at Jeff to take the oars, and we pulled for the marina. An ugly glint of purple flashed at the tunnel mouth—the shoggoth was following! No—it thrust out a tentacle, then quickly withdrew into the tunnel.

"It's gone!" Brad exclaimed.

"Ultra-violet-sensitive, maybe?" said Jeff.

Something sour pushed up my gullet, the horizon whirled, and I leaned over the gunnel and generously sacrificed everything I'd eaten for the past two days to whatever lurked in Port Landsend bay. I hoped they'd choke on it.

"Wow," said Jeff, "that was…"

Green-faced, Brad simply shook his head.

"I wonder how many live in there…"

"Not many, I suspect," said Edward. "Maybe just the one. It may represent a sort of beachhead of the species."

"Can't help but almost feel rather sorry for the thing," said Jeff. "A specialized organism requiring very specific environmental conditions." He stared intently into the tunnel. "Conditions *someone* apparently managed to create."

"Indeed," Edward concurred. "This will have to be investigated by the proper authorities. That thing is too dangerous to be left alone. It—or they—will require monitoring."

"Ivor's doing that," I said. "I'll keep him company."

"So," said Brad, "do we tell just anybody, or…?"

"Gentlemen," said Edward, gravely, "of course, I can't keep anyone from talking. I can't suggest that we not tell the press or publish what might be a ground-breaking account of this." He shook his head. "Whatever 'this' may turn out to be…"

"Jesus," I muttered, "I wonder if they were sacrificing to that thing in there."

"Sara and Ivor think the local police already know," I said, "and possibly don't give a shit."

"So, this becomes a matter for wider investigation," said Edward. "Erich, see if you and your friend can learn about this latest occurrence, and if anyone has been reported missing. We can't let that go by. The implications are grim, to say the least. Meantime, at least we'll have photos to study."

"And that." I pointed to a flap of rubbery purple stuff dangling from Edward's shoe.

"Well, well," he exclaimed, "gentlemen, we have our tissue sample."

89

Dangerous Liason

Wind whistled down Harbor Street, rain poured, the yellow traffic signal swung back and forth. Cold, alone, empty. I headed upstairs, dried my head, hefted my little clay buddy, and sat on the sofa gazing dumbly out on the Harbor Street intersection and beyond to the dark waters of the bay. Hunched figures slouched into the deluge and disappeared. The guys were a thousand miles away, Sara a million. The bass lay on its side. I thought about taking it and serenading her under her window. Instead, I grabbed the jug and took a nice, warm swallow. *Chickenshit.*

Not hardly: We found the damn shoggoth, we faced it down, we escaped, tissue sample and all. Then—nothing. Not even a nocturnal somnambulation. It was as if something simply vacated my brain. A welcome relief. Only, what about that thing in the sewer? A week passed, I did my work and heard nothing behind Jack's mystery door, then came Friday and music, with its own peculiar appetites. It was fun playing that night, joshing with Rick (who seemed oddly preoccupied), talking about the old days of music with Danny, and sharing our secret with Brad and Jeff. What now?

Halloween. The night hadn't meant much to me since childhood, but now I wanted to carve pumpkins with Sara and put on something weird and spend a spooky night together. But no. I hoped she had some psychic sense of my misery. *Sara*, I whispered, as I stroked the viol, *Sara...come back.*

But there was another.

Arla. *Come out with me sometime.* I took a swig. *We can walk by the water.* Okay.

I put the jug down, bundled up, and slipped into the night. Past the Grebe, the Town Tavern, the United Wharf, into a dark stretch. More people scurried by, a lot for a rainy October night. Then, before I saw her, I felt her eyes boring into me from the shadows.

"Hello."

"Arla."

I joined her in the shelter of an alcove. "Well, what brings you out on this miserable night?" Her electric blue eyes made my spine tingle.

"You." I stopped an inch away.

"Ahh," she purred. White teeth flashed, fingertips with long, pointed nails brushed my chest. "Come." She took my arm and led me, head spinning, into a nearby doorway. Smiling, she pressed herself closely to me and planted her mouth on mine. We kissed, our bodies heaving and writhing against each other. "So young," she murmured, "so lovely. Yes, my human—my new—friend. Sex is good, don't you think?

Human? Was she crazy? Well hey, in this particular instance, crazy seemed to work fine.

She took my hand and led me through the door and into a familiar corridor lit by dim bulbs. *Christ—here again!* I felt a shiver—would she suddenly wheel around and sink her canines into my neck?—but I followed dumbly. Every step, every look at her moving figure, every whiff of her salty-spicy scent, made me want her desperately. She led me into a small, empty room, probably a basement of one of the empty Harbor Street buildings, and pulled me to her. "Erich, Erich," she purred, "what are we going to do with you?"

"This." I took her in my arms and kissed her.

We savored the lip-lock a long moment, then she abruptly pulled back. "Now, now," she said, her eyes going black. "You've been a very curious boy, Erich. A pity, too; you're such a lovely specimen."

Specimen?

I looked into her eyes and saw—nothing. And everything. I was stuck in a basement with a nutjob. Again. I let my eyes casually drift up and down the corridor. Her tongue flicked. "Don't think of running, Erich. It wouldn't be polite." She enveloped me, clenched her pointy nails into my back. Even through our clothes I felt it: clammy, soul-freezing *cold*.

All desire had fled, I felt only rising revulsion. "Arla, you're very beautiful. But I belong to someone else."

"No, Erich," she smiled, "you belong to me." Her eyes turned—darker, somehow. And then I smelled it: the alluring aroma of salt air and incense had given way to the stench of an open grave. Nostrils burning, guts churning, I wrenched free of her and ran.

90

The Subterraneans

Down the stinking tube again. One weird labyrinth we had here, and for what? Smuggling, maybe—but smuggling what, exactly? I flashed on dark times, when human beings were treated like commodities. We were beyond all that now, weren't we?

I stopped and listened and heard nothing more than my heart pounding. Arla was back there, I felt her black eyes and blacker soul reaching toward me. She was insane, obviously, but something more—something of pure evil. I ran on and came to a side-aisle; it looked familiar and I thought there was an exit close by. Distant sounds and noxious odors came and went, I couldn't get my bearings. Was I running in circles? I trotted on, rounded a corner, and there they stood. And in the feeble incandescent light I at last came face to face with the truth. I cursed the truth and I cursed the light, for in that ghastly ocherous crepuscule stood what I had been unable to see in my previous encounters: men—maybe—but men with bloated, batrachian lips, and beneath their hoods the unmistakable movement of gills, opening and closing and wheezing, *glub, glub, glub*. At last, I stood, wide-awake, before the midnight hoppers.

My head swam, my vision blurred, I stood staring at eyes that stared back unblinking. Suddenly, there she was, terrible in that arched doorway, terrible and magnificent. Arla. "Erich, don't fight us. Join us." She held out her arms. I was almost touched. But I was more terrified. I wheeled around and bolted down the side-aisle. Behind me, she rasped furiously, "Catch him! Kill him!"

A novel feeling, hearing somebody say that about you. And in another time, I might ponder the existential and eschatological implications of Arla's ejaculation. At this particular time, however, I was more focused on the foul grunting and shuffling that told me the gasping groupers were hot on my tail. At least, as hot as they could be, hopping and shambling out of water. I was glad for their sluggishness and for the scattered few light bulbs, but my spirits sagged as I made one turn then another and saw nothing ahead but more tunnel. The town couldn't be that big—unless of course I had stumbled into some other dimension. That, too, I filed away for later consideration, and I run on, and suddenly there was the faint outline of a door. I jerked it open and burst into the alley just down from Jack's warehouse. Free!

I ran into Gribble Street and turned up toward Harbor. My boots thudded hard on the boardwalk, then went out from under me on the rain-slick wood and dumped me flat on my back. With a sickening crack, the rotted planks gave way and down I went. Splash! Back in the tunnel. Swell. I thrashed to my feet and stood on tiptoe and tried to grab for the opening just overhead, and just out of reach. I sloshed down the tunnel, rain water from the street drains spitting down on me. From far down came ominous shuffling and muttering sounds. Arla and her friends. I dashed on, hoping to get back to the door, and the sound got louder—but instead of voices I heard a hideous hissing and smelled an almighty stink. Shoggoth!

I charged down the brick tube searching desperately in the almost non-existent light for the door, not daring to look back. I knew damn well what was on my ass, and it sounded like it was gaining. On I stumbled through the fetid trough, hoping the horror behind me would lose interest. Where was that damn door? Then I saw something that stopped my heart: a metal grill across the tunnel! *Grunt—hissss!* The thing on my tail was getting dangerously close. I yanked on the grill, but it held fast. Then I saw that it stopped a couple of feet above the floor. Thank you, Unit Marsh! I flopped down and slid beneath it just in time.

Splorf! The hurtling shoggoth plowed into the grill, letting the mother of all farts, and I was safe on the other side of the barrier. With a blasting sigh, it heaved back from the grill and stopped, as if considering its options. Shit—could it compress and squeeze under the gap? It made no further move. I stared in morbid fascination at my nemesis, its ghastly globules pulsating as if about to either implode or explode. I wondered if anyone had ever tried to communicate with it. Perhaps I would be the first: "So, Shoggie," I said, "what's your story? Where do you come from? What do you want from us?" The beast kept its thoughts to itself. I hoped it would tire of hanging out with me and leave, but there it stayed, like a gigantic cow-patty and smelling worse. Was I face-to-face with Man's evolutionary future, or was this an advance guard for our conquerors?

Answers were not forthcoming, so I turned and considered my next move. Before me now gaped a hole half the size of the tunnel, just big enough to crawl through. Where did it go? Anywhere but back to the shoggoth, thank you. I crouched and entered, and was glad to see dim pools of light from overhead storm drains. Grateful also for the lubrication of rain water and algae, I shinned forward to the first drain and pushed hard on the outside grate. It refused to budge. The next one was no more yielding, and then the drains gave out and ahead lay only blackness. On I crawled, toward the inevitable end. Would the tube dump me in the bay, fresh meat for sea lions, or deposit me in some more obscure receptacle?

I crawled on, despairing of a lingering death in a metal pipe. Blackness surrounded me, the water was cold, the air fetid. But everything leads somewhere—I believed it, stoutly. Still do. *This thing can't go on forever,* I told myself. A few more feet, and I shot downward, tumbled into open air, and plunged into icy water.

91

Festival

poosh! I clawed from the depths and surfaced in a vast and shadowy room. Scattered lights flickered through a thick haze, walls curved away on either side of me. The cistern! My clothes kept trying to drag me down, but I made it to the near side and climbed up on the ledge that surrounded the tank. Crouching against the clammy concrete, I shook the water out of my boots and peered into the murk.

Dim figures lined the far wall, and I was glad that none seemed to notice my sudden arrival, but were instead focused on two figures standing at the altar I'd seen before. Beside them, a brazier emitted gouts of noxious smoke. Here and there I picked out familiar faces: the guy from the service station…several Town Tavern and Star Chamber regulars…the marina man…the little creep from the Marsh mansion. All was quiet. Then, a faint, ragged voice began croaking that macabre and all-too familiar mantra—

> *Ya! Ya! Nyarlathotep!*
> *Yog-sothoth! Yog-sothoth!*
> *Ya! Ya! Cthulhu fthagan!*
> *Cthulhu fanaglui!*

The crowd took up the chant, muttering and braying and rending the incantation even more distorted. I heard in the cacophony undertones of slushy slobbering, and saw the source of that loathsome vocalise, that same spine-chilling sound I heard from the apartment, and now beheld the batrachian faces, with drooping lips and bulging eyes and throbbing gills, of those nameless, landless "shut-ins" that I had twice eluded and that Ivor Lumpkin had so eloquently described—shut-in no longer.

Something splashed, I saw sleek forms darting through the water, forms finned and webbed and horned, forms that glared with yellow eyes—forms that could only be the kin of the mystery bones, bones now flesh and blood and life. I didn't scream, I didn't faint, I didn't feel anything, only oddly detached, thinking almost clinically that this was *supposed* to happen. This was what the dreams had been preparing me for.

I hunched close against the wall, hoping to remain inconspicuous, but no one seemed to pay me any notice. All eyes were locked on the two figures at the altar chanting those noxious verses, over and over. I could barely make them out through the smoke and jostling bodies. At last, I saw a glint of shining black hair, a body erect, stately.

Arla.

No—Sara.

I couldn't see her face clearly, she moved slowly, stiffly, as if reluctant. Then, the stout, bullet-headed man next to her stepped in front of her, held up a large container and poured liquid onto the altar: Rule Marsh, the one responsible for this insanity. For insanity it was; insanity, it could only have been, that now drove many of the assembled to fling themselves at the altar and rub the fluid on their foreheads—then leap into the vast pool and meet the Water-Beings, and in an explosion of barking and howling *join* with them. Now, too, the frog-like hybrids hopped into their native element and vanished beneath the surface. I could only gape in amazement at the idea of inhabiting two different worlds. Oh, well, I still had my dreams—if the last few days didn't cure me of that once and for all.

The smoke burned my eyes, the stench seared my lungs, and the sight of Sara made me want to run to her. I wondered if she had been drugged or hypnotized. Another familiar face near the back of the horde looked my way—the Grebe lady. She walked coolly over, a serene expression on her handsome face, and gestured at the frolicking swimmers. "The Water Beings," she said, neck slits on her neck opening and closing. "Aren't they magnificent! They have made the change, some of them many generations ago, and some even now. You're very privileged to bear witness to a great evolution."

Stunned into wordlessness, I could only nod robotically. The howling chant reverberated around the tank and forced me to hunker down on that slimy ledge and cover my ears. The smoke, the flickering lights, the maniacal braying—it was a mass psychosis that conjured the obscene depths of twentieth-century hysteria, when crowds bayed at the moon and burned books and followed lunatics into chaos.

Abruptly, Sara and Rule ceased chanting and walked away from the altar and through the far portal. The crowd fell silent and followed in an orderly line. The water creatures disappeared through some underwater egress, the black surface stilled, and in another moment the cistern was empty. I stared into the void in disbelief. Nothing was real, only me, the swirling mist, the curving walls fading to black. I was wrung-out and blown away, but oddly at peace. Well, whatever happens, happens, right? Sara— she had to know what she was doing. She'd explain it to me, soon. I hoped.

A chilling thought hit me: where was that shoggoth? I looked around and saw that the big metal gate had been closed over the tunnel portal. Necessary, of course, to contain rain water—and to keep Mister Shoggie from crashing the party. I suspected that particular guest would find itself unwelcome even by this bunch. But what of other possible ways in? I listened closely but heard no hissing, no grunting, only the faint sigh of a vast, empty room. Still...I scuttled to the egress and passed into the night.

92

Cthulhu's Back In Town

All human history is a weird tale. You think you've seen and heard and read and imagined it all. Not even hardly. No, we're mere baby steps along the path of our evolutionary potential. I've been fortunate, if you could call it that, to receive certain hints at what may yet be. But then is not now, and now I was staring into the face of madness.

I slipped through the portal, down a narrow passage, and out into a stygian midnight. The rain had stopped, the night clouds hung down like a dingy moth-eaten canopy. The people stood scattered along the beach where Sara and I had gone swimming, and I saw a long line of figures filing over from Point Judson: the shore people contingent, solemn, almost processional. The Water Beings cavorted in the little cove, while two stiff figures surveyed the scene from the nearby street end. The cops. So, the whole town *was* in on it.

Far down at the water's edge, Sara and Rule faced the crowd. I saw him open his mouth, speak to her, saw her say nothing, just stare rigidly ahead. Rule turned, raised his arms high over his head, and resumed the chant, his voice thin in the cool air, his arms rhythmically rising and falling. The others joined in sinister synchronicity, throwing up an unholy curtain of sound. Standing apart from the rest, the shore people moved their arms furiously and howled in guttural unison, the massed voices crescendoed to a blasting roar, repeating again and again, *Ya! Ya! Cthulhu fathagn! Ya! Ya! Cthulhu fanglui!*

I was just beginning to wonder what the point of it all was when the breeze quickened, the water ruffled, and a faint, throbbing hum rose as if from deep underground. An earthquake, or one of the great Cascadian volcanoes erupting? No, the land held its peace. The throbbing hung in middle air and was joined by a rising, rampaging roar impossible to imagine as anything other than the croaking of a million bullfrogs. The sky growled, lumpen blobs sagged from the lowering clouds, and with an ear-searing *rip*, a funnel cloud dropped. A tornado! I looked again—and may I never again see in my addled brain what I saw then, for no sane and rational constituent of twentieth-century America could conjure it—*a tornado with a great starin' bloodshod eye and black tennacles reachin' down outa the clouds!*

It was a ghastly parody of alien life such as some morbid teen might draw: a bloated gray-green mollusk-thing fringed with flapping tentacles, small batlike wings, and surmounted by a purple starfish head with an enormous eye glaring from the center. The Arkham effigy, the idol in the barber shop, incarnate! The eye winked between dim and bright and the thing seemed to go in and out of focus, as if phase-shifting between dimensions, a sulfurous stench filled the air, the bile of another universe suddenly opened. The hovering horror swelled until it blotted out the sky, then abruptly swooped rasping from the sky, tentacles flailing.

All the nightmares, daymares, doubts and delusions, the self-hatred and fetid fantasy and womb memories crowded in, the sky receded, the universe itself faded into irrelevance as the *immediate* swelled into obscene immensity, howling to efface and expunge all previous conceptions of existence, blasting its new reality into every nook, cranny, and orifice of human construction with the charnel stench of a thousand elephant farts, and proclaiming in a belching bellow of naked primal evil,

You belong to me!

The crowd sundered, some frozen in place, others bolting in shrieking, wide-eyed terror, many sustaining the demoniac chant, some laughing hysterically even as they were swept up by the thrashing tentacles! Flailing figures dropped into the bay, others vanished into the pustulant, expanding mass. The shore people stood firm, even as some among them were snatched and ingested by the very thing they were worshipping, and some ran into the water and joined the Water Beings, willing sacrifices to the ravening cult.

I did what any rational red-blooded modern American male would have done: I ran as far as I could into the bushes and heaved my guts into next Tuesday. But I couldn't run away from Sara. After I was thoroughly wrung out, I peered through the branches and tried to see her amid the swirling, panicking mob. *God, don't let that thing get her!* She stood, arms down, facing Rule and shaking her head and looking ready to split. Two of Sara's cousins did bolt, Rule yelled at them and continued in his bizarre obeisance. Sara ducked as a tentacle swept close overhead, I yelled "Sara! Run!" but my voice was lost in the chaos. I ached to dash to her and take her to shelter, but something held me rooted, some dumb inertia that I was momentarily powerless to overcome. Sara knew what she was doing, didn't she? She would resent me for butting in, wouldn't she? Chickenshit.

Aching to do something, I wished for a fire engine loaded with some of Edward's patented shoggoth repellent to blast at the goddamn thing— this jittering, gibbering, giant space turd—profaning our sacred human soil. Oblivious to my concerns, the bloated berserker whirred and flapped and moved as if to engulf the whole town, rasping to high heaven as its terrible protuberances probed for more victims. Sickly purple-gray light washed over the city, time stopped, the thing held its small patch of Earth in possession, as if staking a claim for a vast and diabolical new race. Oh, the irony.

But not for long. As the shattering cosmic horror of it all began to sink in, the crowd disintegrated and the chant faltered, the spell broke, and the monster trembled and flickered, a gargantuan Halloween toy. Sara gestured skyward with raised fist and screamed, Rule rushed at her but she pushed him away, he raised his arms again, but now the purple light darkened, the wings shriveled and the tentacles withdrew, and the great trans-dimensional apparition faded back into the clouds, even as the last flailing tentacle swept a still-howling Rule Marsh into the disappearing horror. With a rasping shriek, the thing from beyond was swallowed by the pitiless sky.

93

Star Dust

"Whoa," said a voice, "that was trippy."

"Fuck...fuck..." whispered another.

Figures stood slack-jawed in the purple dark, paralyzed by the unreality of it. Some wept hysterically, some giggled nervously. Count me among the slack-jawed. The shock still vibrated through my shivering body. Had I really seen *that*?

The Grebe lady walked serenely toward me and nodded approvingly: "Great Cthulhu has received the sacrifice. And he is pleased."

Glad to hear it.

What could I even begin to tell the guys? Edward! I wished I had some way to reach him.

Then, Sara, pale and frazzle-haired and sweaty. I took her in my arms. "Jeez," I croaked, "are you okay?"

"Yeah." She shook violently, her chest heaved. "All things considered."

"I wanted to come get you—I couldn't...I'm..."

"No, sweetie, I'm glad you didn't."

"Rule..."

"I tried to warn him."

"Was that really--?"

She nodded slowly. "Really. But it couldn't hold. Rule fucked up. With a little help from me. And Olin."

"Olin."

"Right here."

The old man loomed up wraithlike, but smiling. "I am sorry, Erich, but we had to move stealthily."

Sara smiled wanly up at her great-uncle. "Olin and I...worked it out..."

"You might say we rendered the spell impotent—used the *Necronomicon* to turn that—energy—back to where it belonged."

"How in hell...?"

"Just a few little tricks the old man on Ponape and our mutual friend Ka'atah'teh showed me. They haven't kept these things locked up for nothing." Olin chuckled with quiet relief. "Well, I guess I really have seen everything."

I kissed Sara. "Sorry about Rule."

"Don't be. He knew what he was getting into."

"Man, once this gets out...reporters, the feds...We'll probably all be quarantined or something."

Sara squeezed me tight, looked into my eyes. "Erich, it can't get out."

"But, how can it not? Everybody saw it."

"Yeah, well, maybe they'll get some attention, and maybe some people will come here to see what it was all about. But they won't find anything. And then, people will just forget." She stared into my eyes and I felt the radiance of telepathic energy. "If reporters or the FBI or whoever actually come here, they'll talk to people and decide we're all crazy."

I could only shrug. I know what I saw. I know what happened. Oh, well. Chalk it up to a freak of nature. The unexplainable. File it under Area 51.

We walked slowly toward town, following the fast-dissipating crowd. On the nearby bluff, two dark forms stood: Olin and Ka'atah'teh, stern sentinels of time immemorial, standing watch over fractious, frivolous, dangerous Man. They hardly looked real, if real they were. But did I see the faintest trace of smiles on their lips? Olin gave a small wave, then they turned and walked away together.

"Sara?" And uncharacteristically sheepish-looking Ivor Lumpkin stepped up. "I might as well get right to it. Sara—uhh—the long and short of it is, as the trambone player said—I'm your dad."

Sara stared at him dumfounded. "My..."

"Your ma—Rebecca. She was my wife. Then she changed over. We didn't have near enough time together."

"Ohhh...So that means I..."

He shook his head slowly.

"I won't make the change?"

"I don't think so. I don't think you got enough of that in you."

"You seem to know a lot about me."

"Been keepin' watch over you right along. Your ma made me promise."

"What happened to her?"

Ivor frowned. "Kilt. Some bad actors mixed it up and she got in the middle of it."

"I'm sorry—Dad."

Ivor stared at his shoes. "She was a good woman. Good all 'round." Ivor cleared his throat and looked at Sara, shaking his head. "It's me who's sorry. Sorry I couldn't be a dad to you, Sara, didn't know how. Maybe I was just too brung down by losin' Rebecca. Felt lost...all shook up." He began crying softly. "Instead o' bein' your dad, I took to the damn bottle. Wish I could've done better by you..."

Sara touched his shoulder. "It's past now. Now, we're together."

A figure moved ghostlike out of the dark and approached us. I could barely whisper, "Hello, Arla." She looked larger than before. Had I actually desired her, not even an hour ago?

She smiled frostily. "Well, Erich, you witnessed the visitation."

"Is that what this was?"

"Let us simply call it an introduction." She focused her black eyes on Sara. "And you, my dear: that was quite a show you put on."

Sara glared back. "It was no show. Whatever it was, it's over."

Arla laughed nastily. "Do you think so? Do you think your puny bungling will stop us?"

"Stop you, from what?"

"Let's just say investment opportunities."

"Investment opportunities."

"Real estate, Erich!" She opened her arms wide. "All of this! And souls, so many lost souls. What have your earthly gods, your tired, moth-eaten religions brought you? Misery, poverty, war...Man is full of desperation—he wants more. And more, we've got."

"'We'? What, you and your little cult?"

She glared contemptuously at me. "You have no idea! We ruled the universe when your earth was a speck of dust. We will rule again, and man will serve us. *You* will serve us!"

"Not fucking likely," Sara snapped. "The spell won't work. He—*it*—can't hold together here."

"Ah, but we will hold together, and hold fast!" She laughed hysterically, her features seeming to vibrate and move around her face—in fact, her face looked oddly bloated now, as if swollen by hysteria. "Man is so weak, so pitiful. What is inevitable cannot be stopped. Cthulhu! Yog-Sothoth! Azathoth! The Great Ones will reign again, forever!"

"The hell they will!" Ivor's one eye glinted eerily "For the good of mankind them things has been locked up, and locked up is where they'll stay!"

"Silly little man," Arla hissed.

"I'll show you silly." Ivor pulled his hand from his pocket and blew a cloud of gray dust in her face.

"Aaaahhh!!" she shrieked. "Fool!" She erupted in a fit of violent coughing and retching

"Well," said Ivor, grinning, "guess these star stones work."

A lightbulb went on in my brain. "Stars! Like in the Star Chamber?"

"Yup. Percy, he wised me up on a lot of things, these stones bein' one of 'em." He kept his eye on Arla as she staggered wildly, gagging and foaming at the mouth.

Ralph stepped from behind him. "Glad to see you're okay, Erich."

"Ralph! You and Ivor...?"

"Yep, me an' Lump. Couldn't let 'em get away with it. Not here in PL."

Arla got a grip and stood up straight and terrible. "Well," she said, her voice a sepulchral parody of its former self, "isn't that touching. It seems I've been found out."

"And who would that be?" I asked.

Her body rattled and shook, her face contorted, her cloak fell away and her dress ripped open, and from the beneath the tattered fabric glared a great, red-veined eye. With the hand I once kissed, she ripped the shreds away, and a thicket of stubby undulating tentacles thrust forth. As her body swelled, her eyes, all three of them, blazed hotly at me. "My name isn't important. People have called me many things, some complimentary, some not. I've been called Circe...Jezebel...Chaos...Others call me Nyarlathotep."

Eyes ablaze with evil, she shuddered and groaned. "Ugghh! This human form...so... confining!" We pulled back, narrowly avoiding her grasping appendages, and with a sulfurous and most unladylike fart the creature rose clumsily into the air. Leathery brown wings popped out and the erstwhile Arla—now a nauseating cross between a giant sea anemone and a bat—screamed, "Aagghh! You—you—humaaiii—*ai-g'nnghth rnmthnsh rrlllll!*" With an eldritch shriek as from a million ravening harpies, the stinking abomination which I had only an hour earlier held in my arms vanished in a blinding blue flash.

94

Hey, Ho, The Wind And The Rain

D rip, drip, drip. My little life, one more raindrop in the sea.
It was all more than passing strange. So, what else is new?
Always the self-pitier, even with my honey beside me.

Her eyes popped open. I'll never get used to that.

"So," I murmured, "were we mass-hallucinating or what?"

"No, my sweet, it was quite real. Rule had some crazy power fantasy.
Poor dumb Eck, my cousin, he got the shit, and Rule just kept right on…"

"It actually worked, didn't it? He actually called that thing out."

"So, which one was it?"

"Cthulhu. I think…"

"Wonder how it would have gone if everybody had been together."

"I wasn't going to let that happen. I started off like Rule said to. But
then it all got crazy, and like, I'm going to remember all those weird spells?
No way! I followed what Olin said, and started saying a bunch of jibberish,
and then I freaked out of my head when that goddamn monster showed
up. I thought we were going to just say some stupid spells and go home!"

She snorted into my chest—"God, it was funny, like, some were saying
'Cthulhu' and some were saying 'Lulu', and some 'Yog-Sothoth'. And the
best part was, where it should have been 'Ee-aa, ee-aa, Rule was saying

'Ya-ya'. It actually makes a difference, but I didn't tell him. He always said he hated know-it-alls."

She twirled her hair and eyed me slyly. "So, what about you and little Miss Arlathop?"

"Oh, it was nothing. She dropped in to the club—guess maybe she kind of fell for me."

"You came on to her."

"She came on to me! But we never did anything. I told her I was a flake, had no future…"

"You better!"

In the middle of a long kiss I felt a tremor. "Shit, what about the shoggoth? It's probably still down there."

"We have to kill it. We can use the star stones like Ivor—Dad—did on your girlfriend. That's what Rule did."

"You saw him?"

"No, but he bragged about it. Said he could control the things, make them do what he wanted. I think he had it kill my cousin."

"The guys and I went in the tunnel after it."

"No way!"

"Almost got us, too, but we sprayed some heavy shit on it and I think it worked—sort of."

"Erich Vann, you're just full of surprises."

"So," I let a moment go by then asked, "are you sad you won't be changing?"

"Not really. I just sort of thought—it might have been—oh, I don't know." She shook her head. "Yes, I do." She took my hands in hers and gripped them tight. "I know what I want, Erich. I want you. I want us to be together. Always. Here, there, or anywhere we want."

And so, we were.

Where does the spirit lie? In the air, the water, the land, or the fifth dimension? I've never been much for existentialist navel-gazing. As far as

I'm concerned, it lies in each of us. There, my trite truism for the day. I had Sara and she had me, there's spirit enough for a lifetime.

Great Cthulhu came, but Sara sent him home. For now, at least. And so, we mind our little earthly business and try to feel bigger than we really are: a voice from Heaven, a godly finger, a golden egg, little two-legged joker. And so, fool that I am, hold out hope that a new world *is* coming. Far off, perhaps, centuries away, yet sure to come. A time when Man—the new Man—and their world will be in balance. When, as the Grebe lady said (and she and I have come to laugh over our little secret), we are at last one with nature and not her enemy, and move in naked beauty between land and water. Torment, torque, agony, entropy, ennui: life—fair, foul, fickle—surrounds us, biding her time, ready to suck us in, here and in a million other quiet backwaters and frozen wastes and sunken islands and fetid swamps and slimy sewers and suburban bedrooms the world over. So, keep smiling.

For days I scanned the Seacoma papers for word of the occurrence at Port Landsend. I found nothing. Somebody or bodies had drawn the invisible veil over it. And that's just as well. Curiosity and man's capacity for mischief-making being what they are, you have to figure that the creepy-crawlies will keep on keeping on. Old PL isn't out of the woods, nor are the rest of us.

Against all predictions, Rick's club not only survived but thrived. I think he made some good connections—and learned about the power of the star stones when it was time to take on the shoggoth. Worked just like Sara said—I almost felt sorry for the poor thing. I hope it was the only one. The guys and I still play there once a month. I told them about the great visitation; I hate secrets so I had to, but I'm not sure if they fully grasp it. Not sure I do, either. I'm just glad to have music. I've found some locals to jam with—old Ralph, for one, a hell of a sax player and a gas to drink beer with and talk about PL's dark side—and a couple of the younger Star Chambers regulars, good gobs once you get past their bulging eyes and blubbery lips and "different" voices. One plays guitar in a startlingly original way and the other sings—well, sort of sings—and I'm digging it totally. Look out, world.

I like to hang out with Ivor at the Lamp Post when the tourists are at their peak. We sip our coffees and eat our pies and needle the wide-mouthed waitress, and we keep our eyes peeled for strangers of a certain ilk—the ilk that treat the world as their playground and have more money than is good for them. And if they start making noises about how PL would be such a nice place to retire to, we explain politely that there's really nothing much to do here, the wind never lets up, and when the rain settles in, it settles in hard.

Postscript

Oh, I almost forgot Jack. I'm still working for him. In fact, he's offered me a partnership in his business and I've accepted. I think we can make this into a good thing. But working for Jack has its quirks. "Erich?" he said one day, "I wonder if you'd mind doing me a little favor and help me clean up some refuge."

Sure, Jack, anything.

After work the next day, he handed me a large garbage sack and said, "The missus don't go out now on account of her condition."

I guess that should have been hint enough. But no. Jack, see, has a way with words. "It's no big deal," he said, "but people make such a fuss. If only we would ed-u-cate ourselves. What do we really know about the truth? What do we really know about all the life in the world, and under the oceans? Just a thimble-full! Most people lack the broad mind to fully comprehend the world. Well, anyhow, it's time for her stories."

He chuckled and lit his pipe and went into the living quarters. I could see him through the opaque yellow curtain, and I could hear him, too, speaking gently as if to a child. Something compelled me to slip into the vestibule and listen. I had yet to lay eyes on Jack's "missus," and I was curious. I went into the vestibule and heard Jack rattling plates and the television prattling. "All right, dear," he said, "here you are. Now, you know you need your rufflage."

I heard another voice, and it took me a moment to acknowledge it, for there was no comprehensible form of human diction in the slopping, slushing, guttural sibilants that answered Jack's call. Only that they seemed to form something like a child's pitiful whining or pleading. Through the opaque yellow screen on the much-soiled vestibule window, I could make out movement, and what moved there might have almost passed for an arm—an elongated, writhing, twisting arm. The protuberance snaked forth and grasped the proffered food, and then there was another, wrestling with the first for its prize—and another, and another. The piping voice mewled and gibbered obscenely, grunting as its owner ingested her meal. The close air of the vestibule, the sickly yellow scrim, and a faint odor of dead meat made me nauseous. But it was the silhouette squatting there behind the waving arms (and arms I will call them), the hunched, froglike outline that emerged for an eyeblink, that will forever remain seared into my mind as it thrust its writhing appendages beyond the screen, grasping hungrily at a box of Purina Dog Chow.

About the Author

Kurt Einar Armbruster is a historian, author, and musician. His books include *Orphan Road, the Railroad Comes to Seattle, 1853-1911* (WSU Press, 1998); *Before Seattle Rocked, a City and its Music* (UW Press, 2011); and *Playing for Change, Burton and Florence James and the Seattle Repertory Playhouse* (University Book Store Press, 2013). Read his short fiction at Extranocredit.com—hear *Shadow and Substance*, by Einar, at Bandcamp. com. Kurt lives in Seattle with his wife, Cedar, and their cat, Moose.